Praise for *The Half Life of Valery K*

"Combine[s] fast-paced action and imaginative settings with beautifully developed queer relationships." —*CrimeReads*, Queer Mysteries and Thrillers to Read All Year Long

"Provocative, unsettling . . . explosive." —*Publishers Weekly* (starred review)

"Pulley's humorous, heartfelt, and occasionally horrifying tale will stay with you long after the last page." —*Paste*, Best Novels of 2022

"An absorbing Cold War thriller." —*The Christian Science Monitor*

"From state tyranny and crimes against humanity to ingenuity and valor under deadly pressure as well as humor and forbidden love, Pulley's brilliantly conceived, vibrantly realized, and complexly suspenseful tale is all the more resounding in the glare of Russia's recklessness at Chernobyl during its latest, horrific invasion of Ukraine." —*Booklist* (starred review)

"An engrossing novel set in Siberia in 1963. The story was inspired by some chilling real events after the cover-up of a radiation leak." —*Independent*

THE
HALF LIFE
OF
VALERY K

THE HALF LIFE OF VALERY K

A NOVEL

NATASHA PULLEY

BLOOMSBURY PUBLISHING
NEW YORK · LONDON · OXFORD · NEW DELHI · SYDNEY

BLOOMSBURY PUBLISHING
Bloomsbury Publishing Inc.
1385 Broadway, New York, NY 10018, USA

BLOOMSBURY, BLOOMSBURY PUBLISHING, and the Diana logo are
trademarks of Bloomsbury Publishing Plc

First published in 2022 in Great Britain
First published in the United States 2022
This paperback edition published 2024

ISBN: HB: 978-1-63557-327-5; PB: 978-1-63973-303-3; eBook: 978-1-63557-328-2

Library of Congress Cataloging-in-Publication Data is available.

2 4 6 8 10 9 7 5 3 1

Typeset by Integra Software Services Pvt. Ltd.
Printed and bound in the U.S.A.

To find out more about our authors and books visit www.bloomsbury.com
and sign up for our newsletters.

Bloomsbury books may be purchased for business or promotional use.
For information on bulk purchases please contact Macmillan Corporate
and Premium Sales Department at specialmarkets@macmillan.com.

For Claire, Larry, and Jacob, who put up with me telling them pointless facts about nuclear physics for the whole of lockdown

1

An Unexpected Departure

Kolyma, Siberia, 1963

Possibly because French made it sound fancy and respectable, the wake-up call for the prisoners was called reveille. In fact it was just one of the guards banging a bit of pipe against an iron bar outside the barracks. If he was in the right mood, the guard would take rhythm requests. On what Valery Kolkhanov didn't yet know was his final morning, it was 'Blue Suede Shoes'.

Valery eased himself upright, one hand in the roots of his hair, because it was frozen to the pillow. The hessian blankets crackled; there was frost on the top side of the weave. He touched the rafters, which were just above his head and sparkling too, and bent forward to stretch out his shoulders. Something fluffy scuffled into his lap and squeaked. Boris the sociable rat. Valery stroked his ears in the dark. For reasons known only to himself, Boris stole nails from all over the camp. He gave Valery the latest and then rolled over to have his tummy scratched.

'Who's a good rat?' Valery said, pleased. Everyone used nails as needles for darning, and if Boris brought four or five a month, Valery could get an entire can of condensed milk just by selling them on. He wasn't sure why Boris had decided he, Valery, ought to get the nails, but he wasn't in the habit of looking gift rats in the mouth.

He bent his neck to see through the small window beside him. The frost was thick on the inside, blurring the halogen lamp on the camp perimeter. He brushed some off. It was snowing.

There was still a clear forty minutes before the start of the labour shift, and those forty minutes stretched out beautifully. He pulled the physics textbook from under the straw mattress and tipped it to the light of the halogen. He preferred to read over the lessons before he had to teach them to the administrator. He would never have needed to – or, not Before – but lately, he could feel his mind effervescing, like one of those headache-cure tablets in a glass of water. He wasn't losing memories, it wasn't as straightforward as that. But it was getting harder and harder to think.

'God's sake, you tart, just lie down and keep the warm in . . .'

This from his bunk-partner, whose name he had forgotten because they rarely spoke. Valery gave him Boris to hold. They didn't know each other well, but in the winter it was a ridiculous idea to sleep alone.

At the barracks doors, the long bar made a grinding noise as the guard pulled it out from the handles. The doors opened, letting in a blast of frozen air, and the old men on light duties. That was a joke, *light duties*; the first thing they did in the morning was light the four lamps. The lamps were kerosene. They sent a clean chemical smell across the musty space, which looked like a barn, but stacked with bunks and men instead of hay bales. Valery read for a little while, then closed the book and slid down to the ground, past two other bunks and four other men.

Hay crunched under his boots. Other eyes followed the boots. He was one of only three men in the barracks who had real boots, not tied-on rags.

'Hand those over,' someone said, someone new.

Valery pushed his sleeve back to show the tattoos on his arm.

'Bugger,' the voice mumbled. 'Sorry.'

On the way out into the black morning, where the darkness was so viscous it felt like being inside an oil slick, Valery bumped the edge of the barracks door. Someone else was coming in just at the same time and they both misjudged their trajectories. It was a tiny knock, just to the knuckles of his first two fingers, but he got a stab of pain anyway that was probably the bones fracturing. He walked shaking his hand in the frozen air, which was as good as any analgesic. Before long his hand was numb.

Calcium deficiency. Annoying but not scurvy. He was fine. He made himself a cigarette, one-and-a-half-handed.

The way to not sink into self-pity and despair – the way to not die – was to look forward to things. Anything; the tinier the better, because then you were more likely to get it. The patterns of ice on the water barrels, the feeling of holding a hot mug. Anything to stop the onset of the terrible docility that came before you gave up. Collect enough bright things, and it was possible to have a good day.

One of the things Valery looked forward to was cigarettes.

All you had to do was find a newspaper from the stack the guards kept for kindling – it was never *Truth* or anything anyone would actually read, just local farmers'-market stuff and news about how somebody had hit somebody else's nephew over the head with a sugar beet – and fold it, one page at a time, into small squares. Then you ripped along the folds. Then you sprinkled tobacco in the middle of a square and rolled it up, tight. The square-tearing had to be precise, or you ended up with something too big that caught fire too enthusiastically and your eyebrows suffered. Valery's favourite thing was the crossword, because it was exactly the right size. Some people took care to find the pictures of Lenin or Stalin, or other things they hated, like marriage banns or cheese adverts, but it was ideal to *do* the crossword and then smoke it. That was a lot of mileage from one piece of paper.

He always had a decent amount of tobacco. The Vory saw to that.

Walking was difficult, because the mud had frozen into solid ruts and troughs, tyre tracks, footprints, some deep, but all hard to see by the halo glow of the far-off halogens in the staff quarter. He had to go in fits and starts, waiting for the white scythe of the tower's rotating searchlight. The camp was quiet at this time, though, so there were no crowds to navigate. In the far distance, from the mines, the whistle of the shift change floated eerie up the hill. Valery breathed smoke into the bitter air, and reminded himself again to be grateful that he was not in the mines. The cigarette moulted firefly embers.

One of the guards at the administration-building door gave him the why-am-I-up-at-four-in-the-morning scowl, and spat to one side. It froze before it hit the ground. Minus sixty degrees.

'Why haven't you taken your hat off for us?' he snapped. There was so much rage in his voice that something else must have gone wrong for him this morning already. He was new. Probably he was as miserable to find himself here as any of the zeks. 'Five paces before you reach a guard!'

He snatched it off, and then roared, because there was a needle in it, probably the only real needle – not a nail – on Valery's side of the camp. It wasn't practical to keep a needle anywhere else. The experienced guards knew that.

There was honest fury in his face, and he lashed out fast with his cattle prod. The electric shock was just as horrible as always, a flash of astonishing pain that zinged right up and down Valery's ribs. Valery forced himself to stay straight instead of doubling over, his hands clamped so hard behind his back that he could feel his nails gouging half-moons into his palms.

He found himself smiling, because he lived for these moments. He loved it when he had a chance to do a real magic trick. There was joy in finding he still could, real raw joy, because what it meant was there was still some iron in him.

'The thermometer's buggered, did you hear?' Valery said, as if nothing had happened.

'What?'

It didn't work if you were big. Valery wasn't. Most people here shaved their heads because it was easier to keep clean, but he didn't; there was a curl to his hair that made him look much younger than he really was, and he poured energy into keeping his shoulders open and his resting expression sunny. It was so out of place here that sometimes, if he hit it exactly right, it cast an illusion that they weren't here at all, but on a street in Moscow, meeting like normal people, with the normal rules.

'The thermometer on the tower. It's only saying minus seventeen. What a joke.'

'What — how does a thermometer go wrong?'

'Probably someone breathed on it while they were doing the reading.'

'Yeah, must have,' the new guard said. He looked confused. 'Yeah.' He put the cattle prod back on his belt as if he'd forgotten why he was holding it.

Abracadabra.

The administrator opened the door before Valery had to knock, freshly ironed like always, despite the hour, but looking anxious. His eyes skipped between Valery and the guards. He hated breaking up fights; it was too undignified. 'Come in then, 745; I'll make your coffee and you can tell me what you've got for me today.'

The heat inside the office was so intense that Valery was instantly too hot. Firewood crackled in the open stove, casting amber light everywhere, nearly as bright as the three gleaming kerosene lamps. He breathed out and let his shoulders sink. It was much easier to inhale in here than it had been outside. The ache down his ribs pulsed.

Valery sat down at the table and skim-read the next section of the textbook for a second time. As the kettle boiled, he touched the dog-eared pages and wondered how much of the science was still up to date. Probably not much. The world would have moved on in six years. One of the upsetting things about any sort of science was that it had about the same half-life as radioactive caesium; after thirty years, at the most, fifty per cent of it turned out to be wrong.

'By the way,' the administrator said, bringing across the coffee, 'today's your last day.'

Something like snow, something heavy and cold, settled over Valery's mind. If he was going to be led away into the woods and shot tonight, then he hadn't done a single useful thing in his life.

'Yes,' the administrator continued, 'you're being sent somewhere else.'

Valery would have been less surprised if the ceiling had fallen in. 'I'm *what*, sorry?'

'I've got a transfer order for you. Not sure where, funny name, I didn't recognise it. Kyshtym mean anything to you? Me neither. Anyway, I'm supposed to put you in a car later this morning.'

'In . . .' Valery trailed off, unable to speak. At some point in the last few years, one he couldn't find now he was looking for it, the world beyond the camp had taken on the feeling of something imaginary – like the Winter King's house, or the grove of silver trees where the dancing princesses danced.

There was no point asking why; the administrator wouldn't know. Valery poured milk into the coffee. It was another of the things he looked forward to, watching it. The spinning patterns were hypnotic.

A transfer order. If the government had remembered his name, it wouldn't be for anything good. It would be because they had realised he had never been properly interrogated. They

6

had noticed, finally, that there might be some useful information sitting in his weakening skull.

It had all been a bit rushed on the day he'd been arrested. They'd had dozens of names to get through at the Lubyanka that morning, and the police had been quite grateful when he'd told them that yes, he'd definitely done whatever it was they had on their list, and they could tick him off straight away thank you, no need to show him the chair with the straps.

'Well? Drink your coffee,' the administrator said.

Valery drank it.

The worst possible approach was to complain. It wasn't because the entire camp administration was evil; they weren't. But if someone complained about normal life, the overwhelming human instinct was to kick them in the head. It was exactly the same feeling that Valery had used to have when he overheard some morose and paunchy faculty member whingeing about how a younger woman was ignoring him.

If you wanted help, you had to let someone arrive at that conclusion alone. You had to make the outline, but never fill it in. He had all morning; maybe he could do it.

'Oh,' said the administrator, annoyed. 'The car's early.' He was looking out the window.

A prison transport van was just pulling in through the camp gates, below the wrought-iron archway sign that said, WORK IS HONOURABLE, GLORIOUS, VALIANT, AND HEROIC.

'Right, well. Off you go, I suppose. Come along.'

Numbly, Valery followed the administrator as he bustled out to the courtyard, the concrete pink now in a dawn that had cathedrals in the clouds. The van was big enough for twenty people in the back, but when the administrator helped him in, Valery was the only one, except for a woman in a KGB uniform, reading a newspaper. The administrator shackled his hands to the wall on a considerately long chain, patted his shoulder, then shut the doors with a clang, which left Valery in the window-less metal cabin with nothing but the KGB lady and a light bulb screwed sideways into the ceiling. Someone banged on the side of the truck, and it rumbled off.

He lost his sense of time. After a while, the KGB lady tipped the newspaper at him to ask if he wanted to read it. He nodded, and stared uncomprehendingly at the front-page articles. It had been six years since he had last seen a copy of *Truth*. They'd changed the font. He read slowly, unable to shake the feeling that he was doing something forbidden. It was all ordinary stuff; the economy, a Lenin Day parade in Moscow, a nicely staged picture of banners and crowds and tanks in Red Square. He read everything, including the weather and the classifieds at the back, and had a strange, untrustworthy warm feeling that after so long away from it all, the world was holding one hand out to him again. When he noticed the feeling, he shut the paper. It was dangerous to start wanting things like that.

He wanted to ask the KGB lady about where they were going, but he couldn't bring himself to. She wouldn't tell him anyway, and if she got angry, she had a baton at her hip. Even though he was only imagining an angry person, not dealing with one, the burn from the cattle prod ached down his ribs again and his heart started to buzz.

He was still working up the courage to try when they stopped. She opened the back doors, and daylight javelined in.

It was an airport. There were people everywhere, normal people, with suitcases and children. When Valery got out of the transport van, the KGB lady gave him a package. It was bulky, brown paper; the paper had been used before, because it was soft from old creases, marked with the address of a KGB station in

Moscow and a ten-kopek postage stamp. He hadn't seen stamps for years. It was enchanting – it showed a miniature portrait of Valentina Tereshkova, the cosmonaut, on a blue and black background that must have been space.

'Clothes,' the KGB lady said. Then an envelope. 'Papers. Right, let's go.'

She took him up the steps, one hand clamped on to his arm. A couple of people with children glanced in their direction, but otherwise the crowds flowed by undisturbed. It was a local airport, small. Most people were dressed for the deep countryside cold in shawls and hats that had probably once belonged to their grandparents; some looked more like officials, walking faster, in neat suits. Here and there, officers in the light grey coat of the KGB stood watching for Valery didn't know what. Their yellow belts were the brightest colour anywhere.

There was a shower room inside. It smelled blessedly of chlorine. He breathed in through his nose, even though it stung, because since his bomb incident, the camp used salt to clean, not chemicals. The salt made everything smell like the seashore on a hot day. The tiles above the sinks here were so clean that the grouting was still white. There were real mirrors.

He saw himself without understanding that the mirrors were mirrors, had a brief uncanny certainty that someone else was here, then shut his teeth when he realised it was only him.

He still looked like himself. That was a surprise. His hair was still red. The scar down his jaw had faded a lot. He looked away before he could see in any detail, full of a sense that it was indecent to know.

The KGB lady sat with a new newspaper, told him to get washed and changed, and that she would shoot him in the knee if he tried anything stupid.

The shower water was hot. He couldn't remember when he'd last had hot water. Not just tepid, from the summer, but *hot*. The shower was the kind where you had to keep pushing the knob to keep the water on, and he ended up staring, entranced, at the way the shiny steel clouded over with new condensation only a few seconds after he'd last pushed it, and at the shapes the steam made as it coiled up for the cold air from the gap above the cubicle door. He felt luminous with joy. Or not joy: the pain-joy that came from trying to memorise it exactly because he would never see anything like it again.

They were going to another camp, they had to be. If he let himself enjoy this too much, he would break when they got there, when it was back to cracking the ice on the frozen barrel with the edge of an axe.

Remember you *like* doing that, remember how satisfying it is when the ice breaks?

God, but that determinedly happy voice sounded hollow.

'Hurry up,' the KGB lady said.

This would seem like a dream when he got to wherever he was going. Just to have some evidence, he tore the Valentina Tereshkova stamp off the brown paper package.

The clothes fitted. It took him a long time to button the shirt. His fingers were definitely fractured from that pathetic knock this morning and that didn't help, but what slowed him down was the feeling of the cotton. It was so soft. He had to hesitate again with the tie, because he'd nearly forgotten how to tie it.

He wondered why she'd given him normal clothes. Probably because people wouldn't like it if they realised unchained prisoners were being transported on the same plane. But then, why an airport, and not one of the red prison trains? Zeks were always transferred by train. A plane implied urgency. He knew a few things, but he couldn't think that any of it would be relevant enough to merit being taken anywhere within hours. He was six years out of date.

He pushed the stamp into his pocket. He had that, whatever was going on. He felt nervous when he wrapped the brown paper over his old clothes, worried that the KGB lady would check and find the stamp was missing, but she only gave him an odd look and slung the whole lot in the bin. He almost dived after it. That coat, with the labels on the back and on the breast pocket that said K 745, had kept him alive for years. He'd looked after it religiously. And he'd need it if they were going to another camp. He was in too much turmoil to think of a clever way to make her listen to him and let him have it.

The KGB lady took him straight to the departure gates, where they boarded a small plane bound for a place called Sverdlovsk. Valery had never heard of it.

2

City 40

S verdlovsk was an ugly industrial city. Outside the airport, it
was so warm that there was a misty rain glinting on the steps
and the lamp posts and the bonnets of the taxis. There was no
need for a coat, even. He was staring at the film of water moving
under someone's windscreen wipers when the KGB lady hailed
a taxi and put him in it.

Immediately Valery was enfolded in the glorious smell of hot
leather and vodka, and what must have been a dab of furniture
polish inside the heater. He moved along the back seat to leave
room, but she didn't get in; she was going to Moscow. Valery
twisted round, taken completely by surprise. Wherever he was
going, it wasn't standard practice for the KGB to just leave a
prisoner alone with a random cab driver.

Again, he wanted to ask what was going on; but if she slammed
his fingers in the door, his bones would turn to powder.

She shut the door and thumped on the roof. The driver
set off.

Maybe the driver wasn't just a cab driver. But none of the
doors were locked. Valery could just hop out at the traffic lights.
There was a set at red outside the airport. He could get out,
and walk off. Perhaps the driver would be able to shoot him,
but perhaps not. He touched the door handle, his fingertips
aching with potential. Get out and go where, with no money

and no other clothes? It was warmer here than Siberia, but that still wasn't *warm*. Sleeping outside would be dangerous. But maybe that would be better than wherever he was going now. He couldn't think properly. It was a shock. He'd wondered this morning – Jesus Christ, only this morning – how much of his mind had dissolved lately, but he hadn't known it was this bad. He felt paralysed.

The lights changed. The driver sped away. He was one of those people who plainly felt that the accelerator should be untouched or floored. Then they were going at forty kilometres an hour, and jumping out would have broken every bone in Valery's body.

Valery scraped up some courage. There was no sign of a gun. It was possible the man wasn't KGB. 'Where are we going?' he tried.

'Can't tell you yet,' said the driver, not in an unfriendly way. 'Settle in, it'll be an hour or so.'

Valery nodded slowly. There were no more traffic lights.

The steel giants that were the Sverdlovsk factories glided by, and soon the car passed the city limits. After that, it was only miles of arrow-straight road, punctuated every so often by more factory towns whose white tower blocks and grid streets looked like they'd all come from identical prefabricated kits. The thrum of the taxi engine was lulling, and he fell half-asleep, his head resting against the window. There was a vodka bottle on the front passenger seat, already three-quarters empty. It made a talkative sloshing sound whenever they went over a bump in the road.

He woke up because the taxi had accelerated. It pressed him back into the seat, and then slung him forward as the driver changed gear. Confused, he looked behind them, then jumped when the driver snapped his fingers at him. The man didn't speak, but he pointed to a sign coming up fast now.

ATTENTION: DO NOT STOP FOR THE FOLLOWING 30KM. PROCEED AT THE FASTEST POSSIBLE SPEED FOR YOUR VEHICLE.

They shot past it at eighty kilometres an hour.

'Because of the poison in the ground,' the driver said.

Valery didn't know what to say to that.

Coming up on their left now were the skeletons of burnt-out houses. The roofs were just blackened sticks, and all that was left of the structures were the stone chimneys. Chimney after chimney, set at angles to each other. The houses would have been wide-spaced, with big gardens – for crops maybe, and animals. Grass and weeds grasped at the ruins. In another few years, they would cover them, and nobody passing by would know what the oddly shaped hillocks had been.

'It was a bomb,' the driver told him. 'You know, an atom bomb, from the Americans. Destroyed everything. All one night. Boom.'

Valery looked up. 'This damage is too widespread for a bomb.'

'Why are the houses burnt, then?'

'I don't know,' he said unhappily. On the right, a blasted church soared by, scraps of gold still winking on its broken domes. Beyond it was an old brick factory, the rafters poking through the roof like ribs.

'I'm telling you. Bomb.' The driver made a bomb noise and opened his hand to sketch a mushroom cloud. 'Yup. We're coming into proper rust country now.'

Valery wondered what that meant.

Apart from those brief open stretches where the burnt towns were, most of the way was forest. Valery had lost the ability to think about anything much except the feeling of violin strings tightening around his lungs, and visions of whatever gutted place lay waiting at the end of this endless road, but he did see that the trees were dying. They were silver birches, but instead of a tall stand of perfect white trunks, the forest was cluttered with trees that listed, trees that had fallen, trees that had shed all their leaves and shrunk to skeletons. They made holes in what should have been a dense thicket. He could see through it in places, sometimes to swampy stretches, sometimes to glimpses of more burnt villages. Whatever the cause, the driver was right about poison in the ground: the land here was sick.

They must have been going uphill, because the birches gave way to pines. Then, even if he had been comatose, he wouldn't have been able to miss it. The birch trees had been unhealthy, but the pines were dead. The whole woodland had turned a weird rust colour. The road was a line of red, dead pine needles; the trees were gingery ruins, and everywhere the trunks had cracked, so badly that it couldn't have been safe to drive beneath them. Even going at eighty kilometres an hour, there was a skitter of falling needles on the roof.

This was right for radiation damage; maybe there *had* been a bomb, but it would need to have been the bomb to end all bombs. And he would have heard. No; actually, he wouldn't. They got no proper newspapers in Kolyma. Half the Soviet Union could have been vaporised for all he knew.

Whatever had happened – was happening – it would kill people just as thoroughly as pines. Maybe they were using zeks to clean it up.

They couldn't be giving every single incoming zek his own personal taxi, though. The two thoughts, radiation clean-up labour versus private taxi, chased each other round his head like two horribly mutated cartoon characters.

The taxi sped on, and above it the dying forest groaned.

Long before they came to any proper buildings, there was a fence. It was metal netting topped with barbed wire, and it stretched out for as far as Valery could see in either direction.

It was broken only by a manned checkpoint, with barriers that swung up and down. The driver pulled up too fast and the wheels skidded. It must have been a regular trick of his, because the soldier in the booth only gave him a wry look.

Valery rolled down his window and handed over his new papers. The guard studied them with no expression. His eyes flicked up to Valery, then down again, then handed the papers back.

'Welcome to Chelyabinsk 40, Dr Kolkhanov.'

Chelyabinsk 40; but this was not Chelyabinsk. That was ninety kilometres back the way they'd come. He'd seen the road signs. And there were not *forty* Chelyabinsks.

The taxi driver went at normal speed now. He had to, because right after the checkpoint they were in a town. A clean, freshly built town. There were people on the pavements and gleaming speed-limit signs. Valery leaned against the window to see out properly, completely discombobulated. All along the road on the way here had been those ominous DRIVE FAST signs, the burnt buildings, deserted land, but here were ordinary people doing ordinary-people things; people with perambulators stopping to talk, kids rushing across the road in school uniform, workers in blue and white caps just starting to cluster outside cafes. There was even a theatre, with pretentious columns outside. On the other side of the road, beyond a row of pretty birch trees – almost healthy, these ones – a tanker was beetling by, cleaning the tarmac. Everything was immaculate.

As well as road signs, there were other signs, bigger. Some of them were billboards set up by traffic lights, some on the sides of buildings. They were bright and colourful, and full of the delicate images of atoms.

GLORY TO SOVIET SCIENCE!

OUR FRIEND THE ATOM!

ANYTHING YOU HEAR HERE, STAYS HERE!

And then one more, a huge poster on the side of a block of flats. In lovely blues and greens, all simple lines, it showed two scientists leaning over something that glowed.

WE ARE KYSHTYM! WE ARE THE SHIELD!

He had no idea what that meant. Whatever it was, all the colours looked over-hopeful in the grey day. It must have been afternoon by now, but he couldn't find the sun. Only low clouds, and the same fine rain there had been in Sverdlovsk. Further off, it was mist. The taxi's wipers squeaked.

It was only a few more minutes before they came to another fence, and another set of gates. This set was even heavier than the first, and beyond the checkpoint, where another soldier scrutinised Valery's papers again, everything was concrete, and every car – shining black and brand new – was identical.

And then they were at the side of a lake, pulling up to a tall building that looked like a prison, and his heart slung itself under his tongue. The people coming in and out were in lab coats. Valery slid down the seat a little way, feeling giddy. Scientists; radiation. God almighty, he was here to be a test subject of a human radiation trial. No wonder no one had told him.

He should have run away at those bloody traffic lights in Sverdlovsk. But oh no, he was too easily confused and too tired, and now he was going to get a dose of intravenous polonium stuck in his arm and dissolve like an idiot.

No; but you didn't give radiation-test subjects their own taxi from the airport.

Did you?

He didn't know how the world worked any more. He'd been out of it for too long. He felt like he might come apart at the seams. People were glued together with logic a lot more than they were glued with the strong nuclear force, and not one atom of any of this made sense.

The taxi was running slowly by the lake shore. The lake itself was black and still. In the middle, some kind of chimney or flue stretched up from the water like a monstrous submarine periscope. There was something wrong about the lake, something odd and dead, and he had to examine it for a clear minute before he could place what it was. A whole section of the nearer half was a lighter colour. It wasn't clouds reflecting on the water; it was that the water was only about a metre deep. Under it was a swathe of solid concrete.

'We're here,' the driver said triumphantly. 'See you round.'

Valery got out, nearly too weak to stand as the car drove away.

At first, he only saw the closest building. It was long and rectangular, and at one end there was a high tower where he could make out washing lines in some of the windows. The whole lot was painted yellow, which couldn't have suited the gloom less. He couldn't tell if it was a prison or not. Beyond it, on a great stretch of land full of diggers and construction supplies, the ground nothing but bare earth and sand, there was another set of buildings, with more fences and gates. Five of them, square, with cooling towers and outbuildings that thrummed, even from here, pipes plunging underground and heavy wheel-locks exposed to the weather. Without meaning to, he glanced at the lake. Wide, cold, unpopulated; he was damned if those buildings didn't house nuclear reactors.

Even as he watched, a crane swung a concrete block into place on a new building. It looked like it was going to be just like the other five. Christ, six reactors; he'd never seen so many. Six nuclear reactors and a whole forest close by that was plainly suffering radiation damage – there must have been some kind of accident.

But he couldn't see any zeks on the building site. Just people in proper work clothes and fluorescent jackets, and hard-hats.

Whatever this place was, it wasn't in the middle of a clean-up operation, and they weren't using prison labour. You didn't get a jacket and a hard-hat if you were on prison labour.

It began to rain, properly. The sound of it on the concrete ground was like stars glittering. Rain, real rain; all the way above zero degrees. Yes, of course it was. It was only October. He had managed to forget that winter wasn't six months long everywhere.

Beyond the construction site was the vast shining stretch of marsh. It was so flat that the horizon seemed much further away than it should have, the sky a grey vault. Somewhere over the wetlands, a blast of mud spurted up about ten metres into the air; there must have been geysers out here.

He should run away.

Only, there was nowhere to run to. They had just come in through the hefty fence around the facility. He had never been here before. He had no idea where to go. Serious people, with the right kind of mind, didn't let that kind of thing bother them. He had seen men escape the gulag before. They were straight-forward. They just walked off the second the opportunity presented itself, some of them hadn't been shot, and he'd never seen them again. Maybe they'd lived.

'Dr Kolkhanov?' A woman in a white cap was standing at the doors. 'Come inside, it's cold.'

Doctor; that was the second time someone today had called him doctor. Nobody called zeks anything but a number. He had the exact opposite of foreboding; a sort of creeping hope, seeping through his chest. The KGB agent had just left him, the driver had just left him. No one was behaving like he was a security risk.

'Today,' the woman in the cap prompted him.

He followed her through the glass doors. They were heavy and they banged shut right behind him. Inside was a broad, pale hallway lined with framed portraits (Lenin, Stalin, Marx) and cork noticeboards with little adverts pinned on them – the nearest had one for a set of political lectures, and someone's lost hat. So definitely not a prison. They wouldn't have glass or drawing pins at a prison. He couldn't convince himself, though. Maybe this was just an administration block.

The woman was looking at him as if she disapproved. 'Wait here, and Comrade Shenkov will come for you shortly.'

Valery wanted to say, *I've got no idea what's going on and I'd be obliged if you'd tell me before I have a nervous attack and collapse*, but it seemed like too much immediately after hello.

He sat down on a plastic chair to wait. Everything was silent. After a few minutes, he had to pull open his collar and yank off his tie, and tell himself firmly that everything was fine.

What was important to notice, the indefatigable over-bright voice in his head said, was that this wasn't like the Lubyanka at all. The Lubyanka was actually rather a nice building, with parquet floors in the main hall and carpets in all the corridors. You couldn't go around linking two places just because they both happened to be sepulchrally quiet. He seriously doubted that this place was silent by law. Nobody was going to lean in and tell you to shut up if you whispered.

As clear as though it were happening right now, with no echo whatever despite the long passageway of the years, he heard someone knocking on the other side of the wall just next to him. *Tap tap, tap-tap-tap.*

He snapped his fingers so he could show his brain the difference between remembered sound and real sound. It helped. The lady in the white cap looked at him like he was insane. He nearly admitted that he probably was. He still dreamed in the Lubyanka knock code.

He'd hoped Shenkov would be a scientist, but the man who came out from a door down the hall to fetch him wore a tailored dark suit and good shoes. KGB, he had to be; nobody else was ever so polished.

'Are you Dr Kolkhanov?' Shenkov said, entirely polite, but looking a lot like he'd hoped for someone different. Valery could see why. Shenkov was tall and powerful, probably about Valery's age, but with the grace of somebody who considered failure to keep fit a betrayal of the Soviet duty of labour. Being little and ill was, Valery suspected, hardly better than mooning the Kremlin.

'Um — yes.'

Shenkov didn't actually say *outstanding*, but he managed to clang it on to the floor like an anvil anyway.

'I'm Konstantin Shenkov, I'm the head of security.' He had an ice-shard of an accent that Valery couldn't place, and he brought with him a clear impression of flint; but it might only have been because of his hair, which was just that colour.

Valery remembered what you were supposed to do next, and stood up to shake his hand. Shenkov was warm.

'Welcome to City 40. This place is called the Lighthouse. It is a radioecological research facility, and over the road is the refinery which supplies most of the plutonium in the Soviet Union.'

Okay; hence six reactors. They were trying to keep up with American plutonium production, for bombs. Valery swallowed. What the hell did *radioecological* mean?

Don't let it be human studies. Do *not*.

'You're here because you're a biochemist,' Shenkov said, looking doubtful that someone as shabby as Valery could be something that useful, and very open to the possibility of some kind of mix-up. For a second — not for two, but certainly a *whole second* — he looked at Valery's boots, which still had the dust of the camp barracks on them. They were the only things the KGB lady hadn't replaced.

It was bewildering to remember he had been a biochemist. It belonged to another time and another Valery, years and miles away.

He must have looked bewildered too, because Shenkov did not seem inspired.

'Come with me.'

Valery had to jog to catch up with him.

'So,' said Shenkov. His grey eyes swept over Valery and he slowed down. Valery felt naked. 'This city is Chelyabinsk 40 or City 40; more informally you might hear it called the Lake. We are a closed city; any written communication reaches us via PO Box 40 in Chelyabinsk. You cannot leave the city without KGB approval; that means you come to my office –' he pointed at it as they passed the door '– and get your papers stamped every time you want to go through the gates. This includes research field trips in the wider Kyshtym area. You will not discuss your research with anyone outside this facility—'

'Sorry, *I'm* doing the research?'

'What did you think you'd be doing?' Light, polite, gentle, and weighted with the suspicion that Valery was a cauliflower in disguise.

'Dying of radiation in a human trial,' Valery said.

'Pardon?'

Valery shook his head once, fascinated despite himself. Men like Shenkov, stark beautiful security officers, generally barked when they spoke. They didn't have this glassen courtesy. It was nearly as confusing as this place, with its DRIVE FAST warnings and the WE ARE KYSHTYM! banners on the apartment blocks.

'I've just come here from the gulag. Six years' hard labour. I was – supposed to do ten.'

'Yes. You'll serve out the rest of your sentence working here as a prisoner scientist,' said Shenkov.

Everything went bright and strange. Valery thought he might faint. He touched the wall and only just managed to hang onto what Shenkov was saying.

'You will not speak to anyone from outside the city. You will submit all your experimental data to me, to be passed on to a special commission that will decide which parts of it are suitable for wider publication.' It had the ring of a required script. 'Meanwhile, someone from my department will be watching your bank account, your post, your telephone calls. This is, we all hope, purely precautionary. I struggle to imagine how stupid you'd have to be to try to communicate with a journalist or a foreigner, but people do surprise me sometimes.'

He didn't look like Valery could ever surprise him.

'Yes. I – Comrade Shenkov, sorry, I don't know anything yet. What experimental data? What's being researched here exactly?'

'Someone will explain in a minute.'

'I don't have a bank account,' Valery added.

'We opened one for you here last week. You can collect the bank book from HR.'

Last week. Someone had known he was coming here that long ago. This time last week he had been curled up in the corner of the guards' coal shed with a spoon and the monthly can of condensed milk, feeling like a king because there was honestly no better treasure in the world. If someone had told him he had such a ridiculous thing as a bank account, he would have asked if he could have some of whatever they'd been smoking.

'Meanwhile, this,' Shenkov said, holding out a small cardboard envelope with a booklet inside, like the kind that came inside library books, pristine and new, 'is a prisoner check-in book. You must come to the security office at eight every morning and eight every night. Another officer or I will stamp it to confirm that you did so. We have a duplicate. If you miss a check-in, it will be treated as an escape attempt. Please do not miss a check-in.'

'No,' Valery agreed numbly.

Shenkov opened a glass door and stepped to one side to let Valery go first. He made it look like the deference of a strong person to a slight one, not an order.

Being told to go first only ever meant a cell.

Shenkov inclined his head to say, *on you go*. Valery wished Shenkov would just shove him. Somehow, being asked politely to make that last step himself was worse than being thrown in.

It wasn't a cell.

It was a laboratory; a standard, baldly lit lab, full of glass boxes where mice and rabbits scuffled, and young people – students or recent graduates – perched around the work benches, chatting and clearly just as newly arrived as he was, backpacks propped against stools and table legs, still marked with airport luggage tags from Moscow.

3

The Lighthouse

The lady who came out of the side office was older than Valery; grandmotherly, shapeless, with the stumping walk of someone who had hip problems. Despite the drab dress, she had bright red shoes. And, incredibly, he knew her.

Dr Resovskaya had been his research supervisor when he did his undergraduate year out in Berlin. She was rounder, older – she had once been stunning and it was faded now into bad health – but it was her. He felt like he was seeing the fairy godmother from a story. It all rushed back. Her husband had run the institute, but everyone had known it was she who really wrote the research papers, very quietly, because the Nazis had been making noises about getting rid of women in scientific institutes. The last time he'd seen her, he had been nineteen and star-struck. She had put his name down on one of her papers as a co-author. He had nearly died of happiness.

'Valery! You look terrible; I see you met Comrade Shenkov,' she said brightly, and engulfed Valery in a hug. She was larger than him all round, so it gave him a nervous flicker. But she smelled familiar; after all these years, she was still using exactly the same lavender-scented soap, and all at once he was nineteen again, getting confused over the effects of gamma rays on rats and feeling hopelessly in awe when she sorted out three weeks of confusion in three minutes. He clung to her.

'Elena. You're just the same.' His voice came out strained, and his own vision had sharpened because his eyes were full of overwhelmed tears.

Dr Resovskaya waved her hand and, he suspected, deliberately misinterpreted. 'Don't worry about Shenkov, he's just here to nanny us.'

Valery couldn't imagine Shenkov being anyone's nanny, unless he was the sort who waited until your parents had gone out and then sold you to an Albanian.

'I'll leave him with you,' Shenkov said to her. Valery had to watch him go, trying to work out just why it was so profoundly disturbing to meet a security officer with that glittering grace. He decided it was because it made him feel like flies probably felt when they veered towards the crystalline strands of a great web for a better look. 'Good afternoon, comrade.'

Everyone in the lab looked relieved once he'd gone. They must all have been Shenkoved on the way in.

Dr Resovskaya took Valery's elbow, very gently, as if he were thirty years older. 'You're the last of the new group to arrive, so let's settle down with some coffee and do the safety briefing.'

'There's coffee?' he said, all his insides burning with happiness and shame rolled up. He was forty-six, for God's sake. Absurdly, he wished Shenkov would come back and be doubtful. If someone trusted you to withstand some coolness, they trusted you not to collapse on the floor. Dr Resovskaya plainly didn't.

She sparkled. She could make her eyes flash when she liked, almost without moving. 'Absolutely there's coffee.' She studied him properly, up and down. 'They sent you straight here?'

'Yes.'

'You won't have brought anything, then? Well, let me take you through, and I'll ring reception and get someone to buy you some clothes from town.'

'That's . . .' He wanted to say kind, but it was beyond kind. He pulled his glasses off and polished them for an excuse to keep his eyes down. 'Did you request me for this?'

'Of course I did.'

He had to swallow the lump in his throat. 'Why?'

She looked dismayed. 'It's not like the Soviet Union has biochemists specialising in radiation coming out of its ears, is it? That was *quite* an administrative cock-up on someone's part. You should have been here years ago.'

'Well – it's not that unusual a . . . there are plenty of other—'

'Not like you.'

'Like me how?'

She laughed. 'Oh, dear. Are you still spending a good sixty per cent of your time trying to work out why you don't always understand other humans and not factoring in how most people's brains are bimbling around in second gear while yours is a fucking jet engine with no off switch?'

Valery couldn't tell if he was being made fun of. 'I don't think I know what's going on any more.'

'Oh, you are! Good stuff. Honestly, I still tell new students that story about how you annihilated Professor Kurchatov at your doctoral defence and you didn't even understand why he got flustered.'

'What?' said Valery, who remembered that Professor Kurchatov – the great, sainted Kurchatov who was now in charge of the whole Soviet nuclear programme – had been cross and dismissive and then inexplicably given him the PhD, but not anything that could possibly be called annihilation.

She patted him. 'Never change. Now off you go. Just through there. Left. Shake some hands, I'll be through in a jiff.'

He had to lean against the wall for a few seconds to get himself together.

Not only was there coffee, but cheese, and real butter, and fresh bread; things he hadn't seen for years. It was all laid out in a neat buffet at the back of a presentation room. At the front was a projector. A technician adjusted something in its workings, and while she did, other people filtered in; the studenty types from the lab, and a couple of supervisors nearer his age. He was surprised when one of the older women smiled and came to say hello.

'You're Valery Kolkhanov? Good to meet an actual grown-up, isn't it?' she said. 'We're from the Biophysics Institute, from the Ministry of Health.'

'Oh, hello,' he said. And then something in the back of his mind lit up and said: the Biophysics Institute. It sounded boring, but it was one of the most secret institutions in Moscow. 'The Institute; are you even allowed to tell me that?'

She laughed, and he laughed too, because she had a brilliant laugh, and brilliant teeth; they were crooked, a child's teeth, but they suited her, and they took the edge off the worry of meeting a person from a secret institute. 'They let you boast. Mind if I sit with you before the children drive me completely insane? Good, thank you,' she said, effusive with exhaustion. He could see what she meant about children. None of the students could have been more than twenty years old.

It wouldn't last; people in isolated labs always rushed to make friends and then calmed down and regretted it later, but all the same, Valery liked her a lot for bothering.

'I'm Ilenko, by the way.' She nodded at the students. 'I'm on mum duty.'

'I doubt that's true,' he offered, awkward. He never knew what to say when women pointed out that they were women and that it was, generally, awful. There was a knee-jerk human instinct to say it couldn't be as bad as all that, like he would have to anyone who was feeling blue, but it was one of those instances where it really was awful, and trying to say it wasn't was somewhere on the spectrum between stupid and criminal.

Dr Resovskaya clipped in, red shoes shining. Valery couldn't make them out perfectly, but he thought they might even have sparkly straps. Ilenko nudged him and pointed indignantly at her own shoes, which were the white, flat kind that nurses wore. He grinned.

Live long enough in an unsafe place, and you got used to it. Valery had become so used to the camp that he'd lost any real awareness that it *was* unsafe. A fourteen-hour labour shift was normal; infection was normal; hunger was normal; the dirty-fingernail-scratching feeling on the back of his neck, the one that reminded him that there were bigger, angrier, more violent men around him all the time, was normal. And now it was gone. Safety was coming up through the floor, glowing from the students, from Ilenko, from Dr Resovskaya at the front.

'Right, everyone,' Dr Resovskaya called from by the projector. 'Listen up or you'll be seeing a lot more of the KGB than you want.'

Dr Resovskaya started with a slide that showed a map of the whole Kyshtym area. It was nearly three thousand square kilometres around the city and its lake, and the territory was divided into rough bands with radiation readings noted on. They weren't neat, and in some of the bands where the radiation was generally less, there were patches of concentration that represented deep lakes connected by the water system to this one.

'Welcome to the Lighthouse, everyone. My name is Elena Resovskaya, I'll be overseeing your research here. Now: the recruitment process for this job was very secretive, yes?'

It wasn't only Valery who laughed. The students did as well.

'I shall explain. New researchers rotate into this institute around this time every year because, as you've noticed, this whole district is irradiated, and all of you will be working daily with irradiated materials. We don't want anyone to get too high a dose. So, we move people in and out a lot. For most of you, this placement will last for nine months, and then you'll go back to your doctoral studies.

'You are all here,' Dr Resovskaya continued over the fluttery sound of the projector's fan, 'to study the effects of radiation on an ecosystem. This is an extraordinary opportunity; nowhere else in the world is it possible. The overarching aim of this facility is to discover which species develop radiation resistance, which do not, and how that affects all the others.'

There was a dazed silence.

An irradiated *ecosystem*.

If Valery had been asked to fill out a form describing what heaven looked like, whatever he wrote would have been pretty damn close to this. It was the bane of any biologist working with radiation; you could only ever work in extremely controlled conditions, in a lab, or worse, a glass box in a lab. You waved some uranium at a rabbit, you waved it for longer at another rabbit, and so forth, and then you wrote down what happened, bored to extinction with the knowledge that all those results would say was how radiation affected rabbits in labs. Yes, you could make guesses about other things, but they were only guesses. You couldn't tell how those rabbits would behave in a natural environment. You couldn't tell how far-reaching the effects of the radiation would be.

Fifteen minutes ago he'd still been terrified.

The massive swing of feeling was already starting to give him a headache. It was coiling round his temples. He slid down in the chair to enjoy it. Ilenko offered him a mint humbug from a paper packet. He took one carefully but didn't open it, worried about crackling the plastic wrapper, but Ilenko crackled away, looking gleeful.

'Now,' Dr Resovskaya was saying, 'that necessitates working in a somewhat radioactive environment, but hold in the hysterics.' She stepped away from the map so they could see properly. The students giggled.

'The radiation in the soil is measured carefully. Immediately by this lake, it's high; but you need not worry about that because, as you can see, there's damn all here for you to work on.' She motioned outside the big window. Part of the view was the black lake and sprawl of the marshes, but part of it was the rest of the research complex, where the ground was bare, and ploughed through with sand that bore heavy machine tracks. 'In the areas where you're going to be walking about, the radiation is never going to be more than five millicuries per square metre. I know not all of you are used to thinking in curies and millicuries, but essentially what that means is that even if you sat on that ground for four hours a day every day, the total radiation you absorbed from it after a year would still be less than the background radiation you get from cosmic rays. Comrade Kolkhanov there is our new resident number genius; am I correct?'

Valery nodded. He had been working it out while she spoke. He was surprised by how readily the figures swam through his head. Assume an average person weighed about a hundred kilograms (given all the cheese), assume you'd only absorb about thirty per cent of the radiation dose . . . 'Ten times less,' he said.

'Scary, isn't he?' Resovskaya said to the students, who laughed. 'I had to put up with that for a whole year once.'

Valery smiled too, but he felt puzzled. That kind of radiation wouldn't hurt anything. It certainly didn't murder forests.

'You'll all get a copy of this map,' Resovskaya was saying, 'so you'll always know which zone you're in. As you probably saw on your way here, the roads and buildings in town are washed down once weekly to get rid of any contamination, and readings inside all the accommodation blocks are wholly within a normal range.

'I imagine you know this, but I can't say this enough: *you will not get even mild radiation sickness unless you are exposed to a hundred roentgen or more in one dose.* You are safe.'

She wrote on the blackboard beside the projector image in capital chalk letters: 100 ROENTGEN=SLIGHTLY ANNOYING. She surrounded it with little stars and sparkles, and everyone laughed again.

Someone raised a hand. 'Will we be issued with dosimeters?'

Dr Resovskaya smiled. When she did that, you could see what she had used to look like; a smoky, sultry film star. She carried herself as if she still looked like that. Valery loved her for it. No despair here; no slouching.

'No. Dosimeters are bloody expensive, and they won't tell you anything that this map doesn't already. That's all been done for you. Relax, enjoy your fieldwork. What we do always say is to limit your outdoor time within a five-hundred-metre radius of this facility to about half an hour a day, just to be on the safe side. We'll give you stopwatches. Putting laundry out is good fun on a timer, I tell you.'

More giggles.

Valery leaned forward to read the notes in each zone on the big map. The numbers there were a patchwork of different units; they were handwritten, and it looked like five or six people had all gone out, measured with different things, done different maths, and stuck on whatever seemed right with no standardisation.

That was odd.

Usually he didn't care if someone mixed up their units. Everyone looking at a chart like that was a grown-up, capable of noticing whether it said metres or centimetres, and doing the very basic necessary maths to get the right idea. But radiation was different.

Radiation measurements were like English spelling; there were half a dozen different systems, nobody normal understood any of it, and the only presiding rule was that if it seemed to make sense, you'd got it wrong.

There were eight standardly used measures of radiation.

Curies measured amounts of actual radioactive material; but one curie was a stupendous amount of radiation, so you almost never had to use it unless you were talking about atomic bombs. Instead it was usually millicuries or, in lab conditions, micro-curies, and helpfully, the abbreviations were *mc* and *mmc*, which meant there were lots of hilarious typos in every research paper ever written.

People who got cross about the curies rubbish used bec-querels instead, which measured the same thing but in smaller units, for common sense.

Then there was radiation as a dosimeter picked it up, roent-gen; that was the unit people had heard of. But then some people objected to calling it after a German, so those people measured in coulombs per kilogram instead.

Either way, those things measured only radiation in *air*, which was useless for measuring radiation that would actually be absorbed by a person; that was a rem, the roentgen-equivalent-man or, because it would be letting the side down by now to have only one unit, the sievert.

Once the radiation was actually inside you, the medical units were different again; it was a rad – radiation absorbed dose – or if there was loads, the higher unit, the one you had to use of people who were dying: the gray.

And of course, the calculations involved in actually working out how many roentgen were in one millicurie of radioactive stuff and how many rems or rads that translated into in different people or organisms were hugely variable and not the kind of thing many people wanted to try without a pencil, a piece of paper, and some headache pills.

Everything was on the map. Roentgen, rem, millicuries, becquerels, even rads, where someone must have got confused and written it instead of rem. Dr Resovskaya must have kept it up as a joke.

Valery glanced at Ilenko, starting to smile, and felt unsettled to find that Ilenko was staring hard at the map, then writing, then staring.

'So, I imagine all of you are keen to know what happened here, and what caused the contamination,' Dr Resovskaya continued.

The next slide was a picture of the black lake.

'In 1957, it came to the attention of the Kremlin that although the world was having a nuclear frenzy, nobody really knew very much about it. The Japanese are a little ahead; they can study Hiroshima and Nagasaki, but they don't like sharing. So, it was decided that, in an area as broad but as unpopulated as possible, with a decently complex ecosystem, a large district would be exposed to radioactive contamination. This was quite a daring thing to do, but they did it. Liquid waste was used to contaminate the water table under a system of these eight lakes here –' she outlined the area on the big map on the wall '– which then contaminated swathes of the local plant life and the general ecosystem of the whole Kyshtym district. This entire region is now a nature reserve.' She smiled. 'All of your research, whether you're looking at plant life, fish or mammals, will help determine whether or not there is resistance to radioactivity in any of the affected species. If there is – that will be quite a discovery, and certainly one that we would publish. Perhaps even beyond the Soviet Union.'

Valery didn't often feel the urge to congratulate the government, but he did have a spark of national pride now.

'As the adorable Comrade Shenkov will have explained to all of you,' Resovskaya was saying, 'there are of course restrictions on what we can publish.'

There was a ripple of laughter.

'Basically, you'll submit all your findings to a special commission of academics in Moscow. That commission will guide you as to which details are all right to publish. As a general rule, we can't publish anything that will give away our location; so, coordinates, and in some cases, specific genera and species of some of our specimens, which are unique to this area. Our research alone is classified; but as you'll have noticed, just along from us are five plutonium reactors and a uranium mine. That is the most secret facility on this side of Moscow. It's where the plutonium for all our bombs comes from, and if the Americans ever discover its location, we could expect an atomic bomb to fall on us within hours.'

Awed nods all round.

Valery inclined his head. It would have been much easier to do all this, to contaminate a large territory, *not* directly over the site of a secret nuclear facility. But then, maybe it was just the logistics of the thing. It would be both difficult and hazardous to transport hundreds of thousands of tonnes of nuclear waste any significant distance.

'Kyshtym is the nuclear shield of the Soviet Union, and its effectiveness relies on the secrecy of its whereabouts,' Dr Resovskaya said. 'You all saw the signs on the way in. We don't talk about our work to a living soul outside this facility, and we don't leave this city unless we are sent. In your rooms you will find a folder, full of suggested cover stories for if anyone does ask too much. I suggest you consult it. Be aware, too, that throughout City 40 there are trained KGB informants. All of them are listening. They're there not to get you in trouble, but to make sure you maintain proper secrecy procedure. If they find that you don't, the consequences could be severe. Comrade Shenkov is not here just to show people around.'

There was a deep quiet in the room now. Dr Resovskaya shook her head and smiled.

'One last thing.' She switched off the projector.

'The city has no real name; people call it the Lake, or Chelyabinsk 40, PO Box 40, or City 40. This practice is called geographic distortion. By suggesting we are in Chelyabinsk, we throw off anyone who's asking too many questions about us. Likewise, you must not call this facility the Lighthouse when you're outside it. Call it the chocolate factory. Even to your families.' She grinned. 'We're all in the business of espionage tradecraft now, which I think is terribly glamorous, and why I feel justified in wearing these ridiculous shoes.' She was perched on the edge of the table, and she waved her legs delicately to show her red kitten heels.

Everyone laughed.

'I imagine you have lots of questions?'

'When will we have assignments?' someone asked.

'Monday. Thought we'd ease you in.'

Valery hesitated. Nobody else asked anything. They were all too excited to be here. In the quiet, there was a distant, odd *pop*. Everyone glanced at the window, just in time to see the mud explosion of one of those geysers in the marsh pattering down. It was nearer than the other one Valery had seen, right on the edge of the lake.

He put his hand up slowly. He couldn't help feeling like everyone else knew something he didn't.

'Comrade Annoying Maths Genius?' Resovskaya said cheerfully.

He glanced at Ilenko, worried he was about to make an idiot of himself, but Ilenko was only watching him intently. 'The figures we were talking about before, a few millicuries per square metre – that's very small. Only a bit more than lab conditions.'

'Yes, that's right.'

Right, good. 'But on the drive here, I saw the forest. It's in a state.'

'Yes, it's fascinating, the effects of only a few roentgen per year.'

She was switching units even while they were talking, a corner of his mind noted. Not like her at all. 'But the mass of a tree is – well, far greater than that of a human, and humans don't show many ill effects short of a hundred roentgen in one dose, so it seems—'

'Extraordinary. I know. And that's partly what we're studying. Isn't it brilliant?'

'That . . . doesn't – sorry. That doesn't sound right. How can the forest be dying from radiation that would barely affect a person—'

'Isn't it funny how men who've been out of the field for years think they can interrupt their old professor just because she's gone grey?' she said to the students, without rancour. She was too graceful to get cross.

Valery had to nod along and shut up, feeling terrible. He had not meant to do that at all.

'Now,' she said, as if there had been no interruption, 'it's Friday, and you're all very tired of listening to me bore on. As I say, I'll hand out all your assignments on Monday. Meanwhile, it's the weekend, the city is full of theatres and cafes, and I urge you to settle in and enjoy it. One final request: please finish all this cheese or the gannets from Shenkov's office will nab it from you.'

Then there was a rush for the cheese. Valery didn't go – he couldn't move that fast anyway – and only watched them, feeling wretched.

'Am I going insane?' he asked Ilenko. 'How does minimal radiation obliterate a forest? Are trees just very susceptible to radiation?'

'Hang on, I'm counting,' she murmured, still looking down at her pencil. She was writing in shorthand, so he couldn't tell what it was.

Valery went to look at the radiation map on the wall. There was no more information given on it than Resovskaya had told them. Three roentgen here, one out in the woods; nothing to say per *what* – hour, day, month, year – nothing to say what the source was, nothing to say when the readings had been taken – even though those things were so basic that it was rare to have to nag even first-year undergrads to remember to note them down. It looked wilfully useless.

He knew Resovskaya was close to him because he could smell the lavender.

'I'm sorry,' he said to her.

She squeezed his shoulder, only lightly, like he was sticky. 'It's all right. I wouldn't do this job if I wasn't up for a few aggressive questions from middle-aged men, would I?'

'I didn't mean to be aggressive,' he said miserably.

'I'm teasing you. Have some cheese, it's Norwegian. It tastes of toffee. Are you listening?' She took his shoulders so that he faced her square on. It made him flicker. The urge to duck away was instant. 'It's safe here. You can calm down. This –' she motioned at the map '– is just what you get when you let bureaucrats have a say in science. They sent half a dozen different people out to do the measurements but there weren't enough dosimeters to go around, so we got measurement Babel. Okay? It's *safe* here.'

He smiled and felt almost better, and decided that in the absence of any other useful apology he could make, he might as well try the special toffee cheese.

He was turning away when he saw Ilenko standing just back from him. He meant to avoid her, but she touched his arm.

'You're right,' she said. 'That map is nonsense. Bullshit does it only take a few millicuries to wreck the trees like that. She's lying to keep the students calm. And she was being a bitch to you just now, I've met crumpets more aggressive than you.'

Valery took a breath, then realised he had nothing to say with it. Not even for a second had it occurred to him that Resovskaya was outright lying. But of course she was. 'I don't think she meant to be a . . . she's allowed to be offended.'

Ilenko pushed her pencil behind her ear. 'Well, personally I don't think she should be taking a hammer to someone quiet and polite and clearly about half an hour off starving to death, but I suppose some of us have impractically strict ideas about chivalry.'

He laughed, reassured.

She smiled too. 'I feel some soil tests coming on, don't you? I'd like to know what we're really dealing with, and not the propaganda figures.'

He wanted to hug her. He didn't dare, and even if he had, something was catching at his attention; a strange, scritching noise coming from the light switch just next to him. Bad wiring, it must have been.

'Cheese,' Ilenko decided.

That was it for the day. Dr Resovskaya passed around keys and directed everyone to an accommodation tower block just next to the facility. Valery expected shared dorms, but when a brand-new lift took them up to the eleventh floor, they each had their own rooms. Inside, it was like a hotel. A bed, a bathroom, a window that looked out over the black lake. And there, on the bed, was a neatly sealed paper bag with three new shirts, two new ties, underwear, pyjamas, and a roll-up wash kit containing the first sharp razor he'd seen in years.

Just because he could, he went straight into the shower and stood under the hot water for nearly half an hour. It was different from the airport. This was real, not a snatched five minutes half-way, perhaps, to somewhere horrible. He had forgotten what it was like to be clean. Not just functionally clean, but really clean, so clean that your hair squeaked and the ends of your nails were white. It only sank in slowly. He stood looking at the burns on his ribs from the cattle prod. He wasn't going to die of an infection. He could say that with a decent amount of confidence for the first time since – well, since Before.

There was a telephone on the desk. Dry and dressed again, he touched the receiver, then stopped. He didn't know anybody who would be interested to hear that he was out of the camp. He let his hand drop again.

It was six years since Valery had been in a room alone.

Camp barracks were never quiet. There would always be fifty men breathing and shifting and sniffing in their sleep, or whispering over dominoes long into the night; there would be rats, and the crunch of the guards' boots as they patrolled outside. It was reassuring. What those rustling nights meant was that if you were ever so ill you couldn't get up, or spiralling too far into bleakness, then there were other humans who would keep checking to see if you were still alive, who might even fetch food or a doctor. With people, it was safe. The only places without people were the solitary confinement cells, and the forest at night.

Nobody came back from either of those.

Even though his forebrain knew that he was safe in here, the rest was positive that he wasn't.

He had to open the window to catch some background noise from the town. There wasn't much; a little traffic, the distant roar of the forest. Better than nothing.

Standing still in the dark, he could hear a tiny, electrical whine, the same as he'd heard in the light switch in the presentation room downstairs. Puzzled, he followed it round the room and found that it was actually coming from three places. The phone, the lamp, and a plug. He wasn't an electrician, though, so he decided it was probably better to leave it alone and tell someone in maintenance in the morning.

He lay down in bed and waited to feel tired. After half an hour, tiredness still wouldn't come, only a rising panic. He tried the radio without much hope, but all the channels were already off-air. He left it on white noise. In the end, he had to build a makeshift person-shape from cushions and pillows next to him in bed, then curl up against it.

4

The River

There were cafes in town. Valery wasn't alone in being excited about that; everybody was, and the next morning, Saturday, when he ventured out early so he could get the stamp in the prisoner book and leave at the same time, everyone else was up early too. Shenkov, the security officer, was at the front door handing out stopwatches. They were beautiful things, proper silver clockwork, all gleaming in a wooden box on a desk. When Valery took his, he paused over it, charmed.

'These are nice. How come . . . ?'

'Cheaper to pick these up from an antique shop than buy normal watches,' Shenkov explained, sounding like he'd said it fourteen times today already. He stamped Valery's book with the KGB seal and wrote his signature over it. 'Set it off the second you're out the door, and don't *stay* outside within five hundred metres of this complex for more than thirty minutes a day. A day, not per journey.'

'That's some fierce radiation,' Valery said.

'No. The thresholds set from Moscow are very low, that's all.' Shenkov was just as polite now as he had been yesterday, but there was something muted about him today. He looked like he hadn't slept either, and KGB or not, Valery felt friendlier towards him. It was good to know he wasn't the only insomniac. 'It's only precautionary.'

Valery studied the silver watch. In his experience, Moscow did not spend money on *only precautionary*. Ilenko must have been right. He took a breath.

'If you say a single word more about radiation,' Shenkov interrupted, not sharply, but with flint that he could have sharpened with a couple of knocks, 'I will not respond well.'

Valery had a stab of sympathy. It must have been a thankless job, to tell a lie to a whole group of people who were qualified to recognise it as such. 'Sorry. I know it must be rough.'

Shenkov turned brittle, as though nobody had said sorry to him and meant it for a long time. Valery stepped back once, in case he had a truncheon. He didn't. He only looked alarmed that Valery had thought he might. 'The soldiers at the perimeter gate have dosimeters. You're scanned as you come in and out, you'll know if there's anything on you.'

'Up to what scale?'

'Three roentgen.'

'Oh,' said Valery, pleased. Well; maybe it wasn't so bad then. Maybe Moscow really *was* being careful about people here. Maybe he had been a zek for too long to have an accurate idea about the value of normal people's lives. Three roentgen was thirty times higher than the annual acceptable dose for everybody except emergency workers, but it probably wouldn't hurt anybody even so, and it was clearly at the very top end of what they expected here. 'Okay. Well, thanks.'

Shenkov nodded once and crossed through a box on a long register, and wrote down the time. Valery slid his prisoner book into his breast pocket, feeling peculiarly safe. Everyone accounted for always, and him particularly; it was bliss after six years of being herded around with a machine gun in the back of his neck, and it meant they really were taking it all seriously.

———

He hesitated by the gate of the research facility and had to watch the soldiers checking other people's papers before he was sure it was all right and nobody was going to say that no, there had been a silly mistake and he was supposed to be in a cell somewhere. He hoped he would see Ilenko, because in some of those sleepless hours he'd rehearsed asking her if she wouldn't mind having some coffee with him, but there was no sign of her. All the while, he could feel the watch ticking in his pocket, so he went up before he was quite ready. Anxiety seeped through him as he reached the booth. The soldier looked at his paperwork, looked at him, made a note in a ledger, then waved him on, just as a truck came in from the other direction. A security guard climbed up to wave a dosimeter over the crates inside. It buzzed urgently.

'It's bananas,' the driver called. 'Sets your stuff off every time, sorry!'

Valery turned away, grinning. Bananas were full of potassium; if you could eat something in the region of a million and a half bananas at one go, you'd get radiation sickness. It was how Dr Resovskaya had taught them to think about amounts of radiation when he was an undergraduate. It worked out at about 0.0001 roentgen per banana, which meant a truck of bananas only needed to be carrying about fifteen hundred of them to get a squeak off a sensitive dosimeter.

He wondered who was getting the bananas. He hadn't seen one since working in that lab in Berlin, or at least, not one you wouldn't have to take out a mortgage to buy.

Just outside the facility was an extremely clean road, bisected with silver birch trees that threw a pleasant shade over the pavements. It was too warm here for frost, incredibly; even though it was October. He stepped out slowly, unable to believe that he was allowed to do it. But, here were people, real people, chatting outside grocery shops and restaurants, and nobody pointed at him or marched him away. Under his hand, the pocket watch ticked. He took it out, meaning to stop the timer, but then hadn't the heart. The watch was old; it must have sat around not doing anything for a long time now. It deserved to run.

He paused outside a stationer's, because there were newspapers, a stand of cigarettes – really *good* cigarettes too, and chocolate; things no one had been able to get even before the war, even in Moscow. And eggs; God, there were hundreds of eggs, just on display. Everything must have been in steady supply too. There was no crowd of people fighting to buy it all, nobody hurrying away with a hundred eggs in a basket looking like they'd won a million roubles. Surreal. He had a powerful urge to steer clear. It would be terrible to get used to things like that.

Because this wasn't going to last forever, whatever Shenkov had said. No one had given him a pardon; he was still in the penal system, even if they were letting him walk about now.

It was tentatively that he went into the cafe. Even then he had to slow down, because he couldn't believe what he was seeing. Carpets, radiators, nicely made tables, newspapers in a rack – among them the *Lake News*, which had a headline that screamed ALIENS IN KYSHTYM!! That made him laugh and think of the song his mother had made up, that there was no truth in *Truth* and no news in *News*.

And there on the counter, a bowl full of grapes. He thought they must just have been for show, but someone saw him looking and said you could buy some; they weren't even expensive. So he did, along with coffee that tasted like it belonged to another age, and sat staring at the bunch of grapes, hypnotised. Real grapes. From another country. Peru, was it, where you got grapes? All he knew about Peru was that there was gold there, and jungles. Unbelievably far away, and yet here was a little part of it.

It was sunny for the first time since he could remember, so he sat outside on the terrace. It overlooked the river, the Techa. The Techa was a broad, inviting span of water, and on the far bank were marshlands where groves of reeds bowed as if there were an invisible tsar in the water.

Cows were nosing around in the shallows. Valery swallowed. He could see how they were swirling up the mud on the river bed. The mud would be nearly as radioactive as on the day it had been contaminated. Caesium-137 and its counterpart isotope, strontium-90, got through only half the neutrons they had to blast out in thirty years; it had only been six years. All those tiny storm systems of neutron shards, still going strong. He wouldn't have wanted to be one of those cows. The thought made him look down at his own coffee and wonder where the milk came from. Not here, hopefully. No – definitely. People would have set off the dosimeters at the Lighthouse perimeter if they were drinking radioactive milk.

Resovskaya was right. He had to relax. It was safe here. Even if she was downplaying the real figures for the students, the city was clearly fine.

He would have loved to know if there was a microscope now that could watch what those neutron shards did inside blood, or how they sliced between the atoms of your bones, atoms so wide-spaced as far as single neutrons were concerned that they would have looked like loosely linked solar systems, through those fragile DNA chains, tearing them to elegant bits, and then going on and on. From the outside, in an acute case, the result looked terrible. A human just melted. But from the point of view of that one neutron, blasted from the heaving core of an unquiet atom, it must have been bewitching.

He decided to ask someone about the state of modern microscope technology.

There was a splash.

Just a short way off was a tiny waterfall where the current rushed over a projecting rock. There were kids playing in it, taking it in turns to jump off, splash, swim to the bank and go again, squeaking with laughter.

What.

Valery stood up. 'Hey.' He found his voice properly. 'Hey!'

They didn't think he was talking to them and paid no attention. He searched for a way down, found some wooden steps, and ran. He grabbed the nearest boy, not caring that he'd never seen a human look so scared as the child did then.

'Don't play in the water. It's toxic, do you understand?'

'What . . .'

'Oi!' The boys' fathers were smoking not far away. 'What the fuck are you doing?'

It was the first time Valery had been grateful to see a group of angry men. 'I'm from the Lighthouse,' he said. 'The water is toxic. The lake is full of nuclear waste; you must know that? Don't let the children anywhere near it.'

'What are you talking about?' one of the men said, but they all glanced at each other.

'Please. *That* is a plutonium refinery,' Valery said, pointing to the new towers opposite the research facility, 'and *that* is where they put quite a lot of radioactive waste.' He waved at the lake. He could hear his voice breaking high, but he couldn't stop it; he couldn't believe the men didn't know. 'That water runs into this river, please – hasn't anyone said? – they *cannot* be in this water.'

'Why don't you just fuck off and leave them alone?' the man said. He was holding a vodka bottle by the neck.

Valery lifted his hands and backed away, hot with a rush of fear. Once he was almost back at the cafe, though, the men hurried the boys out of the water.

Shaken, he trudged back up the terrace and sank back down at the table.

'Are you all right?'

It was the lady who had told him about the grapes. She must have seen everything. Being spoken to unexpectedly by a stranger proved, for the first time since he'd been about six, paralysing, and all he could do was smile and nod.

Horrifyingly, she moved from her table to his.

'You must be new here,' she said, full of kindness.

'Yes.' He managed to laugh, or sort of. 'How can you tell?'

'I've been here donkey's. I came when you weren't allowed to leave at all. Used to be a chemical engineer at the Lighthouse. Retired now, obviously,' she said, and patted her hair, which was bright white. 'In those days they didn't even let you tell your family, it was so secret. They all thought I'd gone missing. Can you imagine! They had a shock when I telephoned after eight years, I tell you. You look suspiciously like a scientist too. Let me guess; physics?'

'Biochemistry,' he said.

'A biochemist at a nuclear plant, whatever for?' She had red lipstick on. A fleck of it had brushed pink between her front teeth.

'Oh, just . . . you know, the effects of the radiation on the plants and things.'

'What radiation?'

He looked up slowly. A chemical engineer would have known bloody well what kind of radiation. 'What's your field exactly?'

She studied him for a long time, a small smile hovering on her face like a cochineal beetle. 'That's better,' she said, in a different voice; one that did not chat to strangers in cafes. 'Remember, Comrade Kolkhanov, loose lips sink ships. No more shouting at children like a madman, now. Enjoy your coffee.' She left, looking ordinary in her flat shoes and her brown coat. Once she was out the door, she put a scarf over her hair, and vanished among all the other old ladies shopping at the grocer's opposite.

The coffee cup juddered in its saucer, because his hand was shaking. For a full five minutes, he tried to calm down, but he only felt more and more trapped, and he had to leave everything and go.

He was only just outside the cafe when a pair of soldiers caught his arms and pushed him into the back of a black van.

His voice shut down. He sat silent in the cold van opposite one of them, who watched him expressionlessly. A camp. They were just going to take him away, exactly like the first time, and no one would know where he'd gone.

He half-closed his eyes, glad he hadn't let himself be taken with the cigarettes, the chocolate, the grapes. None of this was really for him and it was all going to be gone by this time tomorrow. Back to Kolyma for the last four years of his sentence. Well, it had been a nice holiday, for sure. Carefully, and with some difficulty because it was already heavy, he worked at shutting down the front part of his mind, the part that had been waking up since arriving here – noticing things, noticing people, feeling interested in Ilenko, and Resovskaya's shoes, and Shenkov's exquisite courtesy, basking in the hot water. It was good to know that it *could* wake. His mind wasn't atrophying; just dormant. All was well. He could survive another four years. It would be tough to begin with, but he would get into the swing of it again soon, and he would have a marvellous story to tell the camp administrator, and Dima the Vory godfather who still invited him over for tea every Friday. Everyone would laugh at the idea of a bank account and readily available bananas.

The van ground over gravel, and stopped. There was a clunk as the driver slammed his door. The back doors opened. He jerked his head to tell Valery to get out.

They were back at the Lighthouse. They'd only driven half a mile.

He stepped out, expecting a prison transport. But instead one of the men caught his shoulder and marched him inside to Shenkov's office, knocked, left him there, and vanished.

Shenkov didn't look surprised. He nodded Valery into the chair opposite his own at the meticulous desk and asked what had happened, with no ire. He still seemed tired; perhaps he hadn't the energy to be angry.

So clearly there was going to be an obligatory roughing-up session before the prison transport. Spectacular. Expecting a punch in the eye, he was discombobulated when Shenkov gave him a chocolate bar, then put on the kettle. Valery turned round in the chair, strung so tight his whole chest hurt. He was going to be flicked with boiling water, or something.

'Eat all of it,' Shenkov said. 'You'll feel better.'

Very slowly, Valery opened the chocolate packet and snapped off a small piece. His mouth was so dry he had to just hold the chocolate on his tongue, unable to swallow. It was some kind of trick, but the kind he hated, because he couldn't see where it was going. The kettle pinged. Shenkov made some coffee. The hiss and glug of the water, the dank smell of the steam, made Valery's teeth ache. He forced himself to face forward. It was silly to over-dread being beaten up. It would be nasty and then it would stop.

Your bones are sawdust, the old voice said softly.

Shenkov brought back the coffee pot and two matching cups, poured out both and gave Valery one. He didn't sling it at him, only held the rim so that Valery could take the handle. When Valery didn't take it, he put it on the desk.

Nothing happened. Shenkov only sat down again. Valery wanted to tell him to just get it over with. He hated men who made you wait before they hurt you.

'You were told yesterday *not* to speak to anyone from outside the facility.'

Valery waited. However much he despised it, he was good at waiting.

Nothing else was forthcoming.

'Did you hear me?' Shenkov asked. It was mild.

Valery nodded once. He had a feeling that Shenkov was waiting to see if he would break, and he was tempted to tell him not to waste his time. The old men in the camp had cried a lot, the ones who were so broken they couldn't bear it any more if they stepped in a puddle. You had to learn to despise that, not because it wasn't a perfectly human reaction, but because that was how you died, and if you didn't despise it, you would *be* that before long.

Shenkov pushed the coffee nearer to him by another inch or so. He looked unsettled for some unfathomable reason of his own. 'It's standard procedure. The soldiers have a sweepstake in the first week of a new lab intake. Whoever arrests the most scientists wins. Nothing's going to happen to you this time.'

Valery stared at the coffee. If he could just give it another minute, it wouldn't hurt so much if it was dashed out of his hands. He did want it. Never turn down coffee, that was a good rule to live by. Shenkov was lying, of course; it was a standard lie to make you explain yourself.

'Unless I'm so radioactive I'm actually glowing, you're going to offend me soon,' Shenkov said in his petrifying warm way. He was such a powerfully built man that he could have spent his life speaking at nothing above a murmur, and he would still have been plenty frightening. Clearly he knew that.

Valery lifted the cup. He had a scar on his face anyway, and it wasn't as though it mattered how zek biochemists looked.

Shenkov didn't move.

Valery decided to hurry him along. 'There were kids playing in the river. All I did was try to stop them. Surely everyone knows this whole place was contaminated; I mean – it was done on purpose. Half the people in town must work here or at the nuclear plant. Surely people already know the river is dangerous.'

'No. It's kept as quiet as possible. Hence . . . the no-talking rule.'

Valery sipped the coffee. Shenkov, it occurred to him, was too elegant to spray his office with something that would smell for a long time afterwards. 'It was children,' he said.

'You cannot,' Shenkov said, again no louder than the volume at which he always spoke, 'interfere. Whatever's in the river, it isn't much. Those boys will be fine. The more people know about this place, the more chances there are that the Americans will hear about it. Scientists we have to trust, but if you'd come with a family, I'd be telling you now to tell them you work at a chocolate factory. It only takes one child to make one comment on a train with the wrong person on it. If a report were to reach Washington, do you really think the CIA wouldn't be able to work out where we are? If they don't know what we have, then what we also have is the benefit of the doubt. You don't bomb someone whose capabilities you can't judge.'

'Whereas if they knew that all our equipment is made of cardboard and we have at least six times less in the way of bombs than they do, then that would be problematic, yes, I do understand,' Valery said, irritated to have the whole nature of his own state explained to him as if there weren't teenagers who'd worked it out.

'Good, so you see why you won't be talking to any more strangers in rivers,' Shenkov said.

Valery sighed. 'You should at least put barbed wire up. If everyone who goes in the Techa dies of cancer, they'll clock what's going on pretty bloody fast. People aren't stupid.'

'There isn't enough in the Techa to give anyone a cough, never mind cancer.'

'All right, it's all harmless, marvellous. Have you seen the forest?' Valery said.

Shenkov sat back a little, just verging on impatient. 'Nothing is in the Techa, Kolkhanov. Say it.'

'Nothing is in the Techa,' Valery repeated, meeting his eyes so that there was at least a vague jab at sincerity.

Shenkov studied him with something like the beginnings of relief. 'Don't you like chocolate?'

'I do, but is there something in it?' he asked.

'No,' Shenkov said, looking shaken. He was an excellent actor. No security officer would really be shocked to hear someone in their custody wonder aloud if they'd done something terrible to whatever they'd just handed over. He scrutinised Valery for a long time, with rage in his eyes, and Valery wanted to curl forward, because the echo-pain of the cattle prod zinged up his ribs. He stayed straight. 'You can go,' Shenkov said finally. 'I'd prefer not to see you in that chair again.'

Valery paused. 'Sorry, what?'

'What?'

'You're being serious, I can go?'

'Yes? I told you nothing would happen this time.'

'Was that not a lie?'

'It wasn't,' he said.

'Okay,' Valery said gradually. He snapped the bar in two and left half on the desk, smiled, and did not rush as he left. Out in the corridor, the strength in his knees vanished and he had to lean against the wall. No boiling water, no nothing; but maybe Shenkov only deployed that kind of thing rarely, so people would be surprised in contrast with the chocolate.

5

The Importance of Strontium-90

After pausing at the security office for his prisoner-book stamp, Valery looked for Ilenko at breakfast in the canteen on Monday morning. Again, though, she must have been busy with other things. So he sat by himself, lonely but preferring that to the turmoil which would ensue if he tried to start making conversation with someone new. He felt like he was from another species to all the students. It wasn't just that he had to gaze at toast and butter as if it were powdered unicorn, or that the feeling of real cotton sleeves was strange. It was that he had nothing to say. People made conversation by asking after your family, or home, or your last job, or if you'd been watching the ice hockey; he couldn't speak to any of that. He didn't mind, but it was awkward to have to say, *actually I was starving to death last week and I had a rat called Boris.*

He hoped someone was looking after Boris.

He found himself tapping his fingertips against the table in knock code.

Rat rat rat rat rat rat

'Cat,' said Shenkov in passing, in the tone of someone who was saying shut up.

'Does he just say random words now?' said Dr Resovskaya, arriving with a bowl of six boiled eggs.

'I think . . .' Valery couldn't get a sentence together, too puzzled. Some of the officers at the Lubyanka had known a code existed, but none of them bothered to learn it. It hadn't mattered by then. You'd already been arrested.

'Anyway, I'm putting you on field mice to begin with,' she said. She gave him a slim file with a few pages of research goals printed in it, guidelines, regulations. Underlined in bold was *primary aim: evidence of radiation resistance*.

'We need data about strontium-90 retention in their skeletons. You'll need to get outside and lay some traps today, say a hundred or so across a range of contaminated territory. The map's in there.'

'Where did Shenkov come from?' he asked. Shenkov was in the queue now. In the queue, not at the front; he hadn't pushed in, although everyone would have let him. The students behind him had left a clear two metres of space between him and them. They had clustered themselves into an anxious knot.

'Shenkov? He's a foreigner obviously, but I don't know what flavour. Is he Chinese?'

Valery looked at her over his glasses, taken aback, because that sort of comment had been well beneath her when he had known her last, and she wasn't old enough for it to be first instinct. Certainly by the time he'd been at school, it had been distinctly Not On even to notice things like that of any person who didn't have a strong American accent and a sign on their jumper that said I AM DEFINITELY NOT A SPY. His school had been full of propaganda posters showing Communist people of all different races holding hands or playing with their children together, always above the FRIENDS FOREVER slogan. In one way it made you want to be sick in a bag, but in another, it was exactly right. 'I meant immediately prior to the Lake,' he said.

'Not sure. Why?'

He watched her, because it had occurred to him that she *didn't* think like that, and that she was pretending to, and that she was doing it to throw him off – something else. 'What are you not telling me, you unashamed weasel?'

She snorted. 'It would be indelicate.'

'What? You can't say that and then not—'

'Look, get your biochemistry hat on,' she said, a little stern. 'He won't issue you with a pass unless you explain what you're doing and where you'll be. Opportunity to give you another good scare before you go out.'

Valery nodded, but as Resovskaya cracked an egg and rolled it to break the shell, he felt sick and decided that, just now, Shenkov seemed better. He was used to people who liked to be frightening, but he had no internal defences whatever against the boiled egg.

When he let himself into Shenkov's office, it smelled of an expensive cologne and freshly vacuumed carpet. Shenkov himself was holding nothing more offensive than a cup of tea. He looked puzzled; Valery must have seemed happy to see him.

'I'm supposed to be going beyond the perimeter today. Dr Resovskaya said to ask you about the pass.'

'Well, sit down.' Shenkov watched him sit, as though even the way his joints worked was irritating. He took out a form. 'So, strontium-90 in mice. Why strontium-90, what is that?'

Valery suspected the man was just trying to assess whether he was still mentally competent to do the job. He couldn't blame him. After Saturday's performance, Shenkov probably thought he was borderline hysterical. 'A by-product of a nuclear reactor. It's radioactive, which means it has spare neutrons and it fires them out at close to light speed. When strontium is ingested, it seeks bone, because structurally it's similar to calcium. It sits in bone, blasting out radiation, which means the subject gets a long dose over time. Testing for strontium-90 in the bones of animals around this area over a few generations will show us whether it's possible to build resistance to radiation, and also to what extent it affects the animals in question.'

Shenkov nodded slightly. He was taking notes. That faint scritching was coming from the light switch in the new quiet.

'The wiring here is off, isn't it?' Valery said, because it was the third time he'd noticed.

'The wiring?'

'Can you hear that noise?'

Shenkov listened, then shook his head. 'It isn't the wiring. There are bugs in the light switches and the phones. We listen to everything.'

'Oh right,' said Valery. He thought about it. 'That must be boring.'

'It is.' Shenkov looked up. 'So where in the forest are you going?'

'Over some distance. I need to cover three separate radiation zones. A little, more, and the most I can find. To compare the mice from those regions to each other and how they deal with that radiation.'

Shenkov looked at the map taped to his desk – the same one Resovskaya had, with the radiation bands marked on in different colours. Then he tapped some numbers into a calculator. 'Right. Don't stay out for longer than four hours. Set the stopwatch.'

'If the radiation is what we're being told, it wouldn't matter if I camped out there for a fortnight,' Valery said.

'Moscow says four hours.'

That peculiar thing was happening, the one that had happened in Leningrad when Valery was young; everyone knew one thing to be true, but everyone was obliged to keep insisting it wasn't. Gosh, of course everyone who's arrested is guilty. Of course *Truth* only prints the honest-to-God truth, it's in the name.

Of course the radiation is fine.

'Is someone coming with me?' he asked.

'No. Why?'

'You're just giving a zek a car?' Valery said, confused.

'The cars only have thirty kilometres' worth of petrol in the tanks and all of them have trackers in them,' Shenkov said, quite gently. 'Try to run and I'll find you in half an hour. Don't, though; I hate this weather.'

A drizzling rain was pattering at the window behind him.

'Fair enough,' Valery said.

Shenkov shook Valery's hand in both of his, which felt like the subtlest of reminders that he could have crushed it if he liked. 'There's your pass.'

Valery had to show the pass first to the soldier at the facility perimeter, and then again to the soldiers at the city perimeter. They took note not only of his papers, but of the facility Land Rover he'd borrowed from the car park at the Lighthouse, and of the hundred and twelve wildlife traps in the back. They told him politely that the curfew was at sunset, and they would shoot anyone trying to access the gates after that.

It was a relief to drive out over the marsh beyond the fence to the forest. The road was only a little higher than the pools and the tufts of thick marsh grass, and it was beginning to flood in places, gleaming even in the mist. He hadn't driven himself for years and he had forgotten how much he liked it. The Land Rovers were fabulous things, too; brand new, with powerful engines and gearsticks that took the perfect amount of push to shift. He pulled in just under the shade of the trees, and then stepped down and away from the car. Old leaves and twigs cracked under his boots, and without the mumble of the engine, the quiet had roots that delved right into the earth.

Mainly, the trees were silver birches. From a distance, they looked all right, but up close, they had scars. Most of them had lost their branches at some point a few years ago. They were regrowing now, but there were jagged stumps and torn bark where the old limbs should have been. About a quarter of them were dead; they were only standing upright because there hadn't yet been a storm heavy enough to fell them. Valery gazed around. That was all to be expected, but something about the woods felt odd. He couldn't trace what. Perhaps it was only the shush of so many leaves, after he had spent so long out of sight of a single tree. He closed his hand around the silver pocket watch, which was still going; it felt, already, like a talisman from home.

There were birds. That was a good sign. He could see nests and, scanning the forest floor, tracks from little mammals. And big mammals; there were deer round here somewhere. He went down on his knees – they cracked – and turned over a chunk of soil with a knife. Ants – good – and fragile roots where shards of grass were growing.

It was only when he started to walk around, setting out the traps, that he noticed the view through the trees north to south was much clearer than the view east to west. It was so marked that he went in circles for a while, puzzling, and even then he didn't understand until he'd finished with the mouse traps and walked back to the car, on the edge of the woods, where the air was open.

The wind blew from the south; from City 40. The trees had lost their branches only on the windward side.

He turned back to see into the forest again. The windward side. If the radiation was coming from ground contamination, from the water table, the wind shouldn't have had anything to do with it.

Standing so still now, he could feel the stopwatch ticking.

6

The Mouse Room

In the morning, he got up early to avoid Dr Resovskaya and the boiled eggs. He had a lot of catching up to do, if he wanted to be up to date with all the new science. There was a stack of existing research to look through, so he took a sheaf of files to read over breakfast. The first was compiled figures about strontium deposits in soil animals. The data was wonderful; Resovskaya had five years' worth, and it was enough to trace the effects through a dozen generations in some cases. Ants, it seemed, were radiation-proof; the worm population, though, had declined by ninety-nine per cent in comparison with the control group she'd kept in normal conditions.

Poor worms.

Nowhere had she detailed the true radiation readings of her research quadrants; just the difference between them. Usually, that would have been a stunning oversight in a radiation study – it defied the whole point.

Resovskaya wasn't a third-rate academic, though. She was a proper genius. It had to be on purpose.

A wet bang went off outside and he jumped; so did everyone else, but then they all laughed when they saw it was just another of those strange marsh geysers, going off about two hundred yards beyond the lab's broad window, where the lake shore gave way to the wetlands. Some ducks had had a shock too, and whirred off just in time to be sprayed with falling mud.

Valery went back to the soil animal study, rubbing the back of his neck. He was so rickety that being made to jump had twanged one of the nerves that cradled the base of his cranium. Still, his fingers felt stronger now, so the breaks must have been getting better. Once he was healthier, there was nothing stopping him doing some real exercise here. The idea of running, even just on a treadmill, had a dreamy allure.

At the window, some of the students clustered to play geyser bingo and a little cheer went up when another mud fountain poofed up further out into the marshes. It was funny, that; normally you needed proper heat underground for that sort of thing. A geologist he was not, but he would have sworn they weren't near the edges of any tectonic plates out here.

Someone touched his shoulder, which made him gasp, and lifted the prisoner book out of his breast pocket, where he had completely forgotten about it. Shenkov leaned down over him and signed today's eight o'clock box against the table edge, bringing with him the woody scent of his cologne and a freshly ironed shirt. He said nothing about it, and went to join the coffee queue. Valery had to sit there digging his fingernails into his own shoulder. He couldn't remember the last time someone had come up that close to him for no pressing reason and, shamefully, it was sending blood prickling right up and down his arm. He kept his eyes down, hating the idea that Shenkov would see it.

There were fifty mice in the woodland traps the next day. He collected them up into the laboratory's Land Rover and drove back feeling guilty.

'Do we have any anaesthetic?' he asked Dr Resovskaya.

'Anaesthetic, why?'

'For the animals.'

'No, I'm afraid not,' she said. 'No funds for that kind of thing.' She half-laughed when she said it, and her eyes went over his face. Everyone else, of course, was clean-shaven, and there had been a razor in the package she'd sent up to his room. He had only used it selectively. He preferred looking like a floppy poetry-writing liberal to showing the scar across his jaw. If it showed, people would ask how he got it.

There was a particular clunk that was a scalpel cutting through the end of a mouse's tail. After he had three pieces of tail and three distressed mice huddled in their box full of lettuce, he had to stop and pull off his mask and glasses so he could press his hands over his eyes. He wasn't alone in the lab, but other people pretended not to notice. He leaned against the table and faced the wall, waiting to stop feeling so raw.

'So how did you end up in the gulag?' someone asked.

When he looked around, everyone was watching him. Nobody said how they knew. Dr Resovskaya must have mentioned it – she wouldn't think it was anything remarkable. He felt exposed. Ilenko wasn't here still; she must have been assigned to some other lab.

'I did a year abroad as part of my degree, I went to Berlin. It went on record somewhere, and I was arrested in . . . fifty-six.'

'That's all?' a girl said.

Valery took care not to laugh. 'If you spend any time in a capitalist country you'll be sent to the gulag, whatever you did there.'

Unsettled looks slithered between them all.

One boy was annoyed. 'If you were truly loyal to the Party, you'd have been shot before you worked for the enemy though, wouldn't you.'

'They weren't the enemy then, the borders were open. It was nineteen thirty-seven. The Party sent me.'

'But then . . .'

'Every third person in the gulag is an academic,' he said, slowly, because it was bizarre to stumble across someone who didn't know that. He had thought the whole world knew. It had all come out after Stalin died, which was why Valery had almost laughed when he found himself being arrested a good three years after that. You could have papier-mâchéd Siberia with the reams of newsprint written about the arrests and the trials, but under no cover but a penitent air, the Kremlin had kept it going all the same. 'People aren't sent because of what they've *done*, they're sent because of what they *might* do under the right conditions.'

'Why doesn't anyone know that? If there's that many people then why haven't we met any?'

Valery wanted to ask what the boy meant by *anyone*; anyone under twenty-five, it sounded like. But that would have been cruel. 'Because most of those people have no trade skills, so they're assigned to general labour, which is usually mining, in minus sixty degrees, so they die. So you never hear from them.'

'It can't be all that many people then,' the boy said, and Valery heard exactly how maddening he must have sounded when he had tried to tell Ilenko she wasn't on mum duty.

Valery admired her all the more for not having punched him. 'The population of the Soviet Union is now about a hundred and twenty million.' The numbers came quite easily. 'According to the KGB's own records, which have been publicly released to the West and are therefore conservative estimates, twenty million people went through labour camps at some point between nineteen thirty-two and fifty-three. There is no information from before that, and the current numbers are classified. Official estimates are that two million of those twenty million died at the camps, but I should tell you that if someone looks like they're about to die of cold or starvation, they go down on the records as released, not deceased. So one in seven people has been to a labour camp, and if you believe KGB record-keeping, then one in ten of those is dead.'

The phone rang into the silence that followed. It was by Valery, so he picked it up. 'Biology lab.'

'Can you not,' Shenkov said at the other end without bothering to say who it was or how he had overheard from two hundred metres away in the security office, from beyond eight closed doors, 'whip the student population into dissident protests in your first week?'

'Actually they don't look very convinced, I think we're all right,' Valery said.

'It is interesting to have such a determined tightrope walker on staff,' Shenkov told him in his devastatingly mild way, and hung up.

Valery shrugged a little at the students. 'That was Comrade Shenkov telling me to shut up. So draw your own conclusions.'

'That can't be right,' someone else said, sounding angry. 'Everyone would know.'

Valery shook his head, because he had thought about it for years and he still couldn't come up with a way to make it sound factual. A labour camp, the whole witless idea, was the kind of thing fantasists and snuff movie-makers came up with. It felt idiotic to even imagine treating people the way they were treated there. If you spoke for hours and hours, perhaps you'd shift that; but he didn't want to talk about it for five minutes, never mind five hours. 'Everyone does know,' he said.

No doubt they thought he was trying to be mysterious and interesting, and who could blame them; he would have to be philosophical about it if one of them hit him in the head with an ice pick.

Dr Resovskaya stepped out of her office. 'This sudden silence sounds suspiciously like you're all covering up a row,' she said, bright as always. Her shoes sparkled.

The young man turned on her crossly. 'Comrade, we all have to share a lab with a traitor. That's going to look bad on our records, all our records. I worked my *arse* off to be here, and now—'

'And now the Party has placed you here. Problem?' Resovskaya said mildly. If she was flustered to find the beginnings of a mutiny in her lab, she didn't look it.

'No,' he said, but he was still simmering.

'You're dreaming if you imagine that even one in a thousand people sent to the gulag is guilty. Stalin himself said that it was worth arresting a thousand people to find one spy. You understand, don't you, that people were arrested indiscriminately and then tortured into confessing?'

There was a charged quiet that crackled with resentment. Nobody *wanted* to believe things like that, and they certainly didn't want to believe it of someone standing in the room with them. Valery wished she hadn't said it, because he understood why people resented hearing it. If you were the victim of something foul, it gave you the moral high ground, forever. Which meant that all of them now felt defensive about not liking him, because that dislike was a genuine concern, but now it had been made to look frivolous because wasn't he a wonderful martyr and weren't they despicable.

That was a dangerous thing to make anyone feel.

'Not me, though,' Valery said. 'I ratted on everyone I knew the second I got into the Lubyanka, let's not pretend I stood on principle even for forty seconds. Kudos to those people, but I'm a reincarnated mouse.'

Like he'd hoped, it broke the charge and some of the students even laughed.

Resovskaya looked rueful. 'Comrade, come and have a cup of tea with me.'

Valery set the samples aside. As far as he knew, you could still be arrested for association with proven enemies of the state.

Guilt was more infectious than typhus. He wanted to point out that it was hardly unreasonable of any of the students not to want to be seen with him, but he didn't want to argue with Resovskaya.

'It's all right, I'm not marching you somewhere terrible,' Resovskaya said. Like before, her tone was the over-gentle one which she might have taken with an incredibly old person.

Valery managed to smile. He didn't think she meant to be patronising.

She led him out into the bare corridor, where his heart began to tap at his sternum more urgently than usual. He tried to order it to quiet down. Even if she was going to tell him off for how he'd handled the students, he wasn't going to end up stuffed in a bio-waste bin just yet, but the memory of the police van was still so sharp he kept catching himself on it. He could smell the bleach. On cue, the cattle-prod burn on his ribs started to hurt again.

'Are you all right?' Resovskaya asked, sounding alarmed.

Valery realised that he was inclining his head while he listened to his own internal monologue, just as openly as he would have if Inner Valery had been another person standing beside him and talking aloud. He must have looked demented. 'Yes, sorry.'

She pursed her lips a little. 'Because, you know, you can say when you aren't. I don't run one of the labs where people are expected to carry on minus a recently amputated leg. If it's getting too much for you, I need you to say. There aren't many people trained to do what you do, Valery, certainly not to the standard you do it; I can't afford to run you into the ground.' She sounded finished, but then she seemed to hear what she had just said, and because decades of shouty men had made her hard, she looked embarrassed. He felt desperately sorry. 'You'll end up with inaccurate results.'

He forced himself to look at her properly. He had never liked looking anyone full in the face. It felt as invasive as poking them in the chest, and the instinct not to do it was powerful, even if he was surrounded by people who insisted it was the polite thing. It wasn't helped any by a lingering suspicion that everyone was lying. When he was a teenager, everyone had insisted loudly that Stalin was wonderful and obviously your husband must be guilty if he'd been taken away in the night. It had seemed to follow that the validity of eye contact, handshaking, and shouting at people to get things done were also lies of obscure state purpose.

'Comrade, I'm going to be strange for a while, if not permanently. But I'm not unhappy or damaged, or I don't think I am. I've just been growing in different soil. I'm okay.'

She shifted her weight onto one side, plainly uncomfortable. He heard the heel of her shoe creak. 'Only you do occasionally seem to hear things that aren't there,' she said.

'I know. Don't you think, though, that all the best people sometimes indulge in a little bit of auditory hallucination?'

She only nearly laughed. 'Oh, dear. Well, I suppose as long as you know you do it.'

'I know,' he promised. 'Where are we going?'

She brightened, and opened the door they had paused beside. 'The mouse room,' she said, and stood aside to let him go first.

The room smelled of new sawdust. It was a large square space, lined with glass boxes, all bolted together in a great framework that went right the way up to the high ceiling. On each wall was a ladder that would slide along metal rails. Inside each glass box was sawdust, water dispensers, a soft yellow lamp, and white laboratory mice. The whole room was alive with the warm sound of scuffling and claw-clicks. There must have been thousands. Valery smiled. After the bleak corridors and the dead silence of his apartment, being surrounded by so many living things felt like coming out into the sun.

'They're wonderful. What are they for?'

'They're our radiation mice,' Resovskaya explained. 'The wild population study will show us snapshots of how mice in the wider ecosystem are responding to the radiation, but this is the controlled side of that. We expose these mice to regular doses of gamma radiation – gamma because it goes through glass so we don't have to take them out of the boxes – and we monitor mutations and changes in their young. Mice are perfect for intergenerational studies, of course, because you'll get two generations per year.'

'I see,' he said, charmed. He went to the nearest box. A mouse came to peer at him too. 'It must be a low dose? They seem okay.'

'It is. The aim is to irradiate them enough to disrupt forming DNA, but not enough to hurt them. I have to say, the results have been very interesting so far. So if you come over here, this wall is the section that's had the most frequent doses.'

Valery followed her and looked into the eye-level boxes. Even at a glance, the mice inside had all kinds of birth defects. Missing paws, missing eyes, very short tails, very long tails. They all seemed to be getting along happily enough.

'I've never seen anything like this.'

'No,' Resovskaya agreed. 'And that's because what we've found is that a single high dose of radiation won't do much to cause mutations; either it kills the subject, or it causes some cancers and then that's that. That, we think, is why there's no noticeable human mutation around Hiroshima and Nagasaki among the children of the survivors. But what *will* cause mutation is a steady lowish dose. The more frequent the dose and the longer the period over which that dose is given, the higher the rate of offspring mutation.'

Valery looked round. 'This is an experiment to predict the effect of the radiation here on humans,' he said.

She sighed. 'Comrade, I've told you already, the dose *people* receive here is completely negligible—'

'Come on, Elena, the students aren't here,' he said. 'I was arrested at the weekend because I told some kids to get out of the irradiated river. The forest is dying. Obviously people here are getting frequent significant doses.'

She looked hunted, and he watched her teeter over denying it. But then she seemed to see that there would be no earthly point in doing that. 'Well, it will certainly help Moscow understand how much they will need to spend on healthcare here,' she said, stiff, and her eyes went to the main light switch by the door. 'Especially for people who do stray into – the more rusty parts of the forest.'

He gazed at the mice. 'So these are what generation, now?'

'These are our fifteenth and sixteenth generations.'

'And what's the infant death rate?'

'High,' she said. 'Only about forty per cent of the young survive to adulthood.'

'Christ,' he said softly. 'What's the human infant death rate here?'

She looked exasperated. 'Humans aren't mice, Valery; we're rather bigger, and we can absorb a lot more radiation quite happily. Radiation hype is scarier than actual radiation. No one in Kyshtym is going to have horribly mutated children, we're not in an insane science fiction novel.'

He blinked slowly, not quite able to believe that she had just said that to him when he knew bloody well what radiation was and what it did. He almost pointed east, to the forest and the dying trees, which were in turn much bigger than human beings. He didn't.

'Anyway,' she went on, 'I thought this could be your project. You like animals. When you're not running fieldwork, you can keep up with this. We use lead screens to filter out the radiation for our wall of non-irradiated mice and so forth, and – well, it's all in the binder. What do you think?'

He nodded. 'Yes. Thank you.'

'Gets you away from the students too,' she said. She made it sound as though it was the students who were at fault, but he would have bet anything that at least a couple of them had already asked her if it was really necessary to share a lab with the gulag madman who listened to imaginary voices and knock code.

'I'm . . . happy to go to a different lab if you'd rather not leave me with this,' he said.

'There isn't another biology lab,' she said. 'Everything else is for the physics people.'

'Oh right,' he said, and tried to think why he had been so sure there were other labs. He couldn't. 'How do we administer the radiation?' he asked instead.

She pointed at the table, where there was a perfect cube of what looked like lead. 'There's a chunk of uranium in there. Just take the lid off for ten minutes and go for a coffee. Are you quite *sure* you're all right?'

Valery pretended not to hear. Very lightly, he touched the top of the lead box. It was warm. If he were to open the box, the uranium inside would be unspectacular. Uranium was just an inoffensive grey metal. But if you could see further up the electromagnetic spectrum, past visible light, past ultraviolet, to the blasting intensity of gamma rays; it would look like a star. It made him smile, despite all of Resovskaya's lying. It wasn't often that anyone gave you a star in a box.

'Oh,' he said, because he'd remembered. 'If there are no other labs – where's Comrade Ilenko? You know, from the Biophysics Institute?'

Resovskaya withdrew, without moving at all. 'Oh, Ilenko. She had to go back to Moscow unexpectedly. Shenkov told me.'

'Shenkov?' Valery said, puzzled. 'What's he got to do with—'

'For God's sake, Valery,' Resovskaya whisper-snapped. 'You *need* to learn to talk in code. Yes, Shenkov, because Ilenko tried to call a journalist friend who works for *Truth* in Moscow and explain about how everyone is lying about radiation levels and isn't it shocking, and Shenkov had to shoot her.'

No wonder Shenkov looked like he wasn't sleeping.

7

The Institute of Hereditary Biology and Racial Hygiene

Germany, 1937

It was not the first time she'd had to tell him to learn the code.

Although his memory of Before wasn't good any more, he could remember this one, vividly.

He had been nineteen, and he'd arrived in Berlin with Dr Resovskaya and four other undergraduates from Moscow University six months prior, just as part of a traditional yearly exchange. It was the sort of placement people said was a good idea because it was Culturally Expanding, but mainly he'd found that the only thing expanding was him, German food being wonderful and German cafes being everywhere. Dr Resovskaya said he and the other students were actually beginning to look like real people and not ambulatory gardening tools. When he tried to tell the German researchers how you couldn't *get* proper cheese in Moscow, they had thought he was joking, but then been mortified when they realised he wasn't, and he and the other Soviets were still getting through the apology cheese hamper. Seeing it in the fridge made him giggle every morning. He had never met a set of people so easily worried about offending their colleagues. It was the most extraordinary change from Moscow, where you were having a marvellous time if nobody was locking you in the supply cupboard for getting your units wrong.

The lab was small and basic, but working there was fun, and he liked German people a lot. They were direct, and he had been delighted to find that the researchers would correct his pronunciation. It was remarkable how, in other languages, people were loath to do that. He had English language partners too, because so many science journals were in English and he was determined to learn, but English people were useless. If they could hazard the faintest guess at what you might mean, paralysing embarrassment kept them from mentioning that *ee* and *i* were very different sounds, or that you were going to seem peculiar if you chose the wrong one when you tried to say you were going home by ship.

That morning, everyone had been late, because there was a street protest. Valery wasn't very good with German when people were screaming it rather than telling it to him quietly, so he assumed it was something to do with the new government and got on with his paperwork.

'Phew,' one of the German researchers said, reeling in as if he'd had to take a run-up at the door. That in itself was telling. He was about two and a half metres tall. 'Getting hairy out there. There are soldiers and everything.'

'Our windows are pretty high, I'm sure we'll be fine,' Valery said.

'Windows?'

'If they open fire.'

'You're insane. Russians are all insane.'

'Well,' said Valery, not liking to say that Germans were infants who didn't know how to recognise things going wobbly, 'I'll bet you a glass of wine. Is . . . that a jar of eyeballs?' he added, because the researcher was unpacking his briefcase.

'It is indeed,' the man said, setting it down on Valery's desk, 'a jar of eyeballs. Present for you.'

'I love it!' Valery beamed, feeling very happy about the way life was going. He was doing his degree for free, unlike the Germans, who had looked crestfallen when Dr Resovskaya explained that your education all the way up to PhD was free in the Soviet Union; he'd managed by pure blind luck to get a third-year supervisor who was a genius, which undergrads hardly ever did; after university, the government would send him somewhere to do a job that involved being a specialist in radiobiology, unlike the poor Germans who'd have to scrabble around *applying* for things for ages and then end up running a pharmacy somewhere instead. And now, he had his own jar of actual eyeballs. It was the devil's own work to get human tissue at home if you weren't part of the medical school. The medical school were snobs.

The researcher laughed. 'Right, well, here's a challenge for you. See if you can make the irises turn blue. There's a paper here about the possibility of doing it with the right application of radiation; we need to see if we can replicate the findings.'

'Oh,' said Valery, intrigued. He had to blink twice at the journal article to make his brain perceive the German alphabet as sounds and not meaningless lines. It always happened in the first split second, even now that he was close to fluent. 'Why?'

'Peer review.'

It wasn't what Valery had meant, but he decided he didn't care. He scanned the article for numbers and doses. Once he had them, he held up the eyeballs. They bobbed cheerily in their formaldehyde. Some of them spun to look at him. All of them were brown. They looked surprised. He widened his own eyes back at them.

'I've given Valery the eyeball thing,' the German man aimed at Dr Resovskaya, who was just on her way in. She hadn't had to barge anywhere; she was the sort of woman who people let through on the off-chance that she would smile at them.

'Good,' she said, and Valery recognised the tone. She must have demanded they give him something interesting that might help his thesis, not just washing up other people's test tubes.

The German researcher edged away.

Outside, there was some crowd-chanting. Valery couldn't catch the slogan, but people sounded angry. The back of his neck itched. Someone was going to open fire soon, he could feel it coming, so he concentrated on the article, and on replicating the test conditions.

Dr Resovskaya paused by him towards mid-morning to see how he was doing.

'Oh, excellent,' she said, because she had arrived just in time to find a perfectly grey eyeball on Valery's workbench.

'Strips the melanin out pretty well,' Valery said, tapping the syringe, which held a mixture of vicious radioactive isotopes, vicious enough that he was having to wear lead-lined gloves. He paused. 'Funny thing to do, though. You'd blind whoever you injected with this.'

'I wonder if that isn't rather the point,' she said, and film-star walked away. She always wore heels, he suspected as an up yours to the head German researcher, who had made disapproving mumbling noises through his moustache about having women in the lab. Germans were weird about women. For people who seemed very concerned about the economy, they were mad keen to cut off fifty per cent of their workforce. Apparently this was normal in the West. Normal or not, Valery had spent a contented evening yesterday threading horsehair into the head German researcher's cigars.

'I don't . . . understand; never mind,' Valery sighed, not loudly enough for her to hear. It was rare to understand Dr Resovskaya. He had a theory that people who were high up in any organisation spoke a special oblique dialect unknown to normal people.

Outside, there were gunshots. He poked the German researcher who'd given him the eyes, and who now looked scared.

'I like red wine,' he said, to distract him.

'Right! Right.'

Valery forgot about the eyeballs until a few days later, when a severe man in SS uniform arrived. There was instant silence and, almost imperceptibly, Dr Resovskaya moved in front of Valery. It had been on the radio that foreign nationals might like to look into buggering off if they'd be so kind, but it hadn't been made law yet, and Dr Resovskaya said they were leaving when they were sent and not before. Valery agreed, because he was more afraid of her than the Nazis. The Nazis weren't marking his thesis.

'Dr Resovskaya and Dr . . . Kolkhanov?' The SS officer pronounced it Kolkhanoff, but he was smiling. 'Letter for you from the Ministry.' He handed Resovskaya a brown envelope with the eagle stamp on the corner.

He left, and everyone breathed.

Resovskaya opened the envelope and set it on the desk so that Valery could read it too. As always, the German letters were only squiggles for a second.

'Jesus Christ,' she said, having finished first by far. 'Hah.'

'I'm still reading,' Valery admitted.

'The eyeball thing,' she said, unusually bright. 'The results that you confirmed? This is from the researcher who wrote the paper. He says your results were even better than his, he wants to know what you changed. He's inviting us to his lab.'

'Oh,' Valery said, because he had expected to be in trouble.

'Well. Institute of Hereditary Biology and Racial Hygiene, here we come,' she said happily.

Across from them, the head German researcher finally lit one of the cigars Valery had tampered with. The horsehair burned nearly as well as cannon fuse and the whole thing caught fire, and someone had to put the man's stupid moustache out with a cup of tea. Dr Resovskaya gave Valery an assessing look. Valery did his best innocent face. She waited till they were outside before she laughed.

The Institute was a long, white building, part of Berlin University, and it was intimidatingly nice on the inside. A secretary sent them to a well-lit lab on the ground floor, where a big man with a monocle flew out and wrung them both by the hand.

'Hello! Hello, how are you? It's unbearable, but I literally haven't got a spare five minutes to find a cafe, I'm so sorry. Come inside for tea. And have a look at the lab! We've got all sorts today!'

It was infectious enthusiasm, and they both laughed. The man's name was Dr Fischer, and he hurled the lab doors open again just as hard as he'd shot through them a moment before. Inside, half a dozen people were working.

Fischer shouted something across the lab, a name, maybe Joe. 'Come and show them your twins thing while I make the tea! Sorry, you're Dr Resovskaya and . . . Valery, is it?' he said kindly.

'Yes,' Valery said, impressed that the man had bothered to learn his name, and then had to look at the research assistant, Possibly Joe, who was smiling and shaking hands now too. He was dark and handsome, but he seemed not to know; he wasn't snooty, just cheerful.

'You're the radiation people? Excellent. Listen, the twins thing is boring, come and look at what Fischer's working on.'

'Why are they being nice to us?' Valery whispered to Dr Resovskaya.

'Because they're going to make a job offer,' Dr Resovskaya whispered back.

Valery smiled when she nudged his shoulder. She was right. This was *much* nicer than their little polytechnic.

Joe took them across the lab to a long dissection table where, incredibly, there was a whole human cadaver. Valery shot a look at Dr Resovskaya, who widened her eyes back. There was no way in hell that their lab would ever get an entire human.

A small child toddled past, followed closely by an identical one. Valery watched them go, puzzled, then remembered what Dr Fischer had said about twins. Now he was looking, there were three sets, mostly occupied with building blocks in the corner. None of them seemed to have obvious parents. They were laughing, and painfully sweet. It gave him a pang. He loved children, but he knew he would never have any.

'So, I know we've got a reputation, but we are honestly not just about sterilising schizophrenics,' Joe was saying. 'We're starting on some radiation studies. *Our* interest is in the modification of genes. We know radiation changes DNA, obviously, but what we want to start looking into is whether it might change them in a targeted way, to correct genetic errors.'

Valery looked down at the cadaver. He had never seen radiation sickness in a human before, but he had seen it in plenty of rabbits, and he could recognise it well enough to know that that was what the man had died of. Part of him did a happy pirouette. So not just human trials: unfettered human trials. Not hemmed in by miniature dose rates and results so negligible that they might have been caused by radiation, or a chest cold. Another shifted uneasily. It wasn't a very precise or clever trial if they were killing human subjects with it.

'I didn't think we were anywhere near that kind of thing,' Dr Resovskaya said. Her dark eyes were serious now.

'Well, reach for the stars and you might get to the moon,' Joe smiled.

Dr Fischer came over with the tea. He had a natural bounce to his step, and he was modulating it so carefully now that he looked as though he were pretending to roller-skate. 'There we are. What do you think? How would you two like to work here with us?'

'We're Soviet,' Dr Resovskaya said. 'I suspect there will be a passport problem in the next few months.'

'We'll sort it out,' Dr Fischer said. 'Don't worry. Joe's from Frankfurt, for God's sake, and we took him.'

Joe joke-shushed him.

'Anyway, let's have a *proper* tour, shall we? Dr Mengele?' he added grandly to Joe.

'This way,' Joe said, still smiling. 'You look worried?' he asked Valery.

'No,' Valery said slowly. 'No, just . . .'

Dr Resovskaya gave him a death stare which ordered him not to go off in hysterics about the waste of human life and useless suffering like every other pissy undergraduate who went around stating the bloody obvious.

'I was thinking it must be much more difficult for you to get trial volunteers now that you have to declare a death?' he said.

Joe and Fischer both laughed. It was a friendly laugh, but there was something under it that a hyena would have recognised. 'Oh, God, no. They're not volunteers. They're condemned prisoners. Don't worry. No shortage. It's sad, but we have to do the tests on someone and, as you say, we'd not get many volunteers, and certainly not in the genetically diseased groups we're interested in.'

Valery felt queasy.

'What do you think?' Resovskaya asked him as they left, aiming for the tram. 'Fabulous CV fodder.'

She was steering him by the small of his back, something she often did with students here. At home, she would never have

82

touched him, but in Germany, where men stayed boyish well into their thirties, Valery had endless trouble convincing the paper-checking police that he really was nineteen and that he had not forged his passport. He couldn't place how or why, but people from the Soviet Union grew up when they were much younger. If you were being obviously herded by a professor, the effect lessened.

'It's a bit bad they're using prisoners,' he said. It bubbled out before he could stop it.

She tipped her head in a kind of diagonal nod that wasn't whole agreement. 'Mm. But this is a radiation study with human test subjects. It's information that we *have* to know. I'm not impressed by their ethics either, but the horrible thing we all have to accept about working in science is that we have to go where the money is. And career-wise, you will be at a considerable advantage if you've got even a few months working on human trials. It's very prestigious, and it's absolutely the goal of the whole field.'

Valery could feel the weight of her approval, or disapproval, right on the back of his neck. 'I thought it was a little untargeted too.'

'How do you mean?'

'Well, genetic diseases . . . they can't look at everything all at once, can they, from syphilis to cystic fibrosis? Surely they should be looking more closely at one particular thing?'

She gave him a look of such strangeness he remembered it always after. It was sympathy, but it was impatience and disgust as well, and he saw her try to hide the latter, but it crossed her face anyway, only enhanced because of her smoky eyeshadow that enunciated every tiny line. 'Valery. Genetically diseased doesn't mean syphilitic. It means Jews and gypsies and homosexuals. And before you say anything; you can't go around blurting out that they're innocent. Of course they bloody are.

You might as well say the sky is blue and, if you do, everyone will think you're an idiot and you'll never be promoted above a lab technician.'

Valery looked up. 'But they *are* innocent—'

'You can't wave that flag,' she said again, exasperated. 'These tests have to be done. On *someone*. It will be horrendous, whatever happens. But in the end you'll either have done the science, or you won't. If you don't, someone else will, because it's necessary. We need to know how radiation works and what it does. At least here, you can do it on subjects who can't speak to you in your own language, and who you can't be related to. That's as good as it's going to get, I'm afraid. Are you Jewish? Queer?'

'Does it matter?' he said sharply.

'No. Exactly. It doesn't.' She sighed. 'If you don't want this job . . . you're not cut out to specialise in radiation, and I'll transfer you to another department. Microbiology, maybe. Radiobiology is a field where you must always understand that the needs of the many must come before the few. It's a lot to cope with, and not everyone can. Human trials can be very tough indeed. You need a thick skin.'

'Microbiology – they're all pedantic lunatics who—'

'Well, then the question is: do you want to stick with radiobiology?'

He nodded helplessly. This degree was his whole life.

'Good, because it would be a bloody shame if I had to hand you off. You're good at this.'

It was the best thing she'd ever said to him. He smiled awkwardly, not knowing where to look, and thinking about the eyes and whose they had been.

'I'll send Dr Fischer our papers.' Dr Resovskaya gazed down at him for a long time as though she was making sure it was all going in. 'Now: come along,' she said, unexpectedly gentle. She fluffed up his hair, which had turned from an unpleasant squirrelly red to bright gold in the last few weeks, as if the sun had come out somewhere in him. 'I'm buying you a drink. Whatever we think, this is only for a few months. Hitler will declare war and then we'll be sent home.'

In fact it was exactly two months. After that, Valery was called for military service. He didn't know a soul in his unit, but he was too relieved to care.

8

The Body in the Pool

City 40, 1963

Valery let the wild mice go in the morning, each one in the same place he'd found it, and then sat down on a fallen tree to shade in a diagram he'd made of the test areas. Four sections, like there would have been in a controlled experiment; but out here, in a naturally contaminated environment, they weren't neat quarters but a mosaic of different contamination readings. Once it was done, he sighed at it. The data would be useful, but even if he took out the place it was gathered, the time, everything, it was still obviously not a controlled, artificial test space. He couldn't see how that could get past the censorship board. There was only so much use data could be if nobody published it. He looked away through the trees, wondering what the point of the whole facility was, if nobody was ever going to see the results.

No, that was dramatic. Someone would see them. The censorship people would file the data, and then provide it, carefully curated, to heavyweight scientists in whichever fields required it. No one would know where it came from or who collected it, but it would be there. Doing a bit of good.

He became aware that he was sitting opposite a dead man.

Man; boy. He must have been about twenty, the same age as the students at the lab, and he was floating face up in a marshy pool that lapped at the exposed roots of some silver birch trees.

He had been there all along, in full view, very full; he was dressed only in a hospital gown, but there weren't any obvious marks on him. Valery turned around twice. There wasn't a single sign of a path, a track, nothing to say that people ever came this way.

He went back to the Land Rover and picked up the radio. They all had radios. He'd never used one. He pushed the button.

'Er . . . hello?' he said.

The line crackled. 'Hello? Lighthouse security?'

'Y . . . es. I'm one of the biologists at the research base. I'm out in car –' he leaned to see the label in the windscreen '– car 27. I've found a dead man in the woods. He's in a pond.'

'Sorry, a dead body in the – where *are* you?'

He pulled out the map from the glovebox. 'Have you got a pencil? I'm going to have to give you coordinates. I'm about five kilometres from you.'

'Okay. It's a pretty rusty area, so wait in the car, not outside.'

Valery lifted his eyebrow at the map, which claimed there were only a few millicuries here. 'I will, thank you.'

'Is that Valery Kolkhanov?' a voice in the background asked, with a familiar icy accent. Shenkov pronounced it Valerie, like they did in English. For a mad intrigued moment, Valery wondered if he was a super-secret Englishman. That would certainly have landed him in the Lubyanka long enough to learn the knock code. 'If he's been arrested again . . .'

'Hi,' Valery offered. But then, if you *were* a super-secret Englishman, you'd get rid of the accent. Surely. 'I've not been arrested.'

'There's a body,' the operator supplied.

'Kolkhanov,' Shenkov said immediately, 'stay where you are, we'll be with you soon. Do *not* spook and run away, I'm not going to accuse you of murder unless you murdered him.'

'Honestly that hadn't occurred to me,' Valery said, unsettled that it hadn't. It should have; and he should not have trusted

Shenkov to be above board purely because he thought the man was fascinating.

The KGB were there within twenty minutes. It was organised; they came with wading gear so they could reach the corpse, and they had a trolley and a body bag. Shenkov must have been having a dull day, because he came himself. He seemed to feel the cold badly; he had a proper coat on, hands sunk into his pockets. It was the standard officer coat, light grey, but it was tailored, or else he was exactly the shape whoever had designed it had hoped people were.

'No one's been reported missing,' Shenkov murmured as the waders managed to lift the body on to its plastic-lined trolley. They closed a rubber casing straight over the top. 'We should have heard about this by now. He's outside the perimeter, he's been in the water a while, he should have missed at least one curfew.'

'Where's the next nearest town?' asked Valery, who was perched on the bonnet of the Land Rover, because the metal was warm.

'The exclusion zone is a forty-kilometre radius from the plant. So someone we don't know about wandered out here beyond the perimeter fence, attracting the attention of precisely no one, and drowned. Terrific,' Shenkov said, and began to turn away.

'He didn't drown,' Valery said.

'Pardon?'

Valery slid down from the bonnet to go after him. 'Well, maybe he did, but he didn't *just* drown. His hair is gone. It was radiation sickness.'

Shenkov looked down at him. 'From the pool?'

'No, he would have been burned. He must have inhaled something.'

'Then what are you saying?' Shenkov said, his eyes and his voice suddenly full of serrated edges.

Valery had to step back from him. The electric echo of the cattle prod prowled down his ribs. He wished he could make his nervous system shut up. 'I'm just telling you what the data is. He clearly had radiation sickness. I'm sure your coroner will say the same – look, never mind. I'll let you get on.'

'If he had radiation sickness acute enough for hair loss, then that's upward of two hundred roentgen, and we have a leak. Are you telling me that we have a leak of *two hundred roentgen* and no one's reported it to me?'

'Can you stop inferring things?' Valery said unsteadily. He wanted to retreat more, but there was a tree behind him and he was already among the roots. 'I'm not telling you any conclusions, I'm telling you he had radiation sickness. Ask the coroner.'

Shenkov seemed to see he had backed Valery into a tree and stepped back a little. Annoyed with himself, Valery stayed where he was. The part of him that liked doing magic tricks was amazingly unavailable. He was just floundering. 'Keep that to yourself, please.'

'Keep it to *myself*?'

'Before I drown you in that radioactive pool,' Shenkov said softly, 'please assure me that you understand why I'd prefer you *didn't* go back to the Lighthouse and announce to everyone that you found someone dead of radiation sickness five kilometres from the complex?'

Valery shook his head once. 'Whatever caused this, whether it's a leak or something in the ground, or a contaminated object, it is very dangerous indeed. You should be sealing off everything in conceivable walking distance, and you should certainly be warning people in the city to watch out for any signs of radiation sickness.'

'It isn't in the city or we would know about it by now. You don't say a word.'

Right next to Shenkov like this, Valery felt his own fragility. He might as well have been one of those dying pine trees, made of nothing more useful than rusty wood switches and sawdust. He was vividly aware of the black pool right beside him, and the invisible, roiling storm of radiation in the mud at its base.

'Fine,' he said. 'We're all quite safe. I expect he's just a funny-shaped giraffe.'

'I'm not enjoying this tightrope act as much as I was,' Shenkov told him.

'Shoot me, then, see if I care,' Valery said. 'After you've shot me, though, better get some people out here with dosimeters that measure above three roentgen. In hazmat gear.'

The other KGB men seemed eager to get away from the pool; they were already in their Land Rover. The engine came on with an unnecessary snarl. The man driving must have forgotten the size of the thing, because he reversed too fast and straight into a dead silver birch, which snapped. It fell shockingly fast and, although Valery could see what was happening, he couldn't move. He was right beneath the trunk.

Shenkov snatched him out of the way and pulled him to one side as the tree smashed into the pool. He bent forward enough to shield Valery from the splash, then turned him round, much more gently.

'Are you all right?' He sounded honestly frightened.

Mute, Valery nodded. Shenkov's gloved hands were still on his ribs, holding him steady on the uneven ground. It felt so safe it was terrible. He swallowed and found his voice again. 'Thank you. Get that coat off before it soaks through—'

Shenkov pulled it off and lobbed it straight into the pool, where it sank. In the Land Rover, the driver looked terrified.

'The pool isn't radioactive enough to kill anyone straight away, you said?'

'No, no, or it would've killed all the algae. Make you sick, though.'

'Good.'

Shenkov went to the driver's side of the car, dragged the man out, and dumped him in a puddle. Valery had to turn away so the poor man wouldn't see him laughing, then helped him up and offered him a lift back, because the others had already driven off.

While the unfortunate man dripped and complained, Valery drove only half-listening, wondering why Shenkov cared one way or another if a troublesome biologist was crushed under a tree. The way Shenkov had reacted, they could have been blood relatives. Perhaps Valery reminded him of someone else. Or perhaps Shenkov was just a kind person.

The latter thought made Valery nervous. He was in no state to cope with kindness. With no family and no people of your own to build up your resistance to it, kindness was like a triple shot of vodka after being teetotal for years. It went straight to the head.

He was going to have to avoid Shenkov as much as he could, at least until the triple shot wore off.

He spent the rest of the day in the lab, looking down a microscope at the bone samples from the mice. The microscope was better than any he had used before, and it illuminated in needle-sharp detail every strange, frothy malformation in the bones. Half of the samples showed at least the early stages of leukaemia; barely any of the mice were producing white blood cells properly. All of them would be prone to whatever the mouse equivalent of a cold was. He felt horrible when he saw that, because most of them would die now from infection contracted through their wounded tails.

It was a lot of damage for what was marked on the map as a less contaminated area. A lot. Worse than most of the mice in the mouse room, who were irradiated a hundred times more than the figure on the map claimed these mice should have been.

Still, it wasn't as though that was a surprise.

When Valery made his eight o'clock report to the security office in the evening to have the prisoner book stamped, he went out of his way to steer clear of Shenkov, whose office was before the main one, and asked the woman at the desk instead. It was hard not to look to the side as he went back past Shenkov's office door, which was open now.

It was in vain, because after midnight, Shenkov came to the lab. He didn't bang the door, but the clack of the latch was huge in the silence.

'Hi,' he said, and didn't add anything, but he was clearly checking that Valery hadn't gone mad and told everyone about the body with a megaphone.

Valery crushed down a stupid surge of happiness at the sight of him. He couldn't think of anything more off-putting than fawning over a man who had done nothing more than pull a fellow human away from a falling tree. He had to concentrate to keep his own tone brisk.

'Was there a leak?' he asked. Yes, good; businesslike.

'No,' Shenkov said. 'No, the physicists at the plant were as puzzled as we were. And, we aren't missing anyone.'

Valery stood back. 'Then where did he come from? He can't have just wandered in, in a hospital gown. Can he?'

Shenkov shook his head. He had come to the workbench. His eyes went interestedly over the microscope and the cell-sample slides. Valery, who had expected him to just go away once he had decided everyone was behaving themselves, felt as though something Arctic had come to look at him.

'Sometimes people come back into the exclusion zone from outside.'

'Why?'

'It's the people who used to live here, who we moved after the contamination. Things aren't good in the countryside at the moment. A lot of crop failures, and the land's bad anyway. Here it's good, or it looks good. A lot of people didn't understand why they had to move, they didn't know what radiation was. I couldn't explain it.' Shenkov looked straight at him. 'Do you even know?'

Valery nodded, wishing he could say that it was actually hurting him now, for Shenkov to be showing this much interest in speaking to him. He could feel his hastily built levee creaking with the force of the hunger behind it, only this hunger was worse than hunger for food. This was desperate, grasping.

'It's shrapnel, from the broken cores of atoms. That's what a radioactive substance is, something made of atoms whose cores are always in upheaval. The shards get shot out at great speed. If there are only a few shards every so often, it's fine for humans; they go through you, but they don't hit much. At an atomic level we're mainly empty space. If there's a lot all in one go, they shred your DNA and that causes problems like leukaemia later; or if there's even more, you fall apart.'

'That's . . . straightforward.'

'It is,' Valery agreed. 'I don't know why people think it's so mysterious, to be honest.'

Shenkov looked like he might be thinking of smiling. 'What are you doing so late?'

'Test results on the wild mice.' Valery hesitated for a long time. It was beyond stupid to voice anything like concern, especially to the man who had shot Ilenko for doing exactly that, but common sense was losing the battle with the part of him that needed Shenkov to stay and talk more. 'I'm a bit worried.'

'Worried why?' Shenkov said.

Oh, don't encourage us, Normal Valery mumbled.

'They . . . well.' Valery showed him the microscope. Shenkov glanced at him, then bent his neck to see. 'There is significant bone deterioration in *all* of these samples. Lots of birth defects. Not a single perfect specimen. I know we've got more contamination here than what's shown on our maps, but this is ridiculous.'

'Whatever it is, it's inside Moscow's safety parameters.'

Valery was already well beyond the perimeter of safe conversation. He could see the edge of a leather strap against Shenkov's shoulder; a gun harness.

'I know,' he said, and even meant to leave it at that, but then the levee broke, Normal Valery drowned, and the rest decided it was worth risking his life to have just another five minutes of speaking to someone who wanted to listen. 'I know that's what they're saying. But the trees are dying to windward, which means there wasn't just groundwater contamination; it was airborne, the kind you get from a bomb.' Valery felt as though he were being wrenched along by an undertow in the sea now. 'This place is staffed by not one single well-reviewed specialist in the field, but students, convicts, and women who have been elbowed out of better jobs. We're all disposable.' He couldn't stop. Perhaps it was talking, or perhaps it was airing some honest logic rather than the Code, he couldn't tell now. He closed his hands over the edge of the desk. 'The only reason I can think of for this kind of blanket secrecy – flying blatantly in the face of very obvious facts – is that the radiation is so bad it's dangerous for humans to be here.'

It banged into the quiet.

'Unless people here are eating grass in the forest contaminated with strontium-90 like your mice are, I don't see why anyone should worry,' Shenkov said tiredly. He'd closed off. Perhaps that was a good thing. 'If Moscow says it's safe here, it's safe—'

'Are they healthy, your kids?' Valery interrupted. He had begun speaking about the whole thing with no intention of pushing it this far, but the more Shenkov argued, the more Valery had to justify himself, the more sure he was. Now, the undertow was so strong he could feel it wrenching him under. 'You have kids, I've seen the pictures in your office. Their DNA is still building itself, which means it is not closed up yet. It's open, and it can absorb any radiation that happens to pass by in a way that yours or mine wouldn't. Allergies, prone to sickness, bone weakness, any of this sound familiar—'

Shenkov just tapped one hand on the table. But Valery, who had seen it coming and expected him to bang it hard, jumped so badly he dropped the Petri dish he'd been holding. It smashed so delicately on the floor that it almost held its shape, just in pieces. 'Calm down,' Shenkov said, after a pause in which the smash seemed to echo and echo. 'Review your data and find the error. And if you jitter about this to *anyone* else, I will have to shoot you. Do you understand?'

Valery had been in lots of fights; fights about food, non-fights with guards where you just curled up and thought of the motherland, fights with his father. Real fights, not a hushed recommendation from a well-mannered man. He should have been used to it, but he wasn't. He stood at the workbench for a long time after Shenkov had gone, hating how upset he was, and how he'd all but thrown himself into the whole stupid conversation just for the sake of talking when he knew how dangerous that water was. It made him want to shred his own skin off.

He couldn't go to bed feeling like that, so he meant to work all night. He was finished by three, though, which made him feel cheated, so he went walking outside in the dark. Automatic already, he set the stopwatch going at the door, even though he'd decided he didn't care if he was out for more than half an hour. He was still fizzing and ashamed. He had sounded like a gulag-addled neurotic making mountains out of electrons.

Smooth, 745, really bloody smooth.

Normal Valery had not drowned after all.

The birch forest shushed strangely, and out on the lake, reeds bowed in the wind. One of those geysers banged, somewhere off over the marsh.

On the far bank, there were lights. He watched as they moved out over the water. Someone must have been in a boat. Very distinctly, he heard a reel buzz, and the plink of a float.

9

The Village

He could still taste the bleach inside the back of the soldiers' van, and feel the rancid terror he had felt when they escorted him out of the cafe. But splashing about in the Techa was one thing; actually eating irradiated fish was something else altogether. There were some hills you had to die on. He set off across the damp grass.

The way around the lake was dark, but the night was bright. With the halogens of the Lighthouse facility and the town a good way behind him, the marshlands were silver under the stars. In the distance, the forest creaked in the breeze that blew in from the Urals, perhaps a little louder than healthy trees would have. Out into the lake, the weird shallow section looked like a glass spill, the moonlight making ripple shadows on the concrete just under the surface. He had a strong feeling he was walking beside the corpse of a lake, not a living one. There was something fossilised about it. But perhaps that was because, in his mind, the dark water was just a veneer over the smoky pall of radiation on the lake bed, whirling in black plumes where the current pulled it into the Techa and beyond.

On the water, the fisherman in his small boat recast, and the single light on the prow bobbed.

Because Valery was watching that, he almost fell over the bucket of fish propped up in a shallow swim, beside someone's rucksack.

Something pressed into the back of his neck.

'You,' said a hoarse voice, 'had better piss off and leave our catch alone.'

He put his hands up. 'I'm a scientist at the Lighthouse,' he explained. 'I just came out to warn you not to fish here. The lake is irradiated, it's full of nuclear waste. So are the fish. You shouldn't eat them.'

'Well, we've got to,' the voice said crossly.

Valery frowned. 'But everything in town is shipped in. It's all so cheap, you don't need to fish yourself – there's fish in the shops, and—'

'Not for us there's not. Off you fuck, comrade.'

'Can I turn around please?'

The rifle tip lifted from the nape of his neck. The man was dressed in rough clothes, overalls and a jumper with holes in the sleeves, and he was ill. Or rather, starved – he had the pinched look Valery still did, though on Valery it was already softening. Whoever the man was, he was not from City 40.

'Are you living in the exclusion zone?' Valery asked slowly.

'So what if we are?' the man snapped.

'You're living off the *land* here?'

'What do you want?'

'You can't. It's all contaminated—'

'Yes, fuckwit, we know that!' It was real rage, and Valery stepped backwards, once, carefully controlled, which was the halfway point between wanting to stand his ground, and the screaming involuntary need to run away. The man wasn't angry with anyone personally. It was the rage of a starved animal, justified and unmalevolent. Easier to work with.

'The KGB cleared us off in no uncertain terms and burned our fucking houses, didn't they!' The man motioned off towards the woods with his rifle.

Valery nodded, keeping himself very measured. People would copy you, sometimes. 'Then why did you come back?'

The man looked at him as if he were growing a third eye. 'Why do you think? Have you *seen* what's going on in the countryside? There's a famine. Potato blight. Where are any of us supposed to get food? You've shut all this off and whether it's got radiation or not it's still good hunting territory. So fuck off back to the fucking Lighthouse.'

The fear was draining away under the gravity of what the man was telling him. The rifle tip had swung back towards his face, but it didn't matter so much now. Valery touched it with the crook of his finger, to aim it over his shoulder. 'Can you take me back to where you live? I can help you. I can show you which plants are least irradiated, and which lakes. This one is the worst, but – please? I mean it.'

'You'll tell the KGB where we live, they'll clear us out.'

'Blindfold me,' Valery said.

The man hesitated, but then lowered the gun, and flashed his lamp out towards his friend in the fishing boat.

The men had come in through the perimeter fences with wire cutters. They hadn't bothered to be subtle – there were person-shaped holes in the two fences – but they had chosen places immediately at the edge of the reach of the halogen searchlights, places which, to anyone watching from the guard towers, would have seemed the very darkest. Valery still felt sure they were going to hear the rattle of a machine gun at any second as they made the hundred-metre run across open grass to the treeline. His whole spine hurt with the certainty, even though both of the men whispered that they'd done it before.

Nothing, though. The relief made him dizzy. He had closed his hand over the silver watch in his pocket before he remembered it was there. When he took it out, his sense of time went into shock to see that it had only been sixteen minutes since he'd stepped outside.

Tucked into the shadow of a sickly oak was an old farm truck. Valery sat in the back beside the sack of fish, which he couldn't convince them to throw away. When the blindfold went on, his stomach screwed itself into an unhelpful knot, but he could hardly argue now, so he sat rigid, telling himself in a loop that it was fine, it wasn't a trick, no one was taking him back to prison. He should have been freezing, sitting out like that at half past three in the morning, but his shirt was soaked by the time the truck stopped and someone said he could take off the blindfold. He wrenched it off.

One of the men must have noticed. 'You all right, mate?'

He nodded, not trusting himself to speak.

It could not, Valery thought, have been more than about ten miles, because he hadn't had time to go out of his mind. He checked the stopwatch. An hour since leaving the Lighthouse; yes, they'd only driven for forty-five minutes.

They were at the edge of a dense portion of the birch forest. With their silvery undersides, the leaves shimmered in the headlights. Every fourth or fifth tree was dead.

There was no road leading into the forest; they had to leave the truck and walk the last kilometre. They went slowly, half because they had only candles in their lamps, and the way led over fallen trees and patches littered with dead branches, but half because the men kept glancing at him and then at each other, and reining themselves back from going at full pace. He must have looked fragile even to them. The candlelight threw keen shadows over the prints of their boots in the mud.

When Valery saw the first rooftops, he couldn't believe what was in front of him.

The houses were thatched log cabins, made from pale wood that must have been cut from close by. The chimneys were built of fire-blackened bricks that looked like they might have been scavenged from somewhere else. At least ten. Ten houses, ten families. They even had a clearing full of allotments, and another for a graveyard. It would have looked like a perfect medieval village if not for the relics of newer things; a tractor, a tyre swing, even a radio perched on someone's workbench, hooked up to a generator. All of it was spectral in a thin mist and tiny lamps hanging from eaves and trees.

The village was alive already, even though dawn was still four hours away. People looked round when they saw the men had someone new with them, and Valery felt exposed. If they decided not to let him leave, they'd have no trouble stopping him, and no shortage of places to hide a body.

The air was smoky. Someone was cooking pork, and bread.

The men, who looked cheerful now to have brought in such a novelty as a new person, led him to one of the cottages. Its windows – the panes were mosaics of broken glass newly soldered together – were full of candlelight, which cast square patches of gold on to the grass. Inside was an old lady and a dog that might have been mainly wolf. The dog hurried up to them and snuffled at them all.

'Who've you got there?' the lady said.

The men introduced her only as Nanya. Valery couldn't tell if it was her name or her title, but it didn't seem to matter. She was plainly in charge, and plainly the person they had brought him to see. Once they had explained where they'd got him from, she nodded for him to sit down at the kitchen table; solid, well-scrubbed, with flour in the scratches. They had no paper, so he drew out a rough map in chalk on the tabletop to show them where the radiation was. His eyes began to ache in the insufficient light, even though Nanya had moved five or six candles onto the table.

'The radiation is stronger than anyone will tell you,' he said. 'We aren't allowed dosimeters, so I can't tell you how strong, but you can tell from the trees. The more dead trees there are per acre, the more radiation there is in the ground. Try and avoid the lakes completely.'

'This is the first I'm hearing about the lakes,' Nanya remarked, sceptical.

'I know,' he said, feeling helpless. 'I know. The scientists at the facility aren't allowed to tell people in town. I saw some kids playing in the river the other day and someone arrested me when I tried to tell them to stop.'

She gave him a frank study. 'What are you telling us for then, if you might get arrested?'

'I'm hoping none of you will tell anyone I told you.'

'On one of my nice coffee mornings with the lovely KGB man up at the plant?'

He smiled. After the blindfolded drive here and the lamplit walk through the woods, the fight with Shenkov felt like it had happened a long time ago. 'You've met Shenkov, then.'

'Met him; he led the crew who evicted us from our town and burned all the buildings there so we wouldn't come back.' She didn't say it bitterly, only as she might have talked about someone who had said something rude at a dinner party. In the candlelight, she looked more like a terribly weathered statue of a person than a person, the shadows vaulting over her knotted knuckles and the hunger-sharp tendons in her throat. Somewhere in the murk behind her, another animal scuffled. Not the dog; the dog was sitting with its paw on her knee.

No, not another animal; it was outside. When he looked, he jumped, because there were people just outside the window, staring in, silent and unembarrassed.

Nanya had seen them too, but she ignored them. 'Was there anything else you wanted to tell us?'

'Yes. I can give you a list of plant species that we've found to be more radiation resistant than others. And – if you'd like me to, I can take samples of any crops you're growing and find out which are safest.'

The two men looked at her quickly. They weren't so unfussed about living off radioactive land as they had said at the lake, then.

'Sounds sensible,' she said.

'May I have some jam jars?' he asked, looking at her sizeable collection on the kitchen worktop. The candles made them gleam. 'For the samples.'

'If you bring them back. We don't get much glass out here.'

He straightened up. 'I can tell you how to make forest glass if that would help.'

'You what?'

'I'm a chemist, I know how to make glass. It won't be brilliant, but you can do it with what you've got here. All the dead wood will be perfect.'

'Well,' she said, 'aren't you a gem.' She inclined her head. The candle shadows leapt across her again. 'You still haven't said why you want to help.'

'Because I've seen enough pointless loss of human life already,' he said. He aimed it towards the window too. The people were still there.

She was quiet for a moment, and her eyes ticked over him, and then she seemed satisfied. 'Right, you're a zek,' she said, as if gulag prisoners were as recognisable a breed as woodpeckers or huskies. 'All right. Kusnetsov's our blacksmith, so you can show him about the glass. And then you can take samples of whatever you want. But if you tell anyone at the Lighthouse where we are—'

'They blindfolded me—'

'You seem bright, love, I imagine you could work it out,' she said. 'If you tell anyone, I'll send some lads to cut your hands off; fair?'

He nodded, and then took a fast breath when two and two clicked together in his head. 'Nanya – are you missing a man? A young man, about twenty.'

All of them glanced at each other.

'Why would you ask that?' she said, a little hard. The dog was examining Valery too.

'We found a body. He died of radiation sickness.'

There was a small quiet.

'Shit,' one of the men said.

'Sasha,' said the other.

'We thought he just left,' Nanya sighed. 'Well. There you are.'

'He was found in a hospital gown,' Valery said. 'Was he going somewhere for treatment? Is there a town you go to, for doctors, check-ups . . . ?'

The others all snorted. It took Nanya so by surprise that she inhaled at the same time and made a noise that was almost an oink. 'Doctors! No. No; but a hospital gown?'

'Yes. In the middle of the forest.'

'He wasn't sick,' one of the men said. He looked confused. 'Picture of health, Sasha. That's why we thought he'd gone. He could have walked to Sverdlovsk, worked at a factory . . . he was getting tired of living here. Not like we have any mod cons.'

'He was healthy?' Valery repeated, confused.

'Indestructible.'

'How long has he been gone?'

'Four days?'

'Four days,' Valery echoed. 'And we found him yesterday. It takes six hundred roentgen of radiation to kill a person. So in three days, he got six hundred roentgen from somewhere and at some point he also made it to a hospital and left again. That level of radiation is – people never get that, unless they're working in a physics lab and something spills. Have you any idea how he could have . . . ?'

'No,' they all said at once.

Nanya was watching him closely now. 'Are you thinking that there's something dangerous in these woods that neither you nor we know of?'

'I don't know,' Valery said. 'Unless there's an old reactor out here, broken open, I can't think of anything that would give you six hundred roentgen in one go. Is there anything like that? You'd know, it would be huge.'

'No. Who has the body?'

'The KGB.'

There was a long silence.

'Right then.' Nanya clapped her hands, which sent a small plume of flour into the air. 'I'll let you all get on, can't have you entertaining old ladies all day.'

The three of them hurried away before she had to ask again.

After he'd spoken to the blacksmith – a giant with a reedy voice and four scornful cats – Valery took samples from the well, from the allotment soil, the corn, from the bones of the pig carcasses hanging up in the seasoning shed, swabs from the burnt bricks of the chimney stacks, and then from anyone who agreed to let him take blood. To his surprise, people lined up; just to see what he was doing, he thought at first, but no one seemed to mind giving a sample.

He was on the fifth person, a woman about his age, when he saw that the very tip of her little finger was missing. It gave him an unhappy stir and a memory-echo of the scalpel clunking through the mouse's tail, but he put it aside. But then someone else had it too, a girl with thyroid cancer so clear that the tumour was thickening her throat. It must have been leukaemia, or something else that was affecting their bones, making their fingers brittle. He fought to keep his expression normal.

'Can I ask how long you've lived here?' he said to the girl.

'Oh. Nanya brought us – what, three years ago? After they all died from the famine,' she said, waving vaguely. *They* must have been such a presence at the front of her mind that it hadn't occurred to her that he might know who they had been or how many.

Three years. He tried to smile. 'Right. Thanks.'

Someone called for her, a woman hanging out sheets on a long laundry line, with a baby strapped on her back. The baby had no eyes.

10

Radiation Sickness

P art of him had suspected it would happen, and so he wasn't
shocked to see that there were soldiers with torches mend-
ing the holes in the perimeter fence when he got back. It was
six o'clock in the morning; it would be three hours before they
opened the checkpoints. He stood under the trees and watched
them, trying to decide what to do. He didn't have his papers and
the soldiers had been firm in the assertion that they would be
happy to shoot anyone who tried to approach the fence anywhere
other than the checkpoints, but he was not dressed like someone
who lived in the woods, and some of them might even have seen
him enough to recognise him. On balance, it should have been
worth a try, slowly, with his hands up.

He couldn't do it. Even thinking about it made him start to
panic, not because the soldiers at *this* perimeter were definitely
going to shoot him, but because the soldiers at all the *other*
perimeters he knew would have. It was a hard-wired reaction
now, and he couldn't push past it any more than he could force
his own elbow to bend the wrong way.

The second he decided he wasn't going to try, his whole
skeleton relaxed, and all the tiredness he hadn't been feeling since that stupid clash with Shenkov rolled over him. He
sank down at the foot of the crooked oak, his back against
the trunk. All at once, he saw how spectacular the morning

was. The sky was indigo at the crown, but mauve at the hems, shot through with smoky orange clouds that looked for all the world like, beyond the horizon, the Urals were on fire. One of those muddy geysers went off, a long way away. Behind him, the forest whispered, leaning over the rags of mist among its roots. Twigs and leaves pattered down, always. He fell asleep listening to them.

The silver watch said that he had been outside for seven hours when he woke up. When he went to the Lighthouse checkpoint, he showed the soldiers his staff card and explained that he'd done a typical Mad Scientist mental manoeuvre and forgotten the time last night collecting samples. Yes, he had been in the woods all night. They waved the dosimeter at him, and it went off. Yes, he had slept under a tree; sorry.

'It's just the mud on your boots. Get that off and then in you go. Shower straight away.' The soldier gave him a wry look. 'Try not to forget the time again? We get paperwork.'

After a shower and a change of clothes, and an excruciating visit to the security office in which he hid behind a door to avoid Shenkov and then got the prisoner book stamped by a trainee, it was a relief to get back to the familiar antiseptic smell of the lab. The students had just come in with their first catch of fish, so the sink was full of dead perch. Silvery scales were everywhere. Some of the other researchers were annoyed, but it seemed like a good, ordinary, domestic problem to come back to. He tested the blood samples from Nanya's village at his own microscope while he listened to everyone else bicker and laugh.

He ran the samples once, had to go outside for a little while to calm down, then ran them again to be sure, and then took the results straight to Shenkov's office.

'Find your mistake?' Shenkov said when Valery came in. He nodded to the spare chair, which Valery had begun to think of as the Chair of Doom.

'Nope, because there wasn't one.' Perhaps it was just having spent the morning bent over the microscope, but a tight headache was crouched in the front of Valery's skull now. Even the small bump of sitting down made it hurt more. It wasn't the pleasant luxury headache he'd had on the first day here, either. It was winding itself up to be savage.

'I *did* find a village full of people who've moved back into the exclusion zone because the countryside beyond is famine-stricken. I want to show you the results of the samples I took. I'm not submitting them for any kind of publication, or even to Dr Resovskaya; this is just out of interest. Just for you. So don't shoot me, all right?'

Shenkov was frowning. 'Where's this village?'

'No idea, they blindfolded me, but it's where your dead man is from. His name is Sasha. Look at this.' He laid out the findings across Shenkov's desk; one file for the crops, one for animals, one for people, and the bright graphs he'd made to show how they were different to normal counterparts. 'It's very, very bad. They're drinking contaminated water, eating contaminated meat, and contaminated crops. There are visible deformities in the children.' Valery didn't feel nervous now. He was talking about a thing he knew backwards and inside out. Shenkov could never win a reasoned argument with him about this. 'That is caused by radioactive strontium in their bones. A lot of it. Far, far more than any of our figures about the contamination outside suggest, and this, I'd hasten to add, about fifteen kilometres away from this facility. Something out there is not right.' He had to sit back, because he felt dizzy. It had been building beneath the headache, and now he had a powerful urge to stay horizontal for some time.

Shenkov was staring at him hard. Something in his expression was fissuring, though, and real alarm was glowing through the cracks. 'What are you saying?'

Valery decided he'd better plough on while he still had some momentum. 'I'm saying this is not contamination from a controlled leak of radioactive material into the water system. Whatever happened here, it was definitely *not* controlled, it *was* huge, and its effects remain toxic now. *This —*' he set his hand on the results from the village '— is what happens to humans who stay.'

The headache really was distracting now. He'd barely finished talking before he had to tip forward, trying to shift the thumping to his other temple, to give the first one a break. As he did, he had a roll of nausea. Christ, he was going to be annoyed if Resovskaya had been right and he was so fragile he came down with flu after one poxy night outside.

'The villagers also said that Sasha was very healthy. Unlike nearly everyone else there. He was only missing for three days before we found him, so in that time he got six hundred roentgen from somewhere. He even got to a hospital and got out again, maybe he was trying to go home when he died. The only nearby hospitals are *here*, in City 40. So someone knows what happened to him.'

'I've been round every hospital and clinic in City 40 with his photograph. No one has any record of him.'

'Well, then someone has to be lying, someone treated him without paperwork, or . . .' Valery had to stop.

'Kolkhanov?' Shenkov said slowly.

'I'm — I'm okay, sorry.' He sat back, but his hands were shaky. He clenched them, impatient. 'I was outside for the night, I went through a hole in the perimeter fences with some men from the village and they'd been closed when I came back. Didn't dare go up to the soldiers, so I waited, which was . . . probably stupid. I'm immunocompromised something fierce, it's bloody annoying. I must have caught a cold or flu or something.' The dizziness came again and he had to grip the edge of the chair. 'Ugh – can you smell metal?'

Shenkov looked at him like he'd started to strip, then got up, seized his arm, and hauled him out of the office without a word of explanation. Valery gasped, because he could feel the bone in his arm creaking. He tried to pull away, but Shenkov was much stronger and yanked him into the corridor.

The bone made a neat little snap as it broke.

They both froze. There was no pain, just a clear sense of wrongness and a dull ache, like he'd thumped into a doorway at a clumsy angle.

'I didn't mean . . .' Shenkov began. He looked shocked. He had aged in those two seconds.

'I'd better go to the infirmary.'

'I'll take you. I really didn't—'

'I can take myself,' Valery interrupted. 'Thank you, comrade.'

'No . . .' Shenkov glanced down the corridor and lifted his hands as if he meant to grasp Valery's shoulders, but then stopped an inch from touching him. 'No. Kolkhanov – I *have* to take you,' he said softly. 'You might collapse on the way. I think you've got radiation sickness.'

Valery had to look at him for a long time before he could make the words line up properly. 'Oh,' he whispered. 'I have, haven't I.'

Shenkov took him to the infirmary door, but was then shooed out by the doctor. She took one look at Valery, gave him an iodine pill, and hooked him up to a nutrient drip while she set up the X-ray machine. Then she told him off for not coming for a check-up sooner – look at the *state* of you, you were starving a few days ago, obviously your bones are buggered – but it wasn't a real, genuinely cross telling-off. She did it like she would have spoken to someone with dementia or developmental problems, the sort of person who couldn't be trusted with metal cutlery.

Their voices echoed horribly in the high-ceilinged room with its metal bedsteads. Someone, for obscure reasons, had painted them all white. The air tasted of iron. That would be radiation-induced brain damage rather than the actual air, but he still tried to breathe shallowly. He was curled on the bed nearest to the doctor and he regretted that, because he didn't think he could get up again.

'So radiation sickness,' the doctor said, matter-of-fact. 'It's mild; but you are extremely immunocompromised from the camp. Your white blood cells are already on general strike, so this is hitting you harder than it would a healthy person. What happened, were you working in one of the nuclear labs?'

'No,' Valery said. 'I was . . .' It was hard to think through the nausea and the headache. 'I was in the woods. Fieldwork, I'm just a biologist. I got caught out, I spent the night outside.'

The doctor frowned. 'Well, I'll tell you now, I think you absorbed about fifty roentgen in that time. Unless you were cosying up to a chunk of uranium, that shouldn't have happened. Did you fall in the lake?'

'No. No, I just . . . sat down by a tree.'

'You must have touched something.'

'I didn't. Anyway, if it was enough to give me fifty roentgen from one touch, I'd be burnt. Wouldn't I?'

'Yes,' she said. She was scanning him for marks. He turned his good hand over to show her that there were none. Her eyes flicked up again and she lowered her voice. 'Look, you can tell me if you *were* in one of the labs. Accidents happen. You don't have to keep it secret from me, I'm your doctor. I need to know if you inhaled something.'

'I wasn't,' Valery said. 'I promise. I'm not a physicist. Look.' He showed her his staff card.

She only sighed and helped him up so that they could go to the X-ray machine. He tried to tell her again that there had been no lab, no accident, but he gave up quickly, because he understood. She must have come across people too frightened to tell the truth all the time, and perhaps even people involved in projects so secret that their staff cards showed a false profession. He swallowed and tasted iron again as she put on the lead apron. He couldn't still the shudder in his hands any more. She was right, though; it was mild, or he'd be doubled over a bucket by now.

He wanted to think it was the village. But he hadn't touched anything that no one else had, and just being there clearly wasn't this harmful, or everyone else there would have been dead long ago. Radiation extreme enough to make you sick didn't cause mutations in children; you would just end up with a lot of dead foetuses. So the radiation in the village was too low for this, even if it was generally bad.

No; the only thing he'd done differently to anyone in the village was that he'd sat out on the bare soil on the edge of the woods, waiting for the city perimeter to open for the morning.

Fifty roentgen, the doctor had said. That sounded right. It would have taken a hundred roentgen to get a healthy person feeling like this, but as she pointed out, he was a mess, such a mess that his bones were brittle. But fifty roentgen in what had it been – seven hours? And he had only been sitting on the ground for four of those hours.

So the ground immediately outside the plant was so contaminated it was giving off at least seven roentgen per hour. More; he had *absorbed* seven roentgen per hour.

Per *hour*.

'Comrade? I need you to face the machine,' the doctor said, brisk but gentle. Valery must have looked terrible now.

He did as he was told, his heart cantering. The machine banged and thumped, and each bang reverberated around his head.

Seven roentgen per hour.

No wonder they had to use stopwatches.

The X-ray showed a clean break, so it was all straightforward from there. There was a splint and a cast. The break started to hurt a lot and the doctor gave Valery some morphine, which made him feel floaty, and which chased off a good portion of the nausea. He almost didn't notice when Shenkov came in, still looking distressed, and carrying a bar of chocolate.

'How are you?' Shenkov asked, awkward and quiet. He had withdrawn right in on himself, his usual tailored openness all gone.

'Fine,' Valery said, wondering why any KGB officer would care if he'd accidentally broken someone's arm. When you professionally broke people's arms, it was surely a sign of accomplishment.

No; obviously. He was here to ask about the radiation sickness. It was definitely the concern of the head of security if people were swanning around getting radiation sickness even when they were nowhere near the reactors or the physics labs.

'Is it — is it a thing you've always had? The . . . bone weakness.'

But Shenkov didn't only look sorry; he seemed horrified with himself, his whole frame tight, as though he expected to have the offending hand cut off.

'It's not a disease,' Valery explained. 'It's a side effect of a period of starvation; your bones lose all their calcium. It won't last long now, though.'

From the far corner, the doctor gave him a narrow stare over her glasses, one that opined he would definitely liquefy without proper medical supervision.

Shenkov looked haunted before he shut down his own expression. 'Well, that's for you.' He nodded at the chocolate. 'Calcium in there too, I suppose.'

Valery took it, still perplexed. 'Thanks.'

'I didn't know. I wouldn't have touched you if I'd known. I just – wanted to get you here, when you came over . . .' he glanced towards the doctor ' . . . ill.'

'It's okay,' Valery said, waiting for him to ask more about the radiation.

'Is it really that bad in the camps, still, that you don't get enough to eat?'

Completely without meaning to, Valery laughed and Shenkov flinched.

'You must have met zeks before; don't you know what a starving person looks like?'

Shenkov took a breath and then held it without speaking, and Valery realised that he didn't know what starving people looked like; that not many people did, that most people seeing zeks would just think they were shabby and ugly in a general sort of way. It was a leap to understand that they could have looked better.

'I was an athlete,' Valery said. 'Ice hockey. Before. For my university. I'm alive now because I was fit going in.' He paused, aware he was laying it on thick for bad reasons. He wanted Shenkov to feel guilty. Not because he was angry about his arm, or the ignorance of an ordinary person, but because if Shenkov felt guilty, they would talk more.

'Listen – open this, share it with me,' Valery said at last, towards the chocolate. 'Please. But don't give any to the doctor, we don't like her.'

The doctor made a gun out of her fingers and shot herself with it.

'Or definitely not more than two pieces.'

The doctor smiled.

Shenkov did as he was told. 'Kolkhanov . . . where the hell were you, to get radiation sickness?' he asked, well out of the doctor's hearing. 'I need to know. We've got a dead body, and now you. Were you in one of the labs, or . . . ?'

'No.' He couldn't tell any more if it was a stupid idea to tell the truth. The morphine and the radiation were making it hard to think in a straight line. He could still taste iron. He was only upright because he was propped on two pillows. 'I was sitting on exposed soil at the edge of the forest for four or five hours. I was waiting for the perimeter to open.'

Shenkov lifted his eyes, and Valery expected to have another fight, but Shenkov didn't fight. He looked like he was fracturing at the edges. 'How far from the fence?'

'About . . . a hundred metres.' Valery let himself sink into a whisper. 'I think we're talking about seven or eight roentgen per hour, from the soil. I – believe me or don't, but it's easy to test. Go and sit out there for a day and you'll get radiation sickness too if I'm right.'

'No. I believe you.' Shenkov hesitated. 'I believe you,' he said again.

Valery felt so vindicated that he didn't care any more that he had radiation sickness and a broken arm, or that they'd fought before.

'Is that enough to have killed Sasha? If he was out there for three days.'

'Ah . . . maybe? I don't know. But why would he sit out there for three days in a hospital gown?'

Shenkov glanced at the machinery beside them, the light switch, the doctor. 'We can't talk about this here.'

So they watched the news on the small, grainy television in silence, but it was nice silence, and the chocolate was wonderful. Valery couldn't remember the last time he'd watched television properly. He'd never owned a television. He said so. Shenkov called him a savage and seemed to leave it there, but by the time

Valery got back to his flat that night, someone had been in and installed a television on the desk.

He went down to the KGB office the next morning. Boiling water plinked in a samovar. Shenkov was reading a report with a green pen in his hand, hovering the tip down the lines as he read, sometimes underlining things, fast and accurate. Valery stood in the doorway without knocking, just to breathe the scent of the place; coffee and brand-new paper and, nearly imperceptible from here unless you knew to search for it, the bright woodlands in Shenkov's cologne. It was all so clean.

'Valery. How are you?' Shenkov said it so lightly he sounded like a boy, the stones sifted out of his voice.

Accurately, wrecked was the answer. Valery had slept badly because the cast had locked his elbow bent, and the joint had ached more than the broken bone. The radiation headache had got worse around midnight, too intense to sleep through. Then it was a struggle to wash and dress properly in the morning. Getting into a shirt had been such an expedition that he'd nearly called down to the infirmary for help; the only thing that had stopped him was that any human being who made their living as a nurse, looking after people, would be either frightened or angry when they saw the tattoos. He didn't want to frighten anyone, and he couldn't cope with any more angry people.

Shenkov did not need to hear any of that.

'Well entertained. Thank you for the educational equipment you installed in my room, it's already been edifying.' Valery spoke half into the light switch, which scritched with the familiar noise of the bugs. Next door, in the KGB listening room, the officer stationed there in heavy-looking headphones gave him a wave and a thumbs-up. He waved back. He had been telling the light switches jokes as they occurred to him all evening yesterday.

That was all the standing up he could do. He sat down in the Chair of Doom. It was eight o'clock, but the light was getting sparser in the mornings now, and Shenkov had been working by the light of a desk lamp. It threw shadows over the diamond-shaped creases down Shenkov's nearer sleeve, and in the Hoover tracks on the carpet.

Shenkov smiled. It was the first time Valery had seen him do it, and it made him look like someone else altogether, but it faded too quickly as he made the coffee.

'I'm fine,' Valery said, ducking a little to catch his eye. 'I'm up to here in morphine, I'm having the most wonderful time.'

It was true. He was still merry and floaty, even though he was exhausted. It was enough to make him wonder if something similar had happened to Sasha. If a doctor had given him enough morphine – and they would have given him morphine, because extreme radiation sickness was painful – he might have thought he could leave whichever hospital had him, and make it home to Nanya's village on that illusory opioid strength. The haziness that morphine brought might even explain why Sasha had gone out in only the hospital gown instead of his real clothes. Even with much less radiation sickness and much less morphine, Valery suspected that someone could have convinced him that almost anything was an excellent idea now. Walk ten kilometres in the woods in a cotton smock? Great.

Shenkov nodded. 'Milk?' he asked quietly.

'Please.'

Shenkov glanced up. 'How is milk in coffee? Do you like it or is it just for the calcium?'

'I like it.'

'My father always said it was effeminate, so I never tried.' It wasn't an accusation, just a request for permission.

What a nightmare, to be Shenkov's size with *that* kind of father. It was amazing he hadn't become one of those men who felt it was correct and exemplary to hit women over the head with bricks.

Valery tipped his cup. 'But don't you find usually that the people who are most worried about seeming effeminate are the ones with a permanent Friday-evening appointment with a sailor?'

Shenkov choked on the coffee but, thank God, he was laughing. 'Let's take this outside. It's nice seeing the sunrise over the lake. If it – won't make you more sick.'

'It won't for ten minutes. Anyway, everyone should put milk in coffee,' Valery said as he stood up. He lifted the cup carefully by the handle. 'If you're having a wobbly moment, it's reassuring to see that fluid dynamics are the same in a cup as in planetary cloud.'

Shenkov thought about it, then emptied the last of the milk into his cup and followed.

At the door, they both started the silver stopwatches. The dawn was a brilliant pink against a violet sky, though cold, and they walked a little way from the complex, around the lake, where there was now a well-worn path in the long grass. Lots of people must have done the same thing. They stood on an outcrop overlooking the water. Behind them, the noise of traffic on the main road mingled with the hiss of the breeze in the newly planted trees along the pavement. Ahead, there was only the silent lake and muddy glimmer of the marshes.

'We need to be very, very careful now,' Shenkov said after a little quiet. 'I'm the head of security here and no one has mentioned to me, not once, that there is *that* much radiation, *that* close to the city. So it's dangerous for me to know, never mind for you.'

'So shut up about it and ideally forget about it altogether? You didn't need to bring me outside to say that,' Valery said wryly. He was drained even after the short walk. Shenkov had twice had to take his arm to help him navigate around puddles. He felt like he was a hundred years old.

'No; no. Clearly someone's made some kind of – mistake.'

Valery gazed up at him and wondered for the first time, with a strange clarity, how frightened Shenkov must have been these last few years, to talk in code even now, outside, with someone he knew would agree with him. 'Whatever it is, it is not a mistake,' he said. 'I can't be the first person in six years to fall sick on the forest border. Or to notice that something isn't right. How many people have the KGB had to shoot?'

Shenkov looked away. 'A good few.'

Valery inclined his head. 'Why didn't you believe any of them?'

'Because none of them collapsed in my office,' Shenkov said tightly. 'Because no one came to *me* and said, look, this is what I think and why, here's my data; because they just went out and started telling people to get out, or going to the papers, or . . . it just looked like trouble-stirring. We can't have that here. This is the largest nuclear facility in the Soviet Union. If people spook – Moscow will send in the army to get them back to work. I'd rather shoot ten people than have riots and soldiers firing live rounds into crowds.'

'Okay.'

'So you think it's secret because the radiation could hurt people – here? Inside the city.'

'I can't think of any other reason.' Valery paused. 'And, I think the ground is *more* radioactive the closer to the Lighthouse you measure. Seven roentgen an hour is insane. I've never heard of it outside Hiroshima or Nagasaki, and even those places wouldn't have had readings this high, years later. You wouldn't get that without an exposed reactor core. That's a – hah, I want to say significant explosion, but I don't mean that, I mean a terrifying, destroy-a-whole-reactor explosion.'

Shenkov was ashen now. He half-turned away, and then pushed his hands hard into his coat pockets. Valery saw him clench them inside the fabric.

'How long have you been here?' Valery ventured. 'Do you have any idea about what actually happened?'

'They told us it was safe,' Shenkov said. 'Afterwards, they said again and again that it had all been cleaned up and that everyone would be fine.'

Valery's scalp prickled. 'After what?'

'I don't know,' Shenkov said. He sounded helpless. It was strange to hear that from him, when he'd been so unassailable before. Even in distress, he didn't slouch, but he turned breakable. Valery had a surge of protectiveness for him, and a sudden but indelible impression that whoever had hacked Shenkov into shape from that flint bedrock of his character, they had abandoned him out in the elements alone, all his edges too sharp to touch, all prone to fissuring after a determined enough knock. 'Nobody knows, even the people who saw it.'

'Did you see anything?'

Shenkov glanced at his stopwatch. They had already been outside for five minutes. When he spoke next, he spoke fast.

11

Crop Blight

29th September 1957, Chelyabinsk

Shenkov had never imagined he'd be relieved to be in hospital with broken ribs and a shard of bone poking through one lung, but when he came to in the white bed, he was so happy he would have kissed the first person who walked in, even if it was the horrifying Ukrainian nurse with the teeth. He lay staring at the ceiling, listening to the wonderful peaceful sound of other people snuffling in their sleep, or turning the pages of magazines. The sheets were so crisp that the creases were sharp. He had been certain that he was dead, after that fall. He had been fourteen rungs up a ladder, above concrete. Just a lightbulb, at home.

'Where are we?' he asked the man in the next bed.

'Hospital Four.'

'In?'

'Oh.' The man laughed. 'Chelyabinsk.'

He let his head bump down back on to the pillow again, turning his face to it so that the cotton scratched his eyelashes, and two days' stubble. He was propped up, but he could hardly remember having been so comfortable. It was warm, the whole ward, and clean, and there was a big window right opposite. They were high up; he could see half the town and the gleam of the railway beyond as it looped off into the forest. Sitting and looking at it – at the traffic moving on the main road and the people on the pavements, the lady putting out laundry in the tower block opposite – seemed a lot like the best possible thing in the world.

He did exactly that for a couple of hours, then started to doze as twilight smoked rust through the sky. Distantly, he heard a nurse ghost by and check something close to him, morphine or saline or something, but he didn't feel it. Rain clicked on the window-pane, and then hardened into a cosy clatter. He had forgotten how it felt to be outside the Lighthouse; he had been there so long already that being trapped was normal, and he was numb to the presence of the barbed wire, the checkpoints, the tapped phones, the nagging background fear that one of the children would say something wrong at school. To be away from it unexpectedly; he could breathe. It would feel even worse to go back into it, but for now, he could lie here and soak in all this blessed ordinariness.

Every door and window in the building slammed. It jolted him awake, and it made the nurse jump so badly she knocked into the wall. For a shocked, silent moment, they only looked at each other.

'The hell was that? Was it an explosion?' the nurse said, and ran to the window. She slung it open. Down the ward, other people, nurses and patients, were doing the same, but there was nothing to see. There was no smoke, no fire anywhere on the street below, though people there were getting out of cars and hurrying away from buildings.

'Turn on the radio, turn on the radio,' the man in the next bed said to the nurse. 'Maybe it'll be on the news.'

The radio didn't work. 'Piece of shit,' the nurse said, with feeling.

There was another one further down the ward, but that didn't work either. Over the general concerned hum, someone yelled that a heart monitor had switched itself off, and wouldn't come back on again.

Shenkov woke up entirely. He had snapped awake before, but he had still been hazy, and everything had still felt far off. Now, he could feel every centimetre of himself, from the snick of his eyelashes when he blinked, to the little ache of the blanket's weight on the third finger of his left hand, over the old break. He sat up as much as he could and reached for the light switch. *Click, click.* Nothing. He let his arm drop and looked outside again.

People hadn't just stopped their cars. The cars had stopped. A few were just being coaxed back to life now, but most of them refused, and people were getting out, helpless. The traffic lights had all gone dark.

'Some kind of power surge,' one of the nurses decided.

'The heart monitor still won't turn back on!'

He wondered what kind of power surge took out cars. The general gist of the speculation around him was to do with the Americans, but there was no reason for the Americans to do anything peculiar to a boring factory city in the middle of nowhere, seventeen hundred kilometres from Moscow. Chelyabinsk had no military significance. Its largest industry was tractor-building.

'Unless something's happened to Moscow,' the man in the next bed said, uneasy. His eyes flicked over Shenkov. 'You're KGB, right? I saw your coat when you came in. Is something going on?'

'In Moscow?' He hadn't been there for three years. Like always, thinking about it gave him an awful ashamed pang. He felt like he was blaspheming, just speaking its name. 'I don't know.'

The man looked more worried than ever. It was what Shenkov hated about the grey coat. Everyone thought that it made you omniscient. From a policing point of view, that was helpful, but from a personal one, he struggled with it. Everyone thought he was lying when he said he didn't know things. He had a nasty feeling that even his wife believed he spent his whole life hoarding interesting secrets from her like an egomaniacal dragon. The coat was like a code wheel, one that translated things even when you didn't want it to. *I don't know* became *I'm not telling you.*

He wanted to say so, but *no, honestly* would only become *it's terrible, don't ask me again.*

He wondered if it really was terrible, or if it was just the complicated consequence of a confused moth bumping into the wrong part of a power line. On the road now, the few people whose cars were still running nosed through the rest of the stranded traffic. Someone enterprising had already put a huge sign in their back window – ONE ROUBLE TO THE STATION!!!

'Look at that,' he said to the man in the next bed, and felt relieved when the man smiled. The man had fadedly red hair just like Sergei's.

As soon as he thought of that, he had to look away.

They got the heart monitors working again, or some of them, the unease subsided into a generally intrigued hum, and Shenkov slept well into the following morning. He hadn't done that since he was a trainee, and it left him feeling disorientated. He was awake for a long time before his hearing came back, and it was only incrementally that he became aware the ward was much louder than it had been yesterday. There were beds everywhere now, and more being wheeled in. A nurse, not the good one who swore but the terrifying Ukrainian, tapped the foot of his bed as she passed.

'We're going to have to move you upstairs. We don't want you getting sick.'

'Sick – with what?' he asked, still groggy. It must have been the morphine. He'd had nightmares, but now he was awake, he couldn't remember what they'd been about. He only had an after-image of cold sunlight and grey ground and faded red hair sprayed over the earth.

He thought desperately about domestic disturbance by-laws before his brain could rush off and reconstruct the dream. *Undue noise after eight o'clock at night . . .*

'There's quite a bug going round,' the nurse said, nodding down the ward.

There really must have been. All the new people looked queasy and shaky, and a good few of them were being sick in plastic bowls. Everything stank of disinfectant and stomach acid. Another orderly hurried through and helped the nurse move the bed.

The corridor was even louder. As they were coming out, a doctor was persuading a young woman to sit down. There were blisters across her face, like bad eczema, so bad that her skin was peeling. His heart lurched. He twisted as much as he could to see, but then they were past and in the broad lift. Two soldiers who had definitely not been there yesterday were standing on either side, holding guns, and there were more, a lot more, near the far end of the ward. Shenkov was in time to see one of them snatch a camera from someone and dash it onto the floor in a shower of glass and plastic.

Fuck.

Just as the lift doors were closing, a doctor dived through.

'You're Konstantin Shenkov? They brought you in from City 40 – didn't they? You were air-lifted.'

The doors closed and a cheery mechanical voice said, *going up.*

His chest tightened. A stab of pain let him know exactly where the broken bone was, and where the surgery had been. 'No, there's been a mistake there. I'm from Chelyabinsk.'

She ignored him. 'Was anything strange going on when you left? Were they getting ready to test – something?'

'I'm sorry, I don't know what you're talking about.' He glanced at the numbers lighting up above the lift doors. Three, four. There would be more soldiers at the top, and he was far beyond second chances these days. One word and someone was going to take him out to the back courtyard and shoot him, Anna would have to have the baby by herself, and fifty-fifty she'd drown it in the bath because she was acres too clever to just sit in an apartment and look after a baby alone. The whole bargain was that she had them and he looked after them. She couldn't communicate with someone who didn't know what a neutron was.

'Have you seen burns like that before?' the doctor pressed.

They called it a tan, at the plant. 'No.'

'For God's sake!' she snapped. She banged the emergency stop button, right by his head. 'How far away is it? I need to know, Shenkov, I need to know how many fucking ambulances to expect! Should I be diverting people to Hospital Three? Should I be calling in the night shift early?'

It wasn't beyond the higher-ups to have asked her to try and get something out of him. He hadn't left City 40 for three years, and he wouldn't have even now if he hadn't had a punctured lung. Somewhere nearby, someone would be listening. No one in or out, that was the rule, and this was why. There would come a moment when you felt you *had* to tell someone.

'I don't know, comrade, I'm just a policeman,' he said, quiet and polite, because even if she was a spy, he didn't have it in him to start barking. He was tall. Anything but quiet and polite read like he was slinging his weight around, the worst sort of bully. 'I don't know who you think I am. I'm certainly not a doctor. I don't know what your mystery bug is.'

The doctor looked down at him for a long time. 'And how would you feel if I put you in a ward with the rest of them?'

'Why would you do that?'

'You've gone white,' she observed.

'I've just had surgery,' he pointed out.

He hated how good he was at seeming like he was about to kill someone. He hated how well it worked on even the fiercest women. He saw her decide not to push him, how she came up against the wall in her head that nearly all the women he knew had: don't go too far or you're dead.

She punched the emergency button again, and the lift juddered upward. There was perfect silence, and the cheerful lift voice announced that this was the twelfth floor.

'We're keeping everyone who doesn't have this . . . *bug* up here,' the doctor said. She was watching the two new soldiers just beyond the doors. 'To prevent infection.'

The nurse pushed the bed out into the ward. The linoleum squeaked under the bed's wheels. Once they were past the soldiers, the nurse squeezed his shoulder, a lot harder than she needed to. It hurt. Her fingertips were sharp.

'Well done, comrade. You didn't say a word.'

He stared straight ahead.

The ward was full, but only with patients recovering from surgery. A good few of them were ambulatory enough to be clustered by the window, watching whatever was happening on the ground below. Painfully, Shenkov eased upright and went too. Outside the hospital was a queue of ambulances, right down the road. He went straight back to bed and had to sit still for a little while, trying to stop his mind spinning. If the doctor was right and something had gone wrong at City 40, he had to get back there soon, punctured lung or no. He tried to sleep, because he would need all the sleep he could get, but he couldn't.

The radios were working again. There were two on now, tuned to the news, one echoing the other in a way that made the newsreader sound like she was in a cathedral. There wasn't a word about the explosion, or the mystery disease.

He wondered how long *mystery disease* was going to stand up to scrutiny. His instinct was to think not long, but before he went to City 40, he wouldn't have known radiation sickness if it hit him in the face.

'Is there a telephone?' he asked the nurse who wasn't really a nurse. His voice came out sounding as though he was made of rock. He swallowed. It was a struggle. 'I – need to call my wife. She's pregnant.'

'Where is she?'

'She works at the chocolate factory at home.'

The nurse nodded pleasantly to the phone on the wall next to him, as if there was no possible reason to imagine he wouldn't be allowed to. 'Of course.'

He dialled the plutonium laboratory. The line was dead. The home phone just rang and rang.

He had to stay in hospital for three days. When he could walk, he got dressed and escaped without a discharge, but that wasn't difficult. He had thought the hospital was crowded on the first day; now, it was rammed. He called the Lighthouse from a payphone. It was the tenth time he'd tried. Every line was dead, even the security office.

He'd just have to go and see.

He always walked everywhere, but he was only just upright, and he had to get a cab to the station. Down the main road, the traffic was all normal. They waited at a level crossing for a pair of girls with nice coats and prams to go by. He watched them with a tightness in the back of his throat. The doctor had said that that first wave of sick people was all local. Acute radiation sickness; you didn't get that until you hit at least a hundred roentgen. A hundred roentgen, seventy-nine kilometres away from the Lighthouse. What the hell had they got at the reactor plant?

What had Anna got?

He had to stop thinking about that. If he let himself dwell over it, he would panic, and he would lose even the basic common sense to get himself up to City 40.

The station swarmed with people, so dense-packed that watching them all made him feel as queasy as he did if he saw unexpected footage of a beehive. The ticket queues moved at a crawl. He couldn't see why at first; all he could stretch to was standing and not collapsing. But once he was nearer the front, it was clear what the hold-up was. The ticket officers weren't just selling people tickets. They were taking them aside, into little booths. While he was watching, they turned someone away, an ordinary man who looked lost and scared when they told him to go home.

When he got to the front, the officer led him into the small booth and took out a device that hissed and clicked. He waved it over Shenkov twice.

'What's that for?' Shenkov asked quietly. It was a dosimeter, but he wanted to know what they were telling people.

'We're checking for contaminants.'

'Like what?'

'You think they'd tell me?' the ticket officer. 'All I know is that if this goes bananas then I'm not to let you on the train. But it hasn't, so on you go. Single to Pavliok?' It was the closest station to City 40. There was talk of opening one centrally, but he didn't think it would get past Moscow for a long time yet. That would mean letting people in and out. 'You have to be in the front two carriages. Tiny platform.'

'Thanks,' he murmured, and emerged from the booth just in time to see someone else turned away.

———

It was only half an hour to Pavliok, but he was sore by the time they arrived. He was the only person who got off the train there, for which he was grateful, because he would have collapsed in any kind of crowd. Thankfully, there were cabs waiting right outside the station.

Nearly all the rest of the way was through the forest. As they drove, bits of twig and endless pine needles rained on to the car, and once, a branch banged down right in front of them. The driver had to get out and move it. He came back brushing motes of bark off his hands. A few minutes later, he made an annoyed sound and showed Shenkov his palm. It was angry and red.

'I must be allergic,' he said.

Helicopters thunked overhead. Shenkov counted five in the sky as the cab pulled up to the city limits. Inside the Lighthouse perimeter fence, there were bulldozers ploughing up the soil and gathering it into enormous heaps. The administration building was full of people, but not the usual ones. Not labourers. Soldiers. He didn't recognise a single person. He limped inside, looking for anyone familiar.

'Are you Shenkov?' A man was waving from a desk, a phone pinned against his shoulder. 'Thank God. This place is bewildering. I need you to talk to the scientists from Moscow and draft a progress report for me. They're on the lake shore.'

'What happened? Where is everyone?'

'Everyone?'

'From the plant – where are the workers and the staff?'

The man froze, and then sighed. 'You'll see.'

When he reached the lake shore, limping now, there was almost no water left in the lake, and a crater where the furthest half of the reactor had used to be. The rest was torn ruins – mangled girders and concrete, and now, cement trucks everywhere, pumping in concrete waterfalls from at least twenty points around the lake bank. They had barely made a puddle at the base of the ruin a hundred metres below. There were zeks, too, thousands of them, hurling sandbags down into the gulf. It would take them months to fill it.

He found Anna working in a tent with the electrical equipment hooked up to a juddering generator. She and some of the other physicists were fighting with people he didn't know, men, dressed like they were straight from the Kremlin. She saw him coming but didn't stop arguing with whoever she was arguing with – it was something about radiation and contamination, but too technical for him to catch. He slouched forward against a table with a microscope on it. She was alive.

When she did come away, she looked like she might spit.

'Hello lovely. You look horrifying, I thought you were supposed to be in hospital?'

'I tried to call. A lot,' he said, wishing stupidly that she'd look more pleased to see him.

'They've shut down all the phone lines,' she said, shaking her head. 'Nothing in or out except to Moscow. Why are you even out of bed? You shouldn't be walking about—'

'Because people have got radiation sickness *in Chelyabinsk*, Anna, I thought you were dead!'

'Christ, keep your voice down,' she breathed. She took his arm and steered him away, towards the lake, but even then, it didn't take them away from the crowds of people – workers, Moscow men, zeks in grey clothes, digging over the verges, turning the grass.

The wreckage that was the lake bed was worse than he'd thought. It didn't look like anything as simple as an explosion from one particular place. The entire marsh had gone up, from here right to the forest; muck and wreckage and everywhere, absolutely everywhere, the silvery corpses of dead fish. It was too cold for them to smell.

'What . . . happened?'

'The investigators are here trying to work that out now. I don't know. I've never even heard of anything like this before, it's insane.'

'The Americans?'

'God knows,' she said. She glanced behind them, where a man in a black suit had followed, but Shenkov knew a KGB officer from a thousand paces. He had a thrill of unease, the kind he usually gave other people. 'But, it's all being dealt with of course,' she said, a little loudly.

'How are you? Is the baby . . . ?'

'I was at home, indoors.' Her eyes flicked back to the black-suited man again. 'Fortunately, it's been determined that what did look at first like radiation sickness in the immediate vicinity is actually down to spores in the marsh, disturbed by the explosion. There's some kind of blight. Make you ill but nothing to worry about.'

He had to look away, over the blasted marsh. They had spoken to each other like this in Moscow, during the purges, even over their own kitchen table: like they were both characters in a Komsomol manual about how to be good girls and boys. He thought they'd left that behind out here.

He could see the concrete block that housed the reactor. It was ripped open. He wondered how much radiation they were getting just standing here, how much was blasting through Anna, through the baby. He didn't even know what it was, not exactly, but in his mind it was an invisible black smoke, pawing at windows and the branches of the trees.

'Is the – are the spores still in the air? Will they hurt you?'

'It's possible they'll be bad for a foetus,' she said. She sighed, more like someone whose soufflé had sunk than someone whose unborn baby had just been doused in radiation. She was always that way, but it shocked him whenever he saw it. He could never say that: she had told him straight up when they got married that she wasn't a natural mother, that she didn't do very well with small helpless things, because she had been trained to care about electron microscopes, thanks, and obviously she *would* gestate him a small helpless thing to look after if he desperately wanted one, but it would be *his*; she would be present for emotional support et cetera, because she liked him a lot, but there would be no talk of staying at home, nesting, or maternal fussing, because frankly that was nothing but weakness of character in a woman and if he thought differently then he could fuck off.

He had been stupid enough to find it funny at the time, and to think she was underestimating the power of her own heart. She had, as usual, been pristinely accurate.

'It'll be all right,' she said. She smiled, but not much. When she stopped sounding so proper, she was telling the truth. It was a kind of code. 'We're not being evacuated here. A few towns downwind are, just while they deal with the blight.'

'So – you'll be all right? The baby will be all right?'

'Could be,' she said to the bump, as if it might have something to say for itself. 'Never mind if not, though. Or maybe it will be a dragon mutant; that would be variation.'

No pregnancy was a certain thing, working as she did in the lab. There were accidents every second month, as far as he could tell. She had lost three since they'd been here. She would have gone insane if she'd loved them before she knew them. She wasn't hugely interested in the twins even now; she would garner some interest, she said, when they learned the periodic table. He was pretty sure that what she meant was that it would take her that long to feel sure they weren't temporary. 'Speaking of which. I think Dragon Mutant is hungry. I wonder if there are sandwiches.'

'I'll . . . let you get on,' he said, because in his experience, distraught husbands only got in the way. He had to swallow hard. His favourite time, with the children, was sitting in the rocking chair with them while they were still tiny and surprised by everything, like the bright pop-up book about the girl who met the Winter King in the woods. He was always sad when they grew up enough not to want to sit still any more. It was an unspeakable thing to mourn, though. If he even tried to say it, he'd sound like a hysterical moron. It was one of those things you just had to fold away, like the baby clothes.

The buildings around the lake had been bulldozed already. Now, there were trailer offices and tents. Predictably, the KGB had a tent. They would all, Shenkov knew full well, have been far too embarrassed to argue hard for walls and heating. He thought wearily that he had better recruit some women. Women didn't do stupid things just to prove they were really good at being women.

Orders had just come in from Moscow. They were to clear out everyone within forty kilometres of the plant, and maintain the exclusion zone no matter what.

'Only forty kilometres?' Shenkov asked. 'People have radiation sickness in Chelyabinsk, I've just come from there.'

The Moscow officer looked him up and down, and then drew him to one side, behind a trailer full of construction workers in hard-hats, leaning over some plans on a table.

'No one has radiation sickness in Chelyabinsk,' the Moscow man said. 'You're mistaken.'

Shenkov let his breath out impatiently. 'Yes, fine, no one has radiation sickness in Chelyabinsk, but the doctors have clocked it, so—'

The man punched him in the stomach. Shenkov collapsed.

'No one has radiation sickness in Chelyabinsk. As you know, comrade, this was a scheduled contamination, in order that scientists have an irradiated district to study properly. It has been carefully controlled, and obviously Moscow would never allow anything unsafe to happen. There is a toxic blight in Chelyabinsk, that's all; a perfectly natural difficulty. It would be irresponsible to suggest otherwise.'

12

The Alien

1963 (now)

Valery thought about it for a while after Shenkov had finished. There had been a bang, and some electrical equipment shut down ninety kilometres away. Within a few hours, people arrived at the hospital with radiation sickness. The reactor in the lake had been gutted so badly that it had not been rebuilt, but filled in with concrete. If people caught outside in Chelyabinsk had absorbed at least the hundred roentgen required for radiation sickness, then the amount of radioactive material in the air was vast. Vast, however, was not a very specific thing to say.

He pulled his hand across his jaw, frustrated. He felt as if Shenkov had given him everything he needed to know, but if any tests had been done recently to determine exactly what caused what and how, he had no idea. He'd been in prison for too long. When he was arrested, the very first nuclear detonations had happened barely a decade before, and if they were being honest, people knew bugger all about them except that there was a very big bang.

'And the investigators didn't have any conclusions?' he asked at last.

'No,' said Shenkov. 'I think they said a small steam explosion. It looked bad but it was nothing.'

'But you had a radio flash.'

'What's that?'

'What made the electricals short. A nuclear explosion generates an electromagnetic pulse. Fries circuitry.' He paused. 'It would normally have to be above the visible horizon I think, the blast, but maybe we're uphill enough.'

'Yes,' Shenkov said, sounding unsure of himself. 'I thought so anyway, but I was on morphine at the time, and when I asked Anna, she said there couldn't have been, she didn't see how the numbers could line up for that.'

Valery shook his head. 'I don't know enough about it. They must have done tests since I was arrested, I'm six years out of date, but . . . it can't have been a bomb, or City 40 wouldn't be here, a warhead just flattens everything within a kilometre.' He tried to think around the corners of the idea, but it was polyhedral and it had an awful lot of corners. 'But Anna is right, even if the reactor was in disgusting shape, it *still* couldn't have gone up like that.'

'Could they have done it on purpose, like they say?' Shenkov said quietly.

'I don't see what would justify it. A reactor costs millions upon millions, you don't just blow one up. It was really under the lake?'

'It was.'

'We live in a James Bond novel,' Valery said, pleased.

Shenkov smiled, or halfway smiled.

A small mental siren went off to inform Valery that he ought to be enjoying himself less. He had to dredge around for the reason, and then felt terrible when he found it. 'Your baby, was it . . .'

'She's six now. She's all right.'

So there were still miracles. 'Good.'

They were both quiet for a while.

'I suppose the question now is whether Moscow knows there's a problem here, or if the cover-up was so quick that they missed it,' Shenkov said at last.

'They know. They're telling you to limit people's time outside close to the Lighthouse, they're telling you not to let scientists sit around outside. Your own agent told me to wait in the car when I found Sasha. The figures on our maps are rubbish but whoever made your regulations knew very well.'

Shenkov said nothing for a while. 'Can you measure what the radiation readings are inside the city?' he asked. 'Without obviously waving a dosimeter around?'

'Why? What's the point of knowing?'

'Because if we know what we're dealing with, we can take measures ourselves. Barbed wire on the banks of the Techa, like you said. Find reasons to close off anywhere especially bad. Moscow isn't the only one who can bury things under paperwork.'

Valery took a breath to say no, he had no subtle way of measuring it, but then stopped. 'Radiation shows up on film. Yes, film and sticky tape actually, we'll be away.'

Shenkov was staring at him. 'You can make a dosimeter out of some film and some tape.'

'People think science is all specialist expensive stuff, but it's mostly made of kitchen rolls and fridge magnets and we just spray it black when anyone with a news crew turns up.'

Shenkov did not look reassured about the state of modern scientific progress. 'Then what do you do?'

'Pin it up in various places round town for an hour, develop it, see what the results are.'

Shenkov took off his security lanyard and looped it round Valery's neck instead. 'In case anyone stops you.'

'Thank you,' Valery said, surprised, and too touched. He looked down at the pass and brushed the dark cord of the lanyard, 'KGB' woven in yellow on to it ten or twelve times.

Shenkov cradled Valery's shoulder to turn him away. 'Come on, let's go in. I'm cold.' I'm cold, not it's cold, or you'll get cold, or even, remember the radiation. Valery liked him a lot for that.

'What are you doing for the rest of the day?' Valery asked.

Shenkov took a newspaper out of his coat pocket. It was the one Valery had seen at the cafe on Saturday, the ALIENS IN KYSHTYM!! one. 'I've got to frighten a journalist. We don't want anyone investigating funny lights and finding a big secret nuclear installation.'

They went inside laughing, and despite everything Shenkov had told him about the explosion, the extent of it, the radiation, Valery felt happy. It was very good to laugh with someone.

While Shenkov went to frighten his journalist, Valery dissected a film reel and made sixteen badges out of it. He used pin-on staff-card holders. He took eight of them to the mouse room and exposed the first to the uranium block for long enough to give it one roentgen, then the next for two, three, up to eight. Once they were developed, he'd have a clear scale. A light square of film would mean no radiation; a dark one would mean a lot.

The other eight he took out walking. In case they all got irradiated through his pocket, he left seven in a cupboard in the lab and took one out to the lake shore, where he pinned it to a signpost at chest height to stay out for an hour. The second, he pinned to a taxi stand on the main road; the third, on the edge of the school playing field, which was open because people walked their dogs there. Then out to the forest edge. After placing each one, he drew a line on the face of his pocket watch in marker pen to remind himself when he would have to get back to collect them. Nobody asked him why he was in and out so much, even Dr Resovskaya. He was just being Odd Gulag Man.

When he got back, having collected all the badges again after their hour was up, the students were worrying about whether or not slightly radioactive rain might induce balding, and they were deep in negotiations about who to send out for hats. He watched them for a while, tempted to chip in and recommend hazmat suits.

The phone rang before he'd even taken off his coat. It was next to his desk, so he picked it up.

'Biology lab?'

'Valery?' Shenkov said at the other end. Valerie, like English. 'Can you come to the office of the *Lake News* in town? It's next to the theatre.'

'Of course. Why?'

'There's . . . something I need you to look at.'

'Is it an alien?' Valery asked. 'I want an alien.'

'Well,' said Shenkov, sounding pensive, 'I was hoping you could tell me what it is.'

The *News* office wasn't so much an office as the editor's front room. It had a desk with a lamp on it, an old-fashioned printing press in the far corner, and two bespectacled men at high desks scalpelling lines of copy. The walls must have once had wallpaper, but it had either peeled off or been peeled, because now they were bare, paper-stained plywood. Everything smelled of onions, and there was steam drifting through from the kitchen, where a lady in fluffy slippers and hair rollers was making something complicated. Shenkov could not have looked more out of place if he'd tried. He was waiting at the desk with the editor, a young man with lamp eyes and receding hair.

'Hi,' said Valery, curious. 'So what's going on?'

'He won't believe me about the alien,' the young man with the eyes said. 'State oppression, that is.'

Valery thought it was nice that young people felt able to say things like that now. Shenkov looked weary already.

'Show him, please.'

'If you confiscate it, I'll print that too,' the young man said bravely. 'It'll be proof it's something suspicious.'

'Comrade, if you had anything even faintly suspicious, I'd have burned your house down and blamed it on a kitchen accident,' Shenkov sighed.

The young man baulked and came to the side table just by Valery, on which sat a longish box. 'So why's a biologist here, then?'

'Because I want to know what that thing is. Given that what it is not, is an alien,' Shenkov added. Like always, he kept his tone courteous and even quite gentle, but it was translucent. Talking to him, Valery thought, was a lot like ice skating and watching something swimming under you where the water was still liquid, something which knew very well that you couldn't make out whether it was a dolphin or a polar bear, and which quietly enjoyed the confusion.

'Why can't it be an alien? We—'

'Oh,' Valery said, because the young man had opened the box.

Inside, resting on a cotton lining, was a small body. It was a little larger than a standardly sized doll. But it was not a doll. It was a mummified corpse, and it was all wrong. The skull was elongated, reaching what was nearly a point at the crown, and ridged clearly where the bone plates fused. There was no jaw, just a frothy malformation of bone, and the suggestion of a miniature beak of a nose. The arms, crossed over the chest, were too long, there were too many ribs, and the legs were too small.

Shenkov had come up next to him. 'What is it?'

It was a baby.

Valery forced himself to smile. 'It is a very deformed monkey with the tail removed. Whoever gave you this is having you on,' he said to the young editor, who looked briefly crestfallen, before he clawed his way back up to suspicious.

'You're just saying that.'

'Right, comrade, it's definitely an alien.' Valery touched Shenkov's back, wanting to get him away from here *right now*.

'Let him publish whatever he wants, Konstantin, it's a joke. Come on.' He pushed his fingertips into Shenkov's spine, hoping Shenkov would feel it through his coat and understand.

He did. 'Well,' Shenkov said to the editor, 'enjoy your monkey corpse.'

They left together in silence, and only once they were in the street, outside the theatre with its silly Corinthian columns, did Shenkov stop him. 'Valery?'

'That thing was a human foetus,' Valery said softly. He tried to lean close, but he was still getting dizzy spells if he moved too suddenly, and he had to put one hand on Shenkov's lapel to catch his balance. He took it away again, embarrassed, but Shenkov held his shoulders. 'It's been mutated *in utero* to an extent I've never seen before, but it *is* human. It was a little girl. If she was ever born, she wouldn't have lived more than a week. Those mutations, the prominent seals of the skull plates, that lacy bone formation in the face – those are radiation deformities. I see them in our mice. They will have occurred because the mother was exposed for a long time.'

Shenkov's briskness had cracks in it now. 'Are you *sure* it's human?'

'Positive.'

'I didn't know humans could go that wrong.'

Valery inclined his head, because he would have thought Shenkov would have seen, or indeed personally inflicted, worse than that on a few humans himself. Some of the officers at the Lubyanka had been quite imaginative. It was strange to see him rattled by it. 'They can be a lot wronger, but usually a foetus as malformed as that would never make it to term. It's rare that they reach that size.'

'And that's what they look like, after enough radiation to the mother.'

'That's what they look like,' Valery confirmed.

'How many people would *know* that that's what they look like?'

'A lot of women must.'

'Women, why?'

'Well, who've miscarried. Especially physicists in the main labs if they test weapons-grade plu—'

'Oh, don't, don't,' Shenkov said, and put his hand to the wall beside him. He looked ill.

'What?' Valery asked, confused now. He hadn't known there was any such thing as a squeamish KGB officer, and even above that, it was an odd thing to be squeamish about. Weird as irradiated foetuses were, they were fascinating. He used to have one on his desk. It had been called Buttons.

'My wife has had three miscarriages. All late.'

Whenever he thought he was learning to be warmer, and more human, something like this reminded him again that he was only a reptile in disguise.

'She didn't say,' Shenkov said. 'That that's what they look like.'

Valery wanted to say something; that he was sure Anna had only been trying to keep Shenkov clean of the whole idea, or that it had been such a rancid feeling she hadn't been able to talk about it at all, even if she'd wanted to. But he couldn't imagine it would do Shenkov any good to go any further into it.

'We need to find out where that foetus came from,' Valery said instead. 'If the editor bought it on the quiet from someone in the exclusion zone, or someone from a lab, or . . . from inside the city.'

'He said someone from down the road found it in her garden.'

Valery started to nod, but then really heard it. 'People have *gardens?*'

'Gardens, yes? They're shared allotments attached to the . . . towers, you look like you might kill someone.'

'Was the soil all replaced, after the accident?'

'I don't think so. Ours wasn't.'

They both gazed along the street. Everything was smart shopfronts here, but behind the theatre there were apartment blocks and allotments, some of them beautifully tended, some lined up with rows of bamboo canes where people were growing runner beans.

'Did you do the film test?'

'Yes. I'll get it developed when I get back,' Valery said. 'Then we'll know.'

'I don't understand how we don't already know. Secrecy is one thing, the forest is one thing, but children being born here like – like *that* . . . '

'Doctors must know,' Valery said, just as confused.

Shenkov pulled his hand over his face. 'Anyway, I'll go and get the address of the woman who sold them their alien. It can't be from here, someone must have found it in the forest and just buried it here. We can't be surrounded by women who go through *this* all the time and never tell anyone.'

Valery nodded, though he disagreed. He had a needling, frost-forming feeling that that was exactly what was going on.

'And then I suppose I'd better talk to some doctors, not that any of them will tell me anything.'

Valery wished him luck, not sure how much it would take.

Valery visited the facility darkroom, where a technician developed his radiation badges inside an hour and didn't ask what they were for; people must have done odd experiments with film all the time. Even so, Valery didn't dare to take them out of the packet until he was back at the lab. Carefully, he laid them out on the desk.

One to eight, like he'd hoped, showed a spectrum scale. One roentgen was a haze on the film; eight was dark.

Under them, he set out the badges he'd taken to different parts of town. He matched each one to the closest shade on his control scale.

Immediately by the lake, he'd got four roentgen in an hour. Down the main road, there was nothing showing up – that was a relief – but the relief went off the second he saw the one from the edge of the school field. Eight roentgen in an hour. And then the badge he'd left pinned to the oak tree he'd slept against; darker than anything on the control scale.

Seeing it on film felt different to reasoning it out.

He pushed the photographs back into their packet and put the packet in his breast pocket, and then nearly fell over when he tried to stand up. He waited for the dizziness to pass, but it didn't and, feeling defeated, he trailed off to see the doctor.

She gave him another iodine pill and a plastic cup of water, and a lecture about overdoing it. He let it wash over him, too glad to be sitting down to complain. In his pocket, the photographs felt like they had a heat of their own. He found himself gripping Shenkov's security card as hard as anyone ever held a cross.

'Doctor,' he said carefully. 'Do you have a minute for something else?'

'Yes,' she said, looking politely attentive and clearly expecting some kind of troublesome rash.

He laid the images out on her desk. Everything was labelled, so there was no need to explain. As he did, her expression shut down. He saw her glance desperately at the light switch. He shook his head a little to say that he wasn't going to start a lecture about film dosimetry. 'I was just wondering if you see problems related to this sort of thing a lot.'

'Oh. No, I'm afraid not, extremely rare,' she said, aiming bright and clear at the light switch.

Valery leaned over to catch her notepad and wrote, *I'm not an informant.*

She wrote back, *You're friends with Shenkov, I'm not stupid.*

Valery tapped the photograph taken by the school field, urgently. *Shenkov has kids. I did this test FOR him. He wants to make things safer.*

She was twisting and untwisting her hands. Whatever was on her mind, it must have been bothering her for a long time. First do no harm; it must have been hard to keep quiet about anything that was doing harm.

'I'm afraid it's really not my area,' she said, quite loudly, but she took down a file and opened it on the desk for him. Her hands were shaking.

The file was full of pages of tables.

Valery took it slowly and read down the rows. It was done by date, and it was a simple chart: it showed patients diagnosed with low white blood cell counts, the classic hallmark of radiation problems. There was the blood-sample reading, followed by the action taken; discharged, or sent up to Chelyabinsk to see a specialist. At the top of the page was the first of the month, and at the bottom the thirty-first. When he checked back, it was all done like that, calendar month by calendar month. Each month, on the fifteenth, was a red line marked across the whole chart in highlighter pen.

There were a lot of worrying readings; a lot of people with barely enough white blood cells to fight off a cold, far more than he would have expected for one practice in one medium-sized city, and those readings were uniform right down the month. But only the people who were tested before the red line, before the fifteenth, were ever sent to Chelyabinsk to see the specialists. After the fifteenth of each month, everyone, even if they obviously had leukaemia, was discharged with vitamin supplements only.

They had a quota.

'So I'm just on iodine,' he said, and wrote, *Is this the same for every practice in the city?*

'Yes, just as a precaution,' she said tightly. She picked up the pen again. *It is illegal to share this data across practices.*

No wonder Shenkov hadn't heard anything. The only record of the real number of people suffering radiation-related difficulties sat on individual doctors' desks, the data uncollated. Maybe people here generally had noticed that they got colds a lot, that their children had allergies, that there was a high rate of miscarriages, but even someone digging through medical records at the hospitals in Chelyabinsk would find nothing, because the admission rates were artificially low. Nothing after the fifteenth of each month.

Valery swallowed. 'Well. I'll get out of your hair. Thanks, comrade.'

She nodded, and raked her hands through her hair, as if there really was something in it, something poisonous and sticky.

Shenkov wasn't in the office for the rest of the day, so Valery had to wait until the following morning to tell him about the health quota and the photographs. He went to fetch some coffee from the canteen first, though, and while he was in the queue, he saw the morning papers on the rack. The locals all carried the same story.

Two houses had burned down in the night. One belonged to a young man – the editor of another local – and his mother; the other, only a street away, to a professional gardener. Sadly, all three had perished in the respective blazes. In both cases, the fire brigade had found the cause to be chip-pan fires. The articles urged readers to be extra careful about their cooking habits.

'I had to,' Shenkov said when Valery let himself into the office and held up the paper. He looked pale, and although he was still perfectly turned out, he had a heavy jumper on over his shirt, as though he was too tired today to pretend not to feel the cold. He was softer than normal; it was because there was no wax in his hair to hold it swept back, and it was long enough to fall forward on one side, half-redacting him from any conversation. 'Someone called from Moscow after I reported the case last night.'

Valery didn't say anything, but he gave him a chocolate bar. He had a feeling that Shenkov would interpret sympathy in about the same way he would interpret having *faggot* screamed at him across a room.

'Thank you,' Shenkov said, muted.

'Just the prisoner book again,' Valery said for the benefit of the bugs, but laid out the radiation photographs.

Shenkov didn't have to study them for long before he understood. He looked up at Valery wordlessly, raw shock in his eyes.

Valery leaned down against the back of his chair. 'I spoke to the doctor,' he whispered, so quietly he could only just hear himself. 'They have quotas for diagnosing radiation-related illness. They don't diagnose any after the fifteenth of every month. No one looking would know the real extent, and it is illegal for doctors to compare their results across practices.'

'How the hell did you get her to tell you that?'

'I'm a funny harmless little science elf, people tell me things. She showed me the quota sheet.'

Shenkov was turning the pages of his desk diary. He stopped at some point in February and sat still. He didn't write notes to himself there at all; there were crosses by some of the dates, and times that might have been meetings, but nothing else. More security requirements, Valery supposed. 'The fifteenth is the cut-off.'

'Yes.'

'I see,' Shenkov said quietly. He didn't elaborate, and only closed the diary. He was silent for a little while, but he hadn't finished, Valery could see that; he was holding his voice like a shard of glass, looking for a way to lift it without cutting himself. 'Moscow knows exactly what's going on. Like you said.'

Valery nodded. It was painful to keep leaning against the chair, so he perched on the edge of the desk instead, careful to avoid the papers there. He switched the kettle on, but didn't raise his voice above a whisper. 'At least they send us real chocolate and real grapes and real coffee. I reckon I'm okay with being a bit irradiated if I'm allowed to stay happy while it happens.'

Shenkov half-laughed. The small lines around his eyes looked more like scars then. 'What's the fine print? How much does living here cut someone's life expectancy?'

'Depends what you do. People working in offices are much safer than people who work outside.' Valery paused. 'Most of the science doesn't exist yet. We don't know what the long-term effects are. Which is . . . why this place is here. I would think someone in a locked room in Moscow gets the medical notes. Someone will be doing a study on population health in City 40.'

Shenkov was turning the school-field photograph over and over between his fingertips. 'Promise me you won't do anything stupid. No calling the Kremlin, no calling journalists. If I get an order through to shoot you, I will be . . .' his hands flickered and he dropped the photograph, which landed with a tap on the desk '. . . annoyed.'

'I promise,' Valery said. 'What happens about Sasha? The hospital quota thing might explain why he had to leave, but I still don't understand how he ended up dead in a pond. He had to get in and out, and if he was here, inside a hospital, he *wasn't* sitting out there getting this bad a dose.'

'The coroner has the body now. We'll have to see what she says.' The water in the kettle had reached the loudest point of its seething. The switch clicked off. Shenkov had to stop, tip some water out, and put more cold in to start it again before he carried on. Even so, they had to lean so close together that their hair touched. Shenkov smelled of the brightest parts of winter, spices and pine and something else that made Valery think of bonfires in the forest. 'If she says he died of six hundred roentgen then at least that's an excuse to find out where the six hundred came from, but if she doesn't – I don't know. I don't think there's anything else we would be allowed to do. It will go down as an accidental death.' He looked up. 'Thank you, by the way. For doing the dosimetry tests.'

Valery shrugged, because he would have done them whether Shenkov had asked him or not. 'Well. I didn't expect to live out the year before I came here. I know this is very concerning for you, but it's kind of great for me.'

Shenkov smiled, not much. 'If I start asking for the school field to be concreted over, someone will report me to Moscow, it—I was just ordered to kill two people over an alien hoax, never mind actually . . .' He had been holding himself poised all along, but something in him cracked then and Valery realised he was close to tears. He was staring hard at the framed pictures on the shelf opposite; four children, all young enough to be at that school. 'We can't do anything.'

Valery had to look away, because it hurt a lot more to see Shenkov breaking than it had when his arm broke. He didn't dare touch him. The door was open, like it always was. If any other officer walked past to see the boss being openly comforted by the resident lunatic then it would filter outward and there would be mocking murmurs, and for weeks Shenkov would struggle to make anyone do as they were told. That was only if there was no one here who wanted Shenkov's job. If they did, it would turn, by the officious alchemical process of formal reports, into fraternisation with a known enemy of the people. The necessity of Valery's being here to get the prisoner book signed would only stretch so far.

'What if I put these photographs in an official-looking envelope,' Valery whispered, 'and sent them anonymously to the head teacher with a recommendation about concrete? It's in her remit to decide how to spend her own budget. Maybe on six brand-new basketball courts.'

Shenkov laughed, or sort of, and gave him an envelope.

13

The Missing Boy

Valery was wheeling a crate of deer carcasses out to the incinerator two days later when someone appeared from behind the biomass waste bins. It made him jump, but it was only one of the men from the forest village. Looking urgent, the man pressed one finger to his lips and jerked his head. Valery hurried over.

'Meet me on the edge of the woods as soon as you can.'

'Okay,' said Valery, and watched as the man vanished behind the bins again, in the direction of the facility fence. It was a brand-new fence; he couldn't see how the man had got in, but then, perhaps it was safer not to know that. So he told Dr Resovskaya he was moving onto foxes if he could find any, got a fresh permit from the KGB office, bought three bags of groceries from town without being asked even once why he wanted enough coffee and chocolate to feed an army – people must have standardly hoarded it in case Moscow changed its mind about nice things – and drove out to the woodland border, where the man from the village was smoking restlessly.

'Are you all right?' Valery asked.

'What took you so long? Nanya said to bring you. Get in.' He opened the door of the battered old farm truck and held out the blindfold.

'One second,' Valery said. 'I've got some things for you, help me carry the bags.'

'If you've bugged—'

'It's chocolate, you dingbat, not everyone is KGB.'

The man grew a good few centimetres, but then deflated when he noticed just how much smaller Valery was, and the cast, and that he must have meant it as a joke. 'Did you just call me a dingbat?'

'I stand by it,' Valery confirmed.

The man helped him move the bags.

Despite the blindfold, the man took him a different way to last time. Last time had been almost a path; now, the truck eased around tight corners among the trees and tracks so deliberately hidden that sometimes the man had to stop and move aside a veil of branches.

When they arrived at the village, Nanya came out from her cottage and patted the door of the truck to say hello, then clipped across to Valery. She must have been twenty years older than him, but she had a brisk walk. She opened the door for him.

'How are you today, doctor?'

'Well, thank you. We've brought you some things,' he said, before he could forget. 'Coffee and chocolate mainly, and some proper fruit from town. It's in the back, I sort of smuggled it in on a trolley but I can't carry it, if someone could . . .'

She whistled sharp at a pair of girls close by, and they dashed to help.

'That was good of you,' said Nanya. 'Now come along.'

The girls got to the cottage ahead of them, and by the time Valery was sitting down at the kitchen table, Nanya was already sorting through supplies. She had an abacus by the oven, and now she clicked the beads for a short while, and then began dividing up the bags into small portions; one for each family, Valery realised. She was doing it by value of the goods.

'Can I help?' he asked.

'You can make me some coffee.'

Valery did as he was told, glad for something to do. The stove was the old-fashioned kind with a boiler built into the side, so he ladled some water from there into the kettle, which was a tremendously heavy iron thing, and set it on the stove top, where the water soon began to bubble. He listened to it and imagined what the radioactive isotopes inside would look like if you could just see well enough for them. Excitable, swooping around in spirals as they rose up, cooled, sank, and rose again. Little whirlpools of poison. Still, it wasn't like there was anything you could do about that.

'The blacksmith,' Nanya said as he poured the coffee through a makeshift filter – a cloth square from a jam jar, 'is pleased with you, by the way. Your forest-glass instructions worked a treat. He wants to see you, when you're done here, to show you the furnace.'

'Oh, that's excellent,' Valery said, pleased too. 'Did he manage to make some glass?'

'Look at my new jars.'

The new jars on the windowsill were all greenish and irregularly shaped, but they were smooth and solid, and they would last forever if no one dropped them. He used two of them as coffee cups and handed her one.

He was glad his job was over just then, because he felt frayed. He'd had three restless nights with the wretched cast now, and three maddening mornings so stiff that he'd barely been able to stand under the bloody shower, never mind iron a shirt properly and get into it. The latter was a process of trial and error whose results seemed to change daily. And, even though he had been sure when he spoke to Shenkov that he was feeling pretty sunny about the whole thing, he'd had nightmares about radiation sickness: about finding hanks of his hair on the pillow, about that iron taste. He'd jolted awake sweating and shaking, and wished he was back in the frozen barracks at the camp.

'Do you like it?' he asked once Nanya had tried the coffee. 'The real thing.'

'I imagine it's an acquired taste.'

They both laughed.

Across the table, he noticed now, there was a neat arrangement of clockwork parts, each one laid out on a broad cloth with a grid drawn on it in marker pen. It looked complicated, and so did the plans open next to it. Whatever she was making, it would be a fair size. He wondered if they could be engine parts; no, engine parts didn't have cogs. Did they?

'It's the mechanism for a combine harvester,' she explained when she saw him looking. 'The lads have been taking in the crops by hand, but scythes are a bugger to use and we were never farmers, before.'

'You're an engineer?'

'Like I say, we were from an engine factory. Big machinery.' She studied the different packages she'd made up, and then finally came to sit down with him at the table. 'Anyway,' she said. 'There was a big talk about whether to ask you back, and I mention the glass because that's what convinced people in the end. You wouldn't have gone to that trouble if you didn't care what happens here. Or are you one of those who gets more annoyed about people being inefficient than people being unhappy?'

It was so straightforward that he didn't even consider lying. 'Both. But I think it amounts to the same thing.'

She nodded with what might have been approval as she picked up her pipe. 'Light that for me. Now; we've got a problem. Another of our boys is missing. A little boy this time, he's only ten. We can't find him; we've been looking for a day already. I'm not saying we're wonderful trackers here, we're not. But we've had enough people out in the woods that we're pretty sure he's not just lost.'

Valery frowned into her pipe as he held a match to the bowl. 'Is he ill, is there a chance he collapsed somewhere, or . . . ?'

'No. He's the picture of health. Has been always. The other kids suffer here, you saw that I expect, but not Pyotr. Have you heard anything up at the Lighthouse? Have the KGB arrested someone, or the soldiers, or anything like that?'

'I can find out,' he said slowly. 'But I don't think they have. I know the head of security and I think he'd have told me if they had a child in custody.'

Her expression sharpened. 'You mean Shenkov.'

'Yes.' He weighed what he wanted to say next with a lot more care than normal, because the way she had said Shenkov's name was a warning she was watching very, very closely for short measures. 'I think he would want to help find Pyotr, if he knew where he was meant to be looking.'

'No. No KGB. Imagine having to say that to someone,' she said, half-angry and half-quizzical. 'I'm not asking him for piss.'

'You know it wasn't him personally who cleared you out, it was orders from Moscow—'

'Well, he personally set fire to my house,' she snapped. 'They just snatched people and drove us up to some godforsaken hole outside Sverdlovsk. Kicked us out at the bus stop. No money, nowhere to stay, nothing. In the middle of a famine. You can imagine what the local people had to say about that. They're hard up already and then in we come, not even farmers.'

Valery liked her less. There wasn't much that really irritated him now, but whining was on the list. 'What did you expect, a hotel? You're telling me that you honestly think Moscow didn't give him orders to have you all shot in case you talked about the radiation? In a place in the middle of nowhere, when they could easily have told everyone's relatives that you died in an explosion at the engine factory? Christ, you ended up alive and with your family at a bus stop in Sverdlovsk? Dry your eyes, mate.'

She looked like she might hit him. He didn't move, too unimpressed. But at last, she sat back. 'What's it like, in the gulag? Bad?'

'It's Siberia; it's the taiga,' Valery said. 'It's not good or bad, it's just itself.'

'Hm,' she said, nodding for longer than most people would have. It was the faint motion of one of those dolls people stuck to the dashboards of cars, the ones that kept swaying well after the car had reached the end of a bumpy road, after the engine had been switched off. 'Still not asking Shenkov, though,' she told him.

'Okay,' said Valery. 'But you need to find this boy fast. The ground gets more radioactive the closer to the Lighthouse you go. The soil on the forest edge is so contaminated that it will make a child radiation sick after one night spent sleeping on it.'

'I keep hearing all this about radiation, but frankly, comrade, if I can't see it and it doesn't bite, I'm not that worried.'

'Yes, that's why it's so dangerous. You don't feel it coming,' Valery said quietly. 'But I mean it. It's why people here are sick, it's why the children are being born with mutations. We need to find Pyotr soon, or we're not going to find him at all. I honestly think we should tell Shenkov.'

'Don't let me hold you up, you'll be wanting to see the blacksmith. Take him his parcel,' she added, and saw Valery to the door as firmly as any prison officer ever had.

He had only seen her in dim light before, but as she took him out into the daylight, he noticed her hand. The last joint of her little finger was missing, just like those other people he'd tested in the village.

'Comrade,' he said. They couldn't *all* have just trapped their fingers in things. 'What happened to your hand?'

She studied him for a long moment, then let out a breath of pipe smoke. 'There's a scientist who comes here every so often. She tests bone samples. Brings us things. Petrol for the truck and the tractor, all that.'

He nearly asked her to repeat it. 'Someone from the Lighthouse knows you're here. Who?'

'I doubt she told us her real name. Stocky lady, red shoes.' She sniffed. 'Bit stupid to wear them in the woods but she does.'

'Dr Resovskaya.' He had to tell himself to shut his mouth. 'She runs the whole place, I . . . what does she use the samples for, does she say?'

Nanya shrugged. 'Don't care. We just need the petrol.'

'But even Shenkov doesn't know where you . . .' Valcry trailed off. He had thought he'd lost his capacity to be shocked, but he felt blown sideways. 'She's running this place as a human trial.'

'Off you go,' Nanya said. 'Blacksmith.'

14

Skating

At the lab, the students were making fireworks. Valery saw the colourful fizzes from above their Bunsen burners along the back workbench, where a whole row of control-group mice were watching the process with a good deal of curiosity. It was lovely to see everyone giggling after the serious industry of Nanya's doomed village. Healthy, cheerful kids: he wanted to tell them what a miracle they were, and how wonderful it was that they all had eyes and the right number of fingers.

He meant to go straight to Resovskaya. She was running the village for human trial data; it was possible that she had taken Pyotr in for tests, or knew someone who had. She might even know where the radiation hotspots were, the ones which might be bad enough to bring a foraging child down with radiation sickness overnight.

He stopped with his hand right on her office door, because Normal Valery was talking.

Ever hear of not rocking the boat?

Nanya would be unsurprised if he couldn't help. But if Shenkov found out that there was another missing person from the village, and that Valery not only knew and hadn't told him but had made enquiries of his own among the scientists, he would be furious.

If Valery was honest, he was a lot more afraid of that than Nanya's threat. He had liked hearing about the explosion and the hospital, liked talking, actually talking, to someone who didn't think he was broken. He liked being able to lean into the KGB office to say hello. He had been happier in the last week than he had been in a decade. He still had Shenkov's security lanyard, because while he held on to it, there was always a reason to go and talk to him.

Better not to tell anyone at all, and express some vague apology when he next saw Nanya.

But only better for him.

It took him that long to realise that Dr Resovskaya wasn't in the office. He could see through the window blinds now that he was standing close. The light was on inside, but the desk was empty.

'Where *is* Dr Resovskaya?' he said, because it occurred to him that he hadn't seen her for ages.

'I think she has her own lab,' one of the students said. 'Why?'

'No, nothing,' Valery murmured, and tried to think where that lab could be. *This* was the only biology lab. All the others, the main ones where the physicists tested nuclear material, were over the road, in the reactor complex. He couldn't look there; his staff pass was only valid for this building.

He sighed, restless.

Dr Resovskaya reappeared late, after dinner, after the students had gone for the night. He didn't see her come in; she just materialised in her office, the anglepoise lamp on and pointing interestedly at a stack of files. That was quite a magic act. There was no other way into her office except the little back door, which just led straight outside behind the bins, and if she knew about the radiation then she hadn't been wandering around out there. He tapped on the door. She smiled.

'Valery. The doctor said you were sick.'

'Yes, radiation sickness,' he said, because he couldn't think of any other way to do this than frankness. 'Only mild.'

Her expression twisted from sympathy into indignation. 'How did you get it?'

'I was outside, near the perimeter fence,' he said. 'I've almost no immune system at the moment, so it got me sooner than it should have.'

'What were you doing near the . . . ?'

'Could I sit down?'

She nodded at the chair.

He sat. 'I stumbled over your village.'

Immediately she looked sharper. 'What do you mean, my village?'

It needled that her instinct was to pretend not to know even when he'd caught her. 'The village of people who moved back into the exclusion zone, the one the KGB doesn't know about. You've been taking bone samples.'

'Don't be ridiculous—'

'No – no, no.' She was scared, that was all. Not calling him stupid. 'Obviously there's a human study here. I thought it was odd that there wasn't, when I arrived.' He smiled a little. 'It's just that they've lost a child. Pyotr. They're out in the woods looking for him, they're going to get sick if they stray too near here. You haven't got him for tests or anything like that, have you?'

'No,' she said slowly. 'No. That's disturbing. That's the second, recently, is it? They had another man missing, Sasha, and he's turned up dead. I heard you found him.'

'I did.'

'You're rather good at finding things,' she murmured.

'Accidentally.'

'I'd believe that once, but twice is a bit much. Valery . . . you do understand, don't you, why the radiation levels are secret? They're much higher than we can say, but if people in town knew that, there'd be chaos. Even if people didn't try to leave, the restitution funds alone would be astronomical.'

'Of course I understand.'

Her eyes went right down him and right up twice. He had no idea how she could hold a gaze for that long. 'Why are you so worried about this boy Pyotr?' she asked.

'Because someone from the village came to fetch me, to see if I'd help. And he's ten. One night on the soil where I was, he'll be too sick to move, I – why *aren't* you worried?'

'Because when your village is in an irradiated territory, children who wander off into a more contaminated band are likely to succumb. This won't have been the first time, Valery.'

'No, I can see that,' he said, because he was starting to feel tired of being spoken down to. 'But they haven't chosen to be here. There's famine beyond the exclusion zone, and when they were cleared out in the first place they weren't given any money or anywhere to stay. Irradiated territory was better than famine, that wasn't a choice, and now their kids are going missing – we should be helping them.'

'I do, as much as I can. I can't do anything about famine or lack of restitution funds. We have a human population living in an irradiated environment . . . it would be silly not to monitor them,' she said gently. 'Moscow has okayed the project. We need human results, more than any others.'

'They're dying.'

'Yes. And we need to know how, and how quickly, because one day, probably soon, the Americans will find a way to do that to a whole city full of people, not just a village. We have to know what will be needed. You know that – and God, Valery, you know that most of this science . . . doesn't exist yet. We're clawing information from studies like this one.'

Valery had to dig his fingernails into the arm of the chair. 'I didn't mean that, I mean their kids are dying in the woods that we irradiated and which we now lie about to try and convince everyone there is not an area that gives off over eight roentgen per hour—'

'Eight roentgen per – how are you arriving at these figures, there are no dosimeters available to—'

'Please. We could tell Shenkov that they're there, but to leave them alone. The best way to find Pyotr will be to ask the KGB to help. They've got the manpower, cars . . .'

Resovskaya was shaking her head. 'Unless you can think of a way to guarantee that Shenkov will not decide that *his* orders are more important than *our* orders, no. He's been told from day one to clear anyone he finds out of the exclusion zone. If he decides to throw them out, that's all our human data wrecked. And before you say anything about prioritising our data over this boy's life – this data will save the lives of many, many children in years to come, so think extremely carefully.'

Valery looked down at his own hands so that he could think without having to see her, then raised his head again. 'I know the value of the data. But those people have a right to try and live, at least, they—'

'A *right?*' she said, incredulous. 'Christ, that's the most American thing I've heard anyone say in years. Rights are not biological law, you of all people know that. They are a luxury, granted in times of peace and plenty. You're standing on a battlefield and demanding that everybody have access to French patisserie.'

'You say, cosy in a nice lab with electricity and central heating.'

'In an irradiated city that will kill me sooner rather than later,' she said flatly. She lifted her hands a little. 'I can't stop you telling Shenkov. But if you tell him and he jeopardises the study, Moscow will have both of you against a wall.'

'I understand.'

He wondered if in fact the animal studies, the soil sampling, the endless data on ants and fish, might not all be here in order to disguise the human study in Nanya's village. The best way to hide secret work was to bury it under a mountain of stuff so boring that no one in their right mind would plough through it. If a clutch of academics known for their expertise in radiation studies vanished to City 40, but no data at all was published and everything was secret, the entire academic world would guess in thirty seconds that there were human studies here. But set up a research centre out in the open, run endless animal and plant studies, blanket it with restrictions but ensure the data was nonetheless publishable; well, that was what all those scientists were doing, of course. Here were the papers to prove it, full of dull, censored radiation quadrants and slightly ill mice.

Distracted by all that, no one was going to say, *hang on; it sounds awfully like you deliberately trapped people in this irradiated territory, with the KGB on one side and famine on the other.*

Christ's sake. The gulag really had turned him into a vegetable. Six years ago he would have seen what was going on straight away. He had; he had even wondered if he was being brought here for a human study. He just hadn't put it together.

Resovskaya's eyes went over him twice. 'What happened to your arm?'

'It was an accident, my bones are like paper at the moment.'

'I heard a rumour that Shenkov did it.'

Valery looked up properly. He had been doing it in snatches before, then resting his eyes on his knees. 'By accident, like I say. He was trying to get me to the infirmary for the radiation sickness.'

She lifted her eyebrow, and then took out a cigarette and lit it. She didn't have a lighter; she did it with a match. She could do it one-handed, a push of one thumb to scratch the match across the strip on the side of the box. The soft smell of gunpowder reached him as she set the box down again. That habit of lighting up mid-conversation was something he had always hated. She did it to disguise an inability to arrange her face into anything but an honest reflection of her thoughts, and it was no coincidence that the cigarettes came out exactly in the moment that someone less cultured would have told her interlocutor not to be so bloody thick.

'Just a word to the wise,' she said. 'Be careful of Shenkov. He's not your friend. He came here after a spell in prison. He hasn't any grace left with Moscow; if he puts a foot wrong, he's in the gulag. He'll sling you to the wolves if it means saving his own skin.'

'So would anyone,' Valery said. 'In prison for what?'

'I know you want it to be something noble and political, but it was much less salubrious than that. Of course I mustn't say,' she added, and ground out the cigarette, which meant she had finished talking about it.

He watched her for a second. He had made her wary, and that was not a clever way to leave the conversation. She would be surveilling him now, which would mean any effort he made to help find Pyotr, or help the villagers – he found himself determined to do both – would come under scrutiny. He believed her about Moscow having him against a wall if he interfered with the human data.

'Hey,' he said, and arranged his whole demeanour into the same sunny brightness he did when he spoke to the camp guards. 'Sign my cast?'

She laughed, looking relieved. 'Yes.' She drew a cat on it. He went away pretending to be pleased.

He forgot the time after that – part of him was still waiting for the shift-change klaxon and, when he surfaced, he was alarmed to find it was already nine o'clock at night and he was in a deathly silent lab.

Usually, it would have made him uneasy, nothing worse. But he was still at the tail end of the radiation sickness, and a side effect was wrecked nerves.

The silence closed in and screamed, and panic flooded up through his chest. He had to put everything down and leave. When he looked back, he'd left the desk lamp on, but he couldn't bring himself to go into that terrible stillness to switch it off; instead he hurried straight across the deserted corridor and to the lift, where he scanned the apartment buzzers fast. Shenkov was on the ninth floor. Resovskaya was nearer – fifth floor – but he couldn't turn up at a woman's door at nine o'clock.

While he waited for the lift to make its interminable way down, he had to talk aloud to himself just for the sound of a human voice, and so he stood there telling himself what a bad book *Anna Karenina* was until, finally, the lift doors pinged.

When he knocked on Shenkov's door, there was no answer at first. He shut his eyes, trying to breathe through the feeling that his heart was pumping treacle, then tapped again, just in case. Shenkov answered straight away this time. Despite the hour, he was fully dressed. He stood stock-still on the threshold for a second, then slouched against the frame.

'Valery,' he said, sounding young with relief. 'Jesus Christ.'

Valery was lost, then understood and clapped one hand over his mouth. He couldn't believe he'd been so dense. They always came for you at night. 'I'm so sorry,' he whispered. 'I wasn't . . . thinking . . .'

Shenkov shook his head to say forget it. 'Everything all right?'

Valery had meant to say, *hi, I've got your security lanyard still*, but that evaporated. 'No. I got panicky in the lab when I realised I was by myself. It's too quiet. So I – thought I'd bother you.'

'Good timing,' was all Shenkov had to say. He stood aside to let Valery in. 'The ice skating's on.'

'Oh,' Valery said, pleased despite himself. He loved figure skating.

Shenkov poured them both a glass of vodka, and folded down beside him on the couch. He did it much more lightly than he would have if he'd been alone; the cushions barely moved.

Valery sank into the company. The treacle feeling lifted from his heart, and he felt his blood begin to slow down, the panic heat lessen. He hadn't realised he was in such a state.

'My family's in town,' Shenkov explained to the otherwise empty room. It was the same as Valery's, but there was far more evidence of permanence; books on the shelves, photos of children, and a collection of framed maps from all over Asia. 'I'm on call at night here, on weekdays. I go home on Saturday. My turn with the kids or Anna goes mad.'

Valery nodded once. The older he got, the more he noticed how new acquaintances took care to mention their families as a kind of warning; *don't expect too much from me, because on my list of people who I'd rescue from a burning building, you, newcomer, will only ever make it to about number seven and, let's be honest, probably the increasingly radioactive dog would come first.* Even in the camps, people did that.

There was a cheer from the television. One of the skaters had done an impossible-looking spin.

Valery winced. Usually he loved seeing someone skate, but just for now, he felt like he'd been rubbed all over with sandpaper and everything was painful. 'I hate it when they do that. Fifty-fifty they break a leg.' God, he sounded like a whiny little twit. 'Sorry, it's the radiation sickness,' he said. 'It causes depression, I'll be unbearable for another few days.'

Shenkov smiled. 'Surely the whole point of watching this is when they break a leg.'

'You're a horrible person,' Valery said, aching with gratitude. 'Next double loop, you drink if she lands and I drink if she falls.'

Valery tilted his glasses down to give Shenkov a librarian look. 'Don't imagine I don't realise you're trying to condition me into Pavlovian happiness for when she breaks her leg.'

'I don't imagine that at all,' Shenkov said mildly.

They watched the rest of the skater's routine.

'Drink,' Valery told him.

Shenkov drank and tapped him with the empty glass. 'Don't you feel smug now?'

'Yes,' he admitted.

Shenkov laughed. Perhaps he had been lonely too, before Valery arrived.

Valery watched him for a while, Pyotr's name sitting on his tongue like a pebble. The more he saw of Shenkov, the more he was sure that Shenkov was good at acting the part of a frightening man, not a natural.

Shenkov lifted his head a little to ask why he was being so closely studied.

Valery nodded. When he spoke next, he did it softly, under the commentary from the television. If the bugs were old enough to scritch, they wouldn't pick him up through the background noise. 'I went to the village in the woods again today. They're missing a child. Pyotr, he's called. He's only ten. He hasn't . . . I don't know, been arrested, poking around here?'

'No,' Shenkov said, just as softly.

For all 'no' wasn't the best answer, Valery felt lighter for having asked. 'They're worried about him. So am I. If he stays out overnight in one of the most contaminated areas, he'll be dead in three days. The woman who runs the village didn't want to get the KGB involved, she's worried you'll find them and clear them out, and Dr Resovskaya is using the village for human data on radiation effects. I spoke to her earlier tonight. She says we'll both be shot if you touch the place. But we can't not look for him.'

Beside him, Shenkov was dialling the phone.

Christ, he'd been wrong; Shenkov was reporting him, here, right now. He was going to be dead in ten minutes for concealing the village and interfering with KGB orders, or worse, he was going back to the gulag, and instead of getting up and running, he was paralysed.

'It's Shenkov. Yes. We're missing a child. Get the shift together and get them searching the forest. Take the halogens. A boy. Pyotr.' Pause. 'The hell does it matter whose child? Do as you're told. Any adults, leave them alone, they're allowed to be there now.' He put the phone down, lightly; his temper had been pretended. Then he looked at Valery, his expression open and mild again. 'What?'

'Nothing,' said Valery, stunned. It wouldn't go through his head for a good few seconds. He wanted to laugh or weep or something, but nothing would come.

On the television, another skater fell. Shenkov poured himself another vodka, matter-of-fact.

No doubt because Valery had relaxed, tiredness steamrolled over him. He started to curl sideways against the arm of the couch, but then winced when he hit an angle his broken arm didn't like. He straightened up again painfully. Shenkov had watched him do it. Without saying anything, he guided him to the left and shifted so that Valery could rest against his chest. His jumper was soft and laced with that lovely, unplaceable winter scent, so subtle it was only just there. Against the wool, breathing was easier. Shenkov stroked his back, as if he were something nice, like a tame fox. It felt safe.

15

Into the Lubyanka

Leningrad, 1946

In 1946, some elementary tallies would tell an observant person
that the NKVD – that was the KGB in their older jackets – had
arrested a quarter of the entire population of Leningrad. At the
start of the purge, they'd had fun with it, to the point of being
theatrical. The first time Valery was arrested, it was by someone
who had seemed to be a train conductor, until he was right up
close and whipped out the red NKVD identity card. Valery had
quite admired that; the officer had the train conductor's uniform
down to a pin, except maybe that he'd taken a lot more pride in
his shoe polish than did most train conductors. Thinking about
it later, Valery wondered if there had been officers in theatres
and pubs, pretending to be waiters or concierges, dressed up in
feather boas and all sorts. He hoped so.

That first time had been unnerving for the opposite reason of
the one he'd have expected.

Maybe it was his education. He had been trained to think
in formulae, and all a formula was, was a way not to bother
explaining something pedantic for a paragraph and a half. The
most efficient notation was always the laziest. So it had struck
him as utterly unrealistic that anyone in any police district could
possibly be keeping coherent files on everyone. The scale was
too huge and there wasn't enough paper in the Soviet Union.
That the NKVD had extensive, omniscient files on everyone

was an inefficient explanation for what was happening. The efficient explanation was that it was, more or less, random. Every district would have a quota for arrests, and so sometimes they just snatched whoever. It was about numbers, not humans.

If you thought there was a logical system, then when you were arrested, you thought it had to be a mistake; you went along with it because you didn't want to get in any more trouble, and trusted it would all be cleared up. Logically.

If you were pretty damn certain you were being arrested not because you had spent a year once in a capitalist country, but because the officer in question just didn't like redheads, there was no urge to think there had been a mistake, or to clear your name.

You did what Valery had done.

You let the officer put you in the back of a car, you waited while he got into the front passenger seat, and then you dived out the other side and ran away, knowing that they weren't going to bother chasing you when there was a whole street full of other less troublesome people they could arrest.

That afternoon, he put his few things into a suitcase and got on a train to Moscow to see his friend Svetlana, who was now just senior enough in the army to have a nice apartment of her own away from barracks, and then he mysteriously forgot to come back.

She thought the whole thing was so hilarious she inhaled her vodka.

'Ah, *mate*,' was the verdict, after she'd stopped coughing. Valery was terrible at keeping in touch with friends – he was happy to have lunch with anyone and he had moved around too much to have a consistent group of people, what with university and military service – but Svetlana was insistent, and ever since they'd left school, she had scooped Valery up for a drink or for dinner once a month. She had even managed it during the war, and now, if he was upset about someone at work, she offered to kill people for him.

There was no one else who he would even have considered running to. It would have been a risk and a burden for anyone else. But German tanks hadn't bothered Svetlana. Valery definitely didn't bother her, however much trouble he was in. At the most extreme, he was just the evening's entertainment.

'Listen, I'll write to the university in Leningrad and imply there was a super-secret military emergency, and then you can write yourself a reference letter to the Kurchatov Institute here and I will stamp it with the all-powerful nameless stamp of the research unit.' She inclined her head. 'No drama.'

It was Valery's turn to laugh. 'No drama, you dick. If you went to the Grand Ballet they'd all drop dead.'

'I would enjoy that,' she said solemnly.

But she was right; they did exactly what she had said they would, and through only a couple of well-placed lies and one intimidation visit to the office of the director of the Kurchatov Institute, she managed, despite knowing nothing about the intricate power structures within universities, to convince everyone that Valery had had to leave the Leningrad doctoral programme for an unnamed project here, and that she would prefer now that he continued his university work nearer to hand than the other side of the country.

No one, not a single person, asked any questions. Of course they didn't. An army colonel had said that she preferred; that meant the army preferred, and even the local KGB wouldn't argue there.

It worked for ten years. But then, almost to the day, Valery began to notice a man in a black coat who made no secret of following him everywhere. Valery stopped him once to ask, was shown the red badge, and told pleasantly to get on with his day.

'Svetlana,' Valery said, late the same night. The man was smoking just outside Svetlana's dining-room window, leaning against a lamp post. Valery showed him to her.

'Well. Off we go to Archangel or somewhere,' she said, unbothered as always.

It was the *we* that hurt so badly. If she had said you, he would have said yes. 'Don't be ridiculous.'

She lifted her eyebrows. 'If they're going to arrest you, they'll be coming for me as well. Known associates.'

'Yes, exactly.' He swallowed. 'Svet — you can get out of it. Denounce me. Now. I'm going to be arrested anyway, so just — get ahead of the curve. Actually, it will work even better if we get married. If you throw your husband to the NKVD, you'll be a hero at work, and they'll leave you alone forever.'

She studied him for a while. She wasn't one of those people who hurried out of work clothes and into softer things when she got home; she would drink wine at eleven o'clock in full uniform, except for the beret, which sat next to the teapot now, the hammer and sickle insignia winking gold under the laurels of her unit. She didn't have any hair to let down, just a blunt crew cut. 'Or,' she said, as if he was slow, 'we could go to Archangel or Minsk or Kiev.'

'I'm not going anywhere,' Valery said. This was the line he couldn't cross. She had spent her whole life looking after him, matter-of-factly beating up anyone who called him weird, and if he wasn't careful now, she was going to be shot for doing it. 'If you run with me, they're going to come for you no matter what.'

'Not really your decision to make though, mate, is it?'

'I'm not going,' he said, quietly, because he had never fought her before, and he didn't know how. 'I'm never going to do anything useful, but you could be a general soon, you could — do something. For God's sake, look at it like it's numbers and not people. If you get yourself arrested unnecessarily I'll explode from the sheer bloody inefficiency of it all.' He couldn't tell why, but he had both hands around his throat and he couldn't move them. 'Please. I'm not trying to be high-handed, I'm just – I hate it when there's an inefficient equation, it drives me insane and if you go to the gulag because of me I'll kill myself with a belt.'

She nodded slowly. She wore plain gold rings on three of her fingers; she kept those in her pockets at work and put them on at home, because her mum had given them to her and she felt guilty if she didn't get a few hours' wear out of them daily. She took off one from her index finger and put it on him, very gently.

He had to fight the urge to sling it away. It was a symbol of a thing he'd always known he couldn't have. The days of the Tsar were gone: men couldn't go round expecting, like entitled capitalist nutsacks, to get a wife just because they were paid lots of money and they had an impressive job. Everyone was paid the same now. Women were free to marry people who were kind and charming, instead of trudging over to whoever could keep a roof above them. He wasn't charming. He was unsettling. So that was that.

He hadn't realised that he was still sad about it, but it was just under the surface, and now, the weight of the gold was enough to break the ice. It was lonely enough, to know that none of that was for him. It was horrible to imagine *dressing up* as the very thing he couldn't be. Like having always wanted to be a physicist, but doomed to play a mad scientist on a radio advert for toothpaste.

'Thanks,' he said, and made himself smile. 'Registry office, then?'

A week later, the man arrested him on his way to the ice rink for hockey practice and took him to the Lubyanka, along with four other people in the back of a Black Maria from which there was no swift escape. When they arrived, they were herded into a cell that already had thirty men in it.

He hadn't panicked. He could remember that clearly. He just felt like he had lost the game of hide and seek. He listened to the rules with almost no feelings at all.

No talking.

Hands in view at all times.

Move when the guards tell you.

That was that. Some of the others banged on the door and tried to shout that there had been a mistake. One of them was dragged away and returned some hours later with a black eye and blank, shell-shocked stare. The men already in the cell were unsurprised.

Valery slumped into a space by the wall, listening to floorboards creak as thirty silent men shifted. A lot of them had colds, so sometimes there was a cough or a sniff. And very, very softly, there were patterned knocks. He watched the man next to him doing it with his far neighbour and touched his arm to ask what it was. The man nodded and showed him the alphabet scratched out on the floor, and taught him the knocks. The man was slow and thin, dirty, with a scattering of burn scars up his arm and something military about the way he sat. Once he could, Valery asked,

How long have you been here?

Three months.

Valery felt a powerful, bizarre relief. It was all over. No more running or dodging, no more terse awareness of the black uniforms always just in view on the street, the stations, the glint of a red badge when they checked internal passports on the Metro. He let his head bump back against the wall. He had done everything he could and now it was finished: out of his hands.

A guard called his name.

'Confess to whatever they want you to and it'll be fine,' the man next to him whispered. 'It's all made up but you only get the one set of teeth.'

It was fine, in the sense that he didn't come away bleeding. It made him forget the knock code, though, and all he could do when he came back was stare unseeing at the alphabet scratched on the floor, with a hollow where his usually excellent memory stood.

His attention kept catching on the inky mark on the middle finger of his right hand. The pen he'd signed the confession with had been leaky. The document had been full of names he didn't even know, but again, with the peculiar intuition that had seen him straight through the far door of the police car ten years ago, he could see that there was nothing he could do about that. He was dead already and so were all those people. If he'd said no, the interrogator just wouldn't have given back his clothes.

Not Svetlana's name, though, and that was telling. It should have been there. Only informants were immune.

She'd done it, then.

Thank God.

The man shook his arm gently.

OK?

He did it slowly, pointing at the letters.

Valery looked up and wanted to say no; but it would have been precious to make a fuss. The man was missing three teeth and two fingers.

Am fine.

What did you get?

Ten years. Want to play hangman?

The man smiled, relieved.

I'm Shukov btw.

In the deep silence of the cell, the scratch of Shukov's broken fingernail on the letters carved into the floor sounded so loud that someone hissed at him to shut up. Shukov quailed, so Valery stuck his tongue out in the direction of the annoyed someone and got a silent laugh in return.

The silence was already an itch right in the back of his mind.

He didn't speak aloud for six months.

16

The Coroner's Report

City 40, 1963

It wasn't being lifted that woke Valery up, but being set back down again. Some part of his mind must have been certain he was about to be dropped on the floor, but when he jerked awake, he was a few centimetres off a cushion. Shenkov eased him down the rest of the way and set one hand against the side of his head to steady him.

'I'm on the early shift,' Shenkov whispered. 'It's only five o'clock, you can go back to sleep. Are you okay here? This thing is brutal.'

Valery didn't understand at first and had to sit up before he saw he was still on Shenkov's living-room couch, under a fur blanket. The air was cold now, but the heating must have just come on, because the radiators were plinking. 'I'm okay,' he said, wondering why anyone wouldn't be, on a couch full of cushions and blankets.

Shenkov nodded and disappeared.

Five o'clock; it was a gloriously late start. Valery drifted up and made some coffee, admiring how bright but how inoffensive the electric lamps were, and basking in the happy fact that he could have them on for however long he wanted. He coiled up in a kitchen chair to read yesterday's paper, and only when Shenkov reappeared and looked alarmed did he realise he must have been in the way.

'There's some coffee. I'll get out the way—'

'You're not in the way.' Shenkov paused, as if he were about to say something else, but then seemed to decide against it. 'I looked at the guide. Skating's on at eight tonight.'

Valery felt desperately glad, realised it was wildly inappropriate in the face of someone he barely knew, and coughed. 'Oh, right, brilliant,' he said. 'See you later, then.'

And that was that. Valery came round every evening, for the skating or whatever was on – sometimes just the news. Not wanting to push his luck, he made sure he was always back in his own apartment upstairs again by ten o'clock. Or he did for a week, until Shenkov asked if the couch was really that terrible. After that he stayed for most of the time, and slept much better knowing there was someone in the next room. Either Shenkov was an outstandingly polite liar, or he liked strays, because he never seemed to regret the invitation, and if Valery was late, he came to fetch him from the lab.

The KGB had no luck with Pyotr, and nor did anyone else. Quietly, Shenkov said that he had told the search teams to look for a body now, but after two weeks, there was no body, and then they stopped looking. Even so, whenever he went out to do fieldwork, Valery caught himself staring through the trees, hunting for any flicker that might have been a child running. He never saw anything; only the slow reddening of the berries, which announced the coming winter. It was the beginning of November now, and although it didn't feel cold to him after Siberia, the huge marshland sky was greying, the rain poured in the evenings, and in the mornings, a luminous fog hung among the scrubbed tower blocks of City 40.

Dr Resovskaya came round every week with a file full of lists – every lab supply that was available to them – and when Valery flicked through, it quickly turned out they could get anything. There was even a long list of marine creatures you could order.

Including a live octopus. He ordered it just to see what would happen, and then nearly exploded with delight when, only a week later, a tank arrived with a small octopus in it, with a leaflet sticky-taped on top detailing tank requirements, recommended water salinity for the species, acceptable food lists, and a special filtration unit. Valery read it carefully before he opened the locked tank (*it is recommended that you give an octopus something to play with, or it will sulk and refuse to participate in experiments*) to see if the octopus would like to look at a marble. The second the tank was open, though, the octopus flooped straight out and hugged his hand. It sat there on his wrist for ages, pulsing brilliant yellow. It was soft to touch, but not slimy. Charmed, he showed it the marble, which it took, but it kept his hand as well. When he finally persuaded it back into the tank with some tiny crabs from the supply that came in the box (*live food is best. NB: no canned tuna if you don't want it flung at your head*), his hand was covered in miniature kiss marks from the suckers.

'Why?' Resovskaya asked mildly. 'You want to do a saltwater study?'

'No! I want an octopus. No irradiating the octopus.'

'I would say you aren't supposed to use our budget just to buy pets—' she began, and yelled when the octopus squirted a jet of water at her.

'The leaflet says they can be territorial,' Valery said, doing his best at apologetic, but once she'd gone, he gave the octopus all the remaining crabs. It skimmed along the bottom of the tank, hoovering.

It was because the students had come across to play too that Shenkov didn't see the octopus when he leaned in.

'Valery. Come with me a minute.'

Valery stepped out, fighting the sense that he must be in trouble, but Shenkov only steered him out by his shoulder and leaned down so they wouldn't be heard.

'The coroner's given in her report on the man you found in the woods. She says he died of a heart attack, and when I queried radiation, she shut me down. Said I was mistaken.'

'You're not,' said Valery.

'You only glanced at the body.'

'I stared at it for twenty minutes while I waited for the KGB, I have two research doctorates in radiation-focused fields, and I have radiation sickness; how much more qualified do you want me to be?' Valery asked, starting to smile.

Shenkov ducked his head a little. 'Sorry. I was hoping you were going to say you might have made a mistake.'

'I didn't. If he was walking around while his organs were shutting down from the radiation then yes, his heart could have given out, but that isn't a primary cause. Why?'

'Because if you're sure, then the coroner is lying, and now I don't know how many other cases she lied about. I've been looking over the county files, for local deaths. A lot of people seem to die of heart attacks.' He hesitated. 'How many is normal, do you know?'

'One in five of all natural deaths.'

'It's more like one in three here.'

'Okay, that's not heart attacks.'

'I don't know.' Shenkov looked as though he would have liked to say something else. 'Listen, I know I said that we would just have to see what the coroner said, but I didn't expect it to be a flat-out lie. I don't care how well Moscow wants these figures to be hidden – we clearly have something around here that's so radioactive it's killing people within days. It must be a specific place, or people would be dropping like flies, yes?'

'Yes,' Valery said. 'Yes, I agree. And probably not inside the city.'

'If we can find it and seal it off, we'd be saving a lot of trouble. The more people die, the more attention is going to fall on coroners' reports and figures. It's people from the village at the moment, but if this radioactive place, whatever it is, is anywhere near here, it's only a matter of time until something happens to one of our researchers. There will come a point when blowing up a newspaper editor's house won't stop people asking questions, and . . . we can't let people panic. Moscow is never going to evacuate anyone, not from here. They'd bring in the army.'

Valery nodded and said nothing, because he could hear that Shenkov was talking himself into something, much more than he was asking anything.

'If you were to look at the body,' Shenkov said, tentative now, 'is there anything that might tell you . . . I don't know, what kind of radiation it was, how he was exposed . . . ?'

'Yes. Lots of things. Shall we go?'

'You don't have to.' His eyes flicked to Valery's cast, then up and down the rest of him, or rather down and down. Valery was a head smaller. He didn't often look at himself in the mirror, but he knew he looked fragile, even from his own point of view, never mind Shenkov's.

'I know.'

'I'm not asking you as a KGB officer.'

'Yes, don't be so bloody wet,' Valery said, and started down the corridor to keep him from arguing any more.

The morgue was in the same low building as the infirmary, all stainless steel and very, very cold; the heating pipes didn't even run through. The body was in a drawer, along, Valery noticed, with quite a few other labelled drawers. If the population of City 40 was a hundred thousand, like Shenkov had said, the premature death rate must have kept all the morgues busy. Valery perched on a stool and read over the coroner's report. It said very little. Natural death. There wasn't even a mention of radiation exposure.

'Can you do an autopsy?' Shenkov asked quietly. Two of his men had put the body on the autopsy table.

Valery looked, meaning to say it would be useless to do the autopsy again if the coroner had already removed organs during the first one, but the words died when he saw there had been no autopsy.

Not only had there been no autopsy, but there were no radiation precautions whatsoever. The body was covered by a sheet, not a hazmat bag. There were no lead screens. No protective equipment for people working in here. Nothing.

'Yes,' he said slowly. Something odd was going on. Either the coroner had failed to notice that the man had obviously died of radiation sickness and put herself and her entire staff at risk of contamination; or, she knew exactly what had happened already and that it wasn't dangerous. He couldn't see, though, how it could possibly not be dangerous. 'But if he died from contact with something in the woods, he's radioactive. You shouldn't be in here.'

'What about you?'

'If I get sick, I do,' said Valery. 'Outside please.'

'Have you done this before on an irradiated . . . body?'

'Often,' said Valery. 'Go.'

It didn't take him long, because there wasn't much left to look at. The organs were in a state, and under a microscope the marrow and blood were barely recognisable. There was a window that looked out into the corridor, so Valery reported as much as he pulled off the mask and gown. He looked round for somewhere to get rid of them, then slung them into the incinerator.

'So it's definitely radiation,' Shenkov said through the glass.

'He got a dose of about five hundred roentgen over a short period of time,' Valery said. He had to pause, because he had not found what he expected to find. Since the day the body had turned up, he had been sure that Sasha had fallen ill in the forest, found a hospital somehow, and left again. But that was not what had happened. 'I think it was injected,' he said at last. 'There are puncture marks on his arms.'

Shenkov looked confused too. 'Someone *injected* him with . . . ?'

'Yes. With a radioactive isotope. I think it's polonium. That explains why they're not taking any radiation precautions in here.' He motioned around. 'Polonium is an alpha emitter. Human skin blocks it, so if it's inside him, it isn't dangerous to anyone coming into contact with the body.'

Valery realised too late that he was doing the opposite of shedding light on the subject. 'If skin blocks radiation, then why is it dangerous?' Shenkov asked.

'Alpha radiation, only alpha,' Valery said. 'Alpha radiation is when the radioactive atoms chuck whole helium atoms out – that's like throwing cannon balls. They're too big to get through the spaces between the atoms of most substances, so that sits on surfaces. That's why we hose things down that have been exposed. It only kills you if it gets *in* you. Gamma radiation isn't particles, it's very very high-frequency light. It's light-speed cheese wires cutting through you.'

'I see.' Shenkov paused. 'Where do you get polonium? Is it in the ground here?'

'No,' Valery said, feeling heavy now. 'No, you have to extract it from a reactor at exactly the right point, or it fissions into caesium.'

'Then I don't understand.'

Polonium went, as far as Valery knew, mainly to the space programme. It had a good long half-life, but it wasn't so radioactive as to fry circuitry, so the heat that came off a chunk of it was enough to power satellites for years. Probably the cosmonaut on his stolen blue stamp knew all about polonium.

That happy middle ground – radioactive but not devastatingly – made it good for other things too.

'We use polonium on human radiation trials,' Valery explained. 'The effects of injecting it into a human bloodstream are slow. Plenty of time for study. That would explain the hospital gown we found him in.'

Shenkov was taut with unease again. Valery thought he must have had a difficult time as a young officer, given that his feelings etched themselves across his eyes even now. 'If I were injected with polonium – how long would I still be walking about for before it laid me out?'

Valery shook his head a little. 'You'd feel sick and headachey, but you would still be able to walk for a couple of days.'

'So if he was quick about it, he could have run away from whoever injected him.'

Valery nodded.

Shenkov studied him. It was a familiar study; he ran his eyes up and down Valery twice, scanning him for any sign that he was about to break into pieces. 'Hadn't you better get into a shower?'

'I . . . suppose,' Valery said, mainly to his cast. Getting into a shower was an incredible ordeal, not so much because the cast was awkward, but because the bone twanged dangerously if he twisted or moved too much. Twice in one day sounded much worse than whatever mild radiation sickness he may or may not get from faffing about with polonium-contaminated organs.

'There's one out here,' Shenkov prompted him. 'Come on.'

Beneath the shower-cubicle door, Valery could see Shenkov's shadow pacing while he spoke.

'What do you actually mean by a human trial, what's it involve?' he started the moment Valery turned on the water. The noise would be more than enough to confuse any bugs in the room, although Valery could honestly not imagine why any thinking human would ever want to bug the men's changing room at the morgue. Surely there were things even KGB agents didn't want to hear.

Valery took a deep slow breath, hindered by the steam. He wouldn't have thought even a month ago that he would ever whine about hot water, but the humidity made his lungs feel spongy, and trying to think about Berlin gave him the rubbed-over-with-sandpaper feeling again. It was, of course, just the tail end of the tiny spell of radiation sickness; it buggered your ability to fight colds for ages, and it caused this sandpaper variety of depression. Knowing why didn't help.

He had to concentrate hard on the way the water droplets ran down his good arm. 'Well, here, the experimental goal is to investigate radiation resistance. You would identify test subjects who already exhibit a high resistance; so, anyone who seems to be functioning well in a radioactive environment, without the normal cellular problems. You would want the people who continue to stay well even after a long exposure. Then, you would take those subjects into a laboratory environment, and you'd expose them to higher and higher doses, incrementally, and record what makes them sick and what they can recover from, in comparison to an average subject.'

'Why? What's the point?'

'If you could isolate *how* someone has radiation resistance, the next step would be to reproduce it. Give it to soldiers, emergency workers in radioactive places. It would have medical benefits too. You can shrink cancers with radiation therapy, but the therapy is sometimes more savage than the cancer. It gives you low-level radiation sickness, it's terrible. So the . . . yes. The ability to make humans even a small percentage more radiation resistant would save a lot of people.'

Shenkov was quiet for a while. '*Is* there such a thing as radiation resistance? I mean, is anyone immune?'

'I don't know,' Valery said. He sighed. 'No one knows. This is brand-new science. We do know it's not biologically impossible. Ants are immune. Perhaps it's possible for humans to adapt over generations. It would take a *long* time – decades – but I don't know, maybe that's the plan here. This place will be irradiated for centuries. Maybe they're hoping to find children who . . . are different. Or even breed them.'

'That's insane. That sounds like something out of a bloody comic.'

Valery's shoulder blades twitched. He was beginning to notice that he did that when someone said something he really hated: it was slight, but anyone watching him could have been forgiven for thinking he'd been rescued from the woods as a teenager after having been brought up by small, quick birds.

'All new science sounds insane,' he said, and concentrated hard not to lapse into what would sound to Shenkov like hysterical urgency. 'Thirty years ago it would have sounded insane to power cities with a few grams of burning metal. It is *dangerous* to assume anything like this is ridiculous. It is the very fact that so many people believe some things are unthinkably ridiculous that makes them so vulnerable to those who are willing not only to think but to do the ridiculous thing. That's how Stalin arrested tens of millions of innocent people without provoking a revolution; it's so absurd that people didn't believe it was happening. Human radiation studies sound odd, but I guarantee that every nation in the world with nuclear capacity is conducting them in one form or other. Germany was running human studies in the thirties and I know because I worked on them.' He had to screw his eyes shut. 'I worked on them. If I were German, I'd have been condemned in the Nuremberg trials for what happened in those studies. I'd be in prison now for war crimes. It isn't ridiculous.'

He thought he'd controlled his voice well, but beyond the cubicle door, Shenkov stopped pacing, and there was a long silence.

'How old were you?' Shenkov said.

'What?'

'In Germany.'

'Nineteen, I was an undergrad. I worked in the same lab as . . .' Valery pressed one hand over his eyes, because he wanted to cry even though he hadn't cried for years, and dug his fingernails hard into his orbital bone ' . . . Josef fucking Mengele.'

'It wasn't your fault. You were doing as you were told.'

'I could have walked out, I didn't.'

'You were a child,' Shenkov said, half over him. He was just on the other side of the door now. Valery touched it, wanting to open it, and not. 'Anyway, human trials. Tell me how it would work here.'

'Yes. I think Resovskaya is taking data from the village generally, and taking the people who are healthiest to find out how they're healthy. And to see how much radiation they can take before they aren't. I even *asked* her if she had Pyotr, and then I believed her when she said no.'

'I didn't know she was running a village in the forest for human data, for God's sake, and my job is to know things.'

'She must have another lab somewhere. It would explain why she's never around ours. Is there somewhere on-site that could be . . . ?'

'Not that I know, but I'm not feeling very confident about what I know any more,' Shenkov said.

It must have been the awkwardness of using a scalpel left-handed on the body, or stooping too much, because something in his shoulder made a horrible sound and though it didn't hurt exactly, Valery couldn't move it again. He shut his eyes. Of all the most annoying places to be stuck, half-dressed in the morgue shower was surely high on the list.

He agonised, realised he had no choice, and unlocked the door. On the other side, the air was cold. 'I need some help.'

Shenkov nodded.

'Look, before you . . . I have prison tattoos.'

'I wasn't born yesterday,' Shenkov said, starting to smile. 'I've seen Vor tattoos before.'

There was no point saying he probably hadn't seen any like these. Valery handed over his shirt. He had only been holding it, but without anything in his hands, he felt exposed. Without meaning to, he shied backwards when Shenkov stepped in. Separately to his brain, his body had decided it did *not* want to be standing half-naked in front of any more security officers thank you very much. He bumped into the wall. It was involuntary. He wanted to say so and couldn't. His voice had locked down.

Shenkov caught his shoulders. He did it lightly, but firmly enough to hold Valery still even when his whole skeleton twitched again. 'You're safe,' he said quietly. 'It's all right.'

'I know. I'm okay,' Valery said, irritated. 'I'm sorry, it's just – you know, reflex—'

'Right, and you have that for a reason. Just give yourself a second. I'm not going to hurt you.'

'Yes, I know—'

'No, you don't. I broke your arm.' Very gently, Shenkov drew his hands up, which naturally made Valery straighten, then down again to his shoulders, which felt like a cue to breathe out. He hadn't realised he was breathing too quickly. 'You can know something in your head but not everywhere else. I know spiders are harmless but I still nearly jump out the window whenever I see one.'

Valery smiled a little. He had an anaemic sense that Shenkov was still talking to him, but his mind didn't pick it up as words, just a sort of warmth. It was hard to relax, though, because just like it had been by the pool where they had found the body, it nearly hurt to have someone else's hands on him. There was something astonishing and wonderful about coming up close enough to find that Shenkov was a solid human being who could touch him.

There was a desperate grasping need to memorise it and hoard the feeling close, for later, when that aloneness-pressure leaned on him at night; and a terrible shame on top of that, because that sort of desperation was unclean.

'I'm fine,' he said again, needing it to stop.

Shenkov patted his good arm. 'Good,' he said, and stepped behind him to help him into the shirt at last.

The worst thing was that Valery knew exactly what was coming then.

'Christ,' Shenkov said.

Valery could only nod, even though he knew that nodding only drew more attention to the tattoo on his neck, the knife through the top of his spine.

'This says you've killed fifty-three people,' Shenkov said at last, after a pause in which he must have been counting.

'Yes.' Fifty-three crosses. Usually, the Vory didn't ink on crosses for murders – it was other images, more complicated, women or cards, but it would have taken the poor tattooist too long.

Another pause. 'Did you?'

'Yes.'

Shenkov was quiet for a while. 'The knife in the neck means you're for hire.'

'To teach other people how to do – what I did. Not to do it again.' He wrenched some words into some order. 'It was a bomb.'

Shenkov didn't say anything. Finally, he took Valery's wrist and guided his arm through the shirtsleeve. Valery nearly bit through his lip wishing he was somewhere else, with anyone else. He would have cared less what someone else thought. Even though he had turned off the shower only a few minutes before, he felt dirty again. After what felt like a long time, and six buttons, Shenkov said, 'Did they hurt you? The people in the bomb.'

'Men.'

'What?'

'Not people, men. Fifty-three men. No.' By itself, his hand came up to the scar on his jaw. He pulled it away.

Shenkov turned his shirtsleeves back for him.

'Thank you,' Valery whispered.

Shenkov stepped back. 'Let's go.' He didn't say another word about what he thought of the tattoos or the bomb. Valery had a feeling that Shenkov was one of those people who had to think about things for some time before he decided whether he was angry or not. Valery wished he'd just be furious right now. If people like that *did* decide to be angry, it wasn't a sudden brief storm. It was white-hot rage, tempered in the heart of a blast furnace, and it never cooled.

There was no heating, and because he'd acclimatised to the steamy temperature inside the cubicle, the air in the outer changing room felt frozen. He'd come in just his shirt.

'If they're doing human trials, they are,' Valery said at last. 'Resovskaya told me Moscow is behind the village project. This kind of thing is so secret that you'll end up dead in the forest yourself if anyone realises you're looking into it.'

'Taking kids cannot be in their mandate.'

'But if you ring Moscow to check, then it's clear you know about something you shouldn't and you still end up dead in the forest.'

Shenkov took his coat off and put it over Valery's shoulders. Valery looked up at him. It didn't mean for a second that they were all right, however desperately he wanted it to; it was just that Shenkov was involuntarily courteous. 'If someone dies on a trial like this, how do they get rid of the bodies? You said skin blocks alpha radiation, but bodies rot; they must *become* radioactive. What's the procedure? Do they burn them?'

'No. That would be radioactive smoke, so . . .' He couldn't think properly. All his thoughts were roiling too much. Something deep in him was burning hot. He couldn't touch it, but the heat and the shame powering off it were so intense they were distorting everything else. 'Shenkov, clearly no one gives a damn what's radioactive or where, or who gets a face full of it. For all I know they stick them in an incinerator next to the school.'

Shenkov ignored him. 'If you had radioactive bodies to dispose of here, how would you do it? As close to safely as you could.'

'Safely? Lead-lined coffins, buried in the forest to be away from town, but away from the most radioactive band too, for the safety of the workers. No digging the soil by hand even so. Bring in a machine. Bury them deep, fill the graves with concrete to stop any chance of water contamination, get out.'

'So that would mean transporting bodies in lead-lined coffins, digging machinery, and a concrete truck.'

'Yes, which is why I doubt they're doing it like that. It would be expensive.'

Shenkov glanced down at him. '*They* probably feel the same about people's safety as *we* do. They are probably doing everything they can to lessen the exposure to their workers.'

'Within the bounds of the funds available to them,' Valery said, frustrated. 'Dr Resovskaya cares about people normally, but here she's not allowed to, so she had to send students out into a radioactive forest knowing full well they're being exposed to a lot more than they know. If she's running this trial – or whoever is – how it *should* be isn't the same as what they're able to do.'

'All you're saying is that we can't find them. I'm saying that what I *can* do is track every concrete truck, digger, and heavy transport lorry that comes in and out of City 40.'

Valery shook his head. 'Say you do find this lab, say you do walk in and take away some or all of their test subjects, and say one of them is this missing boy Pyotr and you save his life, and it's all heroic and great. Then what? You'll be shot as soon as Moscow hears about it.'

'A child is missing and a man is dead.' Shenkov didn't raise his voice, but he did hone it.

Horribly, that ground against the iron part of Valery's soul. He struggled not to snap. 'Do you know how many children die in labour camps every day? Or on the prison trains? There are carriages full of mothers with babies. Not a lot of them last the whole ten weeks to Siberia, I tell you. Men like you put them there, with none of this moral outrage you're aiming at me now. Life is cheap. At least whoever's on this trial is dying usefully.'

'And you think it *should* be like that, do you?'

'No! But you won't change it by dying too.'

Something icy and frightening flitted through Shenkov's eyes. Valery didn't know for sure what it was, but he could guess.

Big, strong men projected a sacred innocence on to weaker people – on to women and children, and sawdust-fragile biochemists. They had to. It was what stopped them hurting anyone when their tempers were frayed. And of course it was a fairy tale. Women and children could be just as cruel and blood-thirsty as anyone else. But, you couldn't be Shenkov's size and believe that. So, the Shenkovs of the world told each other the fairy tale, and everyone else played along, because they wanted not to be killed in a moment of impatience.

Being told flat out that it was all nonsense must have felt like being told everyone had been lying always.

Valery was pretty sure that was why men throttled women when they found they weren't perfect saints. There was nothing wrong with not being a perfect saint. Except, there was if you were part of what sounded like a big conspiracy to make out that you were the very Madonna. The rage was the smashing of the fairy tale.

He could see it smashing in Shenkov now. He wondered if he was about to die.

'Confirm whether it's polonium or not,' was all Shenkov said, and then vanished down the corridor to the KGB office.

When Valery had been an undergraduate, Dr Resovskaya used to play a game with all the students in his class. She would put random things in a spectrometer – iron, copper, nitrogen, mustard gas, salt – and then hand out ration stamps as prizes if anyone could guess what the substance was just from reading the spectrograms. It had been Valery's favourite thing for ages. He had been good at it, and even now, he associated the spectrometer with free dinners.

All a spectrometer was, was a collection of prisms and lenses that cast a good clear rainbow on to some film, and a little chamber into which you fed a sample. The chamber heated up, and then you fired light through it. Once you'd done that, the rainbow would change, very subtly. There would appear distinct lines across the spectrum. Each set of lines – and this was Valery's favourite thing about all science ever, his own field be damned – corresponded to an element. If there was helium in the sample, it drew itself a sparse pattern that was heavier towards the violet end of the spectrum. If there was oxygen, a more complicated pattern, heaviest in the green. Iron, a much bulkier element, etched a whole chaos across the rainbow that was densest in the blue. Every element had its colour, and no two colours were the same. The explanation was a convoluted thing to do with electron shells and dispersion of light, but the fact remained: put any substance *at all* into the spectrometer, fire its torch, and what you got on the other side was a rainbow photograph, full of lines that showed up every element in it. By looking at how much there was of each, how blurred and complicated the lines, you could judge what the substance was. This was how astronomers could tell the composition of stars; and it was how you could tell if there was polonium in a blood sample. Polonium drew its spectrograph line in a fine shade of violet, and Valery knew it very well indeed.

It was there.

The KGB office was locked for the weekend by the time he got the results, so he stayed in the lab to soak up the human voices before everyone left. He could give Shenkov the envelope on Monday.

'Valery,' said Dr Resovskaya just as the last of the students left. It made him jump, because her office had been empty for hours already and he couldn't tell where she had appeared from. He spun around. She was looking into the spectrometer. 'Why are you running polonium-contaminated human blood through the spectrometer?'

Valery swore silently at the desk. He hadn't yet moved the sample from the spectrometer chamber. It had been next on his list. 'Shenkov gave me some blood from the dead man in the morgue. He's full of polonium.' He tried to hold the accusation well away from his voice.

'What's Shenkov doing giving blood samples to you? What about the coroner?'

'The coroner said the man died of a heart attack, which is rubbish. He died of radiation poisoning; his organs are sludge.'

Valery wished he could think of a way out. If he said nothing about it, she would assume he was up to something stupid. 'He was injected with it. Is this part of your human trial?'

'Valery, you didn't ask me that, and you certainly aren't going to say it to Shenkov. I will not have the KGB jack-booting through my bloody trial.'

'Elena, are you kidnapping people?' Valery asked softly. 'You have that boy, don't you, Pyotr?'

'Listen to me carefully,' she said. She rested her knuckles on the tabletop. They were beginning to twist from arthritis. It looked painful. 'If you give this report to Shenkov, and Shenkov throws everyone out of that village and destroys my trial in a fit of self-redemptive righteousness, that will have been a political decision on your part. You will have taken it upon yourself to disrupt what is probably the most urgent and important clinical trial in the Soviet Union. As you are aware, politics and science are incompatible fields. The last person doing your job here decided to try to combine them. Unfortunately, when Moscow became aware of it, that person was committed to an asylum and diagnosed with schizophrenia.'

'I see,' Valery said.

'I'm not threatening you, I'm just warning you what will happen.' She sighed. 'All of this is classified. You never ran that blood, you did not use this spectrometer, and the man in the morgue died of a heart attack, which is why the coroner said he did. You understand?'

He nodded.

Resovskaya lifted her hands, something like an apology. 'Tell Shenkov you were wrong. Make him believe it, Valery.'

Valery smuggled the octopus into his own apartment on the eleventh floor to have some company in the screaming quiet. The octopus liked the television – it danced when the news jingle came on – so Valery decided once and for all that it was staying. It was a waste of electricity if he kept the television on for himself all day, but in the name of cephalopodal happiness, it was legitimate. The news had been on for an hour or so when the octopus crept out of the tank, stole the remote from him, and changed the channel. He had been feeling hollowed out, but it made him laugh.

17

Tattoos

Kolyma, 1957

After Valery had detonated the bomb, and after the camp administrator had decided for reasons of his own to do nothing about it but take Valery on as a science tutor, the morning felt unreal. It was still dark; embers from the explosion were still floating in the air, and ash had already coated the verges of the muddy path and the side of the administration building. He could feel the heat of the fire burning, even from so far off. The guards must have decided to let it go down by itself.

He didn't know where to go. He hadn't planned this far. He had thought that somebody would have taken him away and shot him by now, and far from being happy to be alive, he was just paralysed by the deviation from the schedule. Slowly, he became aware that the scar on his jaw was aching, that he was too cold standing still, that the rough stitching on the back of the camp-provided coat was scraping his neck – all the stupid human things he had expected not to bother with again.

Two men with tattoos prowled across from the Vory side of the camp. He watched them without moving, because Vory never bothered to talk to political prisoners. They were the gentlemen here: better barracks, better food, lighter duties. People like Valery were invisible to them, unless you lost to them at cards.

But they stopped by him.

'You did that?'

'Yeah,' he said quietly. He didn't sound like himself. He couldn't tell why.

'Dima wants to see you.'

Dima was the camp's Vory godfather. It was always Dima, never Dmitry. He had a full tailcoat of tattoos and he stood in the way that bears do when they aren't sure if they want to eat you or not yet, one shoulder dropped, but he had a soft voice.

'Huh,' he said when his men brought Valery into the criminal barracks. He said it as if Valery was not at all what he had expected. 'I heard you were a professor, in your first life.'

'Yes,' said Valery, who was sure that he was going to die. Maybe one of the men he'd killed had been a Vor. Maybe it had been someone important. The men who had brought him in here were stony and he couldn't tell. One had tattoos right down one side of his face, playing cards and teardrops, and other images too faded for Valery to make out. 'Chemistry.'

Around them, the barracks was significantly nicer than the one Valery had destroyed. There were little lamps everywhere, with funnels made from pipes soldered onto bulbs that held kerosene, the fumes burning with gentle blue flames. People were better dressed, too, with proper coats and boots and jumpers. Nobody looked like they were starving. There was even a loaf of bread sitting on a side table. It would have gone in ten seconds in the other barracks. Valery swallowed hard. He had been hungry for months, almost not in a way he noticed now; but he did notice how badly it slowed him down, and how much weight he had already lost.

He'd thought when he first arrived that the criminals-at-law were healthier because they were just better at stealing. It had been a revelation when he realised that prison ordnances allowed them more food. They were less harmful elements to society, said the rules, than the political prisoners. If you'd been a career thief and ended up with a ten-year sentence here, the administration put you on lighter duties than someone who'd been arrested for speaking English too well.

There was a smell of pine needles in here. Needle-gathering was one of the softest labour details. Someone, God knew why because it was the least scientific thing Valery had heard in his life, had decided that stewing pine needles into a sort of foul medicinal soup was a good way to get vitamin C into prisoners. It wasn't, so Valery always quietly poured his into a hedge, but pine duty existed all the same, and there were always men crossing to and fro between the camp and the forest carrying hessian sacks for it. As if Christmas were this morning over and someone had just taken out the tree, the whole floor was littered with needles.

'Well,' Dima said slowly. 'That's a thing some of my boys wouldn't mind knowing how to do, a bomb like that.'

Valery nodded. He was about to get all his fingers broken, he could feel it coming.

Dima was studying him. 'You're such a little slip of a fox; you're not going to last long without someone to look after you, you know that, right?'

'No, I know.' He blinked, because he couldn't focus, then had to take off his glasses.

'You're a professor. You can teach.'

'Yes. I'll teach whoever you want.'

Dima smiled with just his teeth. 'Really. You know mainly they can't read.'

Valery put his glasses back on, but everything still felt dislocated. 'I can teach them to read as well. It's not difficult.'

'Is it not?' Dima said sharply. 'Because it seems pretty fucking impenetrable to me.'

Valery looked up at him properly, because the part of him that had always been a teacher was annoyed. It was in the background, a very small, modest annoyance, but it was there. 'If it seems impenetrable, it's because your teachers were all idiots who didn't take the time to explain it.'

Dima started to laugh. 'I don't believe you.'

'What?' said Valery. 'It's just code. There are only thirty-three letters and Russian is written basically like it's spoken. I mean it. I can teach you right now. Christ, you're all clever thinking humans.' Now he was having to think about it, he was getting angry. It was farcical that there could be people in nineteen fifty-fucking-seven who had been so failed by school that they couldn't read. 'How many of you here were never taught to read?'

The men with him glanced at Dima, and then few by few, every single man in the barracks flicked his hand up.

'Right,' Valery said, and he didn't care any more if someone *was* coming along later to break all his fingers. 'Everyone who wants to learn, sit down. Is there any chalk?'

'Find him some chalk,' Dima said over his shoulder to a gigantic man with only one eye and a spiderweb tattoo across his head.

'I'm going to use this wall to write on. Get over here and sit down. Not a single one of you is leaving till you know the alphabet. I'm not having it. I know maybe some of you don't think it's for you, but it is, it's for everyone, and if some moron teacher said you were stupid when you were little, then they can fuck off. All of you deserve to know how to do this. Jesus wept.'

All the men did exactly as they were told.

He'd known they would. There was power in looking harmless; people would do things for you that they wouldn't for someone bigger. It happened consistently, in lecture theatre after lecture theatre. Far from being any kind of barrier to teaching, it had always helped. For the same reason, he suspected, that even big hulking men could be at the mercy of a determined kitten, people had a way of wanting to keep him happy.

He supposed it helped to have just blown up a building as well.

He ended up with forty men sitting or kneeling on the floor, a hunk of chalk from the quarry, and writing on the wall. He started with little words – politics and swear words, because you had to be realistic about what would keep people interested – and got everyone to play mix-and-match, and then spot the difference, building them up a few letters at a time so that they were never too lost. After an hour, like he'd thought, because they were all bright and normal, everyone was able to write their own name.

Some of them were so happy they sank in a kind of amazed stupor. Valery nearly cried when he saw that. He could absolutely believe that Moscow thought rapists and murderers were less harmful to the socialist economy than chemistry professors, but something in him just ground and stuck at the idea that there existed primary schoolteachers who would let kids leave school without even knowing the alphabet.

'Same time tomorrow for anyone who wants to learn more,' Dima said after the hour, quite bland, and then touched Valery's shoulder to tilt him away from other people. 'You don't seem afraid. See that man there? He likes to murder redheads.' He looked amused, insofar as a giant bear-person could do that.

Valery smiled a bit. Dima was hazing him, he was nearly sure, in which case, it was kind; and if he wasn't, then being murdered would bring the day back around to plan. 'Would you mind asking him to hold it in until he can spell properly?'

Dima gave a strange look, and tenderly, for no reason Valery could tell, he brushed a strand of Valery's hair back. Beyond him, a lot of the men were still in clusters on the floor, practising carving letters with knives or marking the dust with slim sticks.

'Come with me,' Dima concluded. 'We're going to see the tattooist. You won't last fifteen minutes on your side of the camp otherwise. Animals, the political prisoners. Present company excepted obviously.'

'Hey,' someone said quickly, a young man with a tattoo of a mermaid on his chest. 'It'll take ages. Can we come too and play that word game again?'

'Yes please,' said Valery, charmed. Usually, by the time they got to him, students were tired. He barely ever got to meet someone who was just delighted to learn things. Then, because nobody liked feeling as though you were Doing Them A Favour, 'I think I'll need the distraction.'

Dima smiled; a real, kind smile, the first Valery had seen since arriving at the camp. 'You'll be fine, little fox. We'll look after you.'

18

Chromatography

City 40, 1963

The first snow whirled down into City 40 in the middle of November, and the great flat marshland around the black lake turned grey. Then, crackling with long needles of ice, the deep pools froze, and the grey turned to white. At night, Valery kept a window propped open, because the whole space between the Lighthouse complex and the forest was loud with the bangs and splits of dead branches falling as the cold snapped the last few fibres that had held them to their trees. They sounded like gunshots, but some background noise was better than silence.

He had stayed late at the lab on the first Monday after the tattoos disaster, but Shenkov had not come to fetch him. Valery could only interpret that as having had his standing invitation to the apartment on the ninth floor revoked.

In his own room, he kept jolting awake in the night, certain that he was back at the camp and that the Lighthouse had been a dream. After a week of doing that, what should have been an ordinary sense of aloneness was starting to feel like an entity all of its own, hunched rasping in the corner.

Once or twice, he nearly went down to the KGB office to tell Shenkov to just call the administrator at Kolyma if he wanted, because the administrator would explain about the bomb, but he, Valery, couldn't, in the same way he couldn't breathe carbon dioxide.

It was amazing how debilitating the effect of not sleeping was. He could only think in straight lines in the privacy of his own head; trying to explain anything to the students became fantastically difficult, harder than it had been when he was hungry all the time at the camp. He pushed through, but he started to feel the edges of his mind misting again. Whenever he saw Shenkov at a distance in the cafeteria, his heart lurched, full of reproach to whatever stupid part of his brain had decided that letting him see the bloody tattoos had been a good idea.

Excruciating now was the morning trip down to the KGB offices to get the prisoner book signed. He did all right at first, going to the front desk, but then Shenkov was there on the third day.

'Polonium,' was all he said. 'Yes or no?'

Valery had to look down at the row of stamps in the prisoner book. Things blurred at the edges of his glasses where the thickness of the lenses changed. On his kitchen table, the report about the polonium in Sasha's blood sat untouched. He stood over it for minutes every morning, and every morning he decided to pick it up and take it to Shenkov. Every morning, as he put his hand on it, his mind conjured something so strong it didn't feel like imagination but premonition. There was a grey corridor, lined with doors, and smelling of disinfectant and badly washed people. There were little paper cups that rattled with Thorazine pills, designed to do nothing but clinically lobotomise you. There was the feeling of the very last of his mind fizzing away to nothing.

If he handed the report over, Shenkov would have a choice. He could save a child and smash a radiation trial to save other children. Or he could do nothing, and save a tattooed murderer.

'It wasn't,' Valery said. 'I made a mistake, comrade. Just a natural toxin in the water that caused the same kind of effect.'

Shenkov had put a diamond-tipped drill into his stare. 'What did Resovskaya say to you? Did she threaten you?'

'It was just an accident. I've never seen anything like it before, it . . .' He couldn't keep making things up. 'I can't give you anything. I'm sorry.'

Valery would have liked to be taken outside and shot then. Horribly, Shenkov was looking at him like he had when Valery's arm snapped.

The snow had settled, but the ground had not frozen yet when the incinerator broke. It was something complicated, and within a couple of days, dead field specimens mounted up in the lab. Everyone knew what they were going to have to do, but everyone was too cold already to want to go out and dig in the snow. In the end, Valery reasoned that he was definitely the one who knew most about hard labour and was therefore least put off by it, so he took a shovel out to the lake edge and started to dig in a place with relatively firm, unmarshy ground, close to a pair of nesting cranes, who seemed not to mind.

He was surprised when the students came out in rounds of two or three to help, huddled in down coats and fluffy hats. They all seemed disproportionately impressed that he hadn't ordered any of them to do it for him. It was nice to listen to them talk – they were excited about being allowed to move on to birds from fish soon, and still anxious about the possibly baldness-inducing snow.

'Um, comrade,' one of the students said, sounding puzzled. 'What are these stripy bits in the soil?'

Valery slipped past other people digging to see. The boy was at the lakeside end of the trench, leaning against his shovel now. When he saw Valery, he tapped it against two very clear stripes, right at the base of their trench. One was rusty, and one was nearly silver, slim. Valery knelt down slowly. The silver had a dull gleam, but even as they watched, it was turning black.

'Oop, sorry,' someone said as they walked too close to the edge and displaced some snow on them.

It slid down the strange stripes in the soil, which fizzed just long enough for Valery to catch the nearest two students and drag them bodily behind him. Then it exploded.

Fifteen minutes later, the students were all safely inside. Valery had brushed the stray hunks of soil and soft, strange, discoloured metal from his clothes, and a few grains of it from a graze on his cheek. He went back out with Dr Resovskaya to stand at the edge of the trench, holding the original blueprints of the nuclear plant between them. Nowhere anywhere along the lake shore was anything to indicate any digging work, buildings, nothing.

'And we're sure that's caesium?' Dr Resovskaya said at last. 'The explosion wasn't trapped marsh gas, or . . .'

Valery, who had brought out a cup of coffee, slung the coffee at the silver-black strip at the base of the trench. Where the liquid hit it, it went off with a bang. Dr Resovskaya held up the plans like an umbrella to shield them from the ensuing rain of soil and caesium bits.

'We're sure it's caesium,' she murmured, and touched the back of her own head. 'What the hell is caesium doing just floating about in the bloody topsoil?'

Valery was at a loss too. He'd never seen anything like it. Very tentatively, he picked up a spade and eased more soil away to see further down. There were more layers in it, distinct bands. There must have been at least six. Part of him wanted to dig to see how far it went and what was at the bottom, and another pointed out how stupid that would be.

'What *is* that?' he said. 'Caesium and – what?'

'I have . . . absolutely no idea,' Resovskaya said, and for the first time since he had arrived, Valery believed her without reservation.

The students were still buzzing when they came back in. Given that seven minds were better than one extremely dodgy and recently starved one, Valery put the problem to them, and drew it out on the blackboard at the end of the lab so they could all check and draw on it too if they liked.

'We know this doesn't occur naturally. Caesium has to be extracted from pollucite ore, of which there are no geological strata for a thousand kilometres around us. Anyone who can tell me how we got a perfect seam of raw caesium just lying around in marshland gets a bottle of Stolichnaya.'

'Two,' Resovskaya said.

He'd half-thought they must be missing something obvious, but what followed was studious silence. Gradually, it broke into murmurs and theories between small groups. Valery stayed by himself, holding a pen above a sheet of graph paper. Just to give his hand something to do, he sketched out what they'd found again. The caesium, another seam of something else below it – something more inert, thank Christ – and then more layers still.

The phone rang. Resovskaya picked it up, but the line was so good that Valery could hear Shenkov through it.

'When were you going to report that explosion, comrade?'

'When we knew what it was,' Resovskaya said. 'It's odd. We're working out what it could have been now. It wasn't anything nefarious, comrade, it's . . . well. Something in the soil. Nobody has a bomb.'

Valery could nearly see him looking sceptical in front of the cautionary poster in his office that showed the KGB seal and their unofficial slogan. TRUST BUT VERIFY. 'Send the students who saw it to see me, please.'

Everyone else had heard too. The two students who Valery had wrenched out of the way of the explosion looked worried. Resovskaya nodded at them to do as they were told. There was an unwilling scraping of chairs.

After Valery had finished the sketch, the pen dropped in his hand and pooled an ink splodge on the corner of the page. He watched it seep into the grain of the paper, trying to let his mind go blank. The ink splodge expanded and feathered at its edges.

He sat back slowly. After a frozen few seconds, he shoved the paper pad away. The students had started a *Theories* column on the blackboard, mainly insane, so he added his, and underlined it. They all looked. Resovskaya frowned at it, then got up far faster than she usually did and started gathering glass retorts.

'I think this is what's happened.' Valery tapped the chalk stick against the word. 'Help us design an experiment to test it, all of you.'

As the scramble started, the two students who had been to see Shenkov came back in, looking how people usually did after they had been to see Shenkov.

'He says he's sending people out to see what it—'

Valery snatched up the phone. 'Shenkov, stop being a dick, we're not lying to you. There's something in the ground. If you really have to send anyone out there, make sure it's someone you don't like, because they might explode. We've got an idea. I'll come and see you when we know.' He put the phone down before Shenkov could argue.

'Well,' Resovskaya said in the worried silence that followed, 'if anyone would like to say their final goodbyes to Comrade Kolkhanov before his untimely death?'

But Shenkov didn't come to arrest anyone. From the security office came only quiet, patient as a spider.

By mid-afternoon, they'd confirmed it, and Valery ran to Shenkov's office with a pen and some old receipts.

'Do you know what chromatography is?' Valery asked as he shoved Shenkov's door open, hoping a lot that Shenkov would not *now this instant* turn out to be the sort of person who had fantastically risqué office affairs. Valery had had some suspicions for a good while now, even in the face of no evidence whatsoever. It was a truth universally acknowledged that beautiful women tended despite their natural disadvantages to be virtuous, while beautiful men were invariably bastards. Shenkov might have been doing excellent work of pretending not to, but he could not have failed to notice the wake of flushed people he left behind en route between the canteen and the office every morning.

Shenkov shook his head and sat back with forced poise as Valery rearranged the desk to make a clear space, and requisition a glass of water. Fortunately he did not have to rearrange around a flushed person.

'No. What?'

'Right, so, this is ordinary paper. Blob of ink near the top here. Wind it around the pen to make it hold, balance the pen over this glass, which has just enough water in it to touch the end of the paper. We're going to leave that there and in a minute it will – well, you'll see.'

'Why is this happening?' Shenkov asked, sounding strained.

'I'm telling you. What we found in the soil, what caused that explosion, it's caesium; and other things. Things that couldn't be there naturally in the quantities we found them. They're all stacked on top of each other in layers.'

'If they aren't naturally occurring then how did they get there?'

'Exactly. Do you know how the nuclear reactors dispose of their waste? And where?'

'I don't, but underground. Why is it important? Oh, your thing's doing something.'

Valery looked. The ink from the blob at the top of the paper strip was bleeding down, sucked in by the damp part of the paper. It was black, and it fanned out in a good few dull colours, grey and blue, and an unattractive brown. 'Yes. So that's chromatography; the separation of a mixture on a new medium. In this case the mixture is black ink, which is made up of several colours. Because they have different densities, they separate out at different levels, you see?'

'Like your . . . layers in the soil.'

'Yes. This is what happened in the ground. The soil is the paper. The ink is nuclear waste. The layers in the soil, they're all the elements present in nuclear waste, and the soil has separated them out according to density. Lightest at the top, heaviest below. All the elements will be more or less radioactive, but the main problem is that a lot of them – I mean caesium right down to plutonium – explode in water.'

Shenkov was shaking his head. 'Sorry, why would there be plutonium in nuclear waste? I thought the whole point of a military reactor was to filter it out, for fuel for bombs.'

'It is, but our reactors only get about eighty per cent of it. It isn't a very efficient process. The other twenty per cent gets mixed in with the waste products. So I think the plant has been burying its waste in trenches. We need to know where those are now.' He hesitated, because a tight feeling was growing low in his chest, but he couldn't track why. Traces of plutonium wouldn't hurt anyone. Its radioactivity could be blocked with a sheet of paper, never mind three metres of soil. A tiny bit of it exploding in some water wasn't going to do much either unless it aerosolised and someone breathed it in. 'I think if we're not careful, someone's going to dig somewhere they shouldn't and we'll have more randomly exploding patches of marshland.'

'Yes,' Shenkov said heavily. 'Yes, okay.' He picked up the telephone and dialled an interior line. 'Anna. Sorry to bother you, but I'm coming across with Valery Kolkhanov from the research centre. He needs to talk to you about nuclear waste. Can you call down to the gate and let us in? Thanks.'

'You know people,' Valery said, admiring.

Shenkov looked wry. 'That was my wife.'

Valery started to nod, but then stopped. 'Hang on, your *wife* is *Anna Shenkovna?* The Anna Shenkovna, the nuclear physicist from the Kurchatov Institute.'

'She . . . is.'

'She's royalty. She wrote the standard monograph on the dating of decayed radioactive lead, I've read all her papers.'

'I took her name,' Shenkov said, nodding very slightly in the way of someone still judging whether or not he was being called a dullard who had no business knowing geniuses.

'Okay,' Valery laughed, mainly to hide how funny he was failing to find it. All that felt like a shove in the chest. It had no business feeling that way. He had known Shenkov had a wife, but for reasons that shimmered past him when he tried to grasp them, the prospect of meeting her flooded him with dread.

19

Anna Shenkovna

A t the gates of the reactor complex, the soldiers waved them through, and Shenkov led the way inside. Valery thought they would be ushered carefully to a canteen – neutral territory – by one of the security guards, but instead they went straight upstairs to a lab. People were on lunch break, their lab coats and visors hung up by the door, arrayed now across workbenches.

Anna Shenkovna was a round, luminous person with a bright blonde buzz cut who, when they came in, was reading a physics journal and holding an unlit cigarette like it was a mortal enemy. She had on a black Ukrainian embroidered dress for which she would probably have been arrested in Moscow, socks over black stockings, builder's boots, and despite the backless stool and the extra weight she carried, she sat like a ballerina. About Valery's age, but much better worn.

'Kolkhanov! How are you, infamous one?' she asked, and Valery had a surge of belonging mixed with real fear. God knew what Shenkov had been saying. 'Sit down, sit down, nothing too radioactive lying about just now. Hello, sweetheart,' she added to Shenkov. 'Isn't he a good trophy husband?' she said to Valery. 'He's terribly presentable and sometimes he brings me new things. I've been hearing about you for ages.'

'Oh, dear.'

'No, no, good things.'

Valery glanced at Shenkov. 'Well, he's lying. I just sort of attached myself to him, I go to bits if you leave me by myself.'

Had in fact been going to bits, these last few weeks alone in his own apartment.

She kept a dead-straight face, but she was a terrible actress and there was glitter in her eyes. 'Well, if he was the first thing you saw when you hatched.'

Valery burst out laughing. 'Ugly duckling yourself!'

'Swan, it was a swan, Kolkhanov!' she shouted back at him, as if they'd known each other always. Then, 'Tea, coffee?'

'Coffee, if there is . . .'

She put a kettle over a Bunsen burner and turned it up to full blast, the flame blue. The underside of the kettle looked like it had recently re-entered the atmosphere. 'So, what's going on? Kostya said you needed to ask me things and now I feel desperately important.'

Valery nearly asked who Kostya was before he remembered that obviously Shenkov had a first name and that obviously it was Konstantin.

It was like talking to a delighted pheasant. When he showed her what they thought was going on, she watched him draw, bird-bright, thought about it, then lit her cigarette in the Bunsen burner.

'Yes,' she said. 'I see what's happened. The waste is buried in concrete-lined trenches in the ground. They're twenty metres deep, and so they aren't sealed with concrete on top. We just use the topsoil. It's plenty to block out any radiation from the slurry, so there was no need to go to the expense of the concrete. We thought. At what depth did you find the caesium?'

'Only about half a metre.'

'And what's the soil like at that level?'

'Dry for now, but it'll soak the second we get a thaw.'

She blew out a cloud of smoke. 'Right, so of course you all need to know where the trenches are so that none of your students explode when they're out tagging ducks on the lake.'

'Right. Mark it out, leave it alone, simple.'

'Yes, it would be if the trenches weren't everywhere.'

He straightened up. 'Sorry?'

'I don't know how much you know about this place, but the reactors have been active for ten years. There was a nine-month break in production in fifty-seven, but apart from that, they've run continuously. Each reactor generates thousands of tonnes of liquid nuclear waste every year. The trenches are right across the land between the lake and the forest. All around the facility.'

There it was again, the niggling unease he'd had in Shenkov's office, the feeling that he'd forgotten something big. He could feel his way around the shape of it now. 'They . . . I see. Um. Comrade; these reactors. They still only get about an eighty per cent plutonium yield, is that right? There's still the twenty per cent trace plutonium in the waste.'

She nodded. 'We're going to have to talk to the director.'

Shenkov looked between them. Valery felt graceless for not trying to include him more. Shenkov must have been used to it, because he had only settled with a cigarette of his own and he had been making the coffee – Valery couldn't remember hearing the kettle on the Bunsen burner sing, but it was off now – patient and quiet. 'Why do we need to talk to the director?' he asked.

Valery glanced at Anna, not sure he should be the one to explain. It wouldn't sound real, coming from him.

'Because,' she said, 'a twenty per cent trace of plutonium is nothing in one batch of waste; a few tenths of a gram. But with each reactor producing tonnes of waste every year for ten years . . .' She tipped her head one way and then the other. 'I'd guess there must now be a hundred kilograms or so of plutonium in the ground around the Lighthouse. This wouldn't be a problem, because combined with other elements, plutonium is inert. But as Kolkhanov has just proven, the soil has separated out all the elements in the liquid waste. The plutonium is pure, and it will therefore explode in water. One nuclear bomb, of the kind used at Hiroshima, requires only six kilograms of plutonium.'

Shenkov was silent for a long second. 'You're saying that this facility is sitting – really – on top of twenty atom bombs.'

'Yes,' she said. She was the opposite of Valery; calm, even louche, despite what she was saying. She sipped her coffee. 'And they could well go off in a chain reaction as soon as the groundwater penetrates the plutonium strata.'

They all looked outside, over the black lake. All the time they had been talking, new snow had been tapping at the windows, and now it strengthened just enough to ruffle the surface of the lake, which jumped and skittered, dull under the grey clouds.

20

Albert

'That was quite a catch,' Shenkov said as they walked back to the Lighthouse together in the snow. It wasn't thick yet, but it crunched under their boots. Already it had made the bare earth of the whole complex white, and smoothed over the caterpillar tracks from the diggers and cranes.

'Only by accident. We could just have easily dug somewhere else,' said Valery, who was starting to feel shaky from the nearness of that other future.

Shenkov was quiet for a few paces. 'I called the administrator at Kolyma.'

The blood left Valery's fingers. 'Right.'

'He said he couldn't possibly comment about any alleged accidents at the camp, but he said he knew exactly what I was talking about and that you weren't dangerous.'

'Okay.'

'I want to believe that, but – will you tell me what happened?'

'No. I can't,' Valery said, and then had to slow down, because there was a shushing roar in his ears now. 'Can you leave it?'

'No. I'm not a reptile, for God's sake, I haven't been so brainwashed I can't think for myself. If you had a reason then—'

'*Stop!*'

'What?' Shenkov demanded.

'Oh, Christ . . .' Valery leaned against the fence and tried to breathe normally, but it didn't work. His heart was galloping so hard it felt like it would smash in his chest. Perversely, though, the cold felt much worse than it had a minute ago, and he was shuddering.

Shenkov looked caught somewhere between annoyed and confused. 'Are you all right?'

'I'm having a panic attack, I'll be fine.' He had to slide down towards the ground. 'Go on ahead, they last for a while, it's tedious.'

Shenkov knelt down, a fine line just deepening between his brows. He didn't ever let his expressions develop strongly enough to mark him more. 'But—'

'If you're about to complain that the very mention of something shouldn't be giving me panic attacks then you can get in the queue,' Valery snapped. He heard his own voice go high. 'I agree. I'm as embarrassed as you are.'

'No. I was going to say you can't stay out here for long.' Shenkov held up his stopwatch, which already showed they'd been out for four minutes. He touched Valery's elbows and levered him upright. 'Come on, let's get inside. We need to see the doctor, you're going to collapse if—'

'Oh, get off me,' Valery growled. '*You* collapse. I'm not insane, I don't need *drugging*. It'll go away by itself.'

Shenkov watched him for a second. 'You really can't talk about it.'

'No,' Valery said, on the edge of snapping again, but then understood. 'Shenkov. I don't think you're brainwashed.'

'That's funny, hearing you say that as if it's a ridiculous idea.'

'It *is* a ridiculous idea.' Valery had to pause at the doorway, because his heart was still going as if he had heard machine-gun fire rattle over his head, and it was making him dizzy. 'One second,' he said, exhausted with himself and trying hard to avoid imagining how this must seem to Shenkov.

Shenkov didn't say anything, but he did put his arm around him. Valery thought he was just going to chivvy him inside, but he guided him forwards, against his own chest. Valery stiffened. It was bad enough to be little and calcium-deficient, but to be pathetic enough to have to treat like a child was heinous.

'Don't—'

'No,' Shenkov said. 'It's medicine, you need pressure across your sternum.'

That made no sense. 'What?'

Shenkov shrugged a little. 'Western voodoo.'

Valery stood still, thinking, and trying to feel why that might work; and, after only a few seconds, aware that it *did* work. The hammering in his ribcage was slowing. Shenkov had both arms clamped across his back, tight but not painful. The constriction was, far from unnerving, reassuring in a deep primal way. The panic lost its fangs. Valery had to let his head drop against Shenkov's lapel. He could feel the edges of the KGB badge inside his breast pocket.

'It is shell shock, you know,' Shenkov said quietly.

Valery shook his head once. 'I've never been blown up. This is just weakness of character.'

'No, you can get it from other things than bombs. In the Komsomol, I worked on the building of the White Canal. My unit had to move the bodies of zeks who had died. I went blind one morning. No reason. No bombs, no threat, nothing. I was just having a cup of coffee and it all went dark. The medic, she said it was very common. She got my friend to do this, and it went away in . . . about twenty minutes. She said there are all kinds of bizarre things that can happen to you. It's all shell shock.'

'Oh,' said Valery, feeling strange. Somewhere in a memory archive, he had known that; certainly he had heard of hysterical blindness and paralysis, and all the odd things that happened to soldiers on the front. He had just never applied it to himself. All at once, something heavy lifted away, and he could breathe again. He leaned back a little, almost more disconcerted by that lifting than by the panic itself.

Shenkov let him go. 'All right?'

'Yes,' Valery said gradually. It made him wonder what else humans did in their deep workings that nothing in medical science had so much as brushed on its bumbling way by.

Shenkov sank his hands into his coat pockets as they passed inside and into the long corridor, which smelled of cleaning chemicals and cork from the noticeboards after the sharp clear air outside. 'Now will you please move back into the apartment with me? I've been miserable, you got me used to someone making me coffee at five in the morning, for God's sake.'

Valery started to laugh, which was painful, because his heart was still going hard. 'Oh, God . . . something to confess, then.'

'What?'

'I've got an octopus now, he's been keeping me company. He's called Albert.'

It was telling that Shenkov didn't ask him why or how he'd got hold of an octopus. 'How . . . large an octopus are we talking?'

Valery held his hands apart to about the size of a coconut. He had given Albert half a coconut to play with the day before yesterday, and come home to find what looked like a whole coconut but was in fact Albert tucked up in the half coconut, staying very still and watching his teatime crabs amble nearer in what looked to Valery like a wilfully smug undercover operation.

'Don't they walk about?' Shenkov said carefully. 'Won't it electrocute itself on the television, or . . . ?'

'He uses the remote.'

'Of course it does.'

Neither of them added that all this was only provided the entire facility didn't go up like a super-volcano in the next few weeks.

Talking about Albert and shell shock had been, however brief, a way not to talk about what was going to happen next. Anna had stayed behind because she had to talk to the director of the nuclear plant, and get him to come across here so that someone could show him what was going on. For Valery and Shenkov, the next name on the list was Dr Resovskaya. All the students' work was going to have to stop, at the very least, while the physicists worked out exactly where everything had been dumped, and in the best possible world, everyone was going to have a serious discussion about evacuation. Valery knew already that that would never happen, even before the director of the plant, Anna, and the senior engineer arrived.

The director was a man Shenkov's height who had gone to seed, his nose red with veins and his paunch pressing into the front of his jacket. He was one of those people who found ordinary motion such a struggle that the walk across the snow set him sweating, and as he charged into Shenkov's office, where Valery and Resovskaya waited already, he was loosening his tie. Valery gave him a glass of water. The director took it and thanked him politely, and then seemed to press a switch that spun his character.

'What's all this bollocks about a safety breach?' he demanded of Shenkov. He had a strong Leningrad accent that was subtly wrong. The man wasn't actually from there; he was putting it on to seem like more of a proper, salt-of-the-earth proletarian. Valery watched him with some interest, listening hard now and hoping that it would turn out he was the ashamed grandson of an aristocrat. 'Safety regulations have been followed here *to the letter* since fifty-seven! What qualifies you to say otherwise, Shenkov? Got multiple degrees in physics, have you?'

'Sit down, Borya,' Resovskaya said, dry as radioactive dust. 'Hello, Anna, how are you?'

'Invigorated,' Anna said, taking a chair beside Valery.

'It's all utterly hysterical. I'd think better of you, Elena,' the director snapped, but he did sit down, looking as though he would have preferred it were not by Shenkov. Shenkov watched him without hostility, but his poise became even more immaculate than usual, and the contrast between them was suddenly so marked that it looked like a Western cartoon about the Soviet hope for society versus the sad fact; on the one hand, a portrait of socialist realism with a bewitching soldier, and on the other, actual realism.

The senior engineer ghosted into a chair too, looking like a walking toothache. He was a salt-and-pepper man, ugly in the way people become when they have been indefinably ill for a long time. He was too pale, his face too lined for the age that he was, and though he kept his eyes lowered as he sat down, Valery caught the way that they flickered strangely; very rapid left to right, as if he were asleep, or watching the land go by from a speeding car. As the director began to rail again, the engineer pressed both thin hands over his mouth and yawned.

'Boring you, am I, Polotov?' the director snarled.

Polotov stiffened, scared.

Valery sat back. It was called asthenia, that sourceless fatigue, and he had seen the eye-flicker before too, but never outside a laboratory. It was from chronic radiation sickness.

'As Polotov will tell you if he can be bothered to stir himself,' the director said to all of them, 'all the waste from our plant is disposed of safely. Concrete-lined trenches, in reinforced tanks. Whatever the hell it is you've found in the ground, it isn't from us. Trace amounts from the small volume dumped into the Techa during the experimental contamination, it has to be.'

Experimental contamination; not explosion of apocalyptic proportions. The man sounded like he had been lying so fluently for so long that the truth was beginning to slip his mind.

'It could well be that,' Resovskaya said, nodding. 'This marsh is fed by the Techa. About two million curies' worth of radioactive material has been pumped into it over the last seven or eight years; some of that water will have brought sediment of those radioactive elements into the soil.'

'Two million curies is nothing,' the director put in. 'Three *hundred* million curies are released per kiloton of fission bomb, and the one dropped on Nagasaki was twenty kilotons. Six thousand million curies. And Nagasaki is not drenched in radiation sickness and hysteria, so.'

Valery had to take a deep breath. 'That's like saying you can't drown in a lake because some people were once shipwrecked in the Pacific. And this is not radioactive sediment from the contamination in the Techa. There's too much.' He looked at Anna, willing her to explain how it could have got out if there were waste tanks. She hadn't mentioned those before.

She was, thank God, already nodding. 'If the comrade director remembers,' she said, 'the containment-tanks strategy was abandoned in nineteen fifty-six. We used to use tanks, with cooling systems. But when one of the cooling systems broke down, the cost of replacing it was estimated very high, and the physicists were asked to reassess whether it was necessary.'

'And you reported that it was not,' the director said, raising his voice. 'Your signature is on that document, Shenkovna!'

'Yes, it is, because you said we'd all be arrested if we didn't fiddle the figures to show that it was safe,' she said mildly.

'How dare you!'

'Everyone at this table must be very clear about what happened. Waste at this plant is liquid. It is treated with ammonium nitrate to lessen its radioactivity. Ammonium nitrate, however, degrades and spontaneously combusts with significant force if allowed to. It needs a cooling system. But the budget wouldn't allow for it, so the cooling system was not replaced. The safety report that said it need not be replaced was then interpreted by the Ministry as a reason not to invest in any further containment tanks at all after the incident in fifty-seven, which destroyed all the extant ones. Liquid waste was then dumped straight into the concrete trenches, and covered over with earth. It has been for six years.'

'Ammonium nitrate,' Valery echoed. 'That explains what happened in fifty-seven, doesn't it? An ammonium nitrate explosion set off a chain reaction and . . .'

'*Nothing happened in fifty-seven!*' the director bellowed at him.

It was a absurd thing to do, shout like that. Valery should have been able to laugh at him. But instead all Valery could do was clench his hands in his lap as ghost electric pain shot up and down his ribs, and his whole chest wrenched tight. His heart sped again and, with a distant horror, he wondered if he was going to have yet another of those humiliating attacks right here at this table, in front of all of them. Blood shot away from his hands as fast as the sea receding before a tsunami. It left him icy, waiting for the wave.

Under the table, Shenkov caught his hand and gripped it hard. He was warm.

'So you've been dumping straight into trenches,' Resovskaya summarised, as though nothing had happened. 'You've brought a map of the locations of the waste trenches?'

'No. There is no map.'

'What?'

The director huffed as if it was a stupid idea. 'It's a matter of national security. We don't want to leave around a guide as to where to find exhausted nuclear fuel. People would steal it.'

'We need to talk to the Ministry,' Valery said, because he had had a lot more than enough. 'This whole marsh needs to be drained and covered in concrete. However it got there and whatever happened in fifty-seven, we have a significant layer of plutonium in the soil now, and when water reaches it, it will explode.'

'No – no,' said Resovskaya, laughing a little. 'Hold your horses, Valery. We don't know that we have a significant layer. We know we have it in one particular place, from one trench. For all we know, the others are fine.'

Valery couldn't believe what she'd said at first. He had to listen to the memory again before he was sure he had understood properly. 'How could they be?'

'It's been six years,' she said. 'We've seen no reaction before. It's possible that, mostly, the trenches are deep enough that the groundwater isn't penetrating. Without any further evidence, all we have here is a tiny anomaly.'

Valery nearly choked on that. 'Further evidence? We can't take core samples, and we can't dig. If we hit the plutonium layer and introduce water, we could set off a thermonuclear reaction. There's . . . no safe way to prove what's down there.'

'If we have no proof then why are we talking?' the director said triumphantly.

'Because this whole facility could explode—'

Resovskaya interrupted gently, like she had when he was getting het up as a student. 'You're looking at a match head, and reasoning out a thousand tonnes of TNT.'

'Do you realise what you're asking?' the director demanded, and Valery felt trapped between them. Anna was looking out the window as if she wasn't listening. Shenkov was still holding his hand, though, and if it hadn't been for that, Valery could feel that he would have descended into that foul panic again. 'If we call the Minister, he's going to ask whose *fault* this is. And it's going to be *all* of us, believe you me. Never mind that we were *told* to come up with a way to cut costs in fifty-six.'

'And,' Resovskaya said, much quieter, 'everything here would have to be stopped while the building work is carried out. The reactors would have to stop while a new disposal system was built, the biology fieldwork would be disrupted because draining and covering the entire marsh with concrete will have a massive impact on the ecosystem and on the water table. That would be catastrophic. If our baseline conditions change, we won't be able to tell what has caused any changes in our specimens from now on. That will render all the biological studies here useless. The data would be full of holes. We might as well throw the last year's work in the bin.'

'If it has to stop, it has to stop,' Valery said, but he could see now that he was going to lose this. Like always when she disagreed with him, a terrible instinctive shame drilled its way through Valery's skull. It was like emotional trepanning, even though he knew he was right, would even have bet his life on it, because Anna agreed with him and Anna was in a league beyond either of them.

'No. We know that *one* trench has leaked.' Resovskaya sighed, looking as though she wished she was still his teacher and allowed to shake him. 'I know you're convinced you're right, Valery, and you have an amazing numbers brain, but real life isn't as neat as a mathematical proof. You can't logic out a vast truth from a tiny scrap of data. It could be an anomaly. It could be something we haven't thought of, in the fifteen seconds since we've noticed it.'

Beside him, Anna was still studying the marsh. She must have said everything she wanted to.

'Elena – you don't like me,' Valery said, frustrated. 'You don't like the way I think, you think I'm an idiot. Why did you bother going to the *almighty* administrative effort of getting me out of Kolyma if you don't think anything I say is worthwhile?'

For the first time since he'd known her, Resovskaya looked honestly shocked. 'Valery. Jesus. Academically disagreeing with someone doesn't mean you don't rescue him from certain fucking death when you realise he needs rescuing.'

He didn't know whether to feel better or worse.

The director leaned forward and clasped his hands on the table. 'Comrade Kolkhanov. Say we talk to the Ministry, with just this one piece of evidence. Say that, against the odds, they take it seriously. I don't think you understand what the Ministry is like. If anything goes wrong, all hell breaks loose. If we spend a kopek more than in the previous quarter, all hell breaks loose. If we don't hit our plutonium production quotas, we'll all be sacked, and none of us will work in anything more complicated than cab driving ever again. I don't want to risk anyone's safety, of course I bloody don't, but we have one sample from one trench, as Dr Resovskaya says.' He had taken on the crooning tone of somebody talking to a child who was having a tantrum. 'And Comrade Kolkhanov, I'm sorry, but what's more likely: that this is unexpectedly dense residue from the contamination in the Techa, or a whole new phenomenon nobody but your illustrious self has ever noticed before in the history of science? There's no evidence this is not an isolated incident.'

'There is no evidence that it is,' Valery said. 'Lack of evidence doesn't prove a lack.'

'Comrade, I believe you're sticking so hard to this very shaky hypothesis because you morally object to radiation studies on living subjects,' Dr Resovskaya said in her arid way. 'You're leaping on this for a chance to put a stop to it.'

'What?' Valery said, his voice misting. 'No. Elena—'

'Aha,' the director said, looking satisfied.

'I think we can all agree that the situation bears monitoring,' Dr Resovskaya said. 'I think we can also agree that what has been said in this room remains here. It's no use sparking panic over nothing. We'll declare the marsh off-limits for the students, to be on the safe side.'

Valery looked at Shenkov, not in any hope that Shenkov could do anything, but just to check that another human being thought that this was absurd and terrible. Shenkov, though, was watching Anna, who was still gazing out the window.

'Let's get on with our days, then,' the director growled.

There was a scuffing of chairs on the carpet as the others started to get up and collect pens and papers.

Outside, one of the mud geysers popped, only about fifteen metres from the window. It made everyone jump except Valery, who was too sunken into his own head now to really perceive it until the mud was pattering on to the ground again, and except Anna. She only made a tiny satisfied sound and clapped once. She had been waiting for it, for the whole conversation.

'You know what that is, don't you,' she said cheerfully.

'Volcanic rubbish, isn't it?' the director muttered, clearly embarrassed to have flinched.

'No volcanic activity out here, comrade. That's the marsh water hitting the caesium strata.'

Resovskaya looked at Valery and Anna as if she would have liked to stuff them both with polonium. The director, who had gone a milky colour, was already on the phone, asking the operator for Moscow.

21

MinMac

On the day Valery's cast came off, close to Christmas, someone from the government rang and told them to come to the Kremlin: Valery, Shenkov, Resovskaya, and the director and the senior engineer of the nuclear plant.

They went by military convoy, and then on a military plane, with three soldiers. None of them spoke until they were in the air, everyone too wary of everyone else. Valery stuck close to Shenkov and wished they could talk. He had no idea whether whoever they were meeting in Moscow actually believed them about the plutonium, or if this was meant to be a loud dressing-down, or if they were all going to be arrested and shot. He found himself holding his fist against the scar on his face. Shenkov eased it away. Valery hadn't realised it was enough of a habit for anyone else to notice.

'Why isn't Anna here?' he asked at last, once they were in the air. He had kept expecting her to turn up, separately for whatever reason, but she never had.

'Because it would be unfair to orphan her kids,' the director said palely.

Moscow was full of healthy people. It had been odd enough in City 40, where the population was small, but Moscow was teeming. People poured from the Metro stations, all walking fast and effortless. Party women in fur collars; suited officials; kids in school uniforms, and everyone moved at twice the pace Valery remembered. He was sure there were more cars, swarms of them, beautiful soft-nosed Volgas with silver grilles or the boxy little Ladas; it must have been easier to be assigned a car now. The trolleybuses were still here, trundling along on their electric overhead wires, but like there'd been some kind of tropical invasion at the factory, some of them were bright orange. It was a mad contrast with the snow that fell in streams from the roofs. All of it was fast and bright and completely alien.

Every single person he had known at the camp had talked about trying to go home one day. He had too. It had never occurred to him that there would be no home to go back to. This wasn't his Moscow. He felt indignant that no one had broken it to him beforehand. People were supposed to tell you. They didn't just let you trip over your dead father on the pavement one day and say, *oh, that's right, old Vanya had too much to drink a few years ago, we forgot to say.*

The Ministry of Medium Machine Building, code for all things nuclear, had its headquarters not at the Kremlin, but on Bolshaya Ordynka Street, which was where all the embassies were. It was a gigantic sandstone tower that looked more like a grand hotel from the outside than the state administrative centre for atomic energy. It did a pretty good hotel impression inside too. It had endless corridors and deep carpets that swallowed sound. Everything was new, and everywhere were flags and portraits of Lenin and Stalin. They waited for a long time to see the Minister on nicely upholstered chairs in a smart waiting room, clustered around a low table on which sat a box of brightly wrapped sweets. The box was in the shape of a treasure chest. Nobody took a sweet.

Valery waited longer than the others. He was only there because he was a walking abacus. He sat staring at the horrible carpet for a good twenty minutes (it had an anchor pattern on it – why? Had someone misunderstood in the early days and confused nuclear and nautical?) listening to the secretary unwrap sweets from her own smaller treasure chest on her desk. He quite liked her for doing that.

Shenkov leaned out and motioned for him to come in. He looked anxious. Valery got up, feeling shabbier than ever.

The Minister was a desiccated man in his sixties called Slavsky.

'Come in, Comrade Kolkhanov. Shut the door. Welcome to MinMac.'

MinMac. It only made sense *not* to say the Ministry of Medium Machine Building, but MinMac made it sound like the place was doing its absolute best to seem little and friendly in a way that was so patently not true that Valery felt like he was meeting a boa constrictor dressed up hopefully with bunny ears and a fluffy tail.

'Now,' said Slavsky, over-gently, 'there seems to be some disagreement about safety at City 40. The director here assures me that nuclear waste is being disposed of in strict accordance to Ministry standards, Dr Resovskaya believes there's a fishy-looking anomaly that bears extra investigation, while Comrade Shenkov reports a major risk. I believe they are in danger of killing each other on my nice rug. I wonder if you'd tell me in your own words what it is you found.' He smiled. The effect wasn't good. If someone had admitted that, long ago, they had spilled coffee on him, put him in rice to dry, and then forgotten to take him out, Valery would have believed it.

'Those three views are not mutually exclusive,' Valery said quietly. 'The director is right, nobody is at fault.' The director looked shocked. It hadn't occurred to him, Valery realised, that Shenkov wasn't out to get him. 'The waste has been buried underground in trenches, exactly as the Ministry guidelines say.' He swallowed. He could hear Shenkov's voice inside his head ordering him not to bugger this bit up or he was dead. 'But nuclear waste as it is produced at the Lighthouse plant is liquid. It's poured into those trenches, then covered over with earth. Unfortunately, over several years, the soil has separated out the liquid waste into its component elements according to density. There are now clear strata of caesium, strontium – and maybe others, the most concerning of which is leftover plutonium. This process has never been recorded before, which is why the guidelines do not allow for it, but we believe it is a kind of chromatography. The soil acts as a filter. Given the amount of waste buried around the facility, there could be enough plutonium in the ground now to completely destroy the plant and the city, and cause severe damage as far as Chelyabinsk and Sverdlovsk, if a thermonuclear reaction were to occur. It would be far worse than what happened in nineteen fifty-seven, and it would add significantly to the atmospheric radioactive trace left by that event. American stations in the Arctic would be able to detect it and trace it back to Kyshtym easily.'

'What would cause a thermonuclear reaction?'

'The introduction of water—'

'Minister,' Resovskaya said, low and reasonable and scholarly, 'all of this is speculation. We found one section of affected soil, about a metre wide. Everything else is extrapolation—'

'Let the man talk,' Slavsky said flatly.

Valery wanted to unhear that. Not 'our comrade', which was what Slavsky should have said. A memory of an essay he'd read at school surfaced with an ugly bubbling. *In any given society the degree of woman's emancipation is the natural measure of the general emancipation.*

Slavsky studied him for a long time. His eyes were the colour that hay went right before it caught fire. 'The trench method is exactly what they use at the plutonium refinery in Richland in the United States, and there has never been an accident there. Why would it be different for us, even if this chromatography effect is happening? Plutonium is dense, ergo it is one of the very lowest strata anyway.'

Valery nodded a little. 'Richland is in the desert. City 40 is on marshland.'

'And what action would you recommend?'

'Drain the marsh, with extreme care, and concrete it over.' It was out before he could think about it. That was just as well; he could see all his bridges with Resovskaya blazing into charred ruins. She was holding her expression open and polite, but she would never do otherwise in front of the minister who controlled the Lighthouse budgets. 'But the entire city should be evacuated while that happens, and ideally Chelyabinsk and Sverdlovsk as well. If there is a clear layer of plutonium in the ground and if water hits it, we will lose the entire population of City 40 and a lot of people beyond it.'

Slavsky stood up. There was a bowstring silence. Valery could taste the future where they were all hustled away and shot in the back alley behind the Ministry. Others would be sent out to City 40 to replace them, others who had no idea what was going on but clear orders, and it would all start again.

There was a click that was Slavsky's fingernails on his blazer button. 'Well, comrades. It's unfeasible to evacuate cities,' he said, looking at Valery as if he suspected he had been speaking to a child dressed up as a chemist, 'but I think I'd better come up with a normal-looking reason to ship you an awful lot of concrete.'

Outside, Valery risked a smile at Shenkov, who scooped him close by his neck and kissed his forehead. Valery hugged him back, not sure if he was going to laugh or collapse or both. The way Slavsky had said *man* was still clanging around inside his head.

Shenkov was laughing. 'Christ, Valera. Come on, I'm taking you out.'

Valery tried to cover over how happy he was to be called Valera.

As they made for the stairs, they passed Resovskaya, who was waiting for the lift with the director and the ill engineer. The director gave them a watery smile, one that was clearly relieved to still have all the right organs, never mind a job. Valery hesitated. He couldn't just run away from what Slavsky had done.

'Dr Resovskaya – I'm sorry. I didn't mean—'

'Just piss off, Valery,' she said, sounding utterly weary.

22

Do You Want to Dance?

The whole street was full of nice hotels and nice bars, so they chose one at random and set up there. It was cheerful and dim, strobing with neon lights, but more gently than a club would have. The bar was glass, with a multicoloured display of every sort of liquor bottle ever manufactured in an alcoholic rainbow. Shenkov, happier than Valery had ever seen him, played Spot the Murderer, and made up stories for everyone who ordered a drink. Moscow was, they concluded, full of murderers.

Happiness gave Shenkov a glow even beyond his ordinary elegance, so Valery was not surprised when a woman bought him a drink and saluted from down the bar. Shenkov held up his wedding ring. She shrugged and held up hers. It made him laugh, but he shook his head.

Then Anna was there at the table with them, even though she wasn't. Valery looked down at a paper coaster. He would never come first for anybody, that was silly, but he would have given anything for second. In a desperate rush, he missed Shenkov even though he was sitting right there.

'Smile!' Shenkov chided him. 'It worked, for God's sake, get drunk. You can't be a machine tonight.'

'I'm not purposefully a machine,' Valery protested, and downed the vodka to try and prove it.

He watched Shenkov decide it was because he was shy. 'I'll buy you something expensive if you speak to an actual human woman.'

'I'm not playing. I came here to sit with you, not torture some random stranger.'

Shenkov studied him quietly, without laughing. 'I worry about you, though. You don't have anyone. You need to get into the habit of talking to people.'

Valery nodded. It was Married Person code again: please stop asking for more than precisely one eighth of my available social time. I have too many people already.

He looked along the bar, found a woman about his age with a military haircut like Svetlana's, went over, explained he was being hounded and would she mind talking to him for five minutes. This damselling brought out her chivalrous side, they bought each other a drink and talked about the show she'd just seen at the ballet, toasted each other's pushy friends – she assured him she had an exact Shenkov replica – and parted again.

He made an effort not to look back at Shenkov's table. The man deserved the night to himself and his own thoughts; Valery wasn't so far gone that he didn't understand that other human beings sometimes *wanted* to sit with their own thoughts. After a minute or so, he pulled a newspaper along the bar to read, and turned it over to find the crossword. The *Truth* crossword was much more impressive than the tiny countryside ones. He borrowed a pen from the bartender, ordering himself to feel fortunate. It was, after all, an excellent crossword, with cryptic clues and everything. He could only do some of them. Before long the bartender was also involved. She, it turned out, was a literature graduate, and bar work was what you got for not going into the sciences. A waitress with a history doctorate knew a couple as well.

It was good to sunbathe in their friendliness, though they weren't doing it for the sake of it. They were using Valery to get rid of the pair of unpleasant predatory types lurking at the far edge of the bar. He was a perfect shield. He was wearing a waistcoat and glasses, and his hair was getting its old curl back, so he looked like the boy next door again; but he was also clearly a recent zek, with Vor tattoos showing on his arms where he had turned back his sleeves. Even unpleasant predatory types did not go near that.

It made Valery jump when someone pressed one hand against his back, but it was only Shenkov.

'You're sitting here with a crossword.'

Valery put the pen down. 'You told me to go away. Make up your mind.'

'I didn't! I just thought you might be better if you had an evening with someone who didn't break your arm.'

'Yes, well, and now you're responsible for these poor people having to work out what the hell the newspaper bastards meant about *stately function, badgers foxes*,' Valery said, motioning at his victims.

'You know what, it could be a typo,' the bartender said.

'I think they do it on purpose sometimes so they don't have to give anyone the prize,' put in the history doctor.

'The prize is . . . a cassette player made by a company claiming to be called Robotnik,' Valery reported.

They all laughed. If a machine had to tell people on the box that it was a Worker then something was amiss.

Shenkov ordered some expensive vodka, resting his knee and his shoulder to Valery's because the seats were crammed together. The bartender did a complicated trick that ended with the drinks on fire and sugar caramelising on the surface. It tasted glorious. Valery had to pause after the second round, already more drunk than tipsy, and far too aware of Shenkov next to him – how warm he was, and the way his whole body tightened when he laughed.

'I might go back to the hotel,' he tried.

'You're not going anywhere, I want to know what you're like when you're drunk,' Shenkov said. 'Is . . . that English?' he added, puzzled.

Everyone else had stopped to listen too. There was an odd stillness all through the whole flashing room. Even the bartender had paused. The music was only on quietly, but Shenkov was right – the lyrics were English, over a light drum and a guitar.

'No one report me,' the DJ murmured into the microphone. 'Might have got this special for you.'

She turned it right up just as it hit a climbing scale and swung into a proper melody. Teenagers and students were laughing, disbelieving, but they were jumping up to dance. It was infectious, full of a naive joy like only American music could be, the kind you had to smile to, or smash against a wall; usually you could tell which it would be by whether or not you liked children. It was packed with California sun and the feeling of the beach, and burnt sugar. Shenkov laughed, for all he would probably have lost his job if he'd been found in a bar playing smuggled American radio.

'What's it mean, do you know?'

Valery listened. 'They're saying – do you want to dance.'

He expected Shenkov to say that enough was enough, and they had better go. But Shenkov only asked him to write the lyrics in the margin of the newspaper, which was difficult given that Valery was already struggling to think, and that Shenkov made him drink another shot every time something went wrong. By midnight the bartender and the history doctor had joined in, everyone was helpless laughing, and Valery was trying hard not to enjoy it too much, because, like an echo, he could hear the silence that waited in City 40, and feel how bitter all this would seem when he was back in it, and Shenkov went home to his family.

The hotel room was unexpectedly excellent. It was a double suite, with two bedrooms linked by a living room. They were right opposite the MinMac building, but on the seventeenth floor, so the view looked straight over the top of it. Very much enjoying the ability to finally unfasten his own shirt without serious ado, Valery stood by the window while he did, watching Moscow glimmer. He had never seen it from so high up. Below them, Bolshaya Ordynka Street was a brilliant line that stretched right the way to the glow of Red Square in the north, where floodlights showed up the candy colours of St Basil's meringue-shaped domes. Headlights and tail lights crept along in great chains, and further off, smoother and quicker, like spirits, the front lamps of Metro trains on the circle line.

He put his forearms on the window and rested his head against them, soaking up the sound of the traffic. It was two in the morning, but half of Moscow seemed to be on its way somewhere. Hopefully it would keep up all night. Then things wouldn't get too quiet.

Shenkov folded down on the windowsill just next to him to see out too. Valery tried to remember how he looked here in the electric glow from outside, shirtsleeves turned back, collar open. When his grey eyes came up, tinged violet from the lights of the sign of the hotel opposite, they were full of warmth. 'Everything all right?' Shenkov asked.

'Fine?'

'You look sad.'

'I'm not going to let you have that much alcohol ever again. All this taking an interest is disturbing.'

Shenkov only smiled. 'I take an interest all the time, but usually I have the good judgement to keep it to myself.'

Valery kicked his ankle gently. 'Fuck off, go to bed.'

Shenkov ignored him. 'Are you married?'

'I was,' Valery said to the traffic. 'Before prison. Why?'

'You must want to get back to her.'

'What makes you say that?'

'Those girls at the bar were flirting with you like there was no tomorrow, but you ignored it.'

'Those people were being polite because I was the human shield between them and the rapist-looking nutters in the window. Not everyone looks like you. Some of us are creepy little abacus people.'

'Stop fishing for compliments.'

He tried to laugh, but then it died. 'Do you mind if we don't talk about this? Svetlana and I got married so that she could – well, it wasn't like you and Anna. I'm not *for* any of that. I've never been. Obviously.'

'What do you mean, obviously? Have you looked in a mirror?'

'Don't make fun of me, please.'

Shenkov frowned. 'I'm not.'

'If I look sad it's because this is the happiest I've been for years, and you did that, but you aren't even one tenth mine and you never will be,' Valery snapped. It shocked him, how desperate he was for it to stop, like he would have been if Shenkov had been holding his hand into a fire. 'In five minutes you'll be back with your family, and one day you'll be transferred away, and you won't remember my name, because I'm no one, and that's how it should be, that's how healthy minds think. But I'll just – stop, and you'll always be important. But that's rancid, and so when you're gone, and I think about all this, they won't be good memories; it will just be shameful. I try not to jab sticks in your sore places, Shenkov, so if you'd maybe return the favour.' He had to press his hand over his eyes.

Shenkov touched his wrist and guided it away from his face with one hand, and held his neck with the other. He didn't kiss him, just came an inch more than halfway, then shied back to half. Valery froze hopelessly. It wasn't real. Just alcohol.

Twenty years ago he would have said so. He might even have been angry. But he was too tired to say it now, and had been too tired for years. Being wanted for an hour, even when it was just a mirage of vodka fumes, was a lot better than not at all. At twenty-six, he hadn't understood what *not at all* meant.

He expected to be shoved against the wall. Cheap violence was how these things went and it was always awful as much as it was reassuring. Every nerve in him was braced for it, wound too tight, but it didn't happen. Shenkov stayed sitting, and only interlaced their hands.

When he woke, it was early, and he had a second of total confusion during which he couldn't remember where he was or why, and the horrible thought occurred that the Lighthouse and freedom and all of it were nothing but the rags of fever dream. It came back quickly, though, with the sound of the traffic on the road below. The room was dark, the blackout curtains shut, but there was just enough light where they didn't quite meet to show that it was morning. Moscow; the hotel. Right. He felt himself go slack with relief and then realised someone else's arm was across him. Fitted close to him still, Shenkov was warm against his back.

He stared for a long time at the lamp. There was just enough light to sheen on the steel base. If he could get up now, there was every chance Shenkov had drunk enough yesterday not to remember anything at all, or at least, to remember so hazily that he would never have the confidence to mention it.

And if not; if not, if Shenkov was ashamed enough and humiliated enough, they were never going to talk again.

He knew dimly that there existed people who didn't care one way or another, but he had never met any and he was pretty sure that most of them had been shot by now.

Despite all that, his whole body ached with relief to wake up like this, close to someone else. Too late, he realised his eyes stung; when he blinked, tears tapped against the pillow, and his lashes scratched. The sound seemed immense in the silence. He swallowed hard, painfully aware that his ribs would jolt if his breath caught too badly, and eased Shenkov's arm away, raging at himself.

The phone rang.

Twenty to eight wake-up call.

It made both of them jump. Valery snatched the receiver and dropped it again, fast. He sat with his hand still on it. Shenkov was upright too, just a shadow and a few silver traces in the line of daylight from the curtains. Valery wanted to say something and couldn't. Shenkov didn't either. He must have been cold in the night, because he had a jumper on now, and he was pulling the sleeves over his hands as though he would have liked never to touch anything ever again.

Valery fell asleep almost the moment they were on the plane, and again in the car on the way back to City 40 from the airport. He had a feeling that his psyche was trying to cram in as much sleep as it could while there were other people close by and the thrum of the engine was loud.

It felt like a few seconds before Shenkov was shaking his shoulder to say they were at home again. Groggy, because it hadn't been proper sleep, he dragged himself up and followed.

It was snowing, and everything was strangely, deeply quiet. The cab made dark tracks as it pulled away, and for once, the lights inside the sterile research building looked warm. The journey had taken all day, and in the mauve twilight, everything was still and abandoned; the crane above the new reactor building had stopped at an odd angle, and the usually noisy diggers and bulldozers were quiet under white shrouds. The air had a new, sharp tang to it. The winter, the real winter, was finally rolling in over the Urals.

'I'm going home,' Shenkov said. It was the first he'd spoken since the night before. He was holding the keys to one of the facility cars. 'I'll see you on Monday.'

Of course it was Friday. Echoing, the weekend stretched ahead with all its tenantless hours, and Valery only just remembered to nod. Even though he was certain he wouldn't see him on Monday. Or, perhaps he would, but at a distance. It would only ever be at a distance, from now on.

He turned inside alone. He stole into Shenkov's apartment feeling like a thief to feed Albert, then left fast, into the screaming emptiness of the corridor, and the denser silence of his own flat. There was nothing but the tinny crackle of the bugs. He switched the radio on for voices, and the television, though they clashed. He listened for a long time without hearing, then had to press his hands over his mouth so that he could cry without making a sound, in case anyone in the security office was listening.

23

Stardust

The lab seemed much bigger without anyone in it. It was bright, both from the tall windows that overlooked the lake, and the bleak fluorescents, and without the shadows and shapes of other people to break it up, the light was stark and cold. Valery stood on the threshold for a moment, fighting the urge to turn straight back around and go to the crowded canteen, but after firmly calling himself a moron, he stepped inside. The silence roared and he had to put the radio on. Someone had knocked it, so there was only static at first and his heart clenched, but then he relaxed when he found human voices on the news. He took down an aquarium box of control-group mice. They scuffled excitedly when he gave them some carrots.

He had been working for an hour or so when someone tapped on the door. He looked up, expecting one of the students, and had a lurch of sorrow-joy when he saw it was Shenkov. Shenkov and a little girl with curly hair and freckles. She was about six.

'Hey. This is Tatiana. She was hoping to visit the mice,' Shenkov said. He sounded muted; he didn't want to be here.

Valery wondered what was going on. Not a shouting match, surely; not in front of a little girl. Unless she was here to show Shenkov's moral high ground. As if Valery didn't already know where the high ground was. 'They're not very tame,' he said, wary. 'They bite.'

'I don't care about mice,' Tatiana said, puzzled.

Shenkov was taking on the grim look of an actor who was determined to say his lines properly even though everyone else had forgotten theirs. 'Tanya, say hello to Comrade Kolkhanov.'

'Hello,' she said, cheery despite the mice lie. She bobbed across, ignored the mice, and climbed up on the chair beside Valery to look at the microscope. 'What are you doing?'

'Looking at blood samples.' He moved the eyepiece for her, wishing Shenkov would just go, and take the evidence of his wonderful wholesome family with him.

She leaned down. 'It's like jewels!'

He glanced at Shenkov, who seemed tired. He wasn't dressed for work, just in an ordinary jumper, the same one he had had at the hotel, grey and heavy. It made him look softer, and younger.

'I imagine Dr Kolkhanov has a lot of things you can look at,' he said. Where it rested on the table, his hand was shaking. He pulled it away.

Valery felt the way he had when the soldiers bundled him into the back of the van outside the cafe in town. He didn't want to talk. He would have happily taken all of it to his grave. There was nothing Shenkov could say that Valery didn't already know. People did stupid things after three quarters of a bottle of vodka; people did stupid things when they were relieved about not having been shot.

'I do,' Valery said. Whatever was going on, maybe it would reveal itself once Tatiana was occupied. 'Do you want to see?' he added to Tatiana, who nodded fast. You could tell she was the youngest of a lot of children. If there was something she wanted, she was used to diving on it before anyone else nabbed it.

So he set her up with the spare microscope and a selection of sample slides. Some of them were from leaves, some from fur, or insects. She stared down the scope as if it were a window into another universe. When he took out the watercolour pencils for her, she squeaked and set to straight away with the record sheets. He paused when he noticed her arms. She was covered in rashes, so risen he had thought she was wearing long pinkish sleeves. They looked like nettle stings.

'Sorry to interrupt,' Shenkov said quietly. He had seen Valery notice the marks. 'We can go, if you're busy.'

'No we can't,' Tatiana put in quickly, and rolled the pencils protectively under her hand. 'You said Mum needed a rest—'

'No, I know, but we don't need to take up all of Comrade Kolkhanov's time—'

'So why did we come?'

Shenkov looked like he wanted to die. 'Because he's a doctor and he might be able to tell us why you're so ill.'

Valery pulled his eyes up slowly, then down again at the marks on Tatiana's arms. She was covered in bruises too. He hadn't noticed before; she seemed like the kind of child to be forever slinging herself out of trees and getting into disagreements with hedges, so it hadn't stood out. But there were a lot.

'I'm not ill now, look! All better, I was just being silly this morning.'

'No, you weren't.'

Tatiana looked at Valery. 'We can stay, right?'

'Yes. I didn't make that up for you,' Valery said, nodding at the record sheet. 'I'm terrible at drawing. If you don't do it then it won't get done.'

She beamed.

Some of the tightness eased from Shenkov's shoulders, but not much. 'You said a while ago – or I think you did, I was busy ignoring you . . . you said radiation could cause allergies. She's allergic to everything. She's ill all the time, she bruises like . . .'

'I'm *normal*, Dad, you're just hysterical.' She looked at Valery. 'The other doctors said that.'

Across from them, Shenkov folded his arms as if she'd pelted him with spilled plutonium.

Valery wondered which poor, scared doctor had had to look at their monthly quota for the diagnosis of radiation-related problems, look Shenkov right in the eye, and promise all was well. 'Want to see your own blood under that microscope?'

She stuck her arm out, watched him take the blood sample, and then peeped into the microscope with him when he put a dot of it under a slide. 'It's moving.'

Valery had to force himself to smile, because he could see what was happening to her, even just in those cells. 'Yes, it's supposed to, don't worry. That means you're alive.'

'Can I do you?'

'Yes. Look, new syringe, and then . . .' He showed her how to do it, and how to use the sample slide, and how to put it under the microscope. While Tatiana was drawing red blood cells, Valery nodded at Dr Resovskaya's empty office. 'Your dad and I are just going to get a cup of tea, do you want anything?'

'I'm more of a coffee person,' she said.

'Okay.'

When they shut the office door, Shenkov put his back against it. 'She doesn't really like coffee, she's just heard Anna say that, and . . .'

'No, I know,' Valery said over him, because it would have been cruel to make him speak more than necessary now. 'It's leukaemia. It's a bone disorder. Bone marrow is where we generate white blood cells, which fight infection, but her marrow is generating too many white cells, too quickly; they're not mature, so they can't fight. Hence all the colds and the allergies.'

What was left of Shenkov's calm fissured. 'You can tell that just from one dot of blood on a slide? In two minutes?'

'Yes.'

'I've spent – *years* trying to get the doctors in town to look at her properly. They just say she's . . .' He couldn't finish.

'No. They have those quotas.' Valery remembered why they were supposed to be there and put the kettle on. 'Listen. I'm not a medical doctor, I can't prescribe anything, but the quota cut-off is the fifteenth and it's only the thirteenth today. I'll give you the blood sample and the analysis to show the doctor here, and she'll do the referral to Chelyabinsk. Leukaemia isn't curable, but it is treatable.'

Shenkov was watching a flock of ducks fly across the black lake. 'Is it this place?'

'Leukaemia can be genetic, so perhaps not. But it is a known complication of radiation exposure. Foetal DNA is particularly affected. She was the baby Anna was pregnant with, when . . . ?'

'That Christmas.' Shenkov looked past him, at the window that faced into the lab. Tatiana was working on the slides still. 'How long does she have? Just – be honest, please, don't . . .'

Valery almost smiled, because usually if he had to give an ill person a life expectancy, it was measured in weeks. He was brilliant at it. He had never been hesitant about telling people they wouldn't see Christmas. Dr Fischer had once pointed out, looking shocked, that maybe it wasn't very good to tell a person dying of acute radiation sickness that she should probably do her best to enjoy Halloween.

'About five years, I think, if we can keep her healthy.'

A long, long quiet. Through the glass, Valery could hear the squeak of the pencils as Tatiana coloured in, pressing too hard. Shenkov looked so absent from himself that Valery thought he might collapse. He moved a chair and put him in it.

'Come and look at my drawing!' Tatiana called.

Shenkov looked up and afraid. 'She's going to ask—'

'It's okay, I'll talk to her. Do you want me to tell her, or stall?'

Shenkov didn't say anything.

Valery bent a little to find his eyes again. 'Did you hear me?'

'What?'

He was in no state to decide. 'I said, could you make the coffee?'

Shenkov looked relieved for something to do.

Valery shut the office door behind him and went over to Tatiana. He was genuinely impressed with the drawing; she was good.

'Was Dad being bad?' she asked.

'How do you mean?'

'At school, Comrade Alexandrovna says that if people start sneaking around and doing bad things like whispering and being spies, we have to tell her all about it. I want to catch a spy one day,' she added hopefully.

Valery smiled. 'No. Your dad's boringly good. We were talking about your blood. Some things have gone wrong in it, which is why you're ill. Can I show you?'

She nodded and watched as he put the slide back under the microscope, and refocused it to show her the sick white cells, and how they were different to his own.

'This is what's making you so ill,' he said, sitting back and sharply aware that he smelled of cigarettes, and that she wouldn't want to breathe that for a second longer than she had to. 'It's not something we know how to cure. That means you will probably die of it. Do you know what dying is?'

She nodded again. 'You stop, and you turn back into stars. Mum says everyone's made of stars. Is that true?'

'Yes,' he said, and liked Anna even more than before. 'All matter is forged by nuclear fusion reactions in the hearts of stars. They take hydrogen atoms, which are the littlest bits of the stuff the world is made of, and they bolt them together into bigger and bigger atoms – helium, oxygen, carbon, everything. All the atoms that make you. You're star dust.'

She looked pleased with that. 'And then when my atoms have finished being me, they go off back to the stars?'

'Some of them will be rain, some will be earth, some will float away and light up when the solar wind comes, and that makes the aurora. And like you say, some of them will find their way back into a star.'

'Will I *know*?'

'I don't know. Nobody knows.'

She looked worried.

'That's the best kind of research,' he said gently. 'The chance to find out a thing *no one* knows – that's not something that comes along all the time. It's scary, and you don't know where you'll end up, which is why most people aren't too keen. But every now and then, there's one brilliant person who just dives in. An explorer. Like Valentina Tereshkova. You know who that is?'

Tatiana shook her head.

Valery pushed his hands into his pockets. The stamp was there; he had been moving it religiously between pockets whenever laundry day came around. He still couldn't have said exactly why. He put it on the table. 'She's a cosmonaut.'

Like he'd hoped, Tatiana started to get a little spark. 'When will I go?'

'Hard to say. Before you're grown up, but not right now.'

She thought about it. 'Do you have to pack, for dying?'

'No. You don't take anything, just yourself.'

Her eyes came up fast. 'Like the people on the red trains,' she said quietly.

He had to sit down. He could deal with a six-year-old who wanted to ask about dying, and he could explain nuclear fusion to anyone who was happy to hear him bore on about it, but the idea of the trains hit him like a bullet in the gut. 'No. No, not like that. Where did you see the red trains?'

'At Chelyabinsk station. They go to the bad places.'

'Yes. They do.' He sighed. 'But not you. This is . . . something else altogether. There's no train, for you.'

'Are you sure?'

'I am certain.'

'Okay,' she said. 'Do you think the coffee will be ready soon?'

'It's ready now,' Shenkov said as he came out of the office with it. He looked wrecked but steadier. When he put their cups down beside them, he squeezed Valery's shoulders, very softly. It felt like it might mean they weren't going to have a row quite yet.

Shenkov came back in the evening without her. He was washed out. Valery had just finished replacing the water in Albert's tank. Now, Albert was back inside, flashing alternately red and black to the tune of the nine o'clock news. Valery was on the floor by the coffee table so that he could watch it without his glasses. The newer prescription was giving him a headache in the evenings still, while he got used to it. He had found a patch where the heating pipes ran right underneath. He'd meant only to stay for a minute or two, just for the headlines, while he tried to decide what to do with Albert and the tank now that he wouldn't be coming in here any more.

'I'm sorry, I thought you'd be at home till tomorrow,' Valery said, horribly conscious that Shenkov had probably expected to come back to a nice, empty apartment. He got up fast, meaning to go.

Shenkov dropped down next to where Valery had been on the floor and seemed not to hear. 'The doctor rushed it straight off. Anna's with her in Chelyabinsk,' he said.

Valery nodded a little. 'Good.'

'They're talking about bone marrow transplants. They tested all of us to see if we're . . .' He couldn't find the word and looked at Valery for it.

'Compatible. There's a high chance one of you will be.'

Shenkov looked up. 'Where are you going?'

Valery sat back down again. They watched the news, right into the local-interest stories.

Then, 'Do you remember the story about Sverdlov, from school?' Shenkov said.

'Do I?' Valery asked aloud, because consulting memories from Before felt like requesting them from someone separate, someone who he knew, but not well.

'Early days of the Party. He was sitting in the canteen at headquarters after the revolution. He'd been separated from his family years before in the fighting, hadn't seen them in all that time. Anyway, a soldier comes up to him and she says, *Comrade Sverdlov, I recognise you, you're my father. May I have three roubles to buy lunch?* And Sverdlov says, *Of course, everyone should be able to afford lunch, here you are.* And he goes back to his work.'

Valery had a distant memory of school, and of Svetlana pretending to be sick under the table. 'That rings a bell, now you say.'

'Yes.' Shenkov was quiet for a moment. 'I used to want a chance to be that way. And now this is it. Labour before family.'

Valery wrinkled his nose. 'Really? He sounds like he needed pushing off a bridge.'

Shenkov laughed. 'There's you with your golden halo looking angelic and then what do you come out with? Filth.'

'Angelic isn't what it's cracked up to be,' Valery said, over the instinct to tell Shenkov not to take the piss. He was beginning to wonder, very cautiously, if Shenkov wasn't doing anything of the kind. Self-conscious, he straightened out a curl of his hair to see it. Shenkov was right, it had turned proper gold again. 'I was a choirboy before the war. I was in the Komsomol, I enforced kolkhozes in Ukraine, I reported my parents to the police and everything, sent them to prison. The Party gave me a special award.'

'You did not,' Shenkov said. He looked urgently relieved to have something to think about other than Tatiana, so Valery told him about it.

24

Sand

It had been two weeks since Moscow, and the concrete still hadn't come. Every morning, Valery went down to the KGB office to have the prisoner book stamped and to see if there was any word, and every morning, there was nothing. Shenkov stamped the book and signed it every day, and as Valery had thought, that was all the overlap they had. Talking about Tatiana hadn't mended anything. Valery suspected Shenkov was ashamed of having had to talk to him at all.

The evenings, endless, were in the lab with the radio if there was any conceivable work to do, and in the silent flat if not. He stopped sleeping, again. The nights were all useless panic and the radio or the television tuned to the hallucinatory things that aired at three in the morning. Every ten minutes or so, on a clockwork goldfish loop, he wanted to go and see who was on duty at the security office, as if that would do anything except get him a punch in the eye.

At the start of the third week, he arrived at the security office in time to hear what sounded like the tail end of a row. Anna Shenkovna was there, not shouting exactly but speaking very clearly and fluently in the way people do when they intend to continue even if somebody else comes in with an axe.

'—false economy, given that the not unlikely outcome is the necessity of replacing, this time, not one but *six* reactors—'

'Anna, I know—'

'—and so it seems short-sighted to just nod to Moscow and say yes. Oh, morning Kolkhanov. Have you heard about this?'

'About what?' Valery asked, who was insomnia-slow and hadn't got together the basic wit to stop walking before he reached the door. He wanted to promise he hadn't been eaves-dropping, but trying to catch words this week was like trying to judge distances without his glasses on. He couldn't think of an excuse to turn around and retreat to the lab. Mouse emer-gencies weren't very common, and Anna was already talking again.

'Apparently,' she said, 'they're sending not cement but a large quantity of sand.'

He forgot about everything else. 'Sand.'

'It's cost-effective.'

'It is not cost-effective if six nuclear reactors explode.'

'I'll just open the window and point you both towards Moscow, shall I?' Shenkov said, and unlike Anna, the wreckage of whatever argument they'd just had was still raw in his voice. He pushed the door shut.

Anna ignored him. 'We need to call the Kremlin and tell them to send cement like they agreed in the first place,' she said to Valery. 'I wanted to wait for you; they've spoken to you already, they're not going to take a random call from me.'

Valery put the kettle on, half to have an excuse to stay over the other end of the room from them. Even disagreeing, they were too united a front, too much an *us* against a *you*. Tribunal and criminal. 'If Moscow have decided they don't care if they lose six reactors and a hundred thousand people, then they don't care. We've spoken to Slavsky; there are no more facts to hand over.'

Shenkov was much too restrained to wave at Valery and yell, *yes, that*; he was standing very still, his hands by his sides, but he took a breath as though he wanted to speak, and inclined towards Valery, just a few centimetres, before he caught himself.

'No,' said Anna, 'they assuredly care if they lose six reactors. Some idiot in cost analysis or whatever has down-played it, though, and now Slavsky has got it into his thick skull that this isn't urgent.'

Valery measured out coffee. It felt strange to do it for three people. 'I don't think it was some idiot. It could have been Elena Resovskaya.'

Anna looked confused. It was the first time he had seen her do that. 'I don't understand why she's so against it. All her studies are in the forest. Unless she's doing a study on the effect of exploding mud on the local heron population, I don't see how fixing this will affect anything she does.'

'It's the water table,' Valery explained. 'The water from these lakes feeds everything round here for a hundred kilometres, but if they start damming off parts to keep the marsh drained, then the conditions will change.'

'So we should all explode quietly and without fuss?'

'She doesn't think we will. It came from me and I've a history of disapproving of the studies she works on. I think she thinks I'm . . . doing some moral peacocking.'

'The wonderful thing about telephones,' she said drily, 'is that we can bypass all that if we just call Slavsky.'

'Okay. I'll call him with you.'

'Kolkhanov!' Shenkov said. He went quieter with urgency, not louder; he was so quiet now that Valery had to come nearer to hear him. 'None of us can do that. If we start calling Moscow sounding angry, someone's going to accuse us of criticising the Ministry. It's treason. We'll all be shot.'

'A hundred thousand people live here,' Anna said, incredulous. 'It would be worth getting shot.'

'No, it wouldn't, because you'd be dead and they would still be sending sand,' Shenkov said. He shook his head once, like someone had flicked boiling water at him. 'Losing six reactors and a hundred thousand people isn't what bothers the Ministry. What bothers them is that the West might find out. Any weakness, anything, that gets out and towards the CIA, that's worse. They're not wrong either. They know that our only strength is in how strong we *seem*. If it preserves that illusion, then the loss of six reactors is worth it. Reactors can be rebuilt. The illusion can't be. An explosion happens, the CIA notice, fine: it's weapons testing, look what we can do. Great. Word gets out that the Ministry is acting to make safe something the reactor staff have screwed up so terribly that it could cause a massive accident on a scale never seen before: that's a problem. That's evidence of weakness in a way the blast itself isn't. No?'

Anna glanced at Valery. 'We have to try.'

'Anna – we have four children, please swear to me you're not going to call Moscow—'

'Don't be so bloody American,' she said sharply, and it was the first time she had really sounded angry. Valery wished he could be somewhere else. 'The children would survive without me, they're not idiots. They would not, however, survive a thermonuclear blast encompassing six reactors built less than a kilometre away from where they live.'

'Anna, you can't call anyone, you *can't*,' Shenkov said. His voice was shattering now. 'What if you're wrong? What if it's all fine, what if it's just what Dr Resovskaya thinks? You'll have died for nothing—'

'We're not wrong. Labour before family, Kostya, it's who we are,' she said, this time with real ire. She turned to him like a sniper. 'Or do you want it to be God in heaven and father in the house?'

Shenkov looked utterly helpless. If she had shot him in the chest, it would have been better. Valery didn't know very much about Shenkov's father but even with the tiny snippet he did know, he could see that the idea of becoming that man was Shenkov's own private hell vision.

'What are you doing?' Shenkov said to Valery, who had picked up the phone.

'Calling the Ministry,' Valery said. He looked between them. He couldn't stand hearing them argue any more, and it was giving him the ghost pain of the cattle prod, but he didn't know any magic tricks for this one. 'What? You're both right. Someone needs to call, and whoever calls might get shot. And I'm sorry to contradict noble social ideals with biochemistry, but saying you should forget about your kids is like trying to argue that you shouldn't have arms.'

They both looked ashamed.

'Get out, both of you. Go and talk to someone who'll remember talking to you. And if anyone asks, I snuck in here and used your phone without permission.' They still weren't moving. 'You'd have both saved a lot of time, by the way, if you'd rung me up and said, *Valery, you don't have kids, make this call for us.*'

'We're not nominating you to risk your life just because you happen not to have children,' Anna said, her voice rising. 'That's foul, Kolkhanov, worth isn't conferred on a person according to whether or not they have children. You—'

'It is conferred that way. Don't,' he added to Shenkov, who had taken a step towards him. 'Go on, both of you, out. I'll see you in fifteen minutes.'

It was, after all that, a straightforward phone call. He waited on hold for a minute or so for Slavsky, who, when he did answer, was pleasant. He did question whether the concrete really was necessary, and then whether they could make their *own* concrete with the sand supplies at City 40, but hummed in agreement when Valery pointed out that silica was only one of seven key ingredients in concrete, and that without the sulphur and magnesium, the tensile strength would be damn all, the whole lot would crack and the water problem would be the same as ever. Asphalt or tarmac would be fine too. The equivalent of a large car park. And engineers to drain the marsh. They couldn't pour concrete on soaking ground. Slavsky agreed.

'It was good of you to call, comrade,' he said at last. 'Rather brave, actually.'

The line clicked and died.

Valery supposed that was Slavsky's way of suggesting he enjoy the next few days before he turned up dead under a hedge.

Shenkov tilted the door open. He and Anna were still just outside, exactly where Valery had left them.

'Slavsky says we can have the concrete.'

'Well done,' Anna said. She seemed smaller than before.

'Don't say that yet. Fifty-fifty it doesn't turn up. Right; I'd better get to the lab.'

'Kolkhanov.' She stopped him, only lightly, one arm out shy of his chest. They were the same height, but there was much more of her and he couldn't have gone by if he had tried. 'Don't think we don't realise that we just used our children as human shields.'

'Don't be so stupid,' he said, even though an evil little voice in the back of his mind hissed that that was exactly what they'd done. He stamped on it, hard.

He smiled. 'Anyway, I'd better go.'

Already, there was work going on at the lake bank, over near the main reactor; they were building what must have been the new waste drain, to pump the nuclear slag straight into the water.

Not ideal though that was, the water would look magnificent once there was a decent amount of radioactive waste in it. It would turn the most incredible turquoise. He liked that; a lot of things went a bright colour to warn you that they were poisonous, and it was helpful of even lakes to do the same thing.

The lake surface was dancing. It was raining. Not the fine drizzle that had come down after the first snow a few weeks ago; driving, wetlands rain. It made a cosy sound on the roof, and on the plastic lids of the biowaste bins. Like always, there were diggers and building trucks out in force, at work on the new reactor building, and the workmen were hurrying to and fro with their hard-hats pulled down to shield their eyes.

Out on the marshes, the reed groves nodded, and the pools gleamed grey. Something in the forest cracked – more falling branches probably – audible even over the beep of reversing trucks and the deep, ever-present hum of the reactors.

A fountain of mud exploded just on the nearer lake shore.

'Oop! Points for me. We're playing more geyser bingo,' one of the students said, and drew a little happy face on a chart.

Valery was glad they were cheerful.

'God, already,' Resovskaya said, doing her trick of appearing from what had been her empty office. She was looking at the digging work. 'Our data's going to be worthless.'

He watched for a moment and saw her afresh, properly. He had been seeing her younger film-star self all along, but she was getting old, and ill. Either this place or something else was taking its toll. Her hands looked bad, the knuckles swollen, and he was sure she was walking more awkwardly now than she had even a few weeks ago when he first arrived. She wasn't wearing her sparkly red shoes any more, but flat ones, ugly and comfortable. She was too proud to say that she wanted her human trial done, and the results in and published, somewhere, before she died of whatever was draining her like this. 'I know,' he said. 'Elena, I'm sorry. But what if there really is a hundred kilograms of pluto-nium out there, ready to go off? They can't add any more to it. And they certainly can't keep digging trenches out there.' He hesitated. 'Whatever happens now, whatever the delays, your name is stamped on this place. You're legendary.'

She gave him the bitterest look anyone ever had. 'My name, and yours, will be redacted on every document that comes from here. This isn't about my ego. This is about the work. This trial could be the difference between knowing what to do when the Americans drop a bomb on Moscow, and not. But you object to human radiation studies, so you and the sainted Anna Shenkovna, who wants desperately to get out of here and back to her cosy tenure position at the Kurchatov Institute, spun a stupid story about a bit of caesium. No?'

He took his glasses off to have something in his hands. 'No. It isn't a stupid story, it—'

'—was unevidenced, and you scared the director into talking to the Ministry. Those geysers could be anything, but you pushed this caesium idea because you knew that even while Slavsky would never evacuate this place, you could at least bugger the trial enough to get it shut down. Or did that never once slither across your mind?'

'It honestly didn't,' he said. 'I didn't work out the caesium and the geysers, Anna did, while we were at that table. We didn't – we didn't come up with a story and plot beforehand.'

'Yes,' she said drily, 'it's funny how I don't believe you.'

25

The Asylum

The rain turned to snow again, and the ground froze. This time, it froze properly. The frost arrived instantly, overnight, riming everything with ice after a night that plunged down to minus eighteen degrees. It was a Sunday, and Valery was still curled up in a ball in bed, watching Albert turn his tank heater right up. On the reasoning that an octopus was the best person to know how warm or cool an octopus wanted to be, Valery had shown him how to use it and put an octopus-friendly lever on the dial, in case dripping shorted the electrics. It seemed to work, and it saved him from worrying that Albert would freeze in the night. He blinked slowly. Even his eyes were cold. Albert stayed bobbing on the surface, as near to the heater as he could safely get.

Very carefully, a lot more aware of every single exposed square centimetre of himself than he ever had been at the camp – this was the peril of relative comfort – he went to the window. Outside, everything was white. The lake was frozen. He pulled on another jumper and folded his arms tight for a moment, then gave Albert a huge portion of breakfast crab. Digestion heated you up. Albert flashed yellow and did a victory lap.

Valery wondered exactly *how* frozen the lake was. When he went outside to see, it was frozen perfectly; mirror-smooth, interrupted only where the bulrushes pushed up through the ice.

Two of the students were out doing the same thing. One of them bounced experimentally on the edge of the ice, which didn't even creak.

'We found skates in the supply cupboard,' one of them said. 'What do you think?'

'I think we should get those right now,' said Valery.

They were the kind that went on over your own boots, but that was fine if you pulled the strings tight enough. They all teetered together to the lake shore, laughing, because it was hard to balance on skates on the frozen grass. All of Valery's muscles opened up, relieved, when he reached the ice and he could glide. When he looked back, both of the students had collapsed.

'It looked easier than it is,' reported the one who had been crushed underneath. Valery untangled them and helped them up, and made sure they had their stopwatches.

Maybe other people had noticed them or maybe come out of their own accord, but over the next few minutes, more little groups arrived. Valery's heart did an unpleasant lurch when he saw Shenkov and Tatiana. Tatiana was dressed as the Snow Maiden, including a paper snowflake crown. When she saw Valery, she waved and rushed across. She couldn't skate yet, so she just sort of clunked, and he had to catch her before she went flying. He didn't have the heart to say she shouldn't be skating. Soon, she would be exhausted all the time, and she wouldn't have the energy for any of it. Better to let her do it all while she could.

'Hello!'

'Like the crown,' he said.

'I made it. Can you skate? I'm rubbish, and Dad won't come on the ice. He says tall people fall further.'

Valery offered his hands and skated backwards to tug her along forwards. She told him about the hospital in Chelyabinsk, which she liked, and the market in town where a fake Father Frost was giving everyone sweets.

'The real Father Frost lives in the forest,' she said. 'Mum says that if I'm bad I'll have to go and live with him.'

'Well, he's all right as long as you're polite,' Valery said. He had a dim recollection of a fairy tale that asserted so, anyway.

'No, he's definitely imaginary,' she said severely. 'How do I go backwards?'

He showed her, still holding her hand, very aware that he didn't want her to fall. He didn't know the state of her bones, but it wouldn't be strong. But she had good balance, so very slowly, he straightened up again and taught her how to spin. When it was her turn, he kept his hands to either side of her ribs just in case. He only set her right twice before she got it.

'Arms up like a ballerina – and bow. Nice!'

'Let's show Dad!'

Valery swallowed and took her back to the shore, where Shenkov had been watching with both hands in his pockets.

'You can really skate,' Shenkov said.

'Ice hockey,' Valery explained. He squashed down a blast of memories from an overeager bit of his brain. Hadn't they won something, some inter-university thing that Svetlana had watched in full army uniform to psych out the other team? He didn't want to remember. 'We'd better get off the lake, it's been half an hour.'

'Why is there the half-an-hour rule?' Tatiana asked.

'We'll get too cold,' Shenkov told her. 'I'm already too cold.'

'You're always too cold,' Tatiana told him. 'You should pretend not to be so cold, or everyone will think you're a foreigner and put you in prison.'

'You know there are bits of the Soviet Union that aren't cold. Ones with actual liquid water,' Shenkov said, lifting her off the ice. He glanced at Valery. 'Come with us? We're going to find a cafe. Hot drinks.' It was a politeness offer, not a real one.

'Or,' said Tatiana, patriotically, 'cold ones.'

'Thanks, but I should get to work,' said Valery, balancing to undo the skate laces before he had to step on to the shore again.

'I can't do it,' Tatiana said to her own laces. She studied her fingernails. 'My tools of the patriarchy are getting too long.'

Valery laughed so much he had to pull his sleeve over his eyes. Shenkov only smiled, and then looked emptied out.

As they began to move away, a man in a long coat did the same. He had been sitting on a bench, smoking, for nearly the whole time Valery had been there, just watching people skate, without so much as a newspaper to keep himself entertained. He saw Valery notice him and saluted with his cigarette hand.

'That didn't take long,' Shenkov said. He was looking back too.

'What didn't?' Tatiana asked.

'That man back there is following Comrade Kolkhanov.'

'They only follow you around to make sure you're not evil,' Tatiana said factually. 'And Comrade Kolkhanov's not, so that's fine.'

'I don't think he's just following,' Valery said, because the man was coming closer.

The asylum was cold. So were the thin white clothes. Valery sat by the window, watching the snow. He hadn't said anything on the way, or during processing, when a doctor had explained, doing his absolute best to keep a straight face but not quite succeeding, that Moscow had raised concerns about Valery's mental stability, and it had been decided he ought to stay here for a while. Mixing science and politics was a telltale sign of – well, troubles. Valery didn't ask for how long. He would find out, he supposed, soon enough.

A young man who spoke like a little boy shuffled up to him and gave him a child's story book about a polar bear, so Valery settled him on the windowsill and read it to him. The big room, where patients seemed to be free to do what they liked, smelled of damp. Valery breathed slowly and tried to think, but that was proving difficult.

He was reading the polar-bear story to the young man for the third time when he got himself calm enough to watch the doctors and nurses. They were clipping to and fro casually, without burly orderlies. Nobody here was dangerous, then. That was something.

What he couldn't understand was why anyone had bothered to do this to him when he was still a zek. He could have been sent back to Kolyma if Slavsky were irritated enough. The prison trains went from Chelyabinsk; Tatiana had seen them. It would have been much easier, and no doubt less paperwork.

Unless this was an example. Unless his name was, right now, going in the newspapers here: LIGHTHOUSE SCIENTIST DEEMED UNSTABLE AFTER DEVIANT ACTIVITIES. It would stick, because every student in the lab knew he was odd anyway, and quietly, people would take note, and make sure not to take an interest in soil chromatography, in caesium, or the geysers on the marsh. Perhaps this was happening not because it was easier to send him here, but easier to send other scientists here if they did what he had done. Perhaps even Slavsky was tired of ordering Shenkov to shoot people. This was as good a threat as a gun. Better. They didn't admit to shooting people. Resovskaya had told the students that Ilenko had been called back to Moscow, not killed. This could be a public cautionary tale.

Even that didn't sound right. He was sure he was missing something, but then, that confidence in things being logical was what got you killed. None of it was ever logical. Maybe he was here because it had struck some administrator as a bit more interesting than the gulag, or because the train timetables were being re-done, or a coin toss.

In the evening, they put him in a room on his own. There was a bed and sink, so it was much better than prison. He sank on to the edge of the thin mattress and felt grateful for small mercies. Down the echoey corridor, people were talking. Some were laughing, some were upset or unsettled, he suspected because he was a new person.

The front part of his mind tried to surface, and tried to wonder whether he would be allowed visitors, whether Shenkov knew where he was, if it was worth escaping or if this was just a warning shot and really he would be here only for a month and all he needed to do was wait it out. He didn't have enough information to decide one way or another. The possibilities just chased each other around and around.

A doctor stopped in the doorway, holding a clipboard. She looked as if she had been awake all week.

'I expect you want to ask someone for a lawyer or a phone call,' she said exhaustedly, 'but I'm afraid that isn't going to happen. The application to have you committed has come from your employer, who, because you're a zek, is also your sponsor, so there's no appeal. Sorry about that.'

'Can't do anything if the Ministry says so,' Valery said. 'I understand, don't worry.'

'Not many people are so quiet and polite as you. Are you plotting something?' she said, with the shreds of good humour.

He smiled. 'No. No, it just doesn't seem fair to throw a tantrum. It's not your fault.'

She paused. 'It wasn't the Ministry. In your file I've got down a Dr Resovskaya.' She looked up. She was gaunt, but there was a glint in her. 'Think you probably have the right to know who did this to you, comrade.'

'Thanks,' he said softly.

Of course; if he was demonstrably insane, then everything he had said to Slavsky could be labelled hysteria. Resovskaya was stopping the changes to the marshland and the contamination levels. She might save her human study after all.

He pressed his hands over his eyes. Maybe it really had been hysterical to insist like he had. After all, Resovskaya was right; he had one strip of caesium from one dig site and Anna's guess about some geysers. There was every chance he was wrong, and every chance Resovskaya was right. Historically, she tended to be right. Which would mean that she had done exactly what she had to, to keep together integrity of a study so vital it easily outbalanced one small life.

It was early in the morning and silence was crouched bristling over the ward when a doctor unlocked Valery's door, looking flustered.

'Um, Comrade Kolkhanov; you're to come with me.'

Valery stood up slowly. Yes; of course there was a mistake. Someone had looked at a ledger and realised it was far cheaper to provide for a zek than a mental patient, and the red train was waiting.

26

The Raid

Shenkov was standing in the foyer while five KGB officers destroyed the records office. They were emptying cabinets, taking files, stacking everything into boxes. One of the doctors was trying to protest as Valery came by, and got a truncheon smack over the arm for it. Shenkov had his hands in his coat pockets, flint and austere like always, and managing to hold himself separate from the disinfectant smell of the corridor, and the cold that crept through the high windows. Valery had to stop walking, because it felt like taking a baseball bat to the chest. It was joy and dread at the same time. They'd sent Shenkov to arrest him. Jesus Christ, that was ironic justice right there.

Someone who might have been the director of the place came pounding down the stairs.

'What the *hell* do you think you're doing! This is—'

'One of your doctors is a Western spy,' Shenkov told him. Valery had time to wonder what could possibly be going on. 'Someone seems to be drugging scientists from the Lighthouse with truth serum and taking notes, which are being sent to an embassy in Moscow.' Shenkov held out an envelope to the director. 'This is a search warrant. Your facility will close while we analyse the evidence. Comrade Kolkhanov here will remain in our custody for his own security. You will cooperate with my officers.'

'What! But—'

'Thank you,' Shenkov said, and the director shrank back from him.

Valery's doctor had abandoned him and retreated. Shenkov held both his wrists out to show what he expected Valery to do, then put a pair of handcuffs on him with an efficient click. He did it very gently, fastening them over Valery's sleeves rather than against his skin. Then he turned him by his shoulder and steered him towards the front doors.

Grain by tipping grain, the possibility that there was no train and no camp trickled down into Valery's mind. He tried to stop it. This wasn't rescue, it couldn't be, Shenkov didn't have that sort of authority. It was much more likely that Shenkov was about to explain that he had orders to shoot him. Maybe there would be a chance to run, maybe as far as Nanya's village, but God, it was minus ten now, and the snow was deep.

Numbly, Valery let himself be led outside, up a snowy path that was orange under the street lamps, and into one of the black police cars. It was waiting with the heaters on, blissfully warm, and melting the snow beneath the engine. Shenkov got in beside him and pulled the door shut.

'What's happening?' Valery said, tight.

'I'm taking you home.'

'Then what?'

'Then nothing,' Shenkov said. He tipped forward a little to meet Valery's eyes. 'It's over.'

'What? But – there are charges, and Resovskaya—Moscow will find out in five minutes!' Valery exclaimed. 'You're crazy—'

'I've been police for twenty-five years, I know how to plant evidence,' Shenkov said. He checked the wing mirror and glanced back at the blind spot before he moved out into the road. It was still dark. Their headlights cut bright lines across the new snow. It felt desperately safe, to glide over it in a warm

Faraday cage. 'No one's being sent there for a good while now. If Resovskaya tries that again, I'll arrest her for feeding our spy new sources of information.'

'Thank you,' Valery whispered.

Shenkov didn't take his eyes off the road. 'Are you all right?'

'What? Oh. Yes, of course,' he said, dislocated from himself. 'They had central heating, it was great.' He found himself shaking his head, as if that would dislodge some helpful logic. 'Why did you do that?'

'Why did I– what was I going to do, leave you there?'

'Well – yes?' Valery said.

Shenkov looked hurt, but said nothing else.

The asylum was on the edge of the city, and soon the street lamps and the little tableaux of the apartment-tower windows were denser and brighter. Valery saw snatches of people getting ready for work, scraping snow off car windscreens, steam rising from running engines. The great cautionary posters sprawled over the sides of the shops and high-rises were drained of their colours, except for the vivid ribbons where electric light cut over them. As always in the early mornings, there was a water-tank lorry creeping down the main road, washing down the tarmac.

Turning off for the Lighthouse came with a wave of homecoming.

Constellations of lights sparkled in the reactor complex, which never slept. One of the security guards, anonymous under a heavy cap with fur ear flaps, gave them a friendly wave as they passed her. Gratitude for being allowed to see it all again was making all the details sharp; it was only now they were here, nearly home, that Valery understood how completely he had expected never to be back.

Shenkov pulled into the Lighthouse car park and turned off the engine, but he didn't open the door. 'Will you let me come in and make you some coffee?' he said quietly.

'No,' Valery said. 'No, I'm fine. Thank you. I'll let you get home.'

'No, I'm staying here tonight.'

'I thought you went home at the weekends?'

'Anna wants a divorce.'

Valery couldn't speak at first. 'Why?' he said at last, dreading the answer. Without the engine running, the cold was already flooding in through the windows and the footwells, but it seemed distant.

'Tatiana. It's the last straw.'

That wasn't what he'd expected. 'But that's not your fault.'

'It is. I did something powerfully stupid that got me sent here. All of us.' Shenkov smiled a fraction. 'And now Anna's barely got a thyroid and Tatiana's dying, and I'm fine. I'm healthy, I've never been better.'

'That's . . . to do with your body mass, not ironic justice,' said Valery. 'Unless you grew half a metre since you arrived here.' He hesitated. 'Are you – lying because you mean it's really my fault?' he asked.

'*Your* fault?' Shenkov's voice broke high. 'No. No. Look, if . . . I don't want to intrude if you have other things to do, but if you let me come up with you then I'll tell you about it.'

27

The Lubyanka (again)

The train was so crowded that people were standing up, but Shenkov had a KGB coat, so the seat beside him was empty. He found himself wishing someone would sit there.

When they did, he was surprised to see it was someone he knew. He hadn't seen the man for years, but they'd been in the Komsomol together, working on the construction of the White Canal. Sergei was, a decade later, just the same; his red hair had faded to a fox colour, and there were more lines round his eyes than there should have been on a man of forty, but far from changing him, it just made him look as though someone had put a softer filter over him. Behind him, some of the other passengers were looking disgruntled. He'd actually had to nudge his way through. Shenkov had a surge of gratitude.

'Konstantin,' Sergei said. 'How are you?'

Shenkov took a breath and tried to think of something, anything he could truthfully say in a packed train. *I work for the KGB now*; no, that was obvious; *I miss the White Canal*; no, because that would imply, to anyone listening – and there would be someone listening to him lately, given that he was up for promotion – that he wasn't ecstatic in the KGB. *Good*; no, because that would be a lie. *I'm married now*; who the hell opened with that to a man? No, but people did – didn't they? It seemed just as weird not to mention your own wife.

'Yes,' he said. He couldn't find anything else, feeling stupid. 'Yes.'

'Yes,' Sergei agreed, looking just as anxious as Shenkov felt. He unlooped his scarf and twisted it between his hands.

Shenkov swallowed. He wanted desperately to have a real conversation. He couldn't remember the last time he'd had one. In his bones, desperate. Like he'd been feeling the symptoms for a long, long time, but they'd only just managed to put themselves together at the thinking level of his mind, he realised that something in him was going to break if he didn't talk to someone soon. Talk, not just speak, especially after the shift just past, and the little girl, and the dog.

'Mine's the next stop,' he lied.

'Mine too,' Sergei lied back.

The night at the police station had been typical. It had rained, and when Shenkov got inside, he had to peel off the uniform leather jacket to keep from dripping all over the carpet, which the ferocious cleaners took a lot of pride in. As he walked down the corridor, the Commissioner leaned out of the big office and gave him a sheet of paper.

'Names, lots of names; normal drill, bugs in the phones and all that. And I want you to go in person to the raid on this house. Fellow's quite senior in the Party, he'll frighten the boys if we send them alone. We want his wife too. Both of their communication privileges are to be revoked.'

Shenkov looked up to check. It was what you said to relatives at the prison gates when you wanted them to go away: *nope, sorry, your husband's communication privileges have been revoked.* That was to say, he had been shot in the courtyard. 'He's got kids, hasn't he?'

'Three. Usual drill, there.'

He arranged his face carefully. He hated it when they had to take children. If they had nice relatives, someone would usually find out which orphanage had them and take them in, but if not; he'd started, anonymously, a set of files that he sent out at weekends to charitable institutions frequented by Party ladies, about adopting children. Some of them, babies especially, were all right now, but mainly it didn't work. 'Yes, sir.'

'How's *your* wife, Shenkov?' the Commissioner said brightly. 'I was thinking of organising another big dinner so she could swear at us all some more.'

Shenkov had a familiar electric shock of fear. 'She's very well, sir, she's started as a teacher for the Komsomol. Part-time while she finishes her doctorate.'

'Oh, fabulous, fabulous. Difficult work, that, very difficult.'

Shenkov nodded. It *was* difficult. If you got it wrong and one of the kids reported something you'd said that wasn't quite bang on key with current Marxist–Leninist theory, someone came along to revoke your communication privileges. But Anna was clever. The kids liked her, that was the important thing; people rarely informed on someone they liked. She would be fine. 'Quite an honour, though, sir.'

'Quite, quite,' the Commissioner said. He always said everything twice. He thought about it and pressed one hand to his hair, which was oiled flat so solidly that all of it moved at once, stuck together, with a crackling sound. 'Quite. Well, on you go.'

The raid was standard, and the Party man came to the door fully dressed at one in the morning with a bag packed, and so did his wife. It was unexpected passivity and Shenkov was relieved. Sometimes he was very much in the mood to take a baton to a senior Party member, but it was his fifth night shift in a row, and he was starting to get a sunlight-deprived headache. Once the man and his wife had been taken away in the van, Shenkov herded the three children together as gently as he could. The eldest didn't want to leave the dog. It was a sweet little spaniel, biscuit-coloured.

'But I don't think we know anyone who could look after her,' the girl said seriously. She hadn't complained about being told to put some clothes in a bag, and get on her coat and shoes. Her parents must have told her what would happen.

'You can't take the dog to an orphanage,' Shenkov said, as softly as he could in the hearing of the other officers. He glanced that way. They were doing a search of the study for anti-revolutionary material. If they heard him call her sweetheart, one of them would report him for sympathising with Enemies of the People. All the younger officers were desperate to get off grunt duty and into a warm office of the next job rung up, especially with winter on the way.

'Could *you* look after her, then?' she asked, reasonable as an adult. She was about eight.

He would have loved to. They already had a dog at home, a collie who loved everyone and whose favourite hobby was swishing her tail over the boots of any visiting colleagues of Shenkov's. She could get up a brilliant shine.

'No, I couldn't,' he said.

'But she'll starve!'

One of the younger officers had come to the study door, and now he was watching in the predatory way of someone cold who had smelled good coffee and a nice corner office, his for the taking if he could only elbow Shenkov out of it and into the Lubyanka. 'Got some Tsarist material, comrade,' he said, and waved a framed copy of a proclamation of serf emancipation signed by Tsar Alexander in 1872. There was a stupid piggy gleam in his eyes that gave away how he was hoping Shenkov would snort and tell him where to shove it, a marvellous excuse for arrest if ever there was one. Shenkov kept his expression still and only nodded. Dmitry, aged two and a quarter, had laid more sophisticated traps.

Shenkov shot the dog.

Everything was quiet after that. He drove the children to an orphanage – the same one, not separate ones like he was meant to – and then went back to the office in spitting snow. He went straight to the bathroom to scrub his hands, because after a raid he always felt like there was a film of something foul all over him. He had to stand there with his wrists under the hot water for a long time. He did this job because otherwise a psychopath would do it. If he didn't, kids would go to separate orphanages, and there would be no files sent to charitable institutions, and the teenager who'd been arrested last week for yelling that Comrade Stalin was a pig would be dead, not given a cup of tea and sent home with a note in her pocket for her mum about making sure her teachers knew she'd got that awful medical condition where you couldn't stop swearing.

Throwing your hands up at an organisation like the KGB was no way to solve anything. You had to join, and then you did as many good things as you could, until the evil was a little bit less. He believed that. Or, he had used to. The fact was that to a little girl whose parents had been taken away and whose dog had been shot, it didn't matter if the person with the gun was a psychopath or someone who wanted to do good. Your dog was still dead.

After the train, humid with the rain drying on everyone's clothes and the mouldy smell of damp wool, the clear air on the platform was glorious. Sergei put his scarf back on and Shenkov buttoned his coat. The leather creaked. He saw Sergei give it an uneasy glance, the same glance everyone gave it, but neither of them said anything. Sergei put up an umbrella and took his arm, and they walked close together out of the station, onto a street where the rain gleamed with amber whirls from the lamps, and the car tyres glimmered. Opposite them, outside a bakery with a huge sign that said BREAD, people were already queuing, though it wouldn't be open for another two hours. Someone enterprising had set up a small tent.

'I had to shoot a little girl's dog today,' Shenkov said out of nothing. He hadn't meant to. The second he had, he felt exposed.

'That,' Sergei said with feeling, 'is how I wish I'd spent my day. I work for MiniAg now.' The Ministry of Agronomy. He glanced up at Shenkov. 'They're pushing the Ukrainian grain quotas up again. There are nationalists starting to make noises about not wanting to be in the Soviet Union. Funnily a lot of them are farmers.'

'What about your sisters?' he said, because Sergei was Ukrainian.

'I've told them to get out. Kiev, or something, before everyone starves.'

'You shouldn't say things like that to me,' Shenkov said helplessly.

Sergei looked up at him again, properly this time. 'I would say anything to you.'

Shenkov pulled him into an alley behind a lamp and hugged him, probably too hard, but then stopped caring when he realised that Sergei was clinging to him too.

'Jesus, it's all such a mess, isn't it?' Sergei said, half-laughing. His voice had gone high.

'Steaming.' It was an unbelievable relief to *say* that and not just think it – think it furiously forty times a day, knowing that everyone else must be thinking it too, but never knowing it certainly enough to ever, ever offer it up aloud. 'How's your wife, how's . . .'

'She's a secretary for MiniJust, and all she does now is explain how brilliant everyone is, even at home . . .'

'The house is probably bugged—'

'I know, and I do the same to her, she probably thinks I'm a brainless idiot—'

'Anna too—'

'And the kids are in the fucking Pioneers, they're dead keen to find a spy . . .'

'No, no, no, I win this one. My little boy cheerily told my boss we'd been to America and spoken to the CIA, I nearly had a heart attack. He's two.'

'What did your boss say!'

'He said he was a pirate, in fairness.'

They had been talking over each other so much that neither of them ever quite stopped. It was the only moment in his life Shenkov came close to believing that telepathy was possible.

Sergei laughed. 'My God.' The laugh cracked, and his shoulders shook. 'I'm so tired. I feel like I'm walled into a tower with no windows and no doors.'

'Same.'

Sergei nodded. He let his head bump against Shenkov's shoulder. All at once he seemed like a miracle, trusting a secret policeman enough to do that. 'I don't want to go home,' he said miserably.

'Me neither,' said Shenkov, so they went to find a hotel.

They played dominoes, got drunk, cheated at dominoes, and fell asleep in a heap by the electric fire, because it was a cheap hotel and if you went further away than a metre from the grate, you froze to the thin carpet. Sergei kept his scarf on. They both had a separate nest of cushions and blankets, and Shenkov dozed looking at the pattern on the scarf, nice colours, Ukrainian embroidery on the hem; a risky thing to keep, but then, Sergei must have wanted something from home that was easily hidden.

It felt like an adventure to sleep on the floor, like one of those frozen Komsomol camping trips. He was almost asleep when he felt Sergei take his hand. At any other moment, he would have slapped him away, but now he didn't care. He was a lot more drunk on honesty than on vodka, much more, and he would have done whatever Sergei wanted, even if it was helping to bomb the Kremlin. He dragged him close, worried instantly that he'd hurt him, and felt relief like nothing else when Sergei only shifted to get comfortable.

Someone banged on the door. Four loud, hard thumps.

The Lubyanka was silent. The long corridors were carpeted, so even the guards' boots made no sound. Nobody spoke, and when he glanced to his right to watch another stream of prisoners being led the other way, the guard beside him put one hand on his neck to force his head down. Carpets, in a prison; that had always struck him as bizarre. Right on the edge of hearing, there was a soft wooden noise, like a woodpecker.

He bumped into the wall of the cell and stayed there with his hands against it until the door was locked, to be certain the guards didn't think he meant to fight back. He had expected one of the big cells with a hundred people in it, but it was small, and he was alone. He couldn't tell what that meant. He had only ever brought people to the prison, never gone inside.

He watched the door, expecting someone to step inside. Nobody did. A latch opened and a tray of bread came through. That was it.

Someone tapped on the other side of the wall. It was in a pattern; a code, but he had no idea what it was.

'I don't understand,' he said aloud.

A guard thumped one fist against the iron door. 'Shut up. No speaking.'

There was a long quiet, and then another tap on the wall. *Tap. Taptap. Tap – taptap.* He shook his head at no one.

He understood, after three weeks, that the man in the cell next door was actually teaching him the alphabet. The man did it on a loop every day at nine o'clock, and followed it with something else. When, finally, Shenkov had copied out the knock alphabet in scratches on the wall, he had to rush to find each letter in the second part. His heart nearly broke when he put it together.

What's your name?

He bumped his head against the bricks, full of so much joy that his eyes burned. Haltingly, he tapped his name back, and then, *What's yours?*

Winston.

American?

Yes came to join the Communist cause hahahahahahahahaha haaaaaaaaa.

He laughed, silently. *Bad luck.*

They talked on and off for the rest of the day. Shenkov fell asleep with his temple against the wall. For the first time since they'd brought him, he didn't have nightmares. Even in the dream, he worried about that. Nightmares meant, at least, that none of this was normal. It was amazing how quickly he had got used to the cell otherwise. He had stopped smelling the mildew within a couple of days. He was hungry all the time now, but the hunger was just a presence in the room with him, rather than something urgent. And still, no one opened the cell door. No one asked anything. He would have thought they had forgotten about him, but they couldn't have, or there would have been no food.

For days he'd gone out of his mind worrying about Anna and Dmitry, before coming to the strange calm realisation that there was nothing he could do about whatever it was that was happening to them. The same with Sergei.

He jolted awake when the door banged into the wall. He had no idea what time it was, or what day. A man in uniform stood there; the Commissioner. He could have been a dream from another life.

'Shenkov!' he said cheerily. 'Got a new placement for you. Have you ever heard of City 40?'

28

The Cement Truck

City 40, 1963

In Valery's nearly-empty apartment with its bare walls and the kettle sitting on the windowsill, Shenkov looked more elegant than ever, and out of place. He often seemed that way inside these bleak buildings – he was one of those creatures who, if the world had been arranged properly, nobody would ever have seen except at a distance at great diplomatic conventions, or walking away from a glass-walled boardroom in one of those cities where the tectonic plates of economies shifted; a spirit of the invisible industries, trade or politics or secrets. Impressions like that should have gone away once you'd seen a person ironing shirts, but it kept striking Valery as bizarre that Shenkov could possibly belong in the same room as a linoleum-floored kitchenette and a laundry basket.

Valery poured the coffee that had been brewing while Shenkov spoke. 'They didn't arrest you because of Sergei, though, did they.' He was glad he could speak properly. In the lift on the way up, and for a good while after they were inside, he had been right on the edge of crying with a mixture of relief and shock. He couldn't understand why. The asylum hadn't been awful. But even the tiny zing of the bugs in the light switches was wonderful now.

'What?'

'They arrested you because they wanted Anna to work here,' he said. 'No? She would never have agreed to move out here, not from a tenure-track position at the Kurchatov Institute, so they went after you. They'd have got you for something, whatever happened.'

Shenkov, unlike Valery, usually looked straight at whoever he was speaking to; but all the time he had been talking he had rested his eyes on the floor. They flicked up to Valery now, but as though the sight of him was too heavy, they fell again.

Valery wanted to take his hands and folded his arms to stop himself. 'Solitary for three weeks in the Lubyanka. That's a holiday with full catering.'

Shenkov was leaning back against the wall, his shoulders flat to it as though he didn't like being so tall. He looked at Valery through his lashes. 'I expect your father made you eat roadkill and murdered you nightly in your Arctic shack when you were a lad.'

'*And* I was grateful,' Valery said, hurting with joy to be talking again.

The telephone rang, which was odd, because the only person who ever called him was Shenkov. He picked up the receiver. A nervous voice introduced itself as a junior security officer and asked for Shenkov. Valery handed the phone over, wondering if she had listened, through the bugs, to Shenkov's whole story, or just that she had worked out where he would be if he wasn't at home or in the office.

'Yes?'

'Evening, sir,' the nervous voice said. Valery could hear her clearly. Shenkov motioned that it shouldn't be long. 'There's a cement truck heading to the forest now.' The young woman must have held the phone next to a speaker then, because there was a crackle of evening radio and someone singing in the wholehearted way most people only did when they thought they were alone. 'I've just sent someone after him. You said to call if one went out that way.'

'Good. Keep listening too, I want to know if he talks to anyone when he gets to where he's going.'

'Yes, sir. Night.'

'Night.' Shenkov set the phone back into its cradle. 'If we're lucky we'll know where that bloody lab is soon,' he said, so softly it was hard to hear him even from centimetres away, never mind through the bugs in the phone and the light switches.

'Cement,' Valery said. He turned the kettle on again, and the taps. 'You bugged the trucks even though I wouldn't give you Sasha's results.'

'You wouldn't have been so frightened if you'd found nothing,' Shenkov said.

'It was polonium,' Valery agreed, freshly ashamed. He sighed. 'But you should be frightened too. This is sanctioned from Moscow. You can't just walk in and make them stop. Particularly after shutting down an asylum just for . . .'

'No, but I will tell the newspapers exactly where the lab is, who's running it, and then I'll mysteriously fail to find any of the editors or the printers of the special editions that ensue,' he said.

Valery looked across. 'And then someone comes along to shoot you.'

'They're taking children. You can't talk about why you killed fifty-three men with a chemical bomb and I can't watch them take children Tanya's age. If I get shot, I do.'

Valery had to bite his tongue while he rinsed out the cafetière and made a new round of coffee. He doubted either of them wanted any more coffee, but it was something to do with his hands. The hot water bloomed black, and tiny rainbow bubbles erupted over the surface, and he tried to find that happy voice that enjoyed fluid dynamics and appreciated the crossword-cigarettes. He couldn't. Shenkov was turning brittle again, too ashamed to just be miserable. It was clear he meant what he was saying. He really would do what he could and die for it. He was flint; he couldn't bend, only shatter. The idea of watching him break opened up that thinly covered pit in Valery's mind, the one that went all the way down to the fires, and the bomb, and the red trains. The worst thing was, Valery would survive it; he could survive anything. It was involuntary. He wasn't flint but glass – he broke a lot, but then he vitrified and mended, and he could do it endlessly. He would survive this to see Shenkov in pieces.

'There's an easier way,' he said.

Shenkov had been fetching the milk. 'What?'

'Once we know where this place is, I can just knock on the door. I think I can get myself on to the research team. If there are kids . . . I should be able to find a way to get them out. You can get them to Chelyabinsk on false papers.'

Shenkov watched him for a long time. 'It's Resovskaya's trial. She just had you arrested and sent to that place. I saw the file.'

'I know, but she doesn't know that the arrest actually happened. It's Sunday today. If I turn up for work tomorrow, no one will be any the wiser. If she chases it, she'll find that you've shut the asylum down to intakes from Lighthouse scientists.' He hesitated while he surveyed how certain he was. 'The only reason I'm not already working on her trial is that she thinks I'm trying to sabotage her, but she'll have no choice if I turn up at the door.'

'If she thinks you want to sabotage it, she'll have the inevitable soldiers guarding that door shoot you.'

'I think she would find that overdramatic.' Valery tipped his head. 'She doesn't crack nuts with sledgehammers. She likes elegant solutions.'

Shenkov didn't quite smile. 'I didn't fake three hundred pages of documents at that asylum just to bury you in a pit in the woods.'

Valery nodded, because he didn't have it in him to laugh. 'Yes, no, I know. I really don't think you'll have to do that.

Anyway, listen, I've had all my looking after now. Sod off, for God's sake, salvage the weekend, get some time to yourself. Tell me the coordinates when you know them and I'll drop by your office tomorrow.'

Shenkov didn't move, except to ball his fist and touch the wall with his knuckles, the mime of a punch. 'I didn't mean to make you do anything you didn't want to in Moscow.'

Valery stopped still, because it was so far from what he had expected Shenkov to say that at first, like another language, it was only unconnected sounds.

'I know you must be scared of me, God knows I know, but I'd rather shoot myself than hurt you. I'm not – believe me or don't, but I am not going to just *snatch* you if you let me stay in a room with you for longer than fifteen minutes. I'm sorry, for everything. And I'm sorry to say all this, but watching you contort yourself to be polite in case I lose my temper and kill you is – horrible.'

'What?' Valery said softly.

Shenkov brought his shoulders forward, the barest trace of a shrug to say he didn't know what else to add. He shied when Valery came up close to him, as if he expected a punch in the face. Valery took his hands and pinned them above his shoulders.

'I'm not scared of you. I thought you wanted to be left alone.'

Shenkov shook his head slightly.

Valery let him go, and tilted forward against him until he was resting against his chest. After a long time, Shenkov crossed both arms over his back and bent to press their heads together, all his bones too tight even through his clothes. They didn't ease until Valery put one hand on the nape of his neck, where prison warders would, fingertips between the vertebrae, to remind you they could break it if they had to.

29

The Laboratory

On Monday morning, Valery drove into the forest. He had the coordinates to which the bugged cement truck had driven yesterday, and within half an hour, he had found the place. The path was barely there, and he had to edge the Land Rover through the trees and the undergrowth exactly over the tracks of the truck to get through; even then, gorse and briars squeaked their thorns down the car doors.

The way came out in a clearing. He saw the graves even from the car. There were dozens, lined up in clinical rows. There were no headstones, no markers, but the rectangles of concrete showed clearly in the grass, even the older ones. They were all three metres by one.

He walked around slowly, looking between the trees. If he had been running the project, he wouldn't have wanted to transport radioactive corpses far, particularly knowing that there were researchers from the Lighthouse wandering around, and hunters from the village.

'Hey, you!'

A gun safety catch clicked off behind him. He put his hands up and took a deep, slow breath.

'I'm one of *your* researchers, you flighty bastard,' he called, letting his voice go high with what hopefully sounded like indignation. 'Can you maybe not shoot me on my first day?'

'You're what?' the voice said, anxious.

'My name is Kolkhanov, I specialise in the effects of radiation on human tissue, you can check. I've just come over from the Lighthouse.' He held out his staff badge. 'They only gave me coordinates, I couldn't find the front door. Just that track. Where am I meant to be?'

'I'll take you,' the young soldier said, looking relieved. 'They've given you the wrong directions. This is the back door.'

Valery would never have found the door himself. It was set into a bank of earth at a steep angle, half hidden by the roots of a dying oak tree. When the soldier opened it, there was nothing beyond but a long, long corridor, leading back towards the Lighthouse.

'What?' he said.

'It's under the lake,' the soldier explained.

The way was cold, and it only turned colder. The ground was covered in steel grating, which whickered under his boots like a railway line when a train was coming. Punctuating the corridor, just too far apart from each other, electric lights buzzed in the dark. Valery began to have a sense of weight above him. The lake. Here and there, the passage dripped, and patches of the floor grating were ginger with rust. The air smelled of earth and mould, even though the walls had been panelled with steel bulkheads. He wondered if that was to protect the wiring of the lights from the damp, or people from the radiation. The further he went, the more he thought he could taste the burnt-metal taste of radiation damage, and the harder it became to recognise it was imaginary.

He had Shenkov's security lanyard looped around his knuckles, inside his pocket. He couldn't remember doing that, but he had been gripping it so hard he couldn't open his hand any more. When he reached the door, he wanted to turn back.

Instead he buzzed the intercom.

'Er – hello?' said a puzzled voice through the crackly wiring.

Here we go. He had done harder magic tricks than this; he had.

'Can I come in please? It's freezing out here.'

The lock hummed and opened. On the other side, three people looked up from their workbenches. One of them was Dr Resovskaya.

'Hi,' Valery said, as his heart slammed into his sternum. 'Found you.'

'You can't be here,' someone squeaked.

Just inside the door, two soldiers had trained their rifles on him. He locked his hands behind his head and looked past them to Resovskaya.

'Elena, I was – I thought about what you said, I haven't been able to stop, and I couldn't think of anything else I could do to convince you I didn't mean to harm your trial. I just came to help, if you want another pair of hands.' He paused. 'You can tell me to fuck off, but then I'll have to follow you around with tea all the time and you'll be annoyed. Please . . . let me help.'

There was rank alarm across her face. He didn't blame her. She had expected never to see him again. Now, she must have been trying to work out if he knew anything about the arrest, who had fended it off, how, why, if it had happened and he had, eel-like, managed to writhe his way out of it, or if it had been held up earlier in the bureaucratic chain and he had no idea. He saw it when she pulled down the politic mask.

'Valery, you really *mustn't* break into secret government facilities,' she said, managing to sound genuine and warm.

He had known she was a good liar, but this was impressive.

'Who is he?' one of the other researchers asked, quite high.

'Not a security risk,' Resovskaya said, shaking her head. 'Have you told anyone about this, Valery?'

'No, but please don't shoot me. I'll be much more useful with all my brains on the inside.'

'Oh, just . . . you are a *nuisance*,' she said, smiling. She sighed. 'Come on then, since you're here.'

'Hah,' Valery said happily. It wasn't hard to pretend. Not having two guns aimed into his face was a very happy feeling. Behind the guns, the soldiers looked confused.

Resovskaya herded him by his shoulder into the next room. It was a little office kitchen, with three kettles on the side and a fridge that hummed. 'Is this how you got round Shenkov, just being rather sweetly insane?'

'Yes,' he said, far more shortly than he had meant to.

Shenkov had seemed impossibly, desperately fragile this morning. Standing, it was difficult to notice anything about him except how tall he was, solid muscle and poise, but lying down, his collarbones were clear, and he slept curled on his side with his sleeves pulled over his hands against the cold, unmoving like anyone who had been in the Lubyanka, as though he hated the idea of taking up an inch more space than he had to. Hearing Resovskaya say his name felt like a threat.

She paused. 'Valery, I don't know if you have the stomach for this. You didn't much like the German trial.'

'Well, if I go to pieces, throw me out and shoot me,' he said.

'I'll have to. I can't have you going in hysterics to all and sundry.'

'I do understand, comrade.'

'Not a word. Not to Shenkov, not to random people in cafes. This is serious.'

'I know.'

'I hope so.'

The four rooms had used to be offices. There were still marks on the carpet where the old desks had been. Now, there were beds, shelves, books, televisions, and the old wall that had once hosted all their doors had been taken out and replaced with glass. No one in the rooms could see the others, but they could see out into the corridor. Above the glass, they were all marked one to four.

'Research quadrants,' Resovskaya said, pointing. 'One is the Lighthouse. Irradiated but with the most possible safety measures taken, including imported food and water, and everyone is fully aware of how to keep themselves safe; average yearly intake of about fifty roentgen.'

There was a man inside the cell, watching the television with every sign of enjoying it.

'Quadrant Two is City 40. Irradiated with some safety measures, but the non-scientific populace are unaware of any precautions. We think they get about eighty roentgen annually, from accidental exposure and ingestion of contaminated materials; the river, say, or food grown in garden allotments. Three: the village in the exclusion zone. Irradiated, very few safety precautions taken, contaminated food and water. An average individual absorption rate of a hundred and fifty roentgen annually.'

Valery nodded. In the third cell was a boy who must have been Pyotr. He was asleep.

'Four: control group. Moscow.'

There was a woman in the last cell, reading.

'What we're doing is increasing the dose gradually, to see if there is a universal threshold of radiation tolerance, or if being accustomed to a higher dose to begin with helps with resistance to even higher doses. Moscow's orders are to see if there's a way of increasing resistance.'

Valery looked across at her. 'What do the results suggest so far?'

'There's not enough data to say yet, but it looks like neither. Some people can be pushed much further than others. Oddly we're having most success with the City 40 group. We can't tell why.'

Valery thought about it, rolling around all the factors he didn't know. 'How do you get the subjects? I mean how do you choose?'

She nodded. 'Whenever anyone goes for a hospital check-up, we get their blood work. For those with interesting results, their names then go to the KGB, who arrest them for – you know, whatever – and bring them here. It's not ideal, but it's the only way to get this done.'

'Efficient,' he said. 'Is there any coffee?'

'Coffee, yes.' She laughed. 'You're full of surprises, Valery.'

'Am I?' he said, pretending to be confused.

Part of him was indignant to find how simple it was. Resovskaya thought he was an easily upset, prematurely old man, and so long as he acted a decent caricature of himself, she would keep thinking so. He was too harmless and skittish to be doing anything nefarious. He followed her back into the kitchen, wondering, a bit put out, if he shouldn't have gone into international espionage instead of chemistry. Everything suggested he'd have been outstanding at it.

In the lab, there was data for far more than four people. There had been about sixty test subjects in the last six years. Most, he noticed, were men. That made sense. The more body mass you had, the more diluted any particular dose of radiation was. The numbers were up on a blackboard at one end of the windowless room.

'I have a job for you, if you'd like to get started straight away,' Resovskaya said. 'Chelyabinsk has sent us this week's round of blood samples, we've got about two hundred to plough through. Run them through the spectrometer and find out which ones are carrying any radioactive isotopes. Boring, but it's Item One every Monday.'

Valery nodded. She was right, it was repetitive grunt work, but it was a relief to start with something dull and easy. He didn't know if he would have been able to do an autopsy with equilibrium. 'Of course.'

She lifted up a plastic blue crate that clinked with glass vials slotted into a grid inside, and gave him a wry look. 'Box one of five. Protective gear over there.'

'Elena,' he said.

She had set the crate down on a workbench, and now she was flexing her hands. The arthritis must have been getting very painful indeed. 'Hm?'

'Thank you,' he said, and watched her carefully. 'I can put up with most things, but not your thinking badly of me.'

It took her just a fraction too long to smile.

He let his eyes slip back down to the blood samples. She didn't believe him; which left the question of why she'd let him into her lab. Still, you couldn't have everything at once. Whatever her reason, all he had to do was lean into her inclination to think he was harmless, and find a believable way for Pyotr to escape that bank vault of an observation room. Preferably, a sustainable one that he could pull off whenever any new children turned up.

'Have you seen the paper?' one of the other researchers said. He had been reading while he waited for a centrifuge to finish. 'The KGB have raided the asylum. There's a doctor there drugging patients who used to work at the Lighthouse and wringing them for information, then passing the intelligence on to a foreign embassy.' He looked up and seemed to realise he hadn't produced a pious enough opinion about it. 'The buggers get more and more creative every day, don't they? Imagine abusing one's oath as a doctor, it's inhuman.'

If Valery said nothing, it would seem like he knew too much about it already. 'That doesn't sound very likely. How many

Lighthouse scientists end up in the asylum anyway? They can't be awash with them.'

'Actually,' the man said seriously, 'it's been pretty standard. Make too many doubtful radiation-type noises, chances are you'll end up there. Konstantin Shenkov from Security only comes along to shoot you now if you've done something utterly thick. Talking to journalists, sort of thing. You get a good spell in the asylum as a warning shot these days.'

'Christ,' said Valery. He risked a glance at Resovskaya. 'I'd better watch out, I expect.'

She was observing him in the same quiet, lab-technician way she had when he passed her on the stairs at the Ministry. 'No. I shouldn't think Shenkov would let anything happen to you, would he? You're his little mascot, I think he's rather used to you.'

'Jesus, you're a braver man than me,' the other researcher remarked. 'Shenkov said hello to me once in the coffee queue and my knees didn't stop shaking for a week.'

'Oh, he's not all that,' Resovskaya said, into a filing cabinet. 'You know he was only sent here because he was caught in bed with a Ukrainian nationalist?'

'Oof. Whoops,' the other researcher said, laughing. 'Was he really? That was silly of him.'

It was the self-satisfied laugh of someone in whom the Lubyanka had never shown an interest, and who still imagined that this was down to virtue and not luck. Valery wondered about spilling some polonium on him.

'Oh, yes,' Resovskaya said. Her tired eyes slid twice over Valery. 'A little prone to silliness, our Shenkov.'

30

Boots at the Door

Snow came down in dervishes that evening, throwing speckle shadows across the carpet of Valery's flat. The moonlight was stronger than the small lamp and the television inside. He wasn't watching the television; it was just on the news, for voices. He was marking some graduate papers for Resovskaya. It was nice to mark papers. It was easy, but it required just enough focus for him not to feel the press of the emptiness in the flat. It had crammed itself into the living room and watched him as he crossed to and fro.

Anna was in Chelyabinsk with Tatiana, so Shenkov was at home with the other children. Albert was out and about round the flat, though, and sometimes he left octopus-tracks on the papers, having decided that Valery would pay him more attention and play the marble game if he was sitting on them.

Two in the morning came around, and Valery's brain went on strike. He switched the television off and watched the picture whumpf inward until it was only a single white point, which lingered for a while before it faded. Then the lamp. He stood in the rectangular patch of moonlight. A great nave of clouds led up to the moon, and the snow glowed a strange blue.

He couldn't tell if Resovskaya was going to try to get rid of him another way. He had been half-expecting a bang on the door all night. The asylum would have been ideal for her purposes, but if she just wanted him gone now, there was always the red train and the camps. She would have to be confident that Shenkov wouldn't be able to do anything about it; but Valery couldn't see why she wouldn't be confident, because he was pretty confident himself that Shenkov could do damn all there.

Valery turned away from the window, meaning to go outside and walk around to tire himself out properly, but then stopped. There was still a bright line under the door from the hallway, where the lights were never off. Silhouetted there were two dark places.

Boots.

Someone was standing right outside, on the doorstep, not knocking.

He didn't even think about it. Those kinds of scare tactics only worked if you let them. They didn't stand up too well in the face of someone who invited the police officer in for a cup of tea and a bun. He pulled the door open, ready to ask cheerfully whether the man took milk and sugar.

There was no man. There were three children.

They were different ages, between about ten and fifteen, bundled up still against the cold. He had clearly caught them in the middle of an awkward shuffle about who was going to knock.

'Hello,' he said slowly. 'Wrong door probably? Who are you looking for?'

The eldest squared himself up anxiously, and pulled off his hat in the way of someone whose mother had drilled it into him to be polite to his elders. 'Um, I think it is the right door. You're Comrade Kolkhanov, right? Dad – Dad said you've got red hair.'

Valery still couldn't tell what was going on. 'I am. Sorry, who's your dad?'

'Konstantin Shenkov, comrade. Um, he . . . he told us we should come here and find you.'

All of them had the tight, hollow look of people who had either been given too much morphine, or who had just seen something horrible.

'You'd better come in, then,' Valery said, with a heavy coldness sliding through his bones now. 'Let me make you all some coffee. You look frozen.'

Valery melted some chocolate into their coffee and gave the littlest boy Albert to play with. Once they seemed to have settled, he sat down too. The middle girl took over. She looked very like Shenkov indeed, with dark hair and a lustre.

'They took him away about an hour ago. They wouldn't say what the charges were. We, um . . . they tried to take us to an orphanage, but we ran away.'

'Good,' said Valery. 'Always run. That was exactly right, you did really well.'

'Will they come after us?' the eldest said quietly. He must have known that the Lighthouse was thoroughly bugged, because he kept glancing at the light switch. Valery had already put the television back on, and it was casting harsh shadows over them all while the three-in-the-morning maths professor explained quadratic equations on the screen.

'No. They don't care where you are, the orphanage thing is to upset whoever they're arresting.'

The boy nodded, and they all looked mutedly relieved.

'Did they say what they were arresting him for?' Valery asked.

'Contact with political dissidents.'

So, Valery.

'Right. You didn't have a chance to call your mum, did you?'

'No.' The girl swallowed, her eyes edging over the phone. 'What if they *do* care where we are and they hear us on the bugs?'

'I'll call her,' Valery said.

'But you can't tell her we're here, or . . .'

'I know, don't worry.'

'I don't know the number,' she said suddenly, horrified. 'Oh, God – I'm sorry—'

'I'll find her,' Valery said. 'Easiest thing in the world, I promise. Which hospital has got Tatiana?'

'Um, Chelyabinsk, Hospital Number – Three.'

'Settle in, it'll take me a minute.'

Valery rang the hospital and pretended there was an emergency at the physics labs. It was enough to fluster the nurses into looking up where Anna was staying, and within a few minutes he had the number and the line was ringing. He nodded to the children, who had been watching him hard. While they were distracted, Albert was investigating someone's coffee, dipping in the tip of one arm. He flushed a disgusted shade of green when he realised it was hot.

'Anna,' Valery said brightly when she said a sleepy and bewildered hello. 'It's Valery, from the chocolate factory. Sorry for disturbing you so late. You won't believe this, though. You know your missing kittens? I've just found them, all three. They're with me now.'

There was a long silence at the other end. 'God, you did well,' she said at last. 'Listen, I know they must be climbing up the curtains, but can you sit with them till I get there?'

'They're good as gold. Being terrorised by the octopus, actually.'

'Is . . . the tomcat with them?'

'I think someone else must have decided they wanted him.'

'Well, thanks. I'll see you soon.'

He set the phone down. 'She's coming,' he told them. 'It will take her a little while, though, from Chelyabinsk. Shall we get some blankets in here and you can all sleep by the fire?'

'That sounds like a good idea,' the eldest said with painful seriousness. His shoulders dropped. He was thin; he probably spent a lot of his time looking after the little ones, and he had the harried, too-old look that Svetlana always had.

Valery brought in everything and let them settle themselves, aware that interfering too much would only make it worse. He was a stranger, and he could remember being ten; however kind, strangers had made him nervous, and he could well imagine it was even more the case for the children of a KGB officer and a physicist whose work was so top-secret that they had all been raised thinking this was a chocolate factory. While the elder two moved things around, the littlest came up to him shyly and said they didn't have toothbrushes.

'I'll go and find some. I think they have some in the supplies, for the night-shift people.'

'Comrade – are we going to get him back, once Mum's here? It's just a mistake. Isn't it?'

'I don't know,' said Valery. 'We'll try.'

'But it *must* be a mistake,' the girl said. 'He doesn't *know* any dissidents.'

Valery was quiet for a moment. 'No. The police make things up sometimes.'

'Why?'

'Usually it happens if someone wants your job, or wants you to stop doing your job. It's not fair but it happens. Your dad's not a criminal. Right, sit tight, and I'll be back.'

He gave the girl the key in the hope that they would feel a bit safer, and set out down the corridor. He found himself checking around corners before he walked them. If Resovskaya had managed, God knew how, to have Shenkov arrested, then it would not be long before someone came for Valery again too. In fact he was surprised they hadn't already.

While he had been with the children, there had been the immediacies to think about, the blankets and coffee and whether or not Albert was going to try and squeeze himself into someone's cup. Now, the quiet surged, and so did all the things that he had forced into the background before. He had told the children that he and Anna would try to get Shenkov back, but the truth was that they wouldn't even be able to try. He had no idea where the police would have taken him. There must have been a prison here somewhere, but it was hard to think that the usual protocols would be followed if the arrestee was the head of the local branch of the KGB, and particularly not given that Shenkov already had a prison record. There would not be anything to discuss, no trial to hear.

It was possible that he was already in Chelyabinsk, being slung on to one of the red trains that would run north, and north, north.

Valery was halfway down the stairs when he had to lock his elbow over the rail and stand still while he waited to stop feeling dizzy.

31

The Red Trains

There weren't any secret railway stations. The red trains went from Moscow Central, just along the tracks from the Metro circle line. The carriages were cattle cars, so everyone sat down on the floor, very quiet, and once the car was full, the doors ratcheted closed and the guards pushed home the bolts. There was light, though, because there were sometimes gaps between the planks in the walls. Valery shifted so that, beside him, Shukov – the battered man who had taught him knock code and since become his best prison friend – could stretch his bad knee. Shukov nodded sheepishly. Other people were settling in the same. Everyone knew each other, because they were all from the Lubyanka, all from the same cell.

For Valery, at least, it was a relief to be going. City prisons were just holding stations. You did your ten years at a labour camp, and if he was being honest, he had been looking forward to it for months now. Maybe Siberia was going to be hellish and frozen and all the rest of it, but there was very definitely going to be space to stretch your arms out. Much as he liked everyone else from his cell, he was reaching the point where he would have sold his soul and probably other important pieces of himself just to breathe some air that a dozen other people hadn't already breathed. As far as he was concerned, Siberia sounded like God's own country.

The only thing making him anxious now was that those same fifty people had been crammed into the same carriage, which had even less space in it than the prison cell, and the journey to Siberia from here would take at least ten weeks.

Actually, the carriage had been divided into two. Down the middle was a thick piece of plyboard, but there was a tiny knot-hole in it and on the far side were women's voices. As the train moved off, someone tapped gently on the other side.

'Hello, gents,' a cheerful voice said.

'Ladies,' everyone said automatically. Valery had a weird kind of relief. He hadn't seen or heard a woman for months, and the sound of them was wonderful; there was something much cleaner about them than the way that men muttered, and he had a flash of a memory from when he'd been small and his mother had still taken him to church. They sounded like the choir.

Everyone else must have felt the same, because people started to relax, and the cold air smoked unevenly as everyone began to breathe properly and to talk. It felt like things would be basically okay, now that the women were here.

There was soon quite a lot to complain about, so it was just as well that everyone started more or less happy. There were so many prisoners that it took the guards two hours to get everyone out for toilet breaks, and given that the huge train went slowly anyway, creeping around the sweeps of bleak farmland track, it was completely unrealistic for them to try that more than once a day. It took exactly four days for sympathy to wear out and for the old men to be shunned down the far end of the carriage. Valery felt sorry for them, but not sorry enough to get too close or to stray too far from the stream of clean air coming in through a crack in the carriage wall.

Everyone was used to being hungry, so tempers didn't wear too thin when it became clear there would be one cup of water a day and one meal. Valery was actually grateful about that. He much preferred being hungry to dealing with the old men if someone stuffed them with *three* meals a day. Jesus Christ.

'Um . . . ?' said the woman on the other side of the plywood barrier. 'A.'

'Nope,' he said, and scratched the base of a tiny gallows. About eight of them were playing, but they had elected speakers so it didn't get too chaotic.

'We did agree that no Polish words are allowed, right?'

'Racist,' someone said.

Quiet giggles from the other side. It sounded like sunlight. Valery smiled and wondered for the hundredth time how Svetlana was doing. She didn't giggle, she wasn't that kind of person – she made a kind of muted hiss where most people would have laughed – but it felt warm in the same way.

After two weeks, the weather turned. Summer must have realised it was late and came on all in a rush. They woke up one morning to find that they were gliding under a blue sky, and that it was hot; so hot that it was dizzying. Valery woke with a jolt from a dream of being smothered. He sat up fast and breathed close to the crack in the wall. It made him jump when Shukov pushed him aside, too hard, to get at it instead.

'Ow,' he said.

'Sorry,' Shukov said, back to being the same apologetic person who'd looked after Valery in the Lubyanka cell. 'Sorry, thought I might be dying.'

Valery knocked him gently and felt bad for objecting.

There was a strange scratching sound on their left. Valery frowned through the gloom to try and find it. He was still caught in the dregs of the nightmare, and the idea of having a rat in the compartment with them loomed sharper and nastier than it would have if he'd been properly awake. It was hard to shrug off that fogginess in the morning, and getting harder each day. He wasn't bothered exactly about being hungry and thirsty, but he was starting to feel weak with it, and starting to notice that his mind was turning sticky.

Someone was pulling at the splinters around the knothole in the compartment divider. The air was better on the women's side – they had more cracks in the walls, and a loose plank.

'Hey, can you not?' a woman's voice said on the other side. 'We've got little girls in here.'

'Uh, put up with it,' the man said tiredly. 'We've got old men in here.'

'Hey,' Shukov whispered to the man by the compartment divider. Over the last couple of days, he had been getting a glassiness to his expression. Valery was worried he had a fever. 'Can you *see* them now?'

The man glanced at the slightly enlarged hole. 'Uh . . . yeah.'

Shukov grabbed Valery's shoulder and scrambled over five protesting people to see. 'Hello,' he said happily, his eye to the gap.

Valery winced and pulled his arm. 'Don't, Shukov. Come on, mate, leave them alone.'

'Hi,' a woman on the other side said, very gently. Even to her, he must have looked feverish. 'Everything okay in there?'

'Oh, you're pretty.'

'Nope,' a woman decided, and hung something – a scarf, maybe – on a nail or a splinter above the hole.

'Hey!' This from Shukov and the man who had scratched the hole open a little more. They both sounded like little boys.

With a spike of little-boy anger, the scratching man yanked the scarf to pull it in through. He only succeeded in jamming it, and the angle was too awkward to wrench it all the way.

Valery took a breath, asked the eternal question of *what would Svetlana do*, and banged the man's head against the wall. 'Stop,' he said. 'Now. Look at what you're doing. She said there were little girls in there. Don't scare them.'

'Oh, fuck you, you queer,' the man snapped, but he stopped.

Some of them knocked tentatively and tried to play hangman later, but the women wouldn't answer.

'Stuck-up bitches,' Shukov mumbled. His eyes hazed with tears.

Valery squeezed his arm. He wanted to say that obviously nobody wanted to play after the little performance this morning, but that wouldn't have done any good. He wasn't sure Shukov remembered. 'It's okay. They'll get bored in another couple of days.'

'I don't feel very well,' Shukov whispered.

'I know.' Valery pulled him close despite the heat so that he wasn't propped so awkwardly on the hard floor.

He let his eyes drift around the compartment. Usually, by the afternoon, there was a ripple of conversation, but everything had turned stagnant. Even the younger men, who were normally animated enough to play knucklebones with old nails they'd dug out of the walls, were still and silent. Every so often, people glanced over at the dividing wall, almost as unhappy as Shukov. Valery swallowed. If he was honest, he had been living mostly for hangman too, and those quiet higher voices on the other side of the wall that sounded like home and church windows.

Someone else was scratching at the hole now, trying to free the scarf.

'Stop it,' someone said sharply on the other side.

The man stopped. Valery looked away. If he had been able to string words together properly, he would have tapped on the wall and tried to explain that everyone was miserable, and would it be all right if they could be forgiven now, if everyone agreed they were sorry about before, but even trying to think those things in a logical line gave him a feeling like vertigo. The silence went on.

'I think this bloke's dead,' someone said quietly from the other side of the carriage. 'Is anyone a doctor?'

A brief discussion was enough to elect Valery in the absence of a real doctor. The old man at the back was indeed dead. When the train stopped, it was a relief to get rid of the body.

Wanting to get a look at him in the sun, Valery took Shukov for a tiny walk when it was their turn out. They were on a silent stretch of railway track in the middle of a forest. Valery couldn't have said which forest. The trees were pines, and the heat reflecting from the steel railway tracks was fierce. Shukov had turned still and terse.

'I think it will be me next,' he whispered.

'Don't be silly,' Valery said, but Shukov looked terrible.

The women still wouldn't play.

'We'll play when you stop scratching,' someone said crossly. Valery could hear the glass in her voice too.

Two or three men had been scratching at the plywood barrier now – not, Valery thought, with any purpose, but in the compulsive way of anyone with absolutely nothing else to do. 'You b—'

'Oi,' an ex-navy captain snapped, hard. 'Shut up.'

Four pairs of eyes gleamed crystalline and mutinous in his direction, and Valery felt cold despite the pounding heat.

In the morning, the navy captain was dead. He was in his sixties, and perhaps it was dehydration. But Valery didn't think so. He seemed to be unofficial medical examiner now, and when he looked the man over, he didn't seem in a bad enough way to have died only a few hours after being wholly lucid. He said nothing, though, aware that people were watching him with a wariness that made him think of hyenas. Instead, he sat back on his knees.

'Well. Are the rest of you okay?' he asked the men he was pretty sure had killed the sailor.

A hesitation, then sullen nods. He nodded with them. Sometimes a photon of kindness went a long way.

'Can I have a quick look at you?'

'Okay,' the original scratcher said quietly.

So Valery made a show of looking into their eyes, listening to their hearts, moving their arms gently.

'Good news,' he said. 'You all look good to go for a little while yet. We'll be there soon. Another six days, the guards say. You're all doing beautifully, actually.'

Again like children, they looked pleased with that. 'Thanks, doctor.'

'But you'll tell me, won't you, if you start to feel really bad? One of the signs of dangerous dehydration is sudden anger.' It was a complete lie, but he couldn't think of any other way to make them watch themselves. 'If you feel any sudden rage, that isn't you, that's thirst. You tell me, okay? You're all good boys, we'll get you through.'

'You won't be able to do anything about it, though,' one of them said bleakly.

'We'll be able to talk you down,' Valery said with a confidence he didn't feel at all. 'The worst thing now would be to lose it in a crowded room, right? We'd start World War Three in here and I feel that would be undignified.'

Weak smiles. 'Okay, doctor.'

He smiled back and left them, and felt excruciated, because they *were* good boys. They were good boys turning into something else, though, and when the train stopped next, and the guards helped take out the navy captain's body, Valery touched one of them on the arm and drew him aside.

'I think those boys are going to kill someone,' he said softly. 'If they haven't already.'

The guard sighed. He looked nearly as exhausted as everyone else. 'We're packed full. There's nowhere to put them. Unless you want me to shoot them, you'll have to deal with them.'

Valery looked him over quietly. 'Are you okay?' he asked, not because he was worried, but because in his experience it was a far more powerful thing than getting angry.

In this instance, though, it was the wrong thing. For a terrible second, the man's eyes welled with tears. He caught them before they fell, made himself furious to cover it, and smacked Valery's arm with his truncheon. Valery went down on to the ground hard.

'Shut up. Get back in the compartment.'

Shukov hurried over to scoop him up. 'Come on, up you get. No trouble, okay?' he said quickly to the guard.

'Okay,' said the guard, stony and humiliated still.

The following day, Valery woke to the now-familiar nightmare of suffocating, and to the sound of scratching. There was a wooden squeak as someone pulled a long splinter from the wall. He sat up in time to see Shukov tug the trapped scarf through. Hopelessly, Shukov sank his face into it and breathed. His arm aching, Valery edged across other people's legs to get near enough to speak.

'Morning,' he said softly.

'Look,' whispered Shukov.

Through the gap in the wall, about fist-sized now, the other side of the compartment was brighter than theirs. Across the floor, the women were still asleep. On average, they were young; perhaps the old ladies hadn't managed to survive the Lubyanka. Valery's heart constricted. Despite the dirt and the stifling heat, they looked inhumanly all right, as though the guards had managed to confuse human beings with a clutch of strange things from the woods. So that no one was trodden on too badly if people had to move around, they had all, in perfect order, lined up their shoes along the nearer wall.

'What do you think it's like, not to . . . to get *angry* when you're unhappy?' Shukov asked.

'Clean,' Valery murmured. 'Very clean, I should think.'

'We need to cover this over,' Shukov said. 'Somehow.'

'With what?'

Someone else was awake. 'Let me see.'

It was one of the young men who had been scratching. 'Watch yourself too,' Valery said. 'Remember?'

'I'm not a kid,' the young man snapped, ruffled. 'Shut up.'

Damn.

'Hey,' Shukov said. 'Watch your mouth.'

The young man couldn't reach Shukov, so Valery ended up as proxy. The young man caught the back of his neck and slammed him into the wall. He just caught the edge of the splintered hole and, over the bang of the impact, felt his skin tear, and then almost instantly he was soaked in blood.

The bang woke up the women nearest to the wall.

'Sorry,' Shukov called quietly.

Valery touched his face and regretted it, because his hand came away bloody and of course there was no washing it off. The slice went so deep it had nearly reached his teeth. He couldn't feel it much, though. Perhaps it was because he'd got quite good at shutting his brain off from the things his body wanted. A distant part of him noted that this was, however, bad. He'd be lucky not to die of an infection.

The blow to the wall had splintered off a whole new chunk of plywood. It thumped on to the floor of the carriage, leaving the hole big enough to climb through.

It was a month later that Valery talked himself on to cleaning duty in the camp administrator's apartments. Usually it was a job for the infirm, but the administrator had heard from the guards on the train that he was a doctor, the science kind, and he wanted a tutor, so cleaning was the reward; a sure ticket away from general labour in the mines, which would kill you in a season.

It had earned Valery plenty of resentful looks in the barracks. He ignored them. He wasn't on talking terms with anyone anyway, not after the train, and he was perfectly content with that. He didn't even miss talking to Shukov. Shukov had tried to make up with him three times, increasingly desperate. Maybe it was just righteous bollocks, maybe he was just railing against human nature, but Valery felt sicker each time, and shrugged him off.

In the cleaning cupboard were an amazing number of household chemicals with a great many more uses than tackling limescale.

Valery worked out the proportions, then made the necessary mixture in a big bottle full of nails. He kept it until the early morning, just tucked into the corner of his bunk. It was straightforward. Anyone would think it would be difficult to walk around a labour camp with a bomb, but that depended on who you were. Valery was pretty sure that he could have walked through with a sub-machine gun and everyone would have assumed it was for an art project.

It was still dark, four o'clock in the morning, and the guards tended to unlock the barracks at least an hour before everyone had to be up, because the cleaning units had to come in and take the night-soil barrels away, and all the usual dull life admin of a crowded room with fifty men in it.

The same fifty men from the train.

Valery got up quietly. He was on the top tier of the bunks, so he had to climb past two other people to reach the floor. He slid past the cleaning unit as they came in. They were the old men who had survived the train. Both had proven, when it came to it, to be sprightly.

Three guards were milling outside, blowing on their hands. The band of hot summer had come and gone in only a fortnight. They were high in the north of Siberia now, and the air was already sharp at night. Winter was coming down from the Arctic. When it came, the old hands said, the frost would be two fingers thick on the windows.

'Oh, morning, 745,' one of the guards said. Contrary to Valery's expectations, none of them were vicious people. Mainly they were just tired and despairing, like everyone else. Sometimes one of them did something nasty, locked someone in a shed for a few days, but it wasn't savage. They were still human. 'It's early. I know you're an eager beaver but you can't get started quite yet.'

'I'm not,' said Valery. 'Would you step behind me? Thanks.' He slung the bomb back into the barracks.

It exploded vastly. The windows blasted outward, east and west, and the doors shot open, though they were too solid to blow off. The heat of the fireball was intense, and the roof collapsed. Smoke poured up into the clear sky, orange from the glow below. There wasn't any fuss or screaming; it had been too fast and too final for that.

Very slowly, the guards stepped forward, not quite around Valery.

'What was that?' one of them said at last. He sounded shocked. He was grey with ash.

'Shall I take myself to the administrator or should you?' Valery asked.

'Let's . . . go together, shall we,' one of the other guards said, in the careful way of someone dealing with a madman. He put his hand on Valery's shoulder to steer him in the direction of the administrator's office, but very lightly. All around them, klaxons were keening into the night, and the emergency floodlights banged on around the perimeter.

'He did *what*?' the administrator said, after the guards had explained. He was absolutely blank. '*How?*'

The guards all glanced at Valery. 'Well. He is a scientist,' one of them said, as if scientist was code for magician.

'Okay – *why?*' the administrator managed.

'On the way here,' Valery said, and then found he was struggling to speak. In fifteen minutes he was going to be led into the woods and shot; it didn't seem worth the effort.

There was a long silence. 'Explain yourself, please,' the administrator said, his voice gone high.

In all fairness, the man deserved that. 'On the way here. They threw all the women's bodies into the forest.'

The silence was even longer this time.

'I don't think I quite understand.'

'The carriage was divided into two. Men on one side. Women on the other.' Valery realised he was wrenching his hand round and round his own wrist, but he couldn't stop. 'The men broke through.'

The administrator sat down. 'Yes,' he said at last. 'I see.'

The guards shifted uncertainly. Valery looked at the floor. For the last month he'd been wholly focused on this, on doing *something*, after he'd done nothing on the train. He felt emptied out now that it was over.

The administrator picked up his telephone. 'Yes, tell them to stand down. It was just an accident with some cleaning stuff. No, I know, tell it to Moscow. Bullshit supplies.' He put the receiver down and studied Valery. 'The way I see it,' he said, very softly. They were all still in dealing-with-a-lunatic mode. 'The way I see it, we have short supplies this month. The camp would have been very stretched, and at least fifty men would have died of hunger by November. This unfortunate accident has just evened out our numbers.'

Valery looked up, confused. 'What?'

He expected the guards to argue, but incredibly, the one nearest to him only patted his shoulder.

'Leave him with me. Back to your posts, gentlemen,' the administrator said to them.

They looked relieved to be out of the room, which left Valery alone in the middle of the floor. It felt exposed.

'Tell me now,' the administrator said. 'Did you do that because you feel guilty that you did the same thing those men did?'

'No. I didn't do anything.'

'That sounds sugar-coated.'

'No. You don't understand. I didn't do *anything*,' said Valery. He swallowed, which hurt – there was ash in the back of his throat. 'I just – switched off. I sat in a corner of the train carriage and I didn't move. I didn't help anyone, I didn't even try. It wasn't even cowardice, it was just . . . numbers,' he said, hating that the word for numbers was so neutral, as if having those as the keystones of your soul wasn't horrifying. 'Then I pretended to be dead.'

'Why?'

'I'm small.'

'What? Oh; *oh*.'

Valery made a fresh study of the carpet. He didn't understand how any human being was supposed to function, knowing that forty-nine out of fifty men were nothing but pressure bombs, every single one primed and ready to go off if someone just leaned on them hard enough, and that one in fifty was a machine in disguise, with all the basic humanity of a combine harvester.

Very carefully, he supposed.

The administrator cleared his throat.

'I'm taking you on to my staff. You'll be my secretary. You'll get at least one decent meal a day and in the mornings you'll keep teaching me chemistry. You will not be allowed near any more cleaning cupboards, understand?'

'What?' Valery croaked.

'I will, however, be consulting you sometimes about blasting in the mines. You clearly have an excellent and useful understanding of explosives which it would be foolish of me to waste, and God knows asking you will be cheaper than having a full-time engineer.' He looked pleased. 'Fetch the textbook, will you?'

32

The Demon Core

City 40, 1963

Anna was as good as her word. She arrived at about eight o'clock
in the morning. They didn't speak on the way upstairs. As soon
as Valery opened the door of his flat, the children shot up and
thumped into her, and she had to spend the next few minutes
calming them down. Albert swam up to the surface of his tank
to see what was going on.

'Is that an octopus?' Anna said.

'If you hold your finger out he'll give you a handshake.'

She did, and Albert prodded her fingertip, then furled excit-
ably around the tank to show her his marbles. 'Well,' she said. 'I
might cry now.'

'I know.' Valery gave her a cup of coffee and put the television
on to confuse the bugs. Albert climbed out of the tank and onto
his marble tray, where he leaned over to see into Valery's cup.
Valery prodded him softly. 'It's hot. Not good for octopuses.'
He put a drop on his fingertip and showed him. Albert touched
it, then went green and curled up in a ball. 'See? You know it's
horrible, why do you keep putting yourself through this?'

The littlest boy was looking hopeful, so Valery put Albert in
his hands. Albert took up a noble pose on the boy's shoulder.

'Be very gentle,' Anna said. 'If anything happens to that octopus, you're going in the radioactive lake.'

'Yes, Mum,' the little boy said meekly.

'Actually, Dima, take them downstairs to the canteen and get some breakfast.' It was funny to hear that a little boy was called Dima; in Valery's head, the only Dima there could ever be was the godfather from the camp.

The eldest looked worried. 'But what if they come for us—'

'Nobody has any interest in you whatsoever, darling, I promise.'

All of them looked at Valery.

'Sit near the door that leads into the kitchen,' he said. 'If anyone tries to talk to you, run out the back.'

'Can Albert come?'

'Yes, but he'll have bacon off you at the speed of light, so be careful. Probably better to let him have his own plate. And a jug of water, if you put a tiny bit of salt in it. He'll sit in it if he feels too dried out.'

A little reluctantly, they went. Valery watched Anna. She must have wanted to keep them in the room with her, but she must have realised too he was going to have to talk about this place without calling it a chocolate factory. Once the children were gone, he turned the television on louder to cover his voice as he explained what had happened. Resovskaya, the asylum, Shenkov's raid, the secret lab.

'I think she must have found a way to have him arrested because then that will mean she can get rid of me when she wants to,' Valery said. 'Actually I don't understand why someone hasn't come for me already.' He hesitated for too long, and caught a snatch of a breakfast news programme. 'And I don't understand how she could possibly have the authority to have the head of the KGB arrested.'

Anna was quiet after he finished. Now that he was looking at her properly, she seemed very, very tired; more so than probably she should have, even after the journey from Chelyabinsk. Some clock in her had slowed down too much lately and processed things too sluggishly. A thyroid problem, Shenkov had said.

She was quiet for so long that he had time to feel certain she was going to tell him that whatever had happened to Shenkov, it was none of his business.

'You know what she's done, though,' she said. 'It would have been easy.'

'What?' he said gratefully.

'You said they're running blood samples from the local hospitals; they find their candidates for the human trial from whoever looks promising from the blood work?'

'Yes?'

'His name will have come up in her samples. They ran blood tests on him to see if he would be compatible with Tatiana. Probably it even looked legitimate to the other researchers. He's lived here for seven years but he's never had any radiation-related problems.'

Valery found himself pressing both hands to the sides of his throat, as if he could crush his voice box. 'He's at the lab.'

'He must be,' Anna said. 'I don't think she could have got him for anything else, not this quickly.'

He didn't know what to say, except that she was right.

'How vengeful is she? Resovskaya.'

'Is she going to give him a thousand roentgen right now and watch him melt? No, I think she would say that was a waste of a test subject,' Valery said, furious with himself. He had been right there, holding the blood samples. He had known that Shenkov and Tatiana had been tested in Chelyabinsk. He should have seen straight away that Shenkov was in danger. If he had, he could have warned him.

'Good, then,' said Anna, with her bone-deep practicality. 'So all we need to do is get him out before they give him too much.'

Valery lifted his eyes to find hers. 'If we do that, we have to get him out the country. Ourselves too, and all your children. There's no . . . going back to normal.'

'Obviously,' she said, as if he had just asked her to fetch down some crockery. 'What's the lab like, how hard is this going to be?'

'I don't know if it's manned at night. I can go down early in the morning, four or five, and see.' He pulled his hand through his hair. 'If there are soldiers there twenty-four hours a day, I'm not sure what to do. We'd need some kind of accident. We need them to evacuate the lab, or close it for a few days. But I don't know it well enough to know what would trigger that.'

Anna tipped her head. 'Well. We're living in a plutonium refinery, it would speak to a lack of imagination if I couldn't think of something. How long do you think he has?'

'I don't know,' Valery said softly. 'I think they're trying to find exactly the amount the most resistant person can cope with. They're not *trying* to kill people. But – I don't think he'll be able to move much if we wait long. Within two or three days, he's going to be very ill.'

'Two days,' she said, and nodded. 'I'll think of something.'

Valery risked a study of her. 'Are you sure you're okay to do this?'

She lifted her eyebrows. 'I don't get much fun, Kolkhanov.'

'I'm glad you're a lunatic,' he said. 'But it's a bit much to ask you this. With the divorce, and . . .' He wished immediately that he hadn't mentioned it.

'I have terminal cancer,' she said. 'I don't give a toss if I'm arrested or not. Being shot would be far more dignified than what's coming for me otherwise.'

As if someone had pressed hard on his shoulders, they tacked back by themselves. He should have guessed.

'Does Konstantin know?'

'No. He's already tying himself in knots about Tatiana. I'm not very good with people who tie themselves in knots. Guilt like that, it's a sort of arrogance, you know? An assumption

330

that everything is your own fault when that's clearly absurd. I couldn't watch him do it any more, but likewise this thyroid thing means I'm too exhausted to lie to him all the time. Do you see what I mean?' She sighed. 'I'm not covering myself in glory here. But, I draw the line at letting him liquidise in a basement.'

'What . . . happens to the kids, without him and without you? If this goes wrong.'

'Oh, they'd go to my sister in Moscow where they would live unirradiated ever after. And then once we have him,' she said, as if she hadn't had to pause and think about her children, 'we need to get away *fast*. I think we're going to have to fling ourselves at the Americans or the French.' She paused. 'Having the children will be a good thing there. They're more likely to give asylum to a family. Sentimental like that, aren't they, capitalists.'

'Yes,' he said, and felt the enormity of it hanging above him, brushing the crown of his head. 'Yes.'

Anna was scrutinising him as though he were something in a vial. 'Are *you* all right to do this? You only came here a couple of months ago, but you didn't phrase this as my problem, it's been *us* since I walked in.'

'It's the gulag, it screws you up that way. He was kind to me, so I worship the ground he walks on.' He shrugged slightly. It felt like a lie even though it wasn't. 'It's fucking creepy but that's what it is.'

Anna laughed. 'No, he loves it when he has something fragile to look after. Hence the horde of children. Actually he's desperately unhappy when he doesn't have one, I wasn't surprised when he picked you up.'

Valery nodded once. He couldn't tell if she was talking down to him because she knew, or because she was just such a genius that she sometimes slipped into talking down to anyone and the edge of bitterness in her voice, like over-stewed tea, was just his imagination. He had to click his teeth shut against the chance that she did know, and that she might be angry enough to just abandon them with no way to escape, and leave them to enjoy the gulag together.

Valery was up at four and in Resovskaya's lab by half past. There were indeed two soldiers there, sharing an electric heater that only just brushed the deep night-time cold beneath the lake. They nodded to him, friendly enough. He put the kettle on and made coffee for them, drifted away to do some paperwork for a little while and then, trying to look as absent-minded as he could, started up the steel steps to the sealed vault door that led into the isolation rooms. The second he touched it, one of the soldiers banged the butt of his gun against a pipe with a boom that echoed and echoed.

'Can't go up there without Resovskaya's say-so.'

'But – I was going to ask them if they wanted any coffee,' Valery said.

'Step away from the door, comrade. Now.'

He stepped away from it and retreated to his own bench, his mouth going dry. It was possible to get by that sort of discipline, but you had to have time to build some trust and some routine: weeks. However proud he was of his shabby little collection of magic tricks, he had none that would get him through that door in forty-eight hours.

When Dr Resovskaya arrived towards eight, she watched him with more attention than usual as he put the morning's blood samples through the spectrometer, but she did not say, *aha, Valery, Shenkov is in my vault, your move*; he wished that she would, because he still wasn't sure. Anna was right, it *was* the elegant solution for Resovskaya, pulling Shenkov in for the trial, but he had no idea what other solutions were open to her. Many, perhaps.

When he asked if he could see the patients in the vault, Resovskaya said no. She was at a delicate moment and she wanted – he would understand of course – not to have people traipsing in and out, the trial was her baby, he had to let her have a few eccentricities. He smiled and said yes, and went back to the blood samples. None of them was named, only tagged with medical numbers. He wasn't surprised. The researchers must routinely come across people they knew. It would be hard to crush the instinct to quietly lose the data.

It was a good sign, the cheery gulag voice said inside his head, that she wasn't letting him in. She had no reason not to unless there was a new patient she didn't want him to see.

Or there wasn't, and she really was just feeling possessive about the trial, and Shenkov was already en route to Siberia.

There was nothing he could do, no way to check. He wasn't tall or strong; he couldn't punch Resovskaya and knock out the two men between himself and that door, nor the two soldiers – new ones, because the shift had changed at seven – who were reading magazines at a table in the corner. All he could do was sit here and run two hundred blood samples from six Chelyabinsk hospitals.

He hoped to God Anna had thought of something. He wasn't sure he was in much of a state now to do any thinking at all.

'In America,' Anna said that evening, 'this is called a demon core.' She set two perfect, silvery hemispheres down on the table between them.

They were in Shenkov's apartment again. The children, including Tatiana this time, were playing on the floor with Albert and a small army of the kind of little plasticky toys Valery had always assumed that children hated. Again, the television was on loud. Sometimes, Tatiana pinged a wind-up toy car towards them, so Valery pinged it back. She looked okay, he thought. Perhaps, just perhaps, there were treatments in France or England or America he didn't know about.

'A what core?'

'I know, it sounds dramatic, but actually it's – quite accurate.'

The metal of the hemispheres was beryllium. It was shined up so well it showed warped reflections of them, and light wasn't all it reflected. Beryllium was a neutron reflector. Anna said it with great significance, but Valery, who had never been a physicist, didn't understand at first.

People threw around terms like industrial-grade plutonium and weapons-grade plutonium all the time, she explained, but the difference was this: industrial-grade plutonium, the kind that ran power stations for electricity, was less refined. Weapons-grade plutonium had to go through far more refinement – that was, skimming other elements out of it until it was as pure as it could reasonably be – and this meant it was always close to criticality. Refined plutonium's rate of radioactive decay was so fast that it didn't just degrade and crumble, like other radioactive elements. It exploded. Criticality was the moment the rate of decay increased from normal crumbling to God's own wrath.

But you couldn't just ship atomic bombs around the country without knowing exactly *how close to exploding* they were. If the plutonium was too refined, it would go off by itself and you'd have a crater where Moscow used to be.

So it was important to test it. The demon core was that test.

Put a piece of weapons-grade plutonium into the hemispheres and tip them nearly closed, and the beryllium would reflect all of those loose neutrons back at the plutonium. They'd smash into it with almost the same force as it had slung them out – near to light speed – and in a few seconds, it would be so close to exploding that the beryllium sphere would be hot to touch. But, it was safe once you opened the core again. Let the core close completely, though, and a few seconds later you'd be vaporised.

He sat back from it, even though there was no plutonium anywhere near. 'But that would – Jesus, that would be like the Hiroshima bomb going off. That would take out the whole city.'

'Yes it would, but before it explodes, it does something else a lot more useful. It emits a burst of gamma radiation.'

Valery looked up slowly. 'How much?'

'An absolute fuck tonne,' she said. 'It only takes about half a second.'

'So it just has to do . . . this,' said Valery, and ducked his fingertips towards his thumb. 'The two hemispheres touch for that half a second and then they need to come apart again.'

'Exactly.'

He almost touched it and then couldn't, and took his hand back. 'I can't believe this thing exists. It's the stupidest test I've ever heard of.'

'You ain't heard nothing yet,' she said.

It *was* the stupidest test ever devised, and of course it had been devised by American scientists. American science culture was a lot more about pizazz than peer review (it made Valery feel much better about the flaws in Soviet science) and so rather than people like Anna, it was full of showy young men who were very concerned with seeming like hot stuff for their lab assistants.

One of these showy young men had taken to doing the demon-core test with especial pizazz. He would pop the plutonium into the hemispheres, and then keep them propped open with nothing more technical than a screwdriver; and therefore, nothing but one slip of a screwdriver between him and wholesale annihilation of his entire facility. He did it at dozens of demonstrations for his bosses. Valery wanted not to imagine someone who said *yee-hah*, but that felt like flying in the face of likelihood.

Nobody, it seemed, had thought to suggest to him that this was idiotic, and one day, the screwdriver slipped. The core closed, surrounding the chunk of weapons-grade plutonium with the neutron-reflecting beryllium, bombarding it with neutrons like machine-gun fire. Fortunately, the young scientist had flipped the top hemisphere of beryllium off before the plutonium could actually explode, but not quickly enough. He got a thousand roentgen in the face and, over the following fortnight, disintegrated.

Valery gazed down at the beryllium hemispheres, open at the moment like coconut halves. Inside, his own reflection looked back, a haze of gold-red and the shine of his glasses. 'It's a horrible way to die,' he said quietly.

'Yes. It is. But they'll be doubled up being sick in buckets within twenty minutes, and I can't think of anything else fast enough. If we had time – polonium in a sugar cube would make someone very ill within three days, but that's too slow. An acute dose by injection, great, but you said there are three researchers and two soldiers. You'd only manage one before the others realised, and your bones are very weak. Anyone restraining you would hurt you badly. I'm sure the forest is full of less horrible poisons that would knock someone out for a while, but I'm not a medic, so I've got no idea. A gun won't do you any good; the soldiers would get it off you. Likewise anything like a homemade bomb; they know to look for that stuff. We have to get him out *tomorrow*, we have to take out all five of them at once, and . . . this is what we've got.'

'And if it goes wrong and the plutonium goes critical, we're all dead.'

'Yes.'

'Is there a machine that can make it do that?' He touched his thumb to his fingers. 'Quickly?'

'It's bolted down, I can't take it from our lab. But someone here must know how to build a little mechanism like that?'

'Someone who isn't going to ask what we're doing with it?' Valery said softly. 'I have the mechanical brain of a caterpillar, and I wouldn't trust a single person I know here not to realise what we're doing – the specification is too telling. This thing can't be electrical because the radiation would fry circuitry, it has to be clockwork. Anyone here would know that if I go round asking for clockwork, I'm working with something powerfully radioactive. Which I shouldn't be.' He shook his head a little. 'And I think Resovskaya's watching me very hard. I think she hasn't bothered with me again because she knows I have to shut up with Shenkov gone, but one step wrong, and . . .'

'We'd better think of something, because the only alternative is a bleach bomb in a bucket.'

They both fell into a bleak silence.

'I know someone,' Valery said at last. 'An engineer. She runs the village Resovskaya is using for high-contamination human data.'

'Fantastic.'

'No. She's got her head screwed on. As soon as she finds out what we're doing, she's going to say that she won't help unless we get her people out too. That's – anything between sixty and eighty, I think.'

He thought Anna would wince, but she only looked pensive. 'I think I can do that. We just need a goods lorry.'

'They're going to be radioactive, all of them. Their clothes, their boots – the soldiers at the gate run a dosimeter over everything coming in and out. Even if the villagers come into Resovskaya's lab through the forest door and up on the Lighthouse side, they're still stuck behind the perimeter fence. And we can't drive a truck into the forest to get them.'

'I'll think of something. Go and see her.'

Tatiana, who had been quiet all along, climbed factually into his lap then, with Albert. She was wearing a sticker that said she had been brave at the doctor's.

'Hey,' he said, forcing himself to smile. 'How was Chelyabinsk?'

'A lot of needles and poking,' Tatiana said drowsily, swinging her legs. Her knees were bruised. 'I don't feel very well now.'

'The medicine is vicious,' Anna said. She was watching them with the carefulness that anybody watched a little girl with a strange man.

Valery began to set her down, but then realised she wasn't getting ready to stand up. She had gone to sleep, switched off like a lamp. Anna scooped her up and said they had better be getting home. He saw them to the lift and stood out in the hallway once it had gone down, gazing at nothing. Even if Anna really did want to help him, she would have to do it around a sick child. If Tatiana's reaction to her treatment got any worse than this, there was going to come a point when Anna would have to choose between helping Valery, and going with her little girl to hospital.

Albert squeezed his wrist sympathetically.

33

Octopus Toys

Valery's first instinct, which was childish and formed from reading too many spy novels, had been to find a way to disguise the core or hide it somehow. It only occurred to him when Anna handed over the equipment in a bag that if he had no idea what a criticality test core looked like, then nor would Dr Resovskaya. The beryllium sphere looked impressive and space age, but if someone had just left it on the kitchen table, he would never have guessed what it was. He didn't know what he'd have thought. More than anything it looked like it could have been a novelty indoor fountain, one of those little ones that made happy gurgling noises and everyone wanted because a Japanese person had once said it was zen.

So that was what he did. He took it out of his bag, which was otherwise filled with student papers, and put it together on the table in the underground lab. It took him about ten minutes. The other researchers glanced his way but seemed to put it down to Valery Strangeness. Resovskaya did ask what he was doing, but not with much hope.

'Bloody thing broke at home and the octopus is going nuts without it,' he mumbled.

'What does an octopus going nuts look like, I wonder?' Resovskaya said, sounding resigned.

'You'd think that stealing batteries would electrocute an octopus, wouldn't you, but oh no.'

'O . . . kay,' she said, starting to laugh. She patted his shoulder and went away.

He felt exhausted. It had taken five hours for Nanya to make a clockwork mechanism, scavenged from old combine-harvester parts, which would open and close the demon core accurately enough. Like he had thought, the price was transport away for anyone in the village who wanted to leave.

'I'm not doing this for you unless you can get us out too,' Nanya said over her kitchen table in the candlelight. She looked worse for wear since he had last seen her. He wondered how much radiation she and the other villagers had absorbed, just hunting for Pyotr.

'No, I know.' He swallowed, because he wanted to tell the truth and say, *we've had to organise this in forty seconds because any later and the test subjects will be too far gone to save; I have no idea if any of it will work.* But none of it would without the demon-core mechanism. 'We can do it. We have a truck big enough for everyone.'

Maybe.

'How do I know you won't go without us?' Nanya said.

'Because we need you.' He had rehearsed this in his head on the way to the village. 'If we turn up at an embassy in Moscow claiming to be from some top-secret nuclear installation, no one's going to believe us, even with a few people radiation-sick; we could just be zeks who ran off from a reactor. People come up with stories all the time to get a few American dollars or asylum in France. But if we bring seventy-five people with clear long-term radiation-related health problems and an identical story, they will have to believe us. All of us.'

Nanya hesitated. 'Who's helping you?'

'One of the physicists. Her husband was just taken as a test subject.'

Nanya nodded slowly. 'Okay. But if you screw me over—'

'I know, one of the lads will be by to cut off my hands.'

Then an hour for him to get back to the Lighthouse, another hour to wait for the checkpoints to open. He had brought his papers with him this time, and the soldiers remembered him from before and called him a silly twerp – in a fond kind of way at least.

It was stupid, to wait; but he didn't dare try and get back into the complex through Resovskaya's lab, in case Resovskaya herself was there. Having gone through the checkpoint, though, he was worried he had made the wrong choice. He could have lied to Resovskaya, but the soldiers could have sent the report down to the KGB office, who might then realise he had been in the forest for most of the night. Someone might come along to ask what he had been doing. He didn't know who was in charge now that Shenkov wasn't. There was every chance they were going to put him in a cell to see if he'd say anything interesting once he was scared enough. Which would mean that even if the demon core worked, Shenkov and the other test subjects would still be locked behind the lead doors of the inner laboratory.

Anna, who had been out and come back in the time Valery had been away, gave him a piece of plutonium in an oil capsule. She arranged to meet him by the laboratory's front door, with a truck, at exactly one forty-five. Nanya and the villagers would be at the lab just before that. He hated plans with moving parts and too many people. As far as he could tell, including the test subjects, the villagers, Anna, the children, and him, there would be at least eighty of them.

That was if Anna came.

He thought deliriously that they were all going to die. The entire haphazard plan felt like riding a bicycle for the first time. Obviously someone was going to fall off.

But, he got the core together without any other interruption. The plutonium stayed in its oil capsule, because he didn't dare to take it out too early. On the wall, the clock hands crept round at a fraction of their normal speed. He did paperwork. At exactly ten to one, he took the plutonium from its capsule with a pair of pliers and dropped it into the lower half of the beryllium core, where it landed with an innocent little splat.

Even after a few seconds, the underside of the hemisphere heated up. Jesus, but they really *did* keep weapons-grade pluto-nium close to criticality. He tried to imagine what an arrogant dickhead that American must have been, to prop open an almost-closed core with a screwdriver. It was hard just to force himself to touch it, never mind set the upper hemisphere into its clockwork and wind the springs. He did that while the mech-anism was holding the core wide open.

'I have a theory,' he announced at one o'clock, with sweat slipping down his spine, 'that there is a certain element of quantum entanglement in problems that annoy you and they have a way of sorting themselves out if you stop looking at them.'

'You mean you've been defeated by an octopus toy and now you're going to lunch?' Resovskaya said over her glasses.

'Yes.' He took the key out of the clockwork to set the springs going. The mechanism ticked. To him it sounded deafening, but none of the others looked, not even the soldiers. He gazed around them all for a long moment. He had always known he was invisible, or very near to it. He had never realised just how thorough an invisibility it was. Opposite him, the door that led through to the patient rooms – cells – was shut and locked. It was a heavy vault door, twenty centimetres thick. He closed his eyes as the shapes of numbers skimmed across the front of his mind for the twentieth time. It was enough, more than enough, to keep the patients safe. Even a person bending over

342

the beryllium sphere would have been enough to mostly shield everyone else in the room.

The ticking sang whisperingly, amplified by the hollow space inside the sphere, which was open by a good ten centimetres at the moment. He touched it. It was perhaps a degree warmer than it would have been without the plutonium inside, but nothing anyone would notice.

He set his own stopwatch going too. If Nanya's clockwork worked, then the core would close for exactly half a second, every ten minutes. He had to make sure he timed his return well after the last blast of radiation, but with enough time before the next to get past the vault door and into the patients' cells. The stupidest thing in the world would be to get it wrong and wander back just in time to get a thousand roentgen of gamma radiation to the chest.

This was it. If the core didn't open again, most of the Lighthouse would be destroyed in the ensuing nuclear blast, and not even twenty centimetres of lead would help Shenkov this close to the epicentre of the explosion. There would be nothing left of anyone down here but shadows on the walls.

He turned away and started up the ladder that would lead out to the unobtrusive door behind the main biology lab.

'Valery,' Resovskaya said.

His lungs lithified.

'Your wallet,' she said tolerantly, and handed it up to him. 'Get me a sandwich, will you? Try not to do anything peculiar to it.'

He queued up in the canteen like always. Some of the students were there too, anxious about their papers. He did his best at reassuring them all – quite honestly, because their papers were all excellent so far – and bought a cup of mushroom soup for himself and a packet of sandwiches for Resovskaya, which the canteen lady give him on a paper plate.

Nine minutes. If it was going to go wrong, if the plutonium went critical, they were going to know in the next few seconds. He stared at the sandwich on the paper plate. Maybe the last thing he saw in the world would be those dents around the outside of the plate. He had no idea how they did that; or why. There must have been some kind of vice. Someone would have had to put time and thought into making that.

'Everything all right?'

Another student.

'Oh – yes. Shenkov's gone off somewhere. Normally he winds my clockwork.'

'What a prick,' the boy said kindly, and went away with a banana.

Ten minutes. Nothing exploded.

He sagged with relief and dropped down at the end of a table to drink the soup and read a random newspaper someone had left out. It was *Truth*, yesterday's edition, because it took ages to get anything shipped here.

He hoped Anna would come.

He checked the silver watch. Nineteen minutes.

What if Anna didn't come.

It would take four minutes to walk back. That would be two and a half minutes after the last radiation burst.

He took the sandwich and set off.

He had to stop at the top of the ladder before he could pull together the courage to go down. If they had realised what the core was, if they so much as suspected, then the soldiers would be waiting at the bottom to drag him down. There would be no trial. He would be shot, straight away. He took a deep, slow breath, and eased down one-handed, carrying the sandwich on its plate.

No one grabbed him. He stepped onto the floor, and felt so relieved that for an instant, he didn't care if it had worked or not: they hadn't exploded and he wasn't about to be shot. It felt astonishing.

'Elena, I've got your sandwich,' he said, and then had to look around for her, because the lab was empty.

A bolt of panic slammed into his chest before he saw them all in a miserable row on the floor, backs propped to the wall. Resovskaya gave him a weak smile.

'Valery, be a darling and ring the KGB office. There's been some kind of leak. We're all feeling . . . a bit under the weather.'

On the table, the beryllium core was still ticking away happily. He took the top hemisphere off and put it aside. That was it. Disarmed. Inside, the lump of plutonium looked like a shard of gravel he'd found in the road.

'Okay, don't worry,' he said, and picked up the phone. He only pretended to dial, and pretended to speak to someone at the other end.

By the wall, Resovskaya and the others were all a terrible, claggy shade of white. One of the soldiers jerked up and just made it to the sink before he was sick.

'You should get out of here,' Resovskaya said. 'It could be airborne contaminants or—'

'I shouldn't go anywhere,' Valery said. 'If it's airborne then it's on me now. I'm going to duck in here and check the patients. Hang in there.'

'If you're not sick,' one of the other researchers croaked, 'then we were contaminated either before you started work here, or – or, Jesus Christ, just now . . .'

'Don't be silly, it would have to have been hundreds of roentgen to make us sick instantly,' Resovskaya said, drowsy.

There was blood blooming on her blouse.

'Oh, fuck,' one of the other researchers whispered. 'Jesus *Christ, fuck*! Lesions, we – what the *hell* could have . . .'

'Calm down,' Resovskaya said distantly.

'Calm *down*? We're *dead*!'

'I'll check the patients,' Valery repeated, stepping over them. Resovskaya was staring at him.

'You did this.'

'Yeah,' he said quietly. 'Let me just shuffle you to one side.'

'We're dying.'

'You are,' he agreed.

He had dreaded what he would find. He had been having nightmare visions of the worst, of barely recognisable bodies stretched out and smashed past all recognition by some terrible dose of neutron-shedding poison, but Shenkov was awake. He came straight to the glass.

'Valery!'

'I'm getting you out of here, all of you. How much have they given you, do you know?'

'A hundred roentgen yesterday,' Shenkov said softly. 'They were going to do it again today—'

'A hundred roentgen of what, do you know? Gamma radiation might be okay, but if it's alpha then you need to be in hospital *now*.'

'I don't know, I don't — they just — I don't know where the syringes are.' He sounded helpless. Valery realised he was doing no good whatsoever, only frightening him. 'Get out how? There are soldiers out there—'

'Not any more,' Valery said, wrenching open bolts. 'Come on, all of you. Can you walk?' he added to one of the other men. 'We're leaving, it's going to be okay, but we're going to have to get all of you up a ladder. Do you think you can . . . ?'

'I don't know,' the man said palely. 'Who are you?'

Valery picked up Pyotr, who was awake but drowsy and sick-looking. He was too light, even for a little boy. 'I'm a researcher here. Listen, all of you,' he said, and forced himself to slow down. 'I've just let off a lot of radiation in the next room. The other researchers and the soldiers are very ill now. We're going to just walk out of here, and up a ladder to the surface. At the top, there's going to be a truck waiting for us, and a lady who's going to drive us out past the facility perimeter. If you're all more or less okay, we're going to drive to Moscow. It's going to take two days, but we have to get to an embassy, or the KGB will find us. Okay?'

'I can't go to Moscow,' the last man managed. 'My kids are—'

'You will be shot for even knowing about this place if you don't.'

'He's right,' Shenkov said quietly. 'Come on.'

Valery checked his watch again. How was it twenty to two, where had the minutes gone? Nanya should have been here by now. Fuck it. He pulled the vault door open again and hurried them across the lab, towards the ladder. The other researchers and the soldiers were unconscious, some of them soaked in blood from radiation lesions; perhaps dead already. Resovskaya was holding a bottle of iodine pills in her lap. Shenkov's grey eyes flared with alarm. He looked like he was about to say something, but then there came a thunderous knock on the other door. The one that led to the bicycle tunnel.

Valery pulled it open, and there was Nanya, with a crowd of anxious people behind her. She nodded to him.

'It worked,' he said.

'Of course it bloody worked,' she said. 'Where do we go, up this ladder? Hurry up then.'

What followed would have looked, to anyone watching, like that bizarre act where fifty clowns climb one by one out of a Morris Minor, balloons and all. Only this time, it was sixty-eight people coming out of what seemed to be a tiny storage shed, climbing into the back of a banana delivery lorry.

Dressed in blue overalls, Anna climbed down from the driver's side to help the women with children, even while Valery stared stupidly and tried to think where she had managed to get a banana truck. She had also lined the whole cargo compartment with cushions, blankets, and bags and bags of food and water. Shenkov looked at her like he'd never seen her before.

'The children, are they—'

'At home,' she said. 'We'll all be fine.' And that was all. She didn't say anything else, and Valery remembered that afterwards always. Even though the plan had been for her to come too, with Tatiana and the others. Something must have gone wrong. Maybe Tatiana was ill again, too ill to move. He never found out. 'Into the banana lorry, sweetheart. Don't we live excitingly, that I should have cause to say that?'

Shenkov had to catch the side of the truck's cargo door. He could only just stand, and now there was horror in his eyes, and Valery realised he had no idea what to do if Shenkov refused to go anywhere without his children. 'Anna—'

'No time. Get in. You have no choice, Kostya; if you stand here then we'll all be arrested and shot.'

Valery helped him in. Shenkov didn't look at him. He had gone blank. He was going to hate Valery forever for this, Valery could feel it building, but as Anna said, there was no time, and all he could do was shut the door.

Anna drove. Valery stayed with her on the passenger side. She had got work overalls for him too, and a cap, which was just as well. He couldn't think of anyone else at the Lighthouse with red hair.

The soldiers at the gate stopped the lorry like they stopped everyone.

'You're not Yuri,' a soldier said to Anna.

'No, I'm covering,' Anna said cheerfully. 'He gave me his badge and that.'

'Not strictly okay, you know.'

'Sorry. It was an emergency. He's got this, er, swelling, where you sort of don't want one, so he was embarrassed about—'

'Ugh. Fine. Well,' the soldier said, and then waved a dosimeter vaguely at the truck. The dosimeter squeaked. 'Oh – fuck's sake. Fucking bananas. On you go.'

Anna drove them all the way to Sverdlovsk, then pulled off her overalls to reveal normal clothes underneath, waved goodbye, and got into a taxi back to City 40. It was quick. She didn't open the back of the lorry to say goodbye to Shenkov. It would have been stupid; they were just stopped at the side of the road in a lay-by in the middle of town, next to a whole row of busy grocery shops. There was a police patrol literally opposite, the officers watching the traffic idly over their sandwiches. One of them even watched her as she hailed the taxi. Valery studied the map enough to memorise the way to the main road west, then accelerated fast, certain he was going to hear a siren right behind them. But he never did.

34

The Embassy

The interview room was small and sterile, but nobody wanted it to be frightening, or else they wouldn't have sent the nice lady in with a tray of tea and Bourbon biscuits. Valery sat quietly and dissected a biscuit while he wrote down his statement with a black fountain pen. He did it in English, so nobody would have a chance to misread or mistranslate. He had to go slowly, because his hands had almost seized. Two days' driving; it sounded straightforward enough, but he was so stiff now he wasn't sure he'd ever move his arms properly again.

He looked up when the diplomat came back in. Harrison was exactly what he'd expected; a languid, willowy public school-boy, the kind who'd definitely call himself a boy even though he was Valery's age. Talking to him felt like meeting a dodo. Men like Harrison hadn't existed in Russia since before Valery had been born. He had given Valery a wary twang, but he was surprisingly inoffensive.

'I've been on the telephone,' Harrison said. 'It's all going to take some time to go through channels, I'm afraid, given how extraordinary this is.'

Valery supposed it *was* extraordinary, to knock on the door of the British Embassy at four o'clock in the morning with four people perhaps dying of radiation sickness and seventy refugees from an irradiated research quadrant. 'What does channels mean?' he asked.

'The bureaucracy,' Harrison explained. 'It has to go through a lot of telephones and over a lot of desks.'

Valery nodded. He drew a line of ink on the paper and watched it as the shine faded and dried. 'They'll send us back, won't they?'

Harrison looked honestly shocked. 'No, I doubt that very much. You're all in very clear and present danger. Not to mention that the intelligence you can offer is – well, significant.' He hesitated, awkward. 'Mr Kolkhanov, can I get you anything? You don't look too . . .' He stopped, because Valery had flinched oddly. 'Shall I get a doctor?'

'No.' It had been the 'mister'. He wondered if it would make even one atom of sense to this man, to say that it felt like a jab in the crotch to have his gender pointed out to him every time someone said his name. He had clean forgotten they did that. Mr, Mrs, Herr, Frau; every single person reminded every single time they were named of that one part of them that defined everything they were meant to be, and nobody ever seemed to sit back and say, *but we would never call anyone Penis Harrison; how's mister any different?* They didn't *think* that way. 'This is – going to sound bizarre, but it's comrade, not mister. I'm not mister in the way you mean it.'

Harrison looked blank.

'Never mind,' Valery said. He swallowed. 'How are they? The others.'

'Well,' Harrison said, plainly relieved to have a question he could answer, 'the villagers are having an absolute whale of a time in the staff canteen. Your Mrs Nanya has already told our cook everything that's wrong with her shchi soup and they're getting on famously—'

'Sorry,' Valery said, 'I can't understand what you're saying. Simple English. Please.'

'They like each other,' Harrison amended. He smiled. 'We all speak in dialect and we have no idea.'

'No, you don't,' Valery said, and let Harrison decide if he was agreeing or disagreeing.

'Oh, well, that's very good of you. Anyway, yes; they're fine. The doctors are – well, shocked, though, at the level of radiation complications.'

'So was I. And the people in hospital, are they . . . ?'

'Well, no one's dead yet,' Harrison said, with what he probably hoped was optimism. Shenkov, Pyotr and the other two test subjects were in a hospital now whose location Harrison wouldn't say, under British names. It must have been close by, though. 'With their doses, the doctors say it's fifty-fifty, with medical care.'

'Can I see them?'

'I'm afraid not.'

Valery nodded at the plate of biscuits. With the journey, and now this, he hadn't spoken to Shenkov since they had left City 40. Very slowly, he was beginning to understand that he never would again. Even if Shenkov lived, the only thing he would want with Valery would be to punch him in the eye for forcing him to go without the children.

'The KGB are looking for you,' Harrison said gently. 'We all had telephone calls this morning, all the embassies. They're calling you a mass murderer. Dangerous madman, I believe is the phrase. If I let you out on to the street for even a moment, someone's going to shoot you.'

'Am I going to prison, then?'

'Mr Kolkhanov. I find that when the KGB are at their most hysterical is when there is something extremely serious to cover up. I don't believe a word of it. You don't seem like a man who could kill anyone to me.' He fixed Valery with a careful blue look. 'The claims they're making against you are utterly absurd. Fifty men at a labour camp killed in a chemical bomb, five people in a lab from something they can't even explain; all they're doing is trying to discredit you. But fortunately, you brought seventy-four cases of absolute proof that what you're saying about City 40 is true. And if there's anything in that statement you're writing now to suggest you *aren't* a model citizen who would be entirely suited to being settled in the West, I'll fetch you a fresh sheet of paper and you can correct it.' He leaned across the little table and squeezed Valery's shoulder. 'Between you and me, I think the intelligence boys are going to be very pleased with you indeed.'

Valery studied him and tried to tell if he was acting. There was every chance they were going to make him tell them everything, then hand him over to the KGB. He couldn't refuse to talk, or bargain; he couldn't say he would tell them once everyone was safe in England. They had Shenkov. One word from Harrison and he would be out on the street, with radiation sickness.

Harrison smiled his cheery, open smile. 'Why don't you stop that for now and we'll have dinner.'

Valery had to give up. He had never been able to read between the lines, he had never spoken the special code, and no amount of urgency was ever going to help him learn, any more than it would help him learn to fly.

He knew the new man was from the intelligence services, because he spoke fluent Russian. It wasn't a tourist's stumbling. It was the kind you got from hanging round the Kremlin.

By then, Valery and the villagers had been at the embassy for forty-eight hours, and things were getting difficult. Harrison had locked the place down on the first night – no one from City 40 was to go out, ever – because quietly, unremarkably, Bolshaya Ordynka Street had filled with people who had taken to hanging around outside all the embassies. They knew, Harrison said, that Valery must have brought everyone to one of them, but no one knew which one. Whenever one of the secretaries went out for a coffee, someone followed.

It was hard to keep seventy people hidden in what was not really that large a building, away from all the doors and windows. They'd distributed everyone through the guest bedrooms, six or eight to a room, and they were keeping the curtains shut.

Incredibly, every other embassy on the street was also keeping the curtains of their bedroom windows shut. Harrison must have rung around, and while one part of Valery was amazed that people would bother to do that, another spun with anxiety. The more people Harrison told, the more chance there was that someone would go to the KGB. There would be money involved, or whatever it was that diplomats liked to be paid in. Handshakes, secrets.

The new man's name was George. That was all he would say; he didn't claim to have a surname. Like every spy Valery had ever met, he was nothing like people thought spies were. He had the manner and appearance of a secondary-school maths teacher. A bit shabby, a bit balding, friendly in an impersonal way; forgettable.

'I'm so sorry you've had to wait here for so long,' was the first thing he said. They were in Valery's room. Harrison had given Valery a room to himself. He had framed it as a reward for getting everyone out, but it wasn't. If there was a mole in the building, it would mean that any hand grenade someone threw in through the window would *only* kill him, not a bunch of kids from the village.

Valery shook his head at the carpet. It was deep and cream-coloured, and there were silk Turkish rugs everywhere. And a television, incredibly, that showed the BBC. The BBC: he had inhaled their news for an hour, enraptured. They showed debates in Parliament where MPs yelled at each other and made themselves look like morons. They showed journalists giving the Prime Minister an open bollocking *on the steps* of Downing Street. They interviewed random people on the street who said the government were rubbish and ought to be replaced. And not a single one of them was hurried away by anyone in a grey coat. He was still trying to get to grips with how anyone could run a functioning country like that. 'It's okay.'

'No it bloody isn't,' George said, gently huffy. 'It's a nightmare trying to get a flight into Moscow at the moment, everyone's off on holiday. I should have been here yesterday. How are you doing?'

'Fine,' said Valery, not sure why he was asking. It didn't matter how Valery was doing.

'Okay. Well, as you know, your government isn't the only one which must trust but verify.' He smiled a little. It wasn't Harrison's hopeful schoolboy smile. 'You are all clearly running for your lives. I saw KGB agents hanging around all the embassies on the drive here from the airport. But what I have to ascertain now is, are you running from a generally irradiated zone, and you're telling stories in the hope that the whiff of nice intelligence will make us more likely to grant asylum, or do you actually know anything about City 40?'

Valery nodded.

George was watching him carefully. 'If you need to stop, say the word.'

'Why does everyone think I'm ill? I'm not.'

'I don't think anyone thinks that, comrade. I think everyone thinks you're exhausted, and very frightened.'

Valery looked up properly.

'I have one main question, and if you can answer it correctly, I will believe everything else you tell me, all right?'

'Okay?'

'What is the location of City 40?'

Valery sat away from him and had to clench both hands between his knees. 'No, I can't – please. If I tell you that, the Americans will bomb it, they . . .'

George was already holding up one hand. 'No, no, no, I'm not making myself clear. We already know where it is. But I need to check that you know.'

'You already know,' Valery said slowly. 'What?'

George nodded. 'Listen, I'll tell you what I know. There is a place called City 40. It produces weapons-grade plutonium. At some point, we think in early 1958, there was some kind of accident there, a nuclear accident. We know that Kurchatov, the physicist, was sent away from Moscow for about nine months – we believe to City 40, to sort out what had happened there. We know there is a biological research station there, studying the effects of the radiation on quite a large ecosystem; that isn't a secret, they publish at international conferences. We know there is an enormous radioactive trace in the atmosphere over the site for thousands of miles. It's not the devil's own work to put all that together and come up with a pretty good location, which has been confirmed by satellite images.'

Valery had been in a car crash once. When the car had turned over, slinging everyone inside upside down, and there had been a crystalline millisecond where he saw the windscreen smash and the glass spray, winking, he had felt less tumbled than he did now. 'You know . . . everything. Why is it still there? Why haven't you destroyed it? They're keeping radiation there *secret* from people *living in it*, in case anyone tells the Americans, why—'

'Oh, heavens, no, the CIA flew over ages ago and clocked it. But why blow it up when we know exactly where it is? If we bomb it, they'll have to build another facility elsewhere, which they might hide better. Oh dear.' He lifted his eyebrows and smiled. 'Or even worse, they'll build one in Ukraine, or Poland, where an accident would mean radiation over Europe. We're quite content with leaving City 40 where it is. Point to it on the map and I'll believe everything you say thereafter.' He put a map on the table, showing most of eastern Russia.

Valery marked it on.

George nodded. 'Very good.'

Valery was still struggling. 'Are you saying you've known about it all along?'

'More or less. The Americans saw it when it was being built. I mean they drained a lake and they had about a hundred thousand prison labourers building the place. You don't do that if it's not top-secret.'

'Then it's all pointless. They're letting kids play in an irradiated river so no one will know how bad the radiation is, they won't ever evacuate anyone, even if people are getting radiation sickness en masse, people aren't allowed to leave the city, call anyone outside, nothing, and it's not . . . you *already know.*'

George laid one hand on his arm. 'I'm afraid so.' He smiled. 'We haven't let our press have it, of course. Suits us better if the Kremlin doesn't know we know.'

Valery realised how wonderfully easy it must have been, to run an intelligence service in a country where everyone was convinced the press was omniscient and open. People *believed* what they saw on the news. It was genius.

'Then what do you need us to tell you anything about it for?'

'Well, there are details I'd like to know. Will you take me through it? The security, the labs . . .'

Valery had a floating kind of despair. 'And is that enough to buy us a new life somewhere away from here?'

'Yes. The villagers will be given asylum, and you and the four people in hospital will be put into witness protection in the United Kingdom. You'll be rehoused, and given new names. You'll be set up with clinical work straight away, given your field of expertise. If you cooperate, of course.'

'That sounds far too good to be true.'

'Pardon my saying so,' George said, very gentle now, 'but your idea of normal treatment is to be arrested, abused, beaten, and imprisoned for things that aren't your fault, and which are not crimes. That doesn't happen in England. I know that sounds like some fantastical decadence to you, but it is not. Some promised lands really are milk and honey. On the grand scale of things, milk and honey are easy to come by, and simple to provide.'

'I don't believe you, you know that, right?'

'I know, but the part of my job I really enjoy is proving all my hugely suspicious Russian sources wrong about the West,' he said, smiling his unobjectionable maths-teacher smile. 'Our only difficulty now will be getting you out without anyone noticing. My contact in the air force has just been shot, annoyingly, so it might take me another couple of weeks to arrange something.'

Valery nodded and said nothing, because he didn't feel as though any of it could possibly happen.

'Anyone you know who might help?' George said. 'Military types?'

Valery shook his head.

The three secretaries were upset in the morning. The KGB agents outside the embassies had started to get bored of watching, and they had begun to stop people in the street. They weren't asking directly about Valery; they were just checking papers, but they had taken someone's away because of some flaw on the nationality page, and they had told someone else that hers were invalid for reasons they weren't going to say, and that she could expect to be deported. When Valery came into the dining room, everyone glanced at him, and he felt that same pressure on his chest he had felt at the biology lab in City 40. As though the radiation were still on his clothes, and he was contaminating anyone who came near him. They couldn't last much longer.

The phone in Harrison's office was not bugged, as far as anyone knew.

Valery had no idea if military phones were. Probably.

He tried anyway, half because he was almost certain that Svetlana's home number wouldn't be the same.

But it was.

'If this is you again, Kresnik, I'm going to garotte you with this phone cord.' She sounded exactly the same.

'Hello,' he croaked. 'Is that Svetlana Kolkhanova?'

Silence on the other end of the line.

He swallowed hard. 'Uh, sorry. I'm calling about – window sales. May I have a moment of your time?'

If she didn't recognise his voice, that was it.

Silence again. But then, 'Do you know what? This is seren-dipitous. A kid smashed one of my windows with a baseball yesterday. What have you got?'

'Oh really?' he managed. 'Well, madame, we actually have some of the very best glass just in, made in the UK. But it's going very quickly indeed, so if you'd like to have look at it, it might be best to come to the warehouse soon. We always advise coming to look.'

'Right. I will. Thanks.' She hung up.

He wondered if he had just signed her arrest warrant.

She arrived that evening. She walked straight in through the front door, in full uniform, called Valery a silly bastard, and told him there was a military transport to England setting off in the morning.

35

The West

Durham, 1964 (two months later)

Valery liked airports, always had; he still had a zing of excitement whenever he saw a plane take off, and they were even better when he didn't have to go anywhere but only pick someone up. He had never been more nervous to go anywhere, though, than Newcastle airport that morning. He did *not* like driving in England, with the insane insistence that everything should be on the left, and he did not enjoy English passive-aggressive drivers, either. At least at home, if someone was annoyed then they yelled; here, they just drove much too close for miles and then overtook fast at some inappropriate traffic lights. And they hated it if you didn't know where you were going, even though there were no road signs. He was starting to think that there must be a low-level telepathy among English people.

But he was glad he didn't like English roads, cars or people, because it was a distraction.

The call from Moscow had come at five o'clock that morning. It was George, the intelligence-services man.

'We've got Konstantin Shenkov on a plane to you today. Have you got a pen?' He gave the flight number and the timing, the terminal at Newcastle. Valery had only just managed to write it down.

'How likely is it to actually land rather than ending up diverted to Leningrad?' Valery asked.

'Oh, I should say a healthy sixty per cent,' George said in his honest way. 'I don't think I've got any leaks, but sometimes the KGB are crafty. Anyway, good luck.'

And that was it. All there was to do was go to the airport and hope.

He got there two hours early, because he couldn't sit at home any more. The flight desk did know that the plane had taken off and was still in the air according to the tower; they seemed puzzled that he was so worried.

He settled down at the cafe near arrivals, or tried, and read three newspapers cover to cover. His English had swooped right back up to fluent in the last couple of weeks. Weeks; it was hard to believe he had been here for weeks. For the first few days, he had waited by the phone, but heard nothing; and nothing, and nothing. He'd started to think, after six or seven days, that there was never going to be news. George wouldn't think to tell him if Shenkov was dead, shot behind the hospital or vanished into the Lubyanka. It had made him numb at first, and then it hit him gradually, like he'd fallen down the stairs incredibly slowly, and he felt aching and exhausted even to look at the almost certain future: he was just going to keep doing this now, forever, being a foreigner in a bizarre country, where he was either going to stay alone, or settle down with someone matronly and reassuring, just to have another human around.

The call this morning had raked up all his hope again, and now he was shaking with it.

And with fear. He had wrenched Shenkov out of City 40 without giving him any choice. Life and death it might have been, but Valery had taken him away from his children and made him leave them in an irradiated city with nothing but the hope Anna was clever enough to get them out some other way. It was possible Shenkov had boarded this plane and agreed to come out here not because he wanted to live here, but because he wanted the anorexic closure of smashing Valery's head into a wall.

When the boards changed to say that the plane had landed, he straightened and wondered if it was just automatic or if the tower really had seen it come in. He forced himself to sit still for another ten minutes, then went to the arrivals barrier to wait with the bored-looking people holding name cards. It must have been a diplomatic flight; he couldn't think of many people who would be allowed to travel between Moscow and here.

He leaned forward against the rail and shut his eyes, almost certain he was going to hear a gunshot, or see paramedics sprint past. The KGB just would not let one of their own land here safely to defect, they wouldn't; they weren't as omniscient as people thought, but they were still pretty fucking effective. All it took was one man with one poisoned needle, and maybe people wouldn't even call foul play. Shenkov was fifty-one. A heart attack wouldn't sound mad unless you knew him.

A few men in suits filtered out. If Shenkov was coming, it would take ages. The border officers would hate Soviet papers.

'Valera.'

He looked up slowly.

Shenkov pulled him close, which was just as well, because Valery cried. Very gently, Shenkov touched his jaw to angle his head up and rub some of the tears away. Valery couldn't even get together a hello. Around them, a few people gave them curious glances, but he had a feeling they both looked foreign enough for it not to be as strange. Shenkov, for sure, could never have been English. They didn't *make* people like Shenkov in England. Valery still looked like he'd recently been in prison and no one looked like that here. Shenkov kissed his forehead. It felt like a benediction. Thank Christ, he was crying too. Maybe; maybe it was just possible that he didn't blame Valery for what had happened, or at least, not for now. Maybe they could put it off for a little while.

'Car's outside,' Valery managed at last. 'Can I take anything?'

'No, it's just this.'

'How was the journey, was it . . . ?'

'Amazingly smooth. I really thought the plane would be shot down.'

'So did I.' Valery swallowed. 'Right, so I don't know if George explained, but the cover story is we're brothers. We need to get our details straight, because – people have been asking. You know, the neighbours, and . . . everyone's – very curious.' He tried to think how to describe English curiosity. It wasn't like normal curiosity. People didn't just come up to you and say, *well mate, so where are you from?* They circled the idea and asked questions designed to make you say without asking, and if you accused them of wanting to ask, they were offended.

Shenkov smiled. 'Probably they just want to make sure you're not German.'

'Officially we're Polish. English people think Polish sounds like Russian.'

'Lovely,' Shenkov said.

'Someone's invited us to dinner tomorrow night,' Valery confessed. 'I said you don't speak English, but he was – very insistent and I got nervous and now we're bringing the wine.'

Shenkov laughed. 'It's okay. I won't learn unless I hear it. Who is he?'

'Someone from work, an engineer. There's a lab near a nuclear plant. Nothing like ours. They're working on the use of radiation in cancer therapies.'

'How is it?'

'Boring,' Valery said, and smiled. 'Brilliant.' He hesitated. 'Did they tell you anything about . . . what you could do?'

'Well, English, to start with. There are classes at the university.' He had been watching people coming and going, not Valery, but as they went over the second level crossing, out past the taxi rank, he seemed to see the different layers to Valery's skittishness and took the top one away. 'Do you mind if I drive?'

'Are you sure?' Valery said, trying not to sound too grateful. 'It's all on the wrong side, and . . .'

'I *like* driving,' Shenkov promised. 'Anyway, you'll make me feel useless if you do everything.'

So Valery gave him the keys and it was a huge relief to just look at the map and navigate. Shenkov, of course, didn't hesitate to find everything on the opposite side, even on the roundabout from hell just outside Durham.

The house looked different now that there was someone else to see it with. Valery had a stab of anxiety as the engine quietened; he saw how wild the long garden was, how isolated the house; the next nearest was way at the far end of the field. Shenkov came inside quietly. The stove was still going, so it was warm and wood-smoky, and he just had time to turn back and start to say he had some vodka when Shenkov caught his hips and pinned him to the wall under a deep urgent kiss that was still desperately careful.

'Are you okay?' Shenkov whispered.

Valery nodded and leaned forward a little to kiss their chests together. Shenkov stroked his back slowly, right from the nape of his neck to his tailbone. He hadn't known he'd been holding himself tense for the last two months, but it all drained now, and the dull ache of too-tight ligaments went off. He didn't want to move again.

The following evening, they drove into town, with the promised bottle of wine. Valery was nearly embarrassed to introduce

Shenkov, who was luminous; it felt too close to patriotic bragging. The engineer, who was as rubbish as Valery at disguising what he really thought, let out a surprised little 'oh', and looked nervous when he shook Shenkov's hand.

'Gosh – you don't look alike, do you?'

'No, he got all the good genes,' Valery said.

The interesting thing about language, Valery always found, was that some people could communicate well with barely a word in common, and the engineer's wife was one of those people. She was sociable, and she and Shenkov got on like a house on fire. It was bizarre to understand them both and know they were actually replying quite sensibly to what the other was saying.

'Oop, I'd better get everything together,' she said at the tail end of the first glass of wine, and skimmed into the kitchen.

Valery set his glass down, waiting to be asked to help, but her husband didn't lift a finger and she didn't seem to expect him to. 'Um; do you need another pair of hands?'

She actually laughed. 'Oh, good grief. I don't know how they did things in Poland, but here you shall sit and be fed properly by a proper hostess.'

Valery sat back, shocked, and glanced at Shenkov to make sure he wasn't just being stupid.

'What did she say?'

'She said men don't help,' Valery murmured.

They looked uncomfortably at the engineer. Valery tried to imagine *expecting* Anna to serve them a meal. He couldn't even think what a prick he'd have to have been, and yet here was the engineer, a nice man, sitting back and looking actually quite proud that his wife was behaving like his servant.

'I'm going to make her let me help,' Shenkov said.

'Where's he going?' the engineer asked anxiously.

'We don't . . . sit around while someone else works,' Valery explained slowly, aware it sounded accusing. 'It's rude. And I know that when in Rome, but you can't let everything of your-self go, you know?'

'Oh, goodness. Well, if he feels that strongly I'm sure she won't mind if he *does* want to play housewife,' the engineer said, bewildered.

Valery lifted his eyebrows and decided it would be better not to say anything. 'What does Cecelia do, by the way? I don't think I asked before.'

'Do?'

'Yes, for a job.'

Frank laughed. 'Oh, she's not one of these modern girls. It's a full-time job, looking after me, really.'

'Do you think,' Shenkov said from the kitchen, 'that they'll be impressed if we tell them about electricity? Or the wheel?'

'What's he saying?' Frank asked. 'It's a lovely language.'

'He said you've got a lovely kitchen,' Valery fabricated.

'Better not, they'll think we're witches,' said Shenkov, with total impunity.

But Frank looked pleased. 'Oh, yes. I put in a new one for Cee when we moved in. She adores that fridge, I feel I'm in rather a polygamous relationship with it.'

In the kitchen, Shenkov and Cecelia were doing their trick of having a conversation in two languages.

'No, no, I can do that—'

'You're the size of a wasp, I wouldn't give you a full teacup to carry.'

'I could easily keep you, you know, this is all very chivalrous.'

'Christ. Valera, tell His Lordship to come and sit down.'

'Don't be rude,' Cecelia said.

'That is a well-laundered brain you've got there,' Shenkov told her, serene.

Cecelia, brilliantly, got the gist of his tone enough to blow a raspberry at him, which made him laugh. Valery smiled. He had forgotten how Shenkov sounded when he laughed properly; younger.

'It's the polite thing, is it, for Polish chaps to flirt with the hostess?' Frank said in his helpless eager way.

Valery choked. 'He's not flirting. It's sort of general abuse.'

'I knew it,' Cecelia said, looking righteous over a porcelain jug of gravy.

Shenkov glowed, which didn't do much to reassure Frank, who looked anxious in the way of someone who saw his wife as part of himself, and to whom the idea of her walking off with a handsome Pole equally horrifying as finding his own arms had.

'Cecelia, tell us how you met Frank,' Shenkov said, in his open elegant way, and Valery had a sense of impending doom. 'Did he run over your cat and then punch you romantically in the face?'

'Shut up, or I'm going to inhale this wine,' Valery managed.

Through what Valery could only chalk up to the grace of God, the phone rang. It was for Frank; work. Someone was ill and he was needed. Cecelia hurried up and fetched his coat, even put him into it, and waved him off from the door. When she came back, to Valery's slow horror, she was wiping tears away from her lashes.

'I do hate it when they take him out at night like that. One spends days planning something nice, and then . . .'

'There's more to life than dinner with a couple of random refugees,' Valery said softly, and very, very careful, because she sounded exactly like his mother.

'Goodness, not to my life there's not! I was looking forward to this terribly.'

Shenkov drew out her chair for her and poured her some more wine, then folded down in Frank's chair on her other side. They both kept refilling her glass and telling jokes and complaining about the news, a funnier process than usual because Valery's translation abilities deteriorated dramatically after two glasses of wine and it was soon more like charades. After a while she seemed all right again, or at least, all right enough to laugh. They left her tucked under a blanket with some hot chocolate like a little girl towards midnight.

At home, Valery caught Shenkov and turned him around, still not quite able to believe he was allowed to do that. Shenkov put both hands on his shoulders as if he were checking Valery were still real.

'Are they all like that?'

'So far.'

Shenkov rested their heads together. 'I think we need a designated no-English-people night.'

'Sunday. They're religious, everything's shut.'

'Are you being serious?'

'Yes. Everything. Even the newsagent, it's creepy. I keep expecting the Inquisition to jump out of a hedge.'

'So Sunday. Lock all the doors and windows.'

Outside somewhere, like someone had overheard, bells from two different churches rang midnight. Valery glanced at the window and had a strange deep roll of hopelessness. God in heaven and father in the house; none of it was ever going to change. He wondered how he was going to look Frank in the eye at work, knowing that Frank was just another version of his father, and Cecelia was just as stunted as his mother had been. That probably every doctor he worked with and laughed with in tea breaks probably had an identical wife, all of them keeping women like bonsai trees, a whole wretched forest of them, and all of them together blasting the same poison into their children, as cancerous as any radiation, with as long a half life. Even if everyone changed right now, overnight, that contaminated way of thinking would still be around for a good thirty years. Some of it for far longer.

'She was so upset,' he said uselessly.

Shenkov touched his hair to make him look up again. 'We'll have them round here, I'll make Frank do the washing-up. With proper training comes competence.'

Valery laughed. 'Okay. I don't know why I'm whining. At least we're not being irradiated any more.'

'No.' Shenkov paused. 'Do you think Slavsky ever sent the concrete?'

Valery shook his head slowly. 'No. I think someone's satellite is going to pick up a massive burst of radiation over Kyshtym, sooner or later.' He pressed his hand over his mouth. Tactless. Anna was still there; the kids.

Shenkov read his mind. 'She got them out. I know she did.' It was brittle faith; brittle and necessary. There was nothing he could do about any of it from here. They hadn't spoken about it. Valery got ready to say, *please, there was no other way. If you had stayed, you would have been shot.* He was ready for Shenkov to tell him that that didn't matter, that he would have preferred to see his children one last time and then die than leave them like Valery had forced him to. But for whatever reason, grief or grace, Shenkov hadn't said any of it.

'I'm sorry,' Valery said, because he had to. 'For – taking you away. I just – I didn't know what else to do.'

Shenkov laughed, kind of, a dismayed laugh. 'Valera. Sometimes it's all strawberries and champagne . . . and sometimes you never see your family again. Times we live in. It's not your fault.'

Valery nodded, his throat tight. He hoped that one day in the not-too-distant future, there would be another call from George, another plane coming from Moscow.

'Anyway,' Shenkov said. 'It's Sunday tomorrow.'

'So it is,' Valery agreed, and as Shenkov turned on the record player, Monday seemed like forever away.

AFTERWORD

Shenkov and Valery are fictional, but almost everything that happens to them is real. Or, as real as I could make it. The Lighthouse – Mayak – is now run by ROSATOM, the Russian nuclear science agency, and information about its history is extremely curated.

City 40 is better known now as Chelyabinsk-65 or Ozersk. 'Ozero' just means 'lake', so even that's a kind of code name. In September 1957, an explosion there set off a titan blast that shot at least twenty million curies of radiation into the atmosphere, and caused acute radiation sickness in people as far away as Chelyabinsk, which is sixty miles distant.

That figure, twenty million curies, is probably on the low side. It comes from a report made in 1995 by physicists S. A. Kabakchi and A. V. Putilov, who wrote a short monograph detailing how the accident could be reconstructed from *indirect* data – that is, by measuring radiation levels in the Kyshtym area in flora and fauna now, and gauging the ratios of different radioactive elements like caesium-137 and strontium-90 present in the findings, then back-engineering a theory about what might have caused it all. The direct data – hospital records, radiation levels measured at the time of the accident, photographs of the wreckage, Mayak's own records – are not available. Kabakchi and Putilov guess that what happened was an ammonium nitrate explosion in a storage tank full of liquid radioactive waste from the nuclear plant. The guess lines up, more or less, with what seems to be happening now. But it is only a guess, and it was based on information gathered decades after the fact.

Earlier estimates say at least fifty million curies, which to me at least seems more realistic. To put that in some kind of perspective, the accident at Chernobyl in 1986 released between fifty million and two hundred million curies.

What we know for sure is that the Soviet government declared the entire region around the Mayak facility a nature reserve and barred outside access to it. They opened a radioecological research centre there. We also know that there is a thing called the Southern Urals Radioactive Trace, which dates from the time of the blast; it's an atmospheric trail of radiation over the region. After the incident, whatever it was, thousands of people were evacuated from the area. The surrounding forests died of the radiation.

Whatever happened, the Russian government did not admit to it until 1989, well after scientist Zhores Medvedev outed the incident to the Western press in *New Scientist* in 1976. Medvedev was openly ridiculed when he first spoke of it; many prominent Western scientists couldn't believe they'd never heard of a massive blast that irradiated thousands of square kilometres, or that the Soviet Union could possibly have covered it up. But it had happened. As it turns out, the CIA knew all about it. Declassified files show they had satellite pictures of City 40 quite early on.

The one thing I wrote about here with no basis whatsoever in fact is the human radiation trial at City 40. I have no evidence that this ever happened. It's just a guess. Maybe there were no human trials at City 40, and I think too harshly. I hope so.

Everything else is true. Twenty million people really did go through the gulag under Stalin; out of a Soviet population of only about a hundred and two million in 1950. In the 1950s, scientists really were all but kidnapped, sent to the laboratories at City 40, and forbidden to leave or to communicate with the outside world. They really did refer to the Mayak facility as 'the chocolate factory'. Nuclear waste amounting to at least two million curies has been dumped in the Techa, and for years liquid waste was buried underground. Soil chromatography is a real phenomenon.

The 'alien' baby is called Alyoshenka; her body was discovered in 1996.

The Mayak facility is still a major producer of plutonium and other useful radioactive isotopes – including the polonium-210 which in 2006 was used to poison Alexander Litvinenko.

In 2018, radiation in the Kyshtym region spiked significantly; again.

A NOTE ON THE AUTHOR

NATASHA PULLEY studied English Literature at Oxford University. After stints working at Waterstones as a bookseller, then at Cambridge University Press as a publishing assistant in the astronomy and maths departments, she did the Creative Writing MA at UEA. She later studied in Tokyo, where she lived on a scholarship from the Daiwa Anglo-Japanese Foundation, and she is now an associate lecturer at Bath Spa University and panel tutor at the Cambridge Institute of Continuing Education. Her first novel, *The Watchmaker of Filigree Street*, was an international bestseller, a *Guardian* Summer Read, an Amazon Best Book of the Month, was shortlisted for the Authors' Club Best First Novel Award and won a Betty Trask Award. *The Bedlam Stacks*, her second novel, was published in 2017, followed by *The Lost Future of Pepperharrow* in 2019 and *The Kingdoms* in 2021. She lives in Bristol.

@natasha_pulley

ALSO AVAILABLE FROM NATASHA PULLEY

THE MARS HOUSE

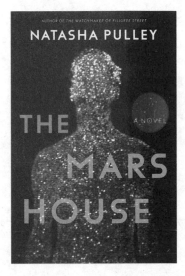

A compulsively readable queer sci-fi novel about a marriage of convenience between a Mars politician and an Earth refugee.

In the wake of an environmental catastrophe, January, once a principal in London's Royal Ballet, has become a refugee in Tharsis, the terraformed colony on Mars. There, January's life is dictated by his status as an Earthstronger—a person whose body is not adjusted to lower gravity and so poses a danger to those born on, or naturalized to, Mars. January's job choices, housing, and even transportation are dictated by this second-class status, and now a xenophobic politician named Aubrey Gale is running on a platform that would make it all worse: Gale wants all Earthstrongers to naturalize, a process that is always disabling and sometimes deadly.

When Gale chooses January for an on-the-spot press junket interview that goes horribly awry, January's life is thrown into chaos, but Gale's political fortunes are damaged, too. Gale proposes a solution to both their problems: a five-year made-for-the-press marriage that would secure January's future without naturalization and ensure Gale's political success. But when January accepts the offer, he discovers that Gale is not at all like they appear in the press. They're kind, compassionate, and much more difficult to hate than January would prefer. As their romantic relationship develops, the political situation worsens, and January discovers Gale has an enemy, someone willing to destroy all of Tharsis to make them pay—and January may be the only person standing in the way.

Unputdownably immersive and utterly timely, Natasha Pulley's new novel is a gripping story about privilege, strength, and life across class divisions, perfect for readers of Sarah Gailey and Tamsyn Muir.